AS TIME GOES BY

Annie Groves lives in the North-West of England and has done so all of her life. She is the author of *Ellie Pride*, *Connie's Courage* and *Hettie of Hope Street*, a series of novels for which she drew upon her family's history, picked up from listening to her grandmother's stories when she was a child. Her most recent novels are *Goodnight Sweetheart*, *Some Sunny Day* and *The Grafton Girls*, which were inspired by wartime recollections from members of her own family who come from the city of Liverpool. Annie Groves also writes under the name Penny Jordan, and is an international bestselling author of over 170 novels with sales of over 67,000,000 copies.

For further information go to www.anniegroves.co.uk and visit www.AuthorTracker.co.uk for exclusive information on you favourite HarperCollins authors.

D1386689

ANNIE GROVES

As Time Goes By

HARPER

This novel is entirely a work of fiction.
The names, characters and incidents portrayed in it are
the work of the author's imagination. Any resemblance to
actual persons, living or dead, events or localities is
entirely coincidental.

Harper
An imprint of HarperCollins*Publishers*
77–85 Fulham Palace Road,
Hammersmith, London W6 8JB

www.harpercollins.co.uk

This paperback edition 2007
1

First published in Great Britain by
HarperCollins*Publishers* 2007

A catalogue record for this book is
available from the British Library

ISBN 978-0-00-785794-4

Set in Sabon by Palimpsest Book Production Limited,
Grangemouth, Stirlingshire

Printed and bound in Great Britain by
Clays Ltd, St Ives plc

Acknowledgements

I would like to thank the following for their invaluable help:

Teresa Chris, my agent.

Susan Opie, my editor at HarperCollins.

Yvonne Holland, whose expertise enables me 'not to have nightmares' about getting things wrong.

Everyone at HarperCollins who contributed to the publication of this book.

My writing friends, especially those wonderfully generous fellow saga authors who have given me so much help and encouragement.

Tony, who once again has done wonders researching the facts I needed.

For my sternest critic, my mother
– who 'was there'

ONE

September 1942

Samantha Grey, or Sam as those closest to her called her, put down her kitbag and wrinkled her nose. A school dormitory! Well, she had had worse billets, she admitted ruefully.

She had travelled to Liverpool by train, sharing a compartment with several other young women in uniform, all of whom had been going to different destinations. One of them knew Liverpool quite well, having once been posted there. She had told Sam that her new billet, in the Wavertree district of the city, had been a small private school occupying a large Victorian house, which the War Office had requisitioned because of its proximity to Liverpool's famous Bluecoat School, which had also been requisitioned. Such requisitioning was a wartime necessity to provide accommodation for the country's service personnel.

There was no sign of the girls Sam would be sharing her new quarters with, which meant that either they had not yet arrived, or they were already on duty.

Sam hadn't been at all pleased when she had been told that she was being posted to Liverpool. She had hoped she might get a really exciting posting like some of the girls she had trained with – maybe even overseas – after all, she had won praise from her tutors on both the ATS courses she had completed, a standard one for typewriting and a second and far more enjoyable one for driving. The latter equipped her for one of the ATS's more exciting jobs, such as being a staff driver to drive visiting 'important' personnel. She suspected that if it hadn't been for the unfortunate set of circumstances that had led to her getting on the wrong side of a certain sense-of-humourless sergeant who hadn't appreciated her pranks, she probably would have had such a posting. After all, she had passed the driving course with higher marks than anyone in her group.

But then she had had the wretched bad luck not just to injure her thumb, larking about demonstrating her skill at 'wheel changing' to the other girls, she had also been caught doing so by the car's owner. Unfortunately she had not been authorised to do any such 'wheel changing', especially not on the duty sergeant's chap's precious MG sports car. It had been rotten bad luck that the duty sergeant and her chap had appeared just when Sam had the wheel completely off the car, and even worse bad luck that in the panic that had followed she had caught her thumb in the wheel spokes, and that the injury she had received had become

2

infected. As a result, she had been hospitalised until the infection had cleared up and then sent to work as a clerk/stenographer in the quartermaster's office at her Aldershot barracks, and denied the opportunity to drive anyone anywhere as punishment for her prank.

A clerk. How her elder brother, Russell, would have laughed at her for that, knowing how much the dullness of such duties would chafe against her exuberant adventure-loving nature. He would, though, have understood her disappointment.

Sam gave a small shake of her cropped golden-blonde hair, a new haircut that had caused her mother such distress.

'Well, the sergeant said that our hair has to clear our collars,' she had told her mother in answer to her bewildered, 'What have you done to your lovely hair?' 'And besides, I like it,' she had added truthfully, giving her mother a mischievous smile. 'At least this way you won't have to worry about men in uniform trying to take advantage of me. From the back now, if I'm wearing slacks I look more like a boy than a girl.'

'Oh, Samantha,' her mother had protested, but Sam had just laughed. It was true, after all. She had never yearned for soft rounded curves instead of her boyish slenderness. Even as a young girl she had preferred tagging along with Russell and scrambling up trees and damming streams rather than dressing up in frocks and playing with dolls.

Nothing could have appealed more to her tomboyish spirit than playing a really active role in defending her country. If there had to be a war, then she very definitely wanted to be a part of it. Having joined up at nineteen after badgering her parents to give their permission, she had hoped to be doing something exciting. But now here she was, being sent to work as a clerk. Some war she was going to have.

She could feel her eyes beginning to smart, so she blinked fiercely. There was no point in feeling sorry for herself, not even if only a month ago she had been here in Liverpool seeing off some of the girls who had joined up at the same time, on the troop ship that would ultimately take them to Cairo where they would have goodness knew what kind of exciting adventures.

Her orders had been to report first to her billet, for her new posting at Deysbrook Barracks, on Deysbrook Lane, which she had managed to find out, via the ATS grapevine, contained amongst other things a large Royal Engineers vehicle workshop and depot, an army stores depot, and some small regular army units of men posted to home duties.

Since officially she wouldn't be on duty until the morning, and as there didn't seem to be anyone around for her to report to, her irrepressible desire for action was rebelling against sitting in an empty dorm waiting for something to happen when she could be outside exploring her new surroundings.

She had no idea which bed was going to be hers, but she knew it must be one of the two that weren't made up, their biscuit mattresses, as the three hard sections of the bed were called, exposed.

That being the case, she might as well take the one closest to the door because it would give her the best chance of reaching the ablutions quickly if she overslept.

Having dropped her kitbag on the bed, she went back the way she had come.

Whilst the dorm might be on the bleak side, the house itself was very handsome, even if the pale green distemper on the walls was flaking and the air smelled of chalk, boiled cabbage and damp mackintoshes, which reminded her of her own schooldays. The stairs she was walking down were quite grand, the banister rail smooth, broad, well polished and intricately carved. Had the house belonged originally to some rich Victorian ship owner or merchant, Sam wondered absently whilst she crossed the empty panelled hall with its black and white tiled floor.

Several doors opened off the hallway, all of them closed. The hallway itself, containing a wooden desk with a chair behind it, plainly intended to be occupied by someone in authority, was empty. Sam wasn't going to waste time waiting for one of those closed doors to open now that she had made up her mind to go out and explore. Without looking back, she pulled open the front door and stepped outside.

The front garden consisted of dank-looking ever-green trees that screened the house from the road beyond, and a lawn into which were set pieces of limestone to form a tired-looking rockery. Sam didn't waste time studying the garden in detail though. Perfectly well aware that she ought to have remained by the unmanned desk in the hallway, dutifully waiting for someone to appear to whom she could report, Sam hurried towards the road.

She suspected that at one time the house would have possessed elegant wrought-iron gates, but these would have been sacrificed for the war effort, melted down to provide much-needed metal for the manufacture of guns and tanks. As she stepped out onto the pavement she could see a bus trundling towards her and she ran to meet it, halting in the middle of the road so that the driver had to stop.

'It's against the rules for us to stop, miss, you know that. And you shouldn't have stood out in the road like that. Could have caused a nasty accident, you could.'

'I'm really sorry, Driver,' Sam said. 'Only I'm new here, and I was hoping you might be able to tell me the best way to get into the city.'

'The city, is it? Well, there's not much of that left, thanks to Hitler and his ruddy Luftwaffe. Bombed the guts out of it, they have.'

'Yes, I heard about the terrible pounding Liverpool took in May last year,' Sam sympathised.

'Seven full days of it, we had, but they couldn't bomb the guts out of *us*, I can tell you that. Missed most of the docks, even if they have flattened whole streets of houses and left families homeless. A bad time for Liverpool, that was. They got the Corn Exchange, Lewis's store in Great Charlotte Street, and Blackler's, an' all. Broke my daughter's heart, that did. She worked in Blackler's, you see, and they'd just taken in a consignment of fully fashioned silk stockings that week. Worth ten thousand pounds, they was, and she'd promised herself a pair. I can tell you, she cursed them bombs every time she had to paint gravy browning down the back of her legs instead of having them silk stockings. A five-hundred-pound bomb fell on the William Brown Library. Every ruddy book on the shelves of the Central Library were burned, along wi' everything in the Music Library. Mind you, it weren't all bad news. In one way old Hitler did some of us a bit of a favour, since India House got set on fire, and all the Inland Revenue records got burned,' he added with a big grin, but then his grin disappeared. 'Seventeen hundred dead, we had, and well over a thousand seriously injured.'

Everything he had told her made Sam more determined to see for herself something of this city that had withstood so much and at such a cost.

As though he read the resolution in her eyes, the driver said abruptly, 'By rights we shouldn't be picking anyone up, seeing as we're on our way back to the depot, but go on then, you might as well hop on. Tell Betty, the conductress, to let you off two stops before the bombed-out church.'

The final notes of the song died away, leaving Sally free to step down from the stage of the Grafton Ballroom. She had been standing in at rehearsal for one of the Waltonettes, the four girls who sang with Charlie Walton and his band. For a good few months now, poor Eileen just couldn't seem to get rid of the cough that was plaguing her, so Sally was singing more regularly than Eileen. But a stand-in was still all she actually was, as Patti enjoyed making clear to her.

Patti, the most senior of the Waltonettes, had been a bit off with her right from the start. Sally knew that Patti looked down on her because she had been working as a lowly cloakroom assistant when Charlie had overheard her singing to herself and had insisted that she was good enough to fill in for Eileen. Patti had tossed her head and told Sally that the only reason Charlie had taken her on was because he was desperate. So Sally was determined to prove herself and to show Patti that she could sing every bit as well as the rest of them.

She could see Patti pulling a face as she announced sharply, 'You was out of tune again, Shirley, in "Dover", and you know how much the lads go mad for it. 'Ere, where do you think you're off to?' she demanded as she caught sight of Sally getting ready to leave.

'I've got to go,' Sally told her, 'otherwise I'm going to be late for picking up my two boys from me neighbour.' When Patti went thin-lipped she reminded her firmly, 'I did tell Charlie when he first asked me to do this that I'd got other obligations. And I'm not a permanent member of the band, after all; I'm only standing in for Eileen.'

'Go on then. But mek sure you're here on time tomorrow for the rehearsal for Saturday night,' Patti warned her.

Nodding, Sally picked up her bag and hurried towards the exit.

Stan Culcheth, the ex-sergeant major who had been invalided out of the army after losing an eye in the action in the desert, and who the owner of the Grafton had taken on to deal with any unwanted rowdiness amongst the large number of service personnel who came to the dance hall every week, gave her a cheery smile as he opened the back door for her.

'Heard from that husband of yours yet?' he asked kindly.

Sally shook her head, pulling up the collar of her coat against the evening air. 'He's probably gone AWOL with some pretty girl he's found,' she joked. But she knew from the look he was giving her that Stan wasn't deceived. The truth was that she *was* worried. How could she not be? There hadn't been a single day not filled with anxiety in the long months since she had received that telegram with the news that Ronnie – her Ronnie, whom she had thought was serving in Africa, but who had in fact been in Singapore with the rest of his unit when the island fell – was now a Japanese prisoner of war.

Unlike the women whose men were German POWs, Sally had not had the comfort of letters from Ronnie, passed on by the Red Cross, who had taken on the task of monitoring the treatment of all POWs and ensuring that it complied with the terms of the Geneva Convention.

'Aye, well, it's early days yet,' Stan offered her comfortingly. 'It takes time for the Red Cross to sort out who's who and where they are. Like as not you'll be hearing from him any day now.'

His voice was too hearty and he couldn't look her in the eye, and of course Sally knew why. Other women almost shrank from her when they knew that Ronnie was a Japanese POW, not knowing what to say, what kind of commiserations or sympathy to offer to her. There were some horrors that even the most stalwart heart could not reasonably contemplate, unthinkably sickening horrific things that had to be kept locked away and not spoken of. Sally tried not to think about them either; that was one of the reasons why she liked to sing. When she was singing, she could pretend that everything was all right, just like it was in the songs.

'Oh, I know that. My Ronnie's not some raw recruit, after all,' Sally answered the doorman stoutly. 'He's seen plenty of action. With the BEF at Nantes, he was, at the time of Dunkirk, and he came through that. Then he got shipped off to Italy, and then the desert supposedly, although seemingly he wasn't going there at all but to Singapore.'

'He'd be proud of you if he could see the way you're coping, lass. When a chap's bin taken prisoner he needs to know that all's well at home. Means the world to him, that does. It's what keeps him going sometimes,' Stan told her, so obviously wanting to sound optimistic that Sally felt obliged to respond in a similar cheery vein, as she said goodbye to him.

After all, she wasn't on her own, she reminded herself, as she made her way home. There was hardly a household in the country in which the women were not worrying about their menfolk, and that included her neighbours on Chestnut Close, in Liverpool's Edge Hill area, as well as the girls she worked with both here at the Grafton and at Littlewoods, where they were making parachutes and barrage balloons for the war effort. It was a matter of everyone at home pulling together to support one another and to give their fighting men the comfort of knowing that those they had left behind were being looked after by their community. A matter of getting on with things as best they could without making a song and dance about it.

But Sally was feeling far from as chirpy as she tried to pretend, and not just because word was creeping back that the Japanese treatment of POWs was so cruel. She also had problems at home. Trying to bring up two exuberant and sometimes mischievous boys wasn't always easy without their father there. It was not even as though the boys had an uncle around who could have shown them a firm hand when things got a bit unruly. Like the other teatime, when three-year-old Tommy, born the day war was announced, had started a scrap with his younger brother, Harry, which had led to them both yelling blue murder.

And then there was that other matter that kept her awake at night, and that seemed to get worse, no matter how hard she tried to get on top of it. She did some anxious mental arithmetic. She knew there were those who disapproved of the fact that she was singing at the Grafton on her night off from her late shift at Littlewoods. After all, with her children under five, and rationing making sure that everyone in the country got their fair share even though it was barely enough to fill people's stomachs, she could have stayed at home with her boys, never mind have taken on two jobs. But they didn't know what she did, and they didn't have to worry about it either. She needed every penny she could earn and somehow it still wasn't enough.

Sally thought she was lucky to have her job at the Grafton, especially with Stan Culcheth there. Stan had a heart of gold, and all the girls who worked there knew that they could turn to him if they ever needed help dealing with the sometimes over-keen admiration of the men who flocked to the ballroom to enjoy themselves. Not that keeping the peace amongst these young men was an easy job at the moment, what with more and more American servicemen arriving at the huge Burtonwood American base near Warrington, all determined to enjoy themselves after their journey across the Atlantic and before they were sent off to join units in other parts of the country.

There had already been several scuffles, and on a handful of occasions more serious fights, between British and American servicemen, sparked off by what the Brits saw as the unfair advantages the Yanks had when it came to getting the prettiest girls.

The American Military Police were very quick to step in and restore order amongst their own men, though – Sally had to give them that.

Personally she did not feel any animosity

towards the Yanks. After all, they were the allies and here to help win the war.

'Oh, well, you would be in sympathy wi' them Yanks, Sally,' Shirley, one of the Waltonettes, had sniffed deprecatingly when Sally had said as much. 'What with your Ronnie being a Jap POW and all them Yanks being took prisoner by the Japs as well, wi' Pearl Harbor and all that.'

When Sally had related this conversation later to her best friend, Molly Brookes, Molly had immediately sympathised and tried to comfort her.

Yes, Molly was a good friend to her, and yet it had been June, her elder sister, whom Sally had palled up with first, when they had been young wives and then young mothers together. But then poor June had been killed during a bombing raid. Molly had gone through her own fair share of heartache, what with one engagement being broken off, and then losing her handsome young Merchant Navy fiancé when his ship had been torpedoed, before June was killed. June and Molly had been particularly close on account of them losing their mother very young, so perhaps it was no wonder that Molly had ended up marrying her sister's husband, in January, and was now mothering June's little girl, Lillibet, just as if she were she own, while waiting for the birth of her and Frank's own baby.

They were already into September and the home front was destined to became harder. At the end of the October the double daylight saving time, introduced so that the country could make the most of the long summer daylight hours, would come to an end and they would be plunged back into the misery of the blackout. Then they would have the winter to live through with only a meagre amout of fuel allowed for fires, and the dreariness of thin soups made from whatever bones and scraps of meat could be had, thickened with whatever winter vegetables were available.

They were fortunate on Chestnut Close, Sally recognised, in that one side of the Close backed on to a row of allotments, maintained in the main by the Close's residents.

Albert Dearden, Molly's dad, had always been kind enough to help out Sally with veggies and the like from his own allotment, treating her almost as though she were another daughter, and her two boys his grandsons.

Yes, the residents of Chestnut Close had pulled together right from the start of the war, when they had set to to erect their communal air-raid shelter, Sally acknowledged half an hour after leaving the Grafton, as she got off the bus and crossed Edge Hill Road to turn into the Close. Not that it had always been plain sailing or happy families. There had been a fair few fall-outs since the war had begun in September 1939, none more spectacular perhaps than those between June Dearden, as she had been then, and her widowed future mother-in-law, Doris Brookes.

Poor June, she had never really taken to Doris, nor Doris to her, and yet really you couldn't have wished to meet two more decent sorts.

It had been Doris, a retired midwife, who had delivered Sally's own first baby, commandeering Molly to help her when Sally had gone into early labour. Doris had refused to seek shelter for herself, despite the warning wail of the air-raid alarm, which had everyone else rushing for the protection of the newly erected shelter. Instead she had bustled Sally upstairs to her spare room, where she had given birth. On that occasion the air-raid warning had simply been a practice drill, but they had all had plenty of opportunity to make use of the air-raid shelters in the second half of 1940, especially in December, and in the May of 1941, when Liverpool had been well and truly blitzed in a week of nonstop bombing, and poor June had been killed.

Sally was on her way to Doris's now to pick up her sons. Littlewoods provided nursery facilities for its workers but the number of places was limited, and whilst Sally had been offered a place for Tommy she had not been able to get one for Harry as well. She wasn't going to have her boys separated, so she had to rely on the kindness of Doris, who luckily worked a day shift at the hospital, and who had offered to have the boys sleeping in her spare room whilst Sally was at work.

What a long day it had been – the factory, the Grafton, now the boys to see to and, always at the back of her mind, worry about Ronnie.

TWO

Betty the conductress might have thought she was
doing Sam a favour by warning her not to try to
walk through the worst of the bombed-out heart
of the city, but the truth was that all she had done
was increase Sam's desire to see it. Not that she
could see very much now that it was growing dark.
A thin drizzle had started to fall, mixing with the
fret of mist coming in off the sea and the dusk,
so that when she peered down streets flattened to
the ground apart from the odd half-destroyed
building, the uninhabited emptiness took on an
almost ghostly otherworldliness that shifted shape
around her. Her footsteps echoed in the mist as
she walked down cobbled streets, mentally reckoning the direction she was taking so that she
wouldn't get lost. So long as she kept the sea on
her left she knew she must turn right to get back
to Lime Street Station, which was the only real
reference point she had, but when she decided she
had had enough and that she might as well go
back, the first street on the right she came to was

closed off with sandbags and a sign that read 'Danger Unexploded Bomb'.

Well, if it was still unexploded then it wasn't that dangerous, was it, Sam decided, and to judge from the faded paint on the sign, the bomb had been around for a while. The main reason the authorities put up such signs was to deter children from playing where it was dangerous – everyone knew that. Besides, this was the only right-turning street she had come across in ages, and she needed to get back.

Determinedly Sam hopped over the sandbags, ignoring the sign.

This street seemed to have suffered less bomb damage than the street she had just been in, with only one large gap where houses had once been. There was just enough light left for her to see the wallpaper hanging from what must have been the bedroom walls of the boarded-up houses either side of the empty space, rubble from the bombed houses spewing out on the pavement and into the street. She had seen newsreel images of streets like this, which, in the secure environment of Aldershot, were as close as she had got to the reality of bomb damage, and naturally she was curious to take a closer look. The street was deserted, and there was no one to see her wriggling past the second 'Danger Unexploded Bomb' warning, to clamber over the mound of broken bricks and wooden beams. She had with her the small torch such as everyone carried around with them because of the blackout, and as soon as she was close enough she felt in her pocket for it, removing it and switching it on.

There below her, and much deeper than she had expected, was the bomb crater, a hole in the ground easily wide enough for a person to fall into.

And be buried alive there? Immediately Sam recoiled, sending some loose pebbles and soil falling noisily into the hole. Thanks to her brother, Russell, and his friends she had an intense and secret dread of being trapped underground, and sometimes still had nightmares about the original cause of that dread. Russell and his friends hadn't meant any harm, of course, when they had persuaded her to crawl into a tunnel they had been digging, which had then collapsed on top of her. Fortunately a neighbour had realised what had happened and quickly dug her out, but it had left her with a terror of being trapped underground and dying there that she knew she would never ever lose.

'Hey, you! What the hell do you think you're doing? Can't you read?'

The sound of an angry male voice from inside the crater startled her so much that she lost her footing, dropping her torch as she did so, and then realising to her dismay that the debris on which she was standing had started to move, the bricks slipping from under her feet, carrying her down into the crater. Her fear was engulfing her now, a feeling of sickness filling her stomach and her heart thudding.

'Don't move. Keep still unless you want to blow us both to kingdom come.'

Did he really think she had any choice in the

matter, Sam wondered frantically as she tried to remain calm and to find a secure foothold in the gathering force of the sliding bricks. She must not panic. *She must not*. But she couldn't stop herself from sliding closer and closer to the crater's edge. Then suddenly the breath was jolted out of her body and she was thrown forward and knocked to the ground onto the rubble by the weight of a man hurling himself on top of her, somehow miraculously stopping her slide.

Relief, dismay, shock and a guilty awareness that she had brought what had happened on herself – Sam was experiencing them all.

It was just as well she was wearing her great-coat otherwise her skin would have been cut to ribbons on the rubble, she decided almost light-headedly, but as she struggled to voice this fact to the man who was now lying on top of her, he shook his head and placed his hand over her mouth.

There was just enough light for her to see how disreputable he looked, even if he was in uniform. He needed a shave, and his dark hair looked in need of a cut, his face was streaked with dirt and the hand he had placed over her mouth smelled of dirt and oil.

He was looking at his watch with a fierce concentration that made Sam wonder if he was some kind of madman. If so, he was soon going to learn that she could look after herself. All she was waiting for was the right opportunity to raise her knee and use it in the way her elder brother had taught her would deter any overeager male.

He was leaning intimately into her now, his hand still covering her mouth.

She could feel his breath against her ear, as he mouthed quietly, 'I hope you know how to run.'

What did *that* mean? She looked up at him, intending to tell him what she thought of him but the look in his eyes made it clear that his words were not intended as some kind of chat-up line. Army rules and regulations must have been instilled in her more than she had known, she recognised as she nodded obediently.

'Good,' said the man in a soft whisper. 'So when I say move, you get to your feet and you run and you do not stop. There's a two-thousand-pound unexploded bomb in that crater, and all it could take to set it off is being hit by one of these bricks. Savvy?'

Knowing now not only that he was completely serious, but also the danger they were in, all thoughts of kneeing him in the groin faded as Sam nodded a second time.

'We've got ten more seconds. If we survive those without it going off, then we've got two minutes to get clear.'

At three and nearly two years old respectively, Sally's sons weren't old enough to be aware of the dark times they were living through, and as usual when Doris let her in and then led the way to her cosy parlour, both Tommy and Harry hurled themselves at her, wrapping their small arms around her knees.

'Have you two been good boys for Auntie Doris

then?' Sally asked them lovingly as she kneeled down to hug and kiss them.

'Yeth,' Harry lisped adorably, whilst Tommy nodded firmly.

'It really is good of you to have them for me, Doris,' Sally thanked Molly's mother-in-law gratefully.

'I wouldn't have it any other way. As fond of your pair of young scamps as if they were me own grandchildren, I am,' Doris Brookes assured Sally affectionately. 'I've given them their tea. Now don't you go saying anything,' she warned Sally firmly. 'I had a bit extra on account of me being on duty at the hospital these last few nights and eating there. I've given our Lillibet her tea as well,' she added, nodding in the direction of Molly's stepdaughter and niece.

'I'm sorry I'm a bit later than I said. I managed to call in at the chemist's, though, and I've collected all the kiddies' orange juice and cod liver oil allowances. Here's Molly's.' Sally handed over the bottles, along with the necessary stamped ration books.

'Lillibet will really thank you for that,' Doris laughed. 'She hates that cod liver oil.'

'Tommy's the same,' Sally agreed. 'But I tell him he won't grow up big and strong like his dad if he doesn't have it.'

'Well, Dr Ross that's to replace old Dr Jennings would certainly agree with you there. He was up at the hospital yesterday and I heard him saying how important it was for kiddies to have it.'

'What's he like?' Sally asked. 'Only he's going to have his work cut out if he's to be as well thought of as Dr Jennings.'

'You're right there, Sally. A good man, was Dr Jennings. Thought a lot of him, folks round here did. This new doctor's a lot younger than I expected. A Scot he is, an' all, and a bit what they call "dour", you know: doesn't say much and looks a bit down in the mouth. He's moving into Dr Jennings's old house, of course, since he's taking over the practice, but I don't know if we're going to see him looking after us like Dr Jennings did. I remember Dr Jennings telling me once when my Frank was little, and I'd bin crying me eyes out on account of him being poorly and me not being able to afford to have a doctor round, that I wasn't to worry because he always charged them patients wot were a bit better off a little bit more so that he could do right by them as didn't have enough to pay him to come out. Ever so good like that, he was. That's why everyone loved him so much. There's many a mother round here has a lot to thank him for, and I can't help wishing that the old doctor had stayed on until after Molly has had her baby.'

'I remember when Harry was a few months old how he had that terrible chest and I was worried sick. Came out to him straight away, Dr Jennings did, and wouldn't take a penny,' Sally agreed, looking lovingly at her two sons.

Like many boys, they were inclined to be a bit too adventurous at times, but they were loving little lads as well as stout-hearted. They were her pride and joy, and woe betide anyone who ever said a word against them. There was nothing she would not do to keep them safe and give them the very best that she could.

'Don't you go tempting fate now saying that,' Doris warned her, breaking off as the back door opened and her daughter-in-law, Molly, called out a cheerful greeting.

'My, Sally, you look glam,' she announced.

Sally pulled a small face. 'I've just bin down the Grafton, practising with the Waltonettes.'

'You've got a lovely voice, Sally,' Doris joined in. 'If you was to ask me I'd say there's not many about that can sing as sweet as you can. I was listening to you in church the other Sunday. Fair lifted me heart, it did, to hear you.'

'Frank's mam's right, Sally, you *have* got a lovely voice,' Molly reiterated ten minutes later as they walked down the Close together at a pace slow enough to accommodate Molly's advancing pregnancy. Sally was pushing Harry in the pushchair she had swapped her pram for, and Tommy walking sturdily alongside them, restrained by the reins Sally was keeping a firm hold of. 'You could be one of them girl singers wi' them bands that tour the munitions factories and go on the wireless, and no mistake.'

'No, I couldn't, Molly, because that'd mean travelling around a bit and I couldn't leave my two little 'uns. It's bad enough as it is, but I can't afford not to work, and I'd have to anyway just as soon as Tommy reaches five, and he's three now.' Sally knew she sounded defensive, but she couldn't even tell Molly, her closest friend, about the shameful secret that woke her up in the night and set her heart pounding with sick dread.

'Five – that's another two years away yet, Sally. I hope this war's over before then.'

'Don't we all, but it doesn't much look like being, does it?' Sally was relieved the conversation had moved away from the subject of her work. 'I reckon if it was about to be over then we wouldn't be having all them Americans pouring into the country, would we?'

'No, you're right,' Molly agreed. 'My Frank was saying that there's bin a fair bit of trouble in some of the pubs between the Americans and the British servicemen, fights and that.'

Sally bent her head ostensibly to check on Tommy's reins but in reality to conceal her expression from her friend. However, as though she had guessed what she was feeling, Molly apologised immediately.

'Oh, Sally, I'm sorry. I wasn't thinking. Me and my big mouth, going on about my Frank when you still haven't heard anything from your Ronnie.'

She'd always had a soft heart, had Molly, and always been ready to put others first, Sally knew. 'It's all right, Molly. After all, it's not your Frank's fault that he's on home duties whilst my Ronnie got posted overseas. 'Sides, your Frank's got that bad hand of his and there's many that would have just sat back and let others get on wi' doing their duty for them, not like your Frank, who practically begged the barracks to find him some work. Your Frank's a good man – Ronnie always said so. Do you remember when Frank and Johnny Everton first joined up and they was asking my Ronnie what it was like to be in the army on account of him already being there?'

Molly nodded.

'That reminds me,' Sally went on. 'I heard the other day that Johnny's back in Liverpool. Seemingly he's with the bomb disposal lot.'

When Molly didn't say anything Sally didn't pursue the subject. After all, Molly had been engaged to Johnny at one time, even if the engagement hadn't lasted very long. Then after Dunkirk, when Johnny's unit had been posted to home duties, Johnny had somehow or other ended up working with one of the army rescue teams at the same time as Molly was with the WVS.

They had reached the gate to the neat small house Sally had been renting since the beginning of the war, and which she now thought of, like the Close itself, as her home far more than she had ever done the noisy terrace in Manchester where she had grown up.

'We'll be back to dark evenings come the end of next month when we lose double summer time. I can't say that I'm looking forward to it,' Molly commented.

'Me neither,' Sally agreed. She had more reason than most to dislike the dark nights. You always got some nosy ARP warden asking you who you were and where you were going, just when you didn't want those kind of questions. 'Harry will be two the first week in October, and the last time my Ronnie was home was just after Dunkirk. Tommy was only a baby then and Harry not even born.'

When Molly reached out and squeezed her arm sympathetically, Sally shook her head.

'Don't pay any attention to me, Molly. I'm just having a bit of a bad day, that's all. It's this war. It gets to us all at times, and don't we know it? I reckon that having a bit of a party for Tommy and Harry, like I said the other week, will cheer us all up. What with Tommy being born the day war broke out I can't bring meself to have a party for him, somehow, and that don't seem fair, so I thought I'd mek it up to him by having one for both of them together. Besides, it meks sense to have one party for them both, especially with all this rationing. You could bring your two round and I'll have the other kiddies from the Close in as well. I'll ask Daisy Cartwright if she wants to come with her lads, and since Harry isn't that keen on eating up all his egg allowance every week, I reckon he won't mind me using a couple of them to make a bit of a cake. I've got some sugar put by, and I dare say Edith will let me have some of her home-made jam. Bless 'em, the little 'uns deserve all the fun we can give them.'

Molly agreed. With three years of war behind them, and increasingly stringent rationing giving her children a bit of fun was something that every mother wanted to do.

Despite it being only September, recent heavy rain meant that the house felt chilly and slightly damp, making Sally dread the coming winter, and think longingly of the days when coal had been plentiful and she would have been able to leave a decent fire banked down against their return home on a cold evening.

This winter, like last winter, she would no doubt have to leave both boys wrapped in their outdoor clothes whilst she got the fire lit, and she knew that she would be blessing Albert Dearden, Molly's father, for his kindness in discreetly tipping into her cellar a good-sized bagful of the coal he would have painstakingly collected whilst he was at work up at the grid iron, as Edge Lane's large goods yard was known locally. The heavily laden wagons passing through the sidings, taking coal to factories, often spilled a bit of coal and the men working the yard had an unofficial 'right' to pick it up for their own use.

When the winter cold really started to bite Molly and Sally took it in turns to have a fire, both families sharing its warmth.

Winter. Sally shivered. No, she didn't want to start thinking about that yet.

She looked at her sons. Tommy was a real live wire and had been early both to walk and talk. Harry had been crawling until he was nearly eighteen months and then had stood up and walked like he had been doing it for months. He still wasn't saying much, though, and when he tried Tommy butted in and spoke for him.

'Come on, you two, let's get you out of your coats.'

She took Harry's off first, because she knew that once Tommy had his off he'd be racing around and then she'd have a job trying to keep Harry from wanting to join him.

The coats were good sturdy Harris tweed, real bargains that Doris Brookes had heard about from someone at the hospital, who had heard that when one of the posh Liverpool boys' private schools had evacuated its pupils it had left behind three trunks filled with only slightly worn second-hand clothes, and they were going to be sold off.

Doris hadn't wasted any time; she had gone straight down to the school and had come back with two bags bursting with good-quality clothes. That had been early on in the war, and Sally acknowledged that both she and Molly had good reason to be grateful to Frank's mother for her foresight. Tommy might complain that his long woollen socks made him itch, but what mattered more to Sally was that they had kept his legs warm all through two winters, and that with two pairs of them she was able to dry one out without him having to go without or wear damp socks.

At least Harry was nearly out of nappies now, she thought thankfully as she removed her younger son's coat, and checked his well-padded behind. It had been a real blessing for her that she had fallen pregnant before war had been declared and that she had had the sense to buy in a really good supply of terrys from that stall on the market that used to sell off factory seconds. That stall, like all the others selling essentials at bargain prices, had long since vanished. Terry nappies were a rationed luxury these days.

Having removed the boys' outdoor clothes, Sally left her sons playing on the floor, Tommy with a set of tin soldiers Frank had given him, and Harry with the wooden train that Ronnie had bought just after Tommy had been born. Toys, like everything else, were hard to come by and cherished by those fortunate enough to have them. The once bright paintwork of the wooden train had faded and was missing completely in places, but that didn't seem to interfere with Harry's enjoyment of it, Sally reflected, listening to him making choo choo noises as she made them their supper. Since Doris had given them their tea, they wouldn't need much tonight, nor a bath either. Doris was a true good Samaritan and the best neighbour a young mother could have, and Sally just wished there was something she could do to show her appreciation.

'Seeing these young 'uns grow up is all the thanks I want or need,' Doris told her whenever Sally tried to thank her. 'Your two are like my own to me, Sally, especially since I delivered both of them.'

As she stirred the soup she was heating, Sally heard an outraged roar. Harry! She turned round just in time to see Tommy trying to prise out of his fat baby hand the soldier he was clutching determinedly.

'Let him have it, Tommy. He's not doing any harm,' she told her elder son tiredly.

'It's mine,' Tommy glowered, still trying to retrieve it, then releasing his brother when Harry threw the solder inexpertly across the room.

Boys! Molly was so lucky. Lillibet was such a little doll and so good, but then little girls were so much easier, so people said, although Doris said that little boys were more loving. Every time she worried about her own two not having their dad around, Sally reminded herself of what a good job Doris had done bringing up her Frank single-handedly as a young widow. Frank was a lovely man. A good son and an even better husband and father. If Molly wasn't so nice it would have been easy to envy her, what with her husband at home, and her family around her.

Sally's own family had urged her to return to Manchester but she had her own reasons for staying where she was, and they weren't reasons she could explain to them. Or to anyone. Her Ronnie had it bad enough being a POW without having to carry the burden of her betraying him and letting everyone know what was going on.

She stiffened as she heard a determined knock on the door. She knew who that would be! She had told him not to come round here, and he had agreed that he wouldn't. But it was him, she just knew it.

THREE

'Run!'

As a girl Sam had prided herself on being able to outrun her brother, but plainly that was not good enough for this man. Not content with issuing that command, he virtually yanked her to her feet, then grabbed hold of her hand, pulling her along with him as he ran down the street at breakneck speed.

'Down . . . down . . .' he yelled at her as soon as they rounded the corner into another street, pushing her down to the pavement and then following her, covering her body with his own.

Her heart was pounding – with exertion, not fear, she assured herself firmly. Her companion showed no awareness of the intimacy of his lying on top of her, and was instead studying his watch, whilst Sam held her breath, waiting for the bomb to explode.

'Looks like the bugger isn't going to blow after all.'

'What?' Sam stared up at him in disbelief. 'You

knew all along that nothing was going to happen, didn't you?' she accused him angrily. 'I suppose you think it's funny acting like that. Well, for your information I've got a good mind to report you,' she told him wildly.

'*You* report me? That's a good one. You're the one who ignored the warning signs and damn-near blew us and the whole street to bits. And if anyone is going to report anyone it will be me reporting you! That's a two-thousand-pound bomb down there,' he reminded her bluntly.

'And you would know, of course,' Sam snapped back smartly.

Instead of responding, he leaned slightly away from her and produced a torch from his pocket, which he shone up at his own shoulder. 'See that?'

Something unpleasant and uncomfortable was gripping Sam's stomach as she stared up at the unmistakable Bomb Disposal Unit insignia on his dust-streaked jacket. Numbly she nodded.

'Know what it means?'

'Bomb Disposal,' Sam offered weakly.

'That's right, which by my reckoning makes it part of my job to be checking up on UXBs, and I'd just as soon be doing that without some bloody silly girl all but setting the ruddy thing off. Three days I've bin checking up on old Kurt there, waiting for the captain to give the order to move in and sort him out, and then you nearly go and blow us both to kingdom come when the ruddy street is closed off as plain as daylight.'

His torch was still on and whilst Sam listened to

him with growing hostility she also registered that beneath the dirt he had the kind of raffish dark good looks that would send some members of her sex giddy with excitement. Some members of her sex, but not her. She was totally immune to dangerously handsome men with war-hardened bodies, who looked as though they knew far more about her sex than it was good for a girl to have them know. And besides, she could just bet that he was the kind who went for chocolate-box soft and pretty girls with curves and dimples.

'So what are you going to do now that the bomb *hasn't* gone off?' she challenged him.

'There's only one thing I can do.' His body moved on hers, and alarm shot through her. He wasn't actually going to try to make an advance to her was he? Because if he was . . .

'Bomb's got to be defused, and that's that.'

Sam felt a thrill of genuine horror ice through her. 'You mean you're going back to do that?'

When he started to laugh her horror turned to chagrined angry pride, her face burning hotly. She had never liked being made fun of.

'It's only commissioned officers that do that – you know, them as wear the posh hats and the egg yolk,' he mocked her, using the current slang expression to describe the gold braiding on top-ranking officers' uniforms. 'Me and the lads only get to mess around in the muck, making sure they can get to the fuses. And that's what we'll be doing come daylight.'

He was moving off her now and getting to his

feet. Quickly Sam followed suit, sucking in her breath when he suddenly turned his torch on her, exposing her face to his scrutiny. For some reason she felt self-conscious and uncomfortably aware of what to him would be her shortcomings, compared with the kind of girl he no doubt admired, and at the same time angry and resentful because something in the way he was studying her was forcing those thoughts on her. It was a relief when the beam of the torch moved downwards.

'ATS. I thought you lot normally hunted in packs,' he said derisively.

Sam was well aware of the low esteem in which some men held girls who had joined up. She had heard all the crude jokes about their supposed lack of morals and their man-chasing, and now her temper was well and truly up.

'That's only if we think there's anything around worth pursuing,' she returned smartly, 'which there isn't right now.'

A bus rumbling past further down the road broke the silence stretching between them. What was she doing standing here trading insults with this stranger? She had been out far longer than she had intended and she still had to find her way back to the billet. The bus was slowing to a stop. Making up her mind, Sam hurried towards it, refusing to give in to the temptation to turn round to see what he was doing and if he was watching her.

*

'I'm afraid I'm rather lost and I need to get back to my billet,' she told the conductress slightly breathlessly, giving her the address.

'You'll need the number sixty-seven. Nearest stop is three streets away.'

Sam's face fell.

'Look, we're on our way back to the depot – if you want to stay on board you'll be able to pick one up there,' the conductress offered.

Thanking her, Sam subsided into a seat, allowing herself to look down the sandbagged street only once they were almost past it, but there was nothing to be seen, and no one to be seen either.

Sally opened the door just enough to allow her to peer out, her heart sinking as her worse fears were confirmed.

'About time. I was just beginning to lose me patience.'

The man standing on her front step was small and squat, with powerful shoulders, the look in his eyes as hard as his voice, but Sally refused to let herself be intimidated.

'You've got no business coming here. I made arrangements with Mr Wade—'

'I don't care what arrangements you made with the old man. Things have changed now, and in future I'll be calling round every week on the dot to collect what's due, and let me warn you, missus, there's new management in charge now and they don't intend to put up with any soft-soaping or sob stories, so if you'll tek my advice you'll have your money ready and waiting when I call round for it, otherwise it will be the worse for you.'

Sally felt sick with a mixture of anger, helplessness and dismay. 'How do I know that you're from Mr Wade?' she challenged him. 'We've all heard about bogus debt collectors setting themselves up and claiming to be working for moneylenders when they're doing no such thing. Mr Wade never said anything to me about there being any changes.'

'Aye, well, mebbe he didn't know there was going to be any hisself.'

'What do you mean?' Sally asked sharply.

'There's some as thought the old man was losing his grip and that folk weren't paying up when they should, so there's bin some changes made. If you don't believe me that's up to you but I ain't leaving here wi'out your payment.'

Sally hesitated. She had half been expecting something like this when she had called round at the anonymous terraced house the moneylender rented to pay her week's money and had found it locked and empty. All manner of rumours abounded about the network of moneylenders, who traditionally had supplied small loans at extortionate rates to the city's poor, being forced to hand over their businesses to those who ran the gangs of the black market spivs. One of the most notorious of all of these gangs was run by 'the Boss', Bertha Harris, and her five sons. It was said that the Harris family thought nothing of administering beatings and breaking limbs when debts went unpaid.

Whilst she worried about what to do, suddenly from upstairs her maternal ear caught the sound of baby Harry waking up.

'Wait here,' she told the man, flushing when he put his foot inside the door before she could close it, wrapping his huge meaty hand round the door edge.

By the time she reached the back parlour her hands were trembling so much she could hardly count out the money from her purse. Not that she needed to count it. After all, she knew to the penny just how many extra hours she had to work every week to pay for the pitifully small sum of money Ronnie had originally borrowed when they had first got married.

She had known nothing about this loan until before the end of Ronnie's last leave. He had been on edge and distant with her, alternating between moody silences and outbursts of angry temper the whole time. Then when she had begged him to tell her what was wrong it had all come pouring out. Tears had filled his eyes as he had admitted how he had borrowed money from a moneylender just before their wedding, primarily to pay off some betting debts he had run up. He had, he said, got in with a crowd of other young soldiers who all wanted to have a good time. The moneylender had persuaded him to borrow a bit extra to help out with the wedding expenses, and to pay for the honeymoon. Everything had been all right at first, he had told her, until he had increased the loan when Tommy had been born, and now he had fallen behind with the payments and Mr Wade's debt collectors were pressing him to make good the deficit.

It gave Sally a sick feeling in the pit of her stomach just thinking about that afternoon even now. At first she had been disbelieving. Ronnie was a serving soldier, earning as much as any other man, and she certainly wasn't an extravagant housewife – far from it; she budgeted carefully and was proud of herself for doing so. Now Ronnie had revealed to her a side of his life she had never dreamed existed: betting, borrowing money and getting into debt. These weren't things that belonged to the kind of life she had believed they had had; the decent respectable safe kind of life that had made her feel so secure and which had deepened her love for Ronnie for being the good provider she had believed he was. Then suddenly she had felt as though a trap door had opened beneath her feet, plunging her into a frightening place. As the reality of what Ronnie was saying to her had sunk in, her shock had given way to anger against him for being so irresponsible. That in turn had given way to compassionate pity when she had seen how sorry and ashamed he was. They were a married couple sharing the good and the bad times together, she had told him firmly as she held him as tightly and protectively as though he were their young son's age. Somehow they would find a way to pay off the money that was owing.

That had been when she had first started working at the Grafton.

But somehow the loan just never seemed to get repaid, and then Ronnie had admitted to her that he had got involved with a betting syndicate during his leave and that he had had to increase their loan to cover his share of its losses. They had had a horrible verbal fight, which had ended up with Ronnie clinging to her and begging her to forgive him whilst promising that it wouldn't happen again. What could she do? He was a soldier about to be sent on overseas duties – how could she let him go without giving him the comfort of her love and her trust, no matter what her inner fears? And so she had hugged him back and held him tightly and told him that he mustn't worry. She had even managed to laugh and say lightly that what with the extra work the Government wanted women to take on for the war effort, she would have the debt repaid by the time he was next home on leave. He had been so grateful for her understanding and so lovingly tender and filled with regret that she had told herself that she had done the right thing. But then when he had gone she had discovered that the amount he had borrowed was far more than he had told her, and she had been filled with angry despair and even resentment.

She had never imagined when she had first met him that Ronnie would turn out to be a betting man. He had seemed far too respectable and decent. She had thought they were the kind of young couple who could keep their heads held up high, and she had even felt sorry for the poor of the city who lived down by the docks, living constantly with the shame of having to borrow against tomorrow to pay for today, opening her purse freely to slip a few pennies to the children she saw begging.

Now the pride she had originally felt in Ronnie and their marriage had given way to fear – and that fear had more than one face. Initially her fear had been because she had discovered that Ronnie wasn't the sensible worldly-wise husband and provider she had believed him to be; the rock she and their children could depend on. But then later had come the fear of the shame she would suffer if their debt became public knowledge, and most of all, fear of how they were going to repay the money and what would happen if they fell behind with their repayments.

When Ronnie had broken down and admitted to her that not only had he foolishly borrowed from a moneylender once but that he had also gone back to him and borrowed again, Sally had struggled to understand how the strong capable Ronnie she loved and depended on so much could have turned into this man who was weak and vulnerable and afraid, and who was admitting to her that he didn't know what to do.

One of the things Sally had loved so much about Ronnie was his dependability. As a child she had grown up in a chaotic family environment with her father often out of work, but well paid when he was in work, and so life had seemed filled with the giddy highs of her mother's excitement when they had money and the frightening lows of her despair when they didn't. Sally had yearned for a life in which those highs and lows were exchanged for the calm of a decent steady man with a nice steady job, and part of the reason she had fallen in love with Ronnie was because he had seemed to embody those virtues. To discover that he had done something that even her own parents had steadfastly refused to do, and gone to a money-lender, had left her feeling as though her whole world had been turned upside down. Only the very poorest of the poor, or the feckless and weak, went to moneylenders, and certainly not people who lived on Chestnut Close.

Sally had known real shame along with her shock and her fear. But she was a young woman with a lot of common sense and courage, and so she had gone to see the moneylender from whom Ronnie had borrowed the money, and they had come to an arrangement whereby she would call on him weekly with their payments instead of him sending round a 'tallyman' to collect it from the house. That way at least she had hoped to keep up a front of respectability.

It had made her feel physically sick to see written down the amount they now owed, so very much more than she had thought. She had told Mr Wade proudly that she wanted to increase their repay-ments so that they could reduce the money owing faster, swallowing back her longing to beg him not to lend Ronnie any more. She could not go behind her husband's back in such a way, and humiliate him.

She admitted now, as she hurried back to the door and handed over the money to the waiting man, that maybe she should have gone back to see Mr Wade and asked him to let her reduce the payments once she realised what a struggle she was going to have meeting the increased amount she had volunteered to pay, but she was desperate to get the loan cleared as quickly as she could, and she had her pride just like everyone else.

It seemed to take for ever for the man to count slowly through the amount she had handed him before he finally gave a grunt of satisfaction and stashed it in his pocket.

He was about to turn away when Sally reminded him firmly, 'Mr Wade always writes the amount down and signs it.'

'Mebbe he did, but that's not the way the new owners do business.'

He had gone before Sally could object, melting into the darkness, leaving her feeling relieved that none of her neighbours had seen him but at the same time highly anxious. This wasn't like worrying about rationing or being bombed; it wasn't an anxiety she could share with anyone else and find comfort in the fact that they were in things together.

It was far later than Sam had planned when the bus finally set her down at the stop closest to her billet. The earlier sea mist had now become a steady downpour, the rain trickling down inside the upturned collar of her greatcoat. Quickly she hurried towards the entrance to the school, dismayed to find that the door now seemed to be locked. Now what was she to do? To her relief, before she had to decide the door was suddenly opened from the inside, allowing her to step inside and quickly close the door behind her to observe the blackout rules about not allowing any light to escape into the night darkness and so potentially provide a target for German bombers.

In the dim light from the bare bulb hanging from the ceiling she could see that the chair behind the desk was now occupied by a very stern-looking warrant officer.

'Private Grey reporting for duty, ma'am,' Sam offered hurriedly, suddenly very conscious of the rubble and brick dust on her greatcoat.

'Strange,' the warrant office marvelled nastily. She was well into her thirties, Sam guessed, with an unusually broad, somehow flattened face and slightly bulbous protruding eyes, 'only we seem to have someone of that name here already, at least according to her kitbag. Got a double, have we, Private?'

'I . . . no . . . that is . . . There wasn't anyone here to report to when I arrived, ma'am,' Sam told her desperately, 'and so I thought I'd just get some fresh air and familiarise myself with the city . . .'

One thin grey eyebrow rose as the warrant officer looked Sam up and down. 'Acquainting yourself with the city, was it? It looks to me more like you've been acquainting yourself with something very different indeed, Private.' She pushed back her chair and stood up. 'Let me explain something to you, Private. Here in this billet and this unit we do not waltz in and dump our kitbags and then waltz out again like we was out of uniform.'

Sam had come across a wide variety of authority figures since she had joined the ATS but never one like this. Instinctively she knew that the woman confronting her now was someone who relished the power her authority gave her. She wouldn't hesitate to bully and terrorise those under her, Sam guessed, and she also deduced that the warrant officer had already made up her mind that Sam was someone she didn't very much like.

Well, that was fine, Sam decided, determinedly ignoring the sickly little feeling in her stomach that said she was upset by the hostility she could sense. She could feel herself starting to shake a bit inside and she was longing for the calming effect of a cigarette.

'Sorry, ma'am,' she apologised dutifully, fixing her gaze on a point to the left of the warrant officer's shoulder rather than risk engaging in eye contact with her. 'It won't happen again.'

Sam could almost sense the warrant officer's disappointment that she wasn't going to give her the opportunity to tear another strip off her. Sam was surprised herself. It wasn't like her to allow herself to be intimated, or to pass up an opportunity to have a bit of fun by coming up with some far-fetched explanation for what she had done.

'No it won't,' the warrant officer agreed meaningfully, 'because—'

The sudden opening of a door behind the desk and the appearance of a tall, slim, grey-haired woman wearing a captain's uniform had the warrant officer along with Sam springing to attention and saluting.

Whatever the warrant officer had been about to say remained unsaid as the captain looked at Sam with surprisingly kind hazel eyes and said calmly, 'Ah, our wanderer has returned has she, Warrant Officer?' The hazel gaze skimmed Sam from head to foot and then paused thoughtfully on her face.

'Took a wrong turning in the blackout, ma'am, and fell over some sandbags,' Sam offered by way of explanation of her appearance.

The captain nodded, then told Sam calmly, 'Warrant Officer Sands will no doubt have informed you of the routine here. First thing after breakfast, transport arrives to take you all to your designated areas of work. You have been assigned to Deysbrook Barracks.'

No supper! And she was very hungry, Sam realised, but of course she didn't say anything.

She stood stiffly at attention until the captain said briskly, 'Dismissed.'

At least she had escaped whatever punishment the warrant officer had no doubt been planning for her, Sam acknowledged, recovering some of her normal insouciance as she made her way to the dormitory where she had left her kitbag.

Not wanting to disturb the other girls, she tried to be as quiet as possible but the discovery that

45

the shape she could feel on the bed closest to the door wasn't her kitbag but the sleeping body of another girl caused both her and the girl in the bed to yelp in protest, and within seconds torches were being switched on all over the dormitory as the noise woke the other girls.

'Sorry, sorry . . .' Sam apologised ruefully, 'only I left my kitbag here . . .'

'The Toad moved it,' a girl in a bed halfway down the room informed her sleepily.

'She means Warrant Officer Sands,' another girl explained unnecessarily, since Sam had quick-wittedly recognised how appropriate the warrant officer's nickname was. 'Lord,' the girl continued, 'when she found your kitbag there without any sign of you, she swelled up so much with fury we thought she was going to burst.'

'Pity she didn't,' someone else announced fervently. 'Gave me jankers for a whole week, she did, just because I hadn't got me cap on straight. Me poor hands were red raw with all that scrubbing and potato peeling in freezing cold water. You want to watch out for her: if she takes a dislike to you you'll know all about it and no mistake.'

'Go on with you, May. Give her a chance to get herself settled in before you start scaring her half to death about old Toad face,' the girl whose bed was next to Sam's spoke up firmly, before warning Sam, 'I don't want to tell you what to do, but if I was you I'd get myself into bed before Toadie comes up here checking up on you. She's got a real mean streak to her and there's nothing she likes better than an excuse to come down heavy on one of us. I'm Corporal Hazel Gibson, by the way.'

'Sam Grey,' Sam reciprocated. 'And thanks for the warning, Hazel, I mean, Corp.' She stifled a sudden yawn. It had been a long day, and she was more than ready for her bed.

'Mind you, at least Toadie's a real live human being, not like that ghost wot's supposed to go walking all over the place at night,' the girl the corporal had addressed as May announced with ghoulish relish.

'A ghost?' a nervously quavering little voice from the bed closest to the door protested shakily.

'Yes. Comes looking for the girl wot got him killed on account of her taking up with someone else and her new lover murdering him,' May told them. 'At least that's what I've bin told.'

'Go on with you, May. You don't half talk a load of rubbish,' the corporal squashed the almost palpable air of nervous tension creeping through the room, leaving Sam free to follow the corporal's advice and make haste to get herself into the only spare bed.

Her new dorm mates seemed a decent crowd, she reflected, especially Hazel Gibson, unlike the warrant officer, and that bossy Bomb Disposal chap. She certainly didn't want to run into him again.

FOUR

'I'm sorry that the warrant officer gave me your bed.'

Sam smiled at the other new girl to join the group, as they emerged from the showers at the same time. She didn't look old enough to have joined up, Sam thought, with her huge hazel eyes and her patent shyness. Sam hadn't missed the nearly bald teddy bear hastily stuffed out of sight before she had got out of bed.

'It wasn't your fault,' Sam assured her with a smile.

The other girl looked relieved. 'I'm Mouse,' she introduced herself. 'At least that's what everyone calls me although I was christened Marianne. I didn't think that they'd be sending me to work in a barracks, I really didn't. I mean, I only joined up because I had to. I didn't want to at all really. It was my aunt's idea . . . She said that with me being on my own . . . I thought I'd be staying close to home, and doing a bit of office work.'

Sam could see that she was close to tears.

Mouse's naïvety, combined with her air of help-lessness made Sam wonder how on earth she had managed to survive the ATS long enough to get through the training weeks. The Government must indeed be desperate for young women to fill the mundane jobs left empty by the men who had been sent on active service.

'Well, that's where you went wrong,' she told her wryly. 'You should have told them you wanted to drive trucks and be posted as far away from home as possible and then you'd have probably ended up being a stenographer.'

'Drive trucks?' Mouse shuddered. 'Oh, no . . . I couldn't possibly do anything like that.'

She was as green as grass and apparently completely devoid of a sense of humour, Sam reflected pityingly. The kind of girl who *should* have been allowed to stay at home with her mother.

'Come on, you two, buck up,' Hazel, who Sam thought would be much more her cup of tea with her jolly no-nonsense manner, called out, warning, as she fastened her own uniform blouse and tucked it into her shirt, 'You're not dressed yet and if you don't get a move on you'll miss breakfast.'

Miss breakfast. Sam's stomach gave a worried growl. She was just about to hurry over to her own bed, when she realised that somehow or other Mouse had already managed to get into the disgusting pink foundation garments that were part of their official uniform whilst in the shower and that she was now trying to keep the towel wrapped protectively around herself as she continued to get dressed.

Shaking her head over such time-consuming and unnecessary primness, Sam reached her bed and grabbed her own clothes.

'You'll never get away with wearing that,' Hazel warned her when she saw the non-uniform white brassiere Sam was fastening. 'Not if Toadie sees it. She likes the thought of us being trussed up in our passionkillers, doesn't she, girls?'

The chorus of assents that greeted Hazel's comment made Sam laugh. With her slim almost boyish figure, the last thing she needed was the one-size-fits-all proportions of the regulation underwear and corsetry supplied to the ATS. In addition to two uniforms, and four pairs of lisle stockings, everyone was also issued with three pairs of khaki lock-knit knickers, two pairs of blue and white striped pyjamas, eight starched collars and two studs, and the bane of Sam's life, three pink brassieres and two pink boned corsets. The corsets Sam was determined never to wear, but the bras had to be worn for the sake of decency, if nothing else, and she had been very grateful when her mother had managed to find a local tailoress who had enough experience of the corset industry to be able to alter the firmly structured cone-shaped cups designed to control to military standard any potentially overexuberant female breasts, to something more appropriate for Sam's much less voluptuous shape. She still felt trussed up and uncomfortable, though. They chafed her skin as well as her desire for freedom, and she would wear her own non-regulation underclothes as long as she could get away with it.

'It was such a pity that my corsets got lost in the laundry at my last posting,' she grinned, her eyes dancing with devilment as she told them mock innocently, 'I was ever so upset about it, but what can you do? They'd just disappeared.'

'Come on,' the sturdily built girl keeping watch by the door hissed down the dorm. 'Toadie's on her way up.'

All around her Sam could see girls moving like lightning, fastening ties, doing up blouses, reaching for shoes and jackets, and at the same time straightening up their beds, the girls who were already dressed quickly leaving their own made-up beds to deal with those of the girls who weren't, so that by the time the warrant officer had reached the doorway, every young woman in the room was fully dressed, and every bed was neatly made.

Sam could have sworn that her glance lingered longer on her than it did on anyone else as they filed past her and headed for the stairs, but she refused to give in to the temptation to look directly at her in order to check.

'Thanks for making up my bed,' she told the pretty fair-haired girl whose bed was next to her own, as she caught up with her on the stairs, five minutes later when they had been dismissed.

'We all help one another out in this unit,' came the smiling response. 'I dare say you'll be repaying the favour.'

'Yeah, by keeping a window open so that you can get back in when you haven't got a late-night pass, Lynsey,' Hazel commented, overhearing their conversation. 'Lynsey here has a raft of men queuing up to take her out and she believes in doing her bit for our boys, don't you, Lynsey?' she teased.

Sam held her breath, half expecting the blonde girl to take offence, but instead she laughed and winked at Sam. 'I certainly do.'

'You want to get her to show you her collection of engagement rings, Sam,' Hazel grinned. 'How many was it at the last count, Lynsey?'

'Eight. It would have been nine, but Pat, that Canadian I was seeing, changed his mind and said that he thought we should just be unofficially engaged. Huh, as if I hadn't worked out what his game was. You could see as plain as anything the white mark on his finger where he'd taken off his wedding ring. The cheek of it, thinking that I wouldn't guess what he was up to.' She gave a disapproving sniff. 'If there's one thing I can't stand it's a married man pretending that he isn't. You'll get a lot of that here in Liverpool, Sam,' she warned. 'There's troop ships arriving every week filled with men who haven't seen a girl in months. Have you got a steady?'

Sam gave a brief shake of her head. Her lack of a young man had recently become a bit of a sore subject, mainly because her elder brother had given her a bit of a lecture on his last leave, warning her that she should start behaving in a more feminine manner and that she frightened off his friends with her tomboy ways. She had shrugged off his criticism, affecting not to care when the following evening, at the dance he had taken her to, she had been left to sit on her own whilst other girls – girls with curls and soft curves and giggling voices – were surrounded by uniformed young men eager to dance with them. That night, lying in bed unable to sleep, she had been forced to recognise that her youthful daydreams in which she had outshot and outdared Robin Hood, outrode and outrobbed Dick Turpin, to win their admiration and the friendship – daydreams that as she had matured had grown into an unacknowledged belief that one day she would fall in love with a real-life hero whose heart she would win with her prowess and her ability to compete with him – were never going to be recognised and that heroes did not fall in love with girls who matched them skill for skill but instead preferred girls dressed in pretty clothes who stood on the sidelines, watching them admiringly.

Sam had told herself that she didn't care, and she wasn't going to change, not even though Rory Blake, the ringleader of her brother's gang, whom she had secretly admired for years, hadn't once asked her to dance, and had laughed at her short hair.

Why should she care? She had more important things to do and think about. There was a war to be fought and won, and that surely was far more exciting than having a steady, she assured herself as the welcome smells of breakfast filled the air of the large panelled room they were all filing into.

*

Sally sighed but gave in when she felt Tommy's eager tug on her arm the minute they drew level with the large furniture van parked outside old Dr Jennings's house. The back of the van was open and, as they watched, two men lifted out a heavy mahogany sideboard and started to carry it towards the house. If furniture was being moved in instead of out – and very good quality furniture too, by the look to it – then that surely meant that the new doctor was moving in as well.

Virtually anything with four wheels enthralled Sally's sons, and Harry, restrained in his pushchair, yelled out excitedly, 'Big car.'

'No, it's not a big car, it's a van, Harry,' Tommy corrected his brother sternly.

Sally hid a small smile.

'Come on now,' she urged her elder son, not wanting anyone who might be in the house to think she was being nosy.

The removal men were carrying a packing case out of the van, and as they crossed the pavement a photograph frame fell out of it, the glass shattering as it lay face up on the pavement.

'No, Tommy, be careful.' Sally hurried over to him with the pushchair, warning, 'You'll cut yourself.' Beneath the shattered glass she could see the photograph quite clearly: a pretty fair-haired young woman smiled towards the camera, a chubby blond baby on her knee whilst her free arm drew an equally fair-haired little boy closer to her. Sally had a similarly posed photograph of herself with her own sons, although the young woman in the photograph was wearing far more expensive clothes than she could ever have afforded, she acknowledged ruefully.

She was so engrossed in the photograph that she didn't see the grim-faced man watching her from the bay window of the house until his shadow darkened the photograph.

'Daddy,' Harry announced proudly with a beaming smile for the stranger, oblivious to his glower, as he showed off his newly learned words.

'That's not Daddy, it's a man,' Tommy corrected him scornfully.

In an attempt to hide her embarrassment, Sally shushed her sons, gasping in protest as Tommy ignored her earlier warning to bend down to pick up the photograph.

'No. Leave it. Don't touch it!'

If the Scots accent was unfamiliar, the harsh anger in the male voice was easily recognisable, causing Tommy to draw back his hand too quickly and then whimper as a piece of broken glass pierced his skin.

'Can't you control your children?' he demanded tightly as he bent down to retrieve the broken photograph.

So this was the new doctor Molly's mother-in-law had told her about. Sally eyed him warily. There was a white line of fury round his mouth; his whole body was rigid with it, Sally saw. He obviously had a nasty temper on him, she thought critically. After all it was only a photograph.

Gathering her now sobbing son into her arms,

she retaliated protectively, 'If you hadn't scared him half to death by shouting at him like that he wouldn't have touched it. He's only a little boy. He didn't mean any harm. You should know what they're like. After all, it looks like you've got two of your own.' She looked meaningfully at the photograph.

The expression of bitterness and loathing he gave both her and the boys shocked Sally as much as though he had physically struck her. He was a doctor, a father, and yet he was looking at her and her boys as though he hated them.

It took one of the removal men's brisk, 'Where do you want this, guv?' to break the tension that that sprung up between them, allowing Sally to turn on her heel and hurry away.

What a dreadful man he was, not fit to step into the old doctor's shoes at all, and the way he had looked at the two poor innocent boys . . . like he hated them, Sally thought indignantly, relieved to see that Tommy's cut had stopped bleeding. And just because little Tommy had touched his precious photograph. She knew his sort, the sort who looked down on her sort. Well, he could look down on her all he liked but she was not having him frighten her little boy like that, she decided, her maternal ire aroused.

She had almost reached the end of the street and some compulsion she couldn't resist made her turn to look back the way she had come, her heart jolting against her ribs when she saw that he was still standing there motionless, watching them.

'S'pose he thinks we aren't good enough to touch his precious kids, not even in a ruddy photograph,' she muttered to herself. 'Stuck up, that's what he is, and no mistake. All that posh furniture, and them kids dressed up like little Lord Fauntleroys!' She had been able to tell just from that one brief glimpse at the photograph and the contents of the van that that been on view that Dr Jennings's replacement could provide his wife and children with a far better standard of living than that that his patients were able to enjoy.

'You're late.'

'Sorry, Patti,' Sally apologised breathlessly as she hurried onto the stage. 'My Tommy cut his finger, and then . . .' She stopped when Patti raised her eyebrows and tutted sharply, 'Yes, we can all see that, there's blood all over your sleeve.'

Sally sighed. None of the other Waltonettes had children so how could she expect them to understand? She sensed that Charlie was beginning to think that he would have preferred to take on a stand-in singer without children had he had the choice. She was lucky to have this well-paid source of extra income, she reminded herself, even if the money wasn't regular, and she certainly couldn't afford to lose it by offending Patti, no matter how much she resented the other girl's high-handed and unsympathetic attitude.

'Come on, let's get on with it,' Sybil demanded impatiently. 'My new chap's taking me out later.'

'If by your new chap you mean that fella wot

was buying you drinks the other night, Syl, I've got news for you,' Shirley chipped in. 'He lives two streets away from me and he's got a wife who'll be down here telling you wot's wot if you don't watch out.'

'He never said owt to me about any wife,' Sybil bridled.

'No, well, they never do, do they?' Shirley countered drily, 'but you've bin told now. Three kiddies, he's got, and another on the way.'

'His wife's welcome to him,' Sybil announced after she had digested this news. 'I didn't think much to him anyway, so he's no loss to me. 'Sides, I've heard that there's some more of them Yanks due to arrive soon. Handsome lads, they are, and free spending too.'

'Come on, you two, stop wasting time and let's get practising.'

Patti might be the lead singer but she was older and not as pretty as either Shirley or Sybil, and Sybil had told Sally when Patti's back had been turned that she reckoned that Patti was jealous of them.

'It's me and Shirl that the chaps come to see, not 'er, and she knows it. Past it, she is, but she won't admit it, allus banging on about how she could have been singing with the BBC lot but for her feeling she owed it to Charlie to stick with him.'

'She's got a good voice.' Sally had felt bound to defend the older girl.

'Not as good as yours, it isn't,' Sybil had

surprised her by saying. 'Not that that will do you any favours in her eyes. You want to watch out, Sally, otherwise, she'll be getting jealous of you and then she'll be tricking you to make it look like you're out of key. Done that a few times to Eileen, she did, until Eileen got wise to her.'

'Ready, girls? We'll start off with "Sunshine" and then go into "Apple Tree", OK?'

'I don't know why we're singing about ruddy sunshine when all we've had for days is rain,' Shirley grumbled under her breath, but Sally could already feel the weight of her problems slipping from her shoulders for a few precious minutes in the joy of singing, her spirits lifted by the music. Singing was her special precious something that enriched her senses, although she would have died of embarrassment if she had ever had to explain to anyone just how she felt about it.

'Thank heavens that's over with,' Sybil grimaced. 'Patti was in that sour a mood she could have curdled milk. Where you off now then, Sally? Back to them kids of yours?'

Sally shook her head. 'I'm doing a night shift at the factory. I had to swap a shift with someone else to get time off to rehearse.'

Sybil wrinkled her nose. 'I dunno know why you do that factory work. I mean, it's not as though you have to, wi' you having them kiddies.'

Sally didn't say anything. What could she say, after all?

*

'And you, Grey, you're to report to the quartermaster's office. They're short of a couple of clerk stenographers down there.'

Sam's heart sank. Of all the bad luck. Working in the quartermaster's office had to be the most boring job in the barracks. The last thing she'd joined up for was to spend the war typing out lists of supplies; typing of any kind was bad enough, but this . . .

'Dismissed.'

Miserably Sam fell into line with the other girls, her attention momentarily distracted by the roar of a motorcycle as a dispatch rider swept past them, the wheels of his motorcycle sending up a spray of water from the puddles. A dispatch rider – now there was a job that would have appealed to her, Sam thought enviously. She could ride a motorbike, after all, having 'borrowed' Russell's – without his knowledge. She wouldn't even have minded being sent to work with one of the ack-ack gun teams, not that girls were actually allowed to fire the guns. Anything would have been better than Supplies, and the typing of tedious lists. Sam longed for the excitement of tracking enemy targets, breaking enemy codes, doing something that made her feel that she had a real part to play in winning the war.

'I'm glad that we're going to be working together, aren't you?'

Mouse's timid comment made Sam's heart sink even further. She had nothing against the other girl, it was just that she simply wasn't her sort.

Deysbrook Barracks had originally been a Territorial Army hall and store, which, like so many others, had been extended to cope with the extra demands of the war. The quartermaster's office was housed in a new concrete building, beyond which lay a vast area of what looked like Nissen huts, stores and storage bays serviced by its own delivery yard. The arrangement of the buildings had created a wind tunnel effect that filled the yard with cold salt sea air, accompanied by a droning buffeting noise from the wind itself, and Sam was not surprised to see Mouse shiver miserably and huddle deeper into her greatcoat.

'This can't be the right place,' she protested, when Sam pushed open the door labelled 'Quartermaster's Office'. The rough concrete floor was so cold that Sam could feel its chill right through the soles of her shoes. The air smelled slightly damp and rank, and the single bulb dangling from a cable and swinging in the draught from the door did nothing to enhance the surroundings.

On a notice board were pinned a raft of MOD leaflets and warnings, but no one was sitting behind the battered desk, and Sam, peering into the dimly lit hinterland of shelving behind the desk, was unable to see anyone.

She was just wondering what they should do when a tall fair-haired man, wearing the insignia of the Royal Engineers, and his sergeant's stripes, appeared out of the murky shadows behind the desk.

'Privates Grey and Hatton reporting for stenographer duties for the quartermaster's office, Sarge,' Sam told him smartly. 'But we can't seem to find anyone to report to.'

'The quartermaster's been called away. He should be back soon.' The sergeant had an unexpectedly kind face, and an injured hand, Sam noticed, which probably explained why he wasn't on active service.

The outer door to the office opened and the young Royal Engineer who came in announced anxiously, 'Sarge, them sleepers you wanted have arrived and they're unloading them in the yard, but Corp Watson says you'd better get over there fast, before some other ruddy unit nicks them.'

It was a good five minutes after the sergeant had gone before the door opened again, this time to admit a short red-faced captain with greying ginger hair. He gave both girls hostile glares before stamping over to the desk.

'Privates Grey and Hatton reporting for duty to Captain Elland—' Sam began.

'I know what you are. What I don't know is why the ruddy hell I've been lumbered with you. ATS, women in uniform and taking on men's jobs. No good will come of it.'

Sam longed to defend her sex and her uniform, but for once caution won out over pride and she managed to swallow back the hot words she itched to speak. There were some men – older men in the main, like this one, but not always – who refused to accept that women had a vitally important role to play in the war. No one could be in the ATS for very long without hearing at least one of the crude insults that were bandied about as to the purpose of the women's uniformed service.

'Done any stores work before, have you?' The captain shot the question out at them.

'We were told we'd be working as stenographers, sir,' Sam informed him.

'Stenographers! What in the name of God is the War Office doing sending me stenographers? This is a barracks, not ruddy Whitehall. I've got two battalions to keep equipped, never mind the rest of them the War Office has seen fit to land us with. A stenographer is as much use to me as a pea shooter is to a Spitfire pilot.'

Sam could hear Mouse's audible indrawn sob, but she was made of sterner stuff and automatically she stiffened her spine and straightened her back.

'Come with me.' Captain Elland threw the order at them, turned on his heel without waiting to see if they were following him and marched into the sour-aired gloom behind the desk at such a pace that they were almost in danger of losing sight of him.

Down between rows of rough shelving stacked with clothing and equipment he led them, finally coming to a halt outside an open doorway behind which lay a space more the size of a cupboard than an actual room. In it was a single desk with a chair either side, a typewriting machine and a telephone. The desk itself was stacked high with piles of paper. One single bulb illuminated the windowless and almost airless room On the wall opposite the door Sam could see what looked like a plan of the stores, individual buildings listed by number and the separate rows of shelving within those buildings listed by letter.

'Right,' said the captain, indicating one of the thick piles of pieces of paper. 'These here are the sheets that come in whenever we get a delivery. No driver leaves my yard until his delivery has been checked off, and if I find you letting them go before you've done that you'll be on a report so fast your feet won't touch the ground. Once it's checked off, the stuff has to be taken to its appropriate storage area, and then once it's there, it gets checked again, and only then do you put the list in this pile here,' he indicated another pile of papers, 'so that one of my lads can check you've got it right. Then you make a copy of it and you put one copy at the end of the shelving the goods are on, you put another copy in the file marked Shelving Number whatever, and you give my sergeant a copy so that he can give it to me, and heaven help you if I find out that all these lists don't tally up when I do my checks. Anyone coming into the stores for anything, no matter what it is, has to sign for what gets taken and you have to put a mark on the lists to show what's gone. Savvy?'

Savvy? Of course she did! Sam gave him a seething look of indignation as he turned away from them, her face burning a dark angry red when she heard him mutter insultingly, as he walked away, 'ATS. Bloody officers' groundsheets, that's what they are!'

Sally knew that a lot of the girls didn't like working the night shift, but she didn't mind. For one thing it meant that she could have time during the day to be with her boys, and for another it meant that she could bargain for extra nights off when she needed them to sing with the Waltonettes, by offering to do other girls' night shifts.

The changeover of shifts meant that there was the usual hectic busyness outside the factory, with those women arriving for work pouring off buses that were then filled up by those waiting to leave.

'War work, I'm sick of it,' one of the women on Sally's shift grumbled as they changed into their overalls and got ready. Sally, like most of the women with longer hair, covered hers with a turban to keep it safely out of the way of the machinery.

'It could be worse,' Sally to her cheerfully. 'We could be working on munitions.'

'Aye, and if we was we'd be earning a fair bit more, an' all.'

'Oh, give over moaning, our Janet, will yer? You was saying only the other day as how you felt sorry for them as worked on munitions and that you'd never do it no matter what you was paid on account of the danger and ending up with yellow skin.'

'Oh, that's typical of you, Zena Harrison,' Janet sniffed. 'If you wasn't me cousin I'd have a few sharp words for you, that I would, allus picking a person up on everything they say.'

''Ere, you lot, you'll never guess what I just heard when I was coming past the medical room.'

'Well, I'm telling you, Wanda, if it was some gossip about some daft lass going crying to the nurse of account of her having been doing what she shouldn't with some chap . . .' Zena started to warn, but the other woman shook her head and laughed.

'No, it's nowt like that. They had some new girls in there waiting to have their medicals and I heard this one saying as how she was scared she wouldn't be able to give a urine sample like you have to, and blow me if the woman next to her in the queue doesn't pipe up loud and clear, "Don't worry about that, lass. You can have some of mine, 'cos I can piss for England."'

Sally could just imagine the reaction of that stuck-up new doctor to their conversation. His wife wouldn't have to work in anything so common as munitions; if she did war work it would be something refined and ladylike like being in charge of a group of WVS women. Just thinking about the way he had looked at her and the boys was like peeling a scab off an unhealed wound, her emotional reaction immediate and sharply painful.

The others were still laughing. The girl who had told them the story shook her head and asked them all, 'Anyone going down the Grafton tomorrow night, only I fancy a bit of a night out?'

The other two girls shook their heads whilst

Sally didn't say anything about the fact that she would be singing. She didn't want them to think she was trying to show off or that she was getting above herself. Not that she kept her singing a secret, she just didn't want to be accused of boasting about it. But the thought banished her anger about the ill-tempered doctor. An evening spent singing with the Waltonettes was something to look forward to.

FIVE

Their work over for the day, the ATS girls crowded onto the bus that would take them back to the school.

'So how did it go then?' Hazel turned round in her seat to ask Sam and Mouse.

Immediately Mouse's eyes filled with tears and she shook her head, unable to speak, leaving Sam to explain tiredly, 'We thought we were going to be doing office work, Corp, but this Captain Elland who we've got to report to had us walking miles up and down the shelves, checking off what was on them against a list he gave us. He wouldn't even let Mouse go to the lavatory until her break-time. Then this afternoon he had us unpacking boxes of Durex to make sure that none were missing.' Sam's expression betrayed her feelings.

'Oh, one of those, is he?' Hazel commented knowingly. 'You do get them – the type that doesn't approve of women in uniform, so they have to try to show us up. That kind, is he?'

'That's him to a T,' Sam confirmed. 'Luckily

there was this decent sort there as well, a sergeant with the Royal Engineers.'

'A decent sort, was he? I see, and good-looking as well, I'll bet,' Lynsey teased her archly.

But as their transport stopped outside their billet for the girls to get off, Sam wasn't in the mood for banter. The captain had infuriated her and bullied poor Mouse all day, sharpening Sam's temper to a fine edge because army rules meant that it was impossible for a mere private to ignore the commands of a captain, no matter how badly that captain was behaving.

'He was just a decent sort, that's all,' she repeated tiredly as they walked towards the billet. 'He told us that the captain was almost as bad with the men and that they all took bets on how difficult he'd make it for them to get stuff out of the stores. He said that the captain couldn't stand women in uniform, and that he'd been brought out of retirement to fill in, on account of the chap that was there before being knocked down by a delivery lorry and ending up with a broken leg and arm. Pity they didn't leave him retired, if you ask me, what with him getting Mouse here so worked up that she was in tears all day, and him keeping on about the ATS being only good for one thing. I don't know how I kept myself from telling him what I thought of him.'

'Yes,' Mouse sniffed as they crossed the hallway and made their way to their dormitory, prior to having their supper. 'And he told Sam that she'd better watch her step otherwise he'd put her on a charge. I never thought it was going to be like this in the ATS.' Fresh tears filled her eyes, causing Sam to stifle a small sigh, and battle with her reluctant sense of responsibility towards the other girl.

'Well, I know what will cheer you up,' Lynsey announced robustly, as soon as they were all in the dormitory with the door closed. 'We're all off duty tomorrow night, I've checked, so why don't we go down to the Grafton and have a bit of fun, seeing as it's a Saturday? It will do us all good, especially you two, and you as well, Corp, what with that chap of yours being down in Dartmouth on that course.'

'What's the Grafton?' Sam asked.

'It's only Liverpool's best dance hall, that's what,' Lynsey informed her enthusiastically. 'We'll have to go early, mind, otherwise we won't get in. All the services boys go there, don't they, Corp?' she appealed to Hazel.

A dance hall! Sam's heart sank. As skilled as she was at sports, and as fleet of foot as she had been at racing her brother, somehow she had never managed to get to grips properly with dancing.

'It's because you want to lead like a man,' Russell had laughed at her. 'Girls don't do that, Sam.'

She would have preferred it if Lynsey had suggested going to the pictures rather than going out dancing, and she was just about to say as much when Mouse burst out, horrified, 'A dance hall! Oh, I couldn't possibly go to one of those. The minister of our church warned me about them when I joined up.'

Behind Mouse's stiffly outraged back Hazel

pulled a rueful face at Sam and muttered under her breath, 'Poor bloody kid, she's so scared of living she might as well be dead. It's a crying shame, and we'll have to do something about it.'

'There's no harm in having a bit of fun,' Lynsey was telling Mouse determinedly. 'Not if you ask me, and not when you remember that there's a war on and wot that Hitler is going to do to us if he has his way.'

Her comment caught Sam like a blow. No matter how much they tried to put it out of their minds, or hide it behind a cheerful mask of banter and determination, for the whole country the fear they shared was never really very far away.

'Lynsey's right, there's nothing wrong in going to a dance, Mouse,' Hazel smiled.

'In fact,' Lynsey added, 'I reckon that it's our duty to think about those poor boys of ours, fighting to save this country and risking their lives for us. It wouldn't be right to deny them the opportunity to have a bit of fun in their off-duty time, and it certainly wouldn't be Christian,' she told Mouse mock piously, adding, 'Anyway, me and others are going, and Sam's coming along too, aren't you, Sam?'

Sam was now caught out fair and square. And there was certainly no way she wanted to be lumped with Mouse and the pair of them turned into a couple of killjoy miseries, avoided by the other girls.

'Yes, of course I am,' she agreed, forcing a hearty enthusiasm she couldn't feel. 'And you're coming as well, Mouse. You don't have to dance,' she told her, shrewdly devising a way out of her own fear of making a complete fool of herself on the dance floor. 'Not if you don't want to, but you can't stay here on your own.'

'No . . . I wouldn't want to do that,' Mouse agreed 'Do you think there really is a ghost here, like May said last night?'

Sam laughed. 'Of course there isn't.'

'Well, that's not what I've heard,' May defended her story stoutly. 'Like I said, I've bin told they was thinking of closing it down as a school on account of the number of girls wot had been taken bad after seeing it and having to be sent home.'

'And the moon's made of green cheese. I'll bet they were making it up just so they could get out of lessons,' Hazel scoffed, adding, 'I'm going down for my supper. Fair starved, I am. I heard one of the other girls saying that it was toad-in-the-hole tonight, and that's one of the few things that Cook serves up that's halfway decent.'

'So come on, Sam, and tell us all about this sergeant you've taken a shine to then,' Lynsey demanded.

They were sitting together at the supper table, and Sam's could feel her face burning with self-consciousness.

'Don't talk such rot. Sergeant Brookes is—'

'Oh ho, so it's Sergeant Brookes, is it? Bet that's not what you call him when you're on your own with him, is it, girls?' Lynsey teased Sam, winking across the table at the other girls.

Sam knew that it was silly to feel so self-conscious and defensive about her good-natured teasing but she couldn't help it. Whilst there had been kindness in the tall fair-haired Royal Engineer's eyes and voice, there had been none of the male appreciation she had seen men exhibiting towards girls they found attractive – nothing improper in any way, in fact. The truth was that she just wasn't the sort that got those kinds of looks from men, and she was sensitively aware of that fact even if the girls ribbing her weren't.

'You'll have to drop a hint to him that you'll be at the Grafton on Saturday,' Lynsey told her knowledgeably. 'If he's got anything about him he'll be there looking out for you. Nothing like a slow smoochy dance to help you to get to know someone.'

'Not eating that, are you, Mouse?' May asked cheerfully, eyeing Mouse's barely touched food. ''Cos if you aren't you can pass your plate over here.'

Sam frowned as she saw the relief in Mouse's expression as she handed over her supper. She had noticed that Mouse had only had a few bites out of the sandwiches they'd been given for their midday meal, and now she wasn't eating her supper.

'You've got to eat something,' she told her, 'especially if Captain Elland is going to keep us working the way he did today.'

Just the mention of the captain's name was enough to have Mouse trembling and blinking back tears, and Sam cursed herself inwardly. She had never come across anyone like Mouse before and her pity for her warred with her own far more robust temperament.

Later in the evening, when the girls were enjoying an hour's relaxation in their shared common room, Hazel confirmed Sam's own opinion of Mouse by commenting to her quietly, 'That poor kid, she should never have been allowed to join up. Pity that no one's seen that and sent her home. She's far too nervy to be in uniform. We'll need to keep an eye on her.'

'I thought she was going to break down in tears and run off when Captain Elland refused to let her go to the lavatory,' Sam confided. 'Mind you, it was a rotten thing to do to the poor kid.'

'It sounds to me as though you're going to have to watch out with him, Sam,' Hazel warned her, looking serious. 'You do get that sort sometimes, worse luck, and sadistic bastards they are too. Toadie's another of the same breed. Wants bringing down a peg or two, she does. Pity we can't give her a dose of her own medicine, not that I should be saying so. I think we'd better talk about something else.' She looked pointedly at her corporal's stripes and then took a deep breath and told Sam lightly, 'I hope you've brought a decent dance frock with you. I dare say I should warn you that there's a strong bit of competition between the services here in Liverpool to see whose girls can look the best. All the more so because we've got a fair contingent of Wrens based here, working at Derby

House.' A small shadow sobered her expression. 'They are the Senior Service, of course, and don't they know it. Their uniforms make ours look very poor, especially their stockings.' She gave Sam a rueful smile. 'Of course, we should be thinking about far higher-minded things than stockings. There is a war on, after all, but sometimes . . . If you are keen on this sergeant I'd advise you to keep him away from them.'

'I'm not keen on him, not at all,' Sam denied quickly, 'and as for the dance,' she gave a small shrug and tried not to look as uncomfortable as she felt, 'to be honest I'm not really one for frocks.'

'So what are you going to wear?' Hazel asked her bluntly. 'A siren suit?'

Sam forced herself to laugh, knowing that was the response Hazel was expecting, but the truth was that she would have felt far more comfortable in a siren suit, as people had nicknamed the all-in-one padded suits people wore at night to keep them warm in the air-raid shelters, than she ever could in a pretty dance frock.

She could remember the disappointment creasing her mother's face when she had refused to wear the pretty dresses she had made for her, especially when she was older and of an age to go to dances. She hadn't been able to explain to her how awkward and ugly they made her feel, like a fish out of water, as she struggled with the restrictions they forced on her.

'I'll probably wear my uniform,' she told Hazel carelessly.

'You can't do that. Not with the Wrens there showing off theirs,' Hazel told her firmly. 'Look, if you haven't brought a frock with you then I've got a spare and we're much the same size. I don't mind lending it to you.'

'Oh, no, I couldn't possibly . . .' Sam protested.

'Don't be silly, of course you can,' Hazel contradicted her. 'And that's an order, Private,' she added with a grin.

Sam tried to look enthusiastic and grateful, knowing there was nothing else she could do, but knowing too that a pretty dress was all too likely to do more to underline her lack of femininity rather than enhance it.

It had been a long day, and after a cheerful game of cards she was more than ready for her bed. Mouse, who had been sitting in a corner knitting, had already gone up to the dormitory and when Sam got there she found her lying on her bed fully dressed, sobbing her heart out, surrounded by some of the other girls.

'It's her teddy,' Hazel whispered to Sam, with a small grimace, pulling her away from the bed whilst one of the other girls comforted Mouse. 'Toadie, the beast, came in and saw it and took it off her. The poor kid's beside herself.'

Whilst Sam might feel that Mouse was too old to need a teddy bear, she was still outraged by the warrant officer's behaviour.

'She had no right to do that. It's Mouse's private property.'

Hazel gave a tired shrug, 'You'll soon learn that

when it comes to what's right, Toadie makes up her own rules. She really is a beast. Fancy picking on poor little Mouse.'

'What will she have done with the teddy?' Sam asked her, thinking quickly. If the warrant officer was not officially entitled to remove it then she was certainly prepared to mount a daring raid to get it back! It was just the kind of challenge she most enjoyed.

'She'll probably have taken it down to that office of hers she likes to lurk in, by the front door, waiting to catch one of us out like she did you last night,' Hazel informed her.

Sam mentally pictured the spot. So far she had seen only the door to the broom cupboard-like space, standing open.

'Does she lock it when she isn't there, do you know?' she asked.

Hazel gave her a searching look. 'You're not really planning to do what I think you're planning to do, are you, because if you are . . . ?'

Sam tried to look innocent but she couldn't keep the mischief from sparkling in her eyes. 'I've no idea what you could possibly mean, Corp,' she stated unconvincingly.

'Sam, I know you mean well, but Toadie isn't someone you'd want to get on the wrong side of,' Hazel warned her. 'There was a girl here before you she had a real down on, and she really broke her.'

'Well, she won't break me,' Sam assured her.

What Hazel had just said had strengthened her

determination to get Mouse's teddy back rather than weakened it.

'She guards that cubbyhole of hers like it was the War Office itself,' Hazel said, 'and I have heard that she's got a couple of girls from another group so much under her thumb that they keep her informed of everything that goes on. Probably bullied them into it, of course, and I'm thankful that they aren't here in my dorm.'

'Well, they won't be able to inform her about anything I'm doing because I don't plan to do anything,' Sam told her.

Hazel sighed. 'I wish I could believe that. You do know, don't you, that it's my duty as your corporal to warn you not to go getting yourself into trouble?'

'I won't do that,' Sam assured her, but she was already making her plans. It shouldn't be so very difficult to sneak into the warrant officer's cubbyhole and retrieve the bear. After all, it was no more than a grown-up version of the games she had played with Russell, when they would take it in turns to outdo one another by surreptitiously 'removing' items from each other's bedroom. She had ended up with a much larger collection of his Dinky toys than he had of her precious treasure-trove of interesting stones and fossils. All she needed to do was to find out when the warrant officer was most likely to be away from her cubbyhole for long enough for her to get Mouse's teddy back.

A thoughtful look darkened her eyes. The

warrant officer was heavily built and Sam had seen for herself how much she enjoyed her food. If she could somehow manage to slip away during breakfast . . . She ran a few options quickly through her head, discarding most of them and then happily settling on the one she thought would work best. It would mean her sacrificing her own breakfast, but it would be worth it to put one over on the warrant officer, and of course to get poor Mouse's bear back for her.

It had been a long night, and in twelve hours' time she would be singing at the Grafton, Sally reminded herself tiredly, as she let herself into the house, bustling her two sons, just up from their beds at Doris Brookes's, inside in front of her whilst she yawned into the early morning air. There was a small folded slightly grubby piece of paper on the hall floor. She stared at it tiredly for several seconds before finally bending to pick it up. It would probably just be a note from one of her neighbours about the birthday party she was planning, but her hands trembled as she opened it. After all, no neighbour was going to waste precious paper writing a note when they could just as easily call in, or leave a message with Doris.

The note was brief, the writing an untidy scrawl: 'Got a message for yer from the Boss. Be in tomorrow dinner.'

Sally could feel the clammy sickness gripping her insides. She felt icy cold with fear and yet at the same time her face was burning with heat.

'Cor, Mum, our Harry needs his nappy changing,' Tommy protested, wrinkling up his nose, forcing her to try to conquer the fear that reading the note had brought her so that she could concentrate on her sons. They must never ever know this fear that terrified her. They must not grow up in the shadow of their father's debts. She had to be strong for them, she had to protect them from that. She pushed the note into her pocket and forced her lips into a painful smile.

Her boys, her sons – she loved them so much. And their father – did she still love him too? Sally buried her face in the warmth of her baby son's neck as she tried to bury she guilt she was feeling. What sort of daft question was that? How could she not love him? Ronnie was her husband, they were married, and he was a POW held captive by the Japs.

SIX

Sam exhaled slowly, pausing to check behind her before straightening up from the agonised position she had assumed in the dining room, gripping her stomach and doubling over as though in pain whilst complaining that her stomach felt too bad for her to eat any breakfast.

'Got yer monthlies, have yer, love?' one of the women serving up the food had asked her sympathetically, unwittingly aiding her deceit. 'A nice cup of tea and a lie-down with a hot-water bottle is what you want.'

When Sam had made her exit from the room under the grim unblinking stare of the warrant officer, she had told herself that her lack of sympathy would make her own victory in retrieving Mouse's bear all the sweeter. Poor Mouse. She looked so miserable, her face all blotchy from her tears. The other recruits had all seen the way she had visibly flinched when they had walked in past the warrant officer.

Toadie had a good appetite, and since she

wouldn't sit down to eat until she had made sure all the girls were up and in the dining room, Sam reckoned she had plenty of time to achieve her mission and get back to the dorm without being found out – providing there was no one around by the front door to see her.

That was the part of her plan that had kept her awake last night. With no chance of doing a recce beforehand, she would have to trust to her own memory and the breakfast routine of the billet.

Toadie was bound to want to be downstairs ready to pounce on them as they left on the buses for work, which meant that she probably had a maximum of twenty minutes in which to get the bear – providing the cubbyhole wasn't locked.

As she had hoped, the hallway was deserted, the front doors closed. Sam found that she was holding her breath. The cubbyhole door was closed. And locked? There was only one way she was going to find out.

Quickly looking over her shoulder to check that there was no one around, Sam slipped behind the reception desk and headed for the door. If the captain was in her office and heard or saw her, she would have to come up with a pretty good excuse for being here. Her mouth had gone dry. Her heart was pounding with the kind of reckless excitement she could remember from her childhood forays into Russell's often booby-trapped room. Hopefully Toadie would not have rigged up a bag of flour to empty itself on her head if she tried to open the door, as Russell might have done.

A small bubble of laughter formed in her throat. The warrant officer waste precious flour – of course she wouldn't. But she could inflict far more serious reprisals on her than Russell, Sam reminded herself, if she should be caught.

But she wasn't going to be caught. She reached for the door handle, turning it carefully and exhaling in relief when the door opened.

At least once she was inside she could close the door so that she couldn't be seen. And be caught red-handed if she had got her estimates wrong and Toadie appeared.

The small room smelled of stale sweat and cigarette smoke. Sam wrinkled her nose in distaste. The shelves lining the walls were unexpectedly untidy, jammed with papers and books as well as various items that looked as though, like Mouse's bear, they had been confiscated. The bear! Where was it? It should be easy enough to find. Sam scanned the shelves intently, frowning when she couldn't see it. It must be here. It had to be. She looked at her watch. Fifteen minute since she had left the dining room – which meant she had only five minutes left at most.

She looked down at the small desk pushed back against the shelves and then stiffened as she saw the telltale pieces of golden fur on the floor besides a wastepaper bin. Sam picked up the bin. Pieces of fur fabric and kapok filled the bottom of it. She could see one beady brown eye staring up at her. To her own astonishment she could feel her own eyes starting to sting with tears. She reached down into the bin, her hand shaking slightly as she gently turned the eye into the fabric. Poor, poor bear and poor, poor Mouse. She must never know about this. Hazel had been right to say that the warrant officer was sadistic. She must have known what destroying her bear would do to Mouse.

Shakily she put down the bin and opened the door. The hallway was still empty. She stepped out of the room, closing the door.

She was halfway across the hall when a girl she didn't know appeared at the top of the stairs.

As she headed for them herself Sam said as nonchalantly as she could, 'I thought I'd try and get some fresh air but the front door doesn't seem to be open.'

'No, it won't be yet,' the other girl replied 'The warrant officer should be on her way down to open it, though, if you want to wait . . .'

Waiting for the warrant officer was the last thing Sam wanted to do but the other girl seemed to be standing in her way. Deliberately?

Sam raised her hand to her mouth and made a small choking sound, keeping her head down as she whispered, 'I'm sorry . . . please excuse me. I need the bathroom,' and dived past her. Her nausea wasn't faked either. She was still in shock from seeing that poor bear.

'Toadie's bin looking for you,' May warned her, coming out of the dorm as Sam headed in. 'Corp told her that you was in the lavvy throwing up.'

Sam opened the dormitory door. Hazel's crisply businesslike, 'Feeling any better, Grey?' warned Sam of the warrant officer's presence before she saw her standing in the shadows.

'Sorry about that, Corp,' she apologised. 'It must have been something I ate. I'll feel better once I've had a bit of fresh air,' she added, remembering the girl on the stairs.

'Private Hatton isn't very well either. In fact she's seeing the MO now,' Hazel informed her in a neutral voice. 'I dare say it must have been something you ate when you were working together yesterday.'

'Yes,' Sam agreed quickly. 'I did think that sandwich we bought in the Naafi smelled a bit off.'

'Has anyone seen the warrant officer, only the captain's asking for her?' a breathless voice called out urgently from outside the dormitory, causing Sam and Hazel to exchange looks of relief.

'What *is* wrong with Mouse?' Sam asked Hazel as soon as she was sure the warrant officer was out of earshot.

'I don't know. Toadie tried to force her to eat her breakfast. She was goading her, asking her if she didn't want to eat because Teddy wasn't there. Mouse was white as a sheet. She tried to force down a couple of mouthfuls, but then she passed out in a dead faint. If you ask me the MO is going to send her home, and to be honest it would probably be for the best.'

'If he does, she'll have to go without her bear,' Sam told her, colouring up when she saw the look Hazel was giving her.

'I'm your corporal, don't forget,' she warned Sam firmly. 'And—'

'Toadie's cut it up – the bear.' Sam was unable to hold back the words. They rushed out, filled with her own disbelief and disgust. Fresh tears burned the backs of her eyes. 'How could she do something so rotten? She must know . . .'

She could feel Hazel's fingers fastening round her arm as she gave her a small firm shake, and told her quietly, 'I know you're upset but it doesn't do to show it. Better to get a grip.' She waited a few seconds whilst Sam struggled to bring her emotions under control and then said approvingly, 'Good show. Now come on, we'd better get on that bus before Toadie comes back up.'

'What about Mouse?' Sam protested. 'Shouldn't we wait in case—'

'We can't do anything for her right now. Let's hope that the MO has pronounced her unfit to serve, because if he hasn't, Toadie is going to make her life hell. It was the captain who called the MO when she saw Mouse faint. Toadie won't like that and she'll make Mouse pay for it.'

'Where's your mate today?'

Sam had been so busy checking off the items on the shelves that she hadn't seen the nice fair-haired sergeant, and the sound of his voice made her colour up self-consciously. Not that she was imagining anything silly, like hoping he might have deliberately sought her out. She wasn't that daft, was she? No, of course she wasn't, she reassured herself. He was just being pleasant, that was all, and she had better not go making a fool of herself thinking any different, nor let on to anyone else that she was actually thinking of how she wouldn't have minded one little bit if he had been.

'She isn't very well,' she told him. 'She isn't really cut out for war work, at least not in the services. There was a bit of an upset last night.'

He looked and sounded so sympathetic that she was tempted to confide in him, but just in time she reminded herself of their respective professional roles. 'I'm sorry. You don't want to hear about any of this,' she apologised. He probably thought she was as soppy as Mouse.

'It isn't easy settling down into service life,' he told her with a kind smile that made her think all over again how really nice he was. 'And it's easy for those of us who have already done it to forget how grateful we ought to be to you girls for what you're doing.'

His praise made Sam glow with pride and pleasure.

'I'd like to do more,' she told him enthusiastically. 'The girls I trained with are on their way to Egypt now. When I joined up I expected to be doing something exciting and worthwhile, and instead I'm stuck here doing a dull boring job with dull boring people.' She gave a small sigh and then flushed as she realised what she had said. 'Oh, I didn't mean you, it's just that . . .'

To her relief he was laughing. 'I know what you meant and it must seem hard to have missed out on going with your pals, but the work we're doing here is every bit as important as all the exciting stuff.'

Sam grimaced.

'It's true,' he insisted. 'The chap who flies the plane that bombs the enemy is a hero but he couldn't do it if someone somewhere hadn't made sure that he had everything he needed for his mission, could he?'

'I suppose not,' Sam agreed grudgingly.

'You see, the way I see it is that we're all part of a team, working together to beat Hitler, and a good team is only as strong as its weakest link.'

What he was saying made sense and it also lifted her spirits – or was *he* the reason they had lifted rather than what he had said, Sam wondered a bit giddily, as somehow without intending to she took a couple of steps towards him.

'Sorry to butt in but if one of you . . .'

Sam had been so totally wrapped up in their conversation that she hadn't realised that they weren't on their own any more. She started to turn away and then froze as the other man stepped into the light and she was able to see him properly.

Even without the uniform she would have recognised him. Those dangerously handsome features of his were printed on her memory for all time.

'Johnny!' she could hear the sergeant exclaiming in a pleased voice. 'Private Grey, let me introduce you to Sergeant Everton, and I warn you, you're going to need to keep your guard up against him,' giving her an almost paternally protective look, which caused her face to burn.

Sam could well imagine the derision there would be in those dark eyes at the thought of her being in any danger from him. Sergeant Brookes, of course, was far too kind and nice to think that a girl like her was simply not the sort to attract a man like Sergeant Everton – 'Johnny', as he had called the other man.

'If you don't,' Sergeant Brookes was continuing with a grin, 'he'll have these shelves stripped of whatever he and his team need without leaving you any paperwork to show for it. Johnny, let me introduce you to our new recruit—'

'Private Grey and I have already met,' he informed the sergeant in a coldly hostile voice.

Sergeant Brookes looked at Sam and then back at his friend, one eyebrow arching in mute enquiry.

'I lost my way and accidentally walked up a street with a UXB in it,' Sam told him unsteadily.

Was Sergeant Everton going to give her away and say that it had not been an accident? Before she could find out, a transport truck, pulled into the yard. Sergeant Brookes apologised to them both. 'I've got to go, but remember, Sam, don't let this chap sweet-talk you.'

Silently Sam watched Sergeant Brookes stride away, wishing that the other man had gone with him.

'You know that he's a married man, and that his wife's having a baby, don't you, *Sam*?'

The sharp words made her face sting. 'No, I didn't,' she answered without turning round. How dreadful she felt now about thinking earlier that

89

she wouldn't have minded if Sergeant Brookes had shown an interest in her. She stood up straight and announced firmly, 'Because there's no reason why I should know.'

'Oh, yeah? That wasn't the impression I got when I walked in here.'

'We were just talking, that's all,' Sam defended herself.

'Frank may have been just talking, but you were looking at him like a moonstruck kid.'

For a few seconds she was too shocked to respond. Was that really how she had been behaving, like a silly girl on the verge of starting a crush? That wasn't how she wanted to think of herself at all and it certainly wasn't how she wanted others to think of her. She felt mortified. But she was determined to defend herself, despite her humiliation.

'That's not true,' she denied 'And you have no right—'

'Mind you, Molly won't need to worry about any competition,' he cut her off forthrightly. 'Frank'd be a fool to risk losing her. Sam. Huh! What kind of a name is that for a girl, anyway?'

'The kind I happen to like,' Sam told him fiercely. She could see Captain Elland marching towards the hangar, in that stiff-kneed way he had, bristling with the irritation and impatience poor Mouse dreaded so much. If anyone had told her yesterday that she'd ever feel glad to see him she would have called them a liar, but then yesterday she hadn't realised that she was going to be brought slap-bang up against *this* man again.

'What's going on in here?' the captain demanded sharply. 'You're supposed to be checking off goods, not lolling around talking to the men. Bloody women in uniform . . . waste of time . . .'

To be accused of flirtatious behaviour with two different men in the space of ten minutes would be enough to make any girl feel like defending herself, Sam thought as she struggled to suppress the hot words burning her tongue.

Sam looked unenthusiastically at her lunchtime sandwiches. Tomato with a thin scraping of something that was supposed to be butter.

So Sergeant Brookes was married. Well, that was nothing to her, was it? Of course it wasn't. But suddenly she had lost her appetite – because of the way Sergeant Everton had spoken to her and the way he had made her feel, not because she was disappointed that Sergeant Brookes was married. What rotten bad luck it had been that she had had to bump into *him* again. Johnny . . . Sergeant Everton, she corrected herself quickly. She would take a bet that *he* wasn't married. No sane woman would be foolish enough to want to marry a man like that. It would be far too much of a risk – and not just because of his work.

Even though she had been waiting for it ever since she had read the note, when the knock on the door finally came, Sally felt a shock as powerfully as if it had been an air-raid warning.

Thankfully Molly had called round and offered

to take the boys down to the allotments with her, so at least she didn't have to worry about them being here.

When she opened the door, she was aware that her neighbour across the road was peering out from behind her curtains.

'I've told you before, I don't want you coming round here,' she said to the burly man who followed her into the hallway, as she closed the door.

'And I've told you, missus, it isn't what you want that matters. The Boss has heard that you do a bit of singing down at the Grafton.'

Sally stared at him. 'What if I do?' she challenged him.

'She said to tell you that she wants you round at her local a week Saturday night, so that you can do a bit of singing for a few friends she's going to be entertaining, seeing as it's her birthday.'

'I can't do that. I work Saturday nights.'

'Listen, you, when the Boss says she wants something she gets it, understand? You'd better, otherwise it will be the worse for you.'

'I can't,' Sally protested. 'I've just told you, I work Saturday nights.'

'Got two kiddies, haven't you?' the man commented, ignoring her.

Sally felt as though the blood in her veins had turned to ice.

'Seven o'clock, Saturday. Corner of Mitchell Street. Oh, and the Boss said to tell you that her favourite song is "Danny Boy". I'll let meself out . . .'

Five minutes, that's all the time it had taken to fill her life with despair. Five minutes . . .

She leaned against the door she had just closed, her whole body shaking and her heart pounding with fear.

SEVEN

'Sam, I feel sorry for little Mouse as well, but being glum isn't going to do anyone any good,' Hazel told Sam firmly as they walked back from the showers together. 'At least she's bucked up enough to say she wants to come to the Grafton with the rest of us this evening.'

'That's only because she's afraid of being left here on her own,' Sam felt bound to point out, guiltily aware that her lack of good spirits had as much if not more to do with what had happened earlier in the day when Sergeant Johnny Everton had seen fit to haul her over the coals for talking quite innocently to another woman's husband. She might not be one of the pretty feminine girls who attracted men like bees to honey but that did not mean that she was the desperate, pathetic type who mistook a man's pleasant good manners for something far more meaningful.

'Well, she's not the only one who needs a bit of fun to cheer her up,' Hazel said so pointedly that Sam looked uncertainly at her. 'I don't normally believe in talking too much about one's personal affairs, but since you're bound to hear about it sooner or later, I may as well come clean and tell you straight out.' She paused and sighed. 'Lynsey told me earlier that it's all off with her current beau so no doubt she'll be on the lookout for someone to take his place tonight.' A small shadow crossed her face, and Sam saw her look down at her bare left hand. 'I wish I had her knack of getting proposals, or at least getting one. The thing is that I've been dating my chap for over six months now – he's Senior Service, and down in Dartmouth at the moment on a course – and I'm getting a bit tired of waiting for him to tell me if we're going to have a future together. After all, a girl can't ask a chap outright what his intentions are, can she? He's expecting to get a new sea posting soon; they've made up him to lieutenant,' she told Sam proudly before sighing again faintly. 'That's going to mean I'll see even less of him. And you know what they say about sailors, especially the handsome ones, which he is. Sometimes I think I'd be better off calling it a day and being fancy free.'

She looked so despondent that all Sam could do was shake her head and say stoutly, 'I'm sure things will work out, Hazel.'

'Well, yes, I'm sure they will, but I'd still like a hint of which way. Come on,' she rallied briskly. 'We'd better go and make sure that dress of mine will fit you.'

'I don't mind wearing my uniform, honestly,'

Sam tried to assure her, but she could tell that Hazel wasn't listening. Perhaps busying herself with organising *her* for their night out might in part help Hazel to put her worries about her relationship to one side for a little while, Sam acknowledged. And that being the case, didn't she owe it to the other girl to ignore her own self-consciousness about wearing a dress?

'Oh, Sally love, you look a real treat,' Doris commented approvingly when she arrived to babysit. 'Mind you,' she pursed her lips and put her head to one side, studying Sally's slender silhouette in the dark blue satin frock that Molly had virtually remade for Sally from an old dress bought from the Red Cross, 'you could do with a bit more weight on your bones. You don't want to start looking haggard. Not that you're likely to, a bonny young girl like you,' she added fondly.

Sharp tears stung Sally's eyes. She didn't know what was the matter with her these days. Just the slightest thing seemed to set her off feeling all emotional, be it kind words or cruel ones. It was plain daft acting all soppy and silly at her age, especially when she was the mother of two boys. How were they going to grow up confident like boys should be with a mother who was spouting tears all the time? And how were they going to grow up with a father who gambled and got into debt? She mustn't think like that, Sally told herself as she hugged Doris.

'You're all sorted out for your kiddies' party now, are you?' Doris asked.

'Yes, thanks to you and Molly,' Sally smiled. 'Daisy came over earlier and said that she'd make up a couple of plates of sandwiches for the kids. She said she'd let me have a tin of fruit as well. I thought I'd put it in a jelly – I can make it go a bit further that way. Molly's dad said he'd paint up them toy soldiers your Frank gave me – I've told Molly I'll make sure she gets them back if this new baby is a boy.'

'It's hard on the kiddies having to grow up in this war, bless 'em,' Doris said quietly.

'I've got to go,' Sally told her, calling over her shoulder as she hurried down the hallway, 'I'll be back around half twelve as usual.'

No, she shouldn't think badly of Ronnie, not with him being where he was, she told herself fiercely as she stepped out into the street, her heart thumping. Sometimes she missed him so much she could hardly bear her longing to see him, whilst at other times she felt so angry with him that she couldn't bear the thought of ever seeing him again. One thing she did know was that he wouldn't have meant to leave her with all this mess, but he could be such a softie, for all that he was a soldier.

The continual dull ache of her anxiety for him since she had been told he had been taken prisoner when Singapore had surrendered, which she had banked down as best she could, unexpectedly burst into a surge of panic and fear. No one wanted to talk about it openly but everyone had heard the horribly graphic reports coming out of the Far East of the way the Japanese treated their prisoners. She had read about it herself in *Picture Post*, and only the other day another woman had broken down on her shift and said that she almost wished her son had been killed outright rather than her having to think about what might be happening to him.

Sally broke into a faster walk. Sometimes there were things it just didn't do to think about.

Hazel's rueful, 'Oh dear' as she finished fastening the last of the white buttons, which ran from the square neckline of the cornflower-blue and white floral frock she was loaning Sam to just short of the hem of its flared skirt, confirmed all of Sam's own worst fears. She obviously looked every bit as dreadful in the dress as she had feared, despite the fact that it was very pretty, and should have suited her fair colouring.

'Lynsey, May, come and look at this,' she called without taking her gaze off Sam. Obediently the other girls came over and, like Hazel, stood in front of Sam and frowned.

'It's me,' Sam told them desperately. Her face was so hot she felt sure it must be the colour of a tomato. 'I'm just not frock person. They don't suit me.'

'It's the waist, that's what it is,' Lynsey announced, totally ignoring Sam. 'She's a lot smaller than you, Hazel. Put a belt round her waist to pull it in a bit and it will be fine, won't it, May?'

'Have you got a belt, Sam?' Hazel asked. 'A white one would be best.'

Sam shook her head.

'I've got one,' Mouse suddenly piped up, surprising them all. 'I've got a cousin who used to work in a dress shop before the war and she gave it to me.'

'Let's have a look at it then, Mouse,' May encouraged.

When Mouse handed over a wide white patent leather belt she had all the girls oohing with envy.

'I can't wear that,' Sam protested. Somehow the belt epitomised everything she knew she could never be. It was made to encircle the waist of someone dainty and pretty, with curls and dimples, not a girl like her, but it was no use her protesting. Hazel was already cinching the belt around her waist.

'My heavens, will you just look at that,' May breathed.

'What is it? What's wrong?' Sam demanded tensely.

'Nothing's wrong,' Lynsey told her, 'excepting that nearly every other girl at the Grafton tonight will be wanting to kill you for having such a tiny waist, you lucky thing.'

'Lynsey's right, Sam,' Hazel agreed. 'That belt sets the frock off perfectly and it pulls in the loose fabric on the waist.'

'But maybe Mouse wanted to wear her belt herself,' Sam pointed out, struggling to get used to the odd sensation of both the belt and the skirt.

'Not with that skirt and blouse she won't,' Lynsey pronounced firmly. 'It won't go with them.'

'Sam, stop arguing, you look terrific, and put these shoes on,' Hazel ordered. 'If we don't get a move on we're going to be late. All you need now is a bit of lipstick. You've even got a lovely tan on your legs.'

It was no use protesting, Sam could see that, and besides, she didn't want to spoil the evening for the other girls, who were all obviously very eager to go dancing. Even Mouse seemed to have forgotten that she had originally flatly refused to go, but then poor Mouse would probably rather have done anything than be left here at their billet on her own with the warrant officer.

'Here's our stop. Lord, will you look at the queue,' May said as the bus pulled into the kerb.

A long wide queue of various groups of girls, young men in uniform, and couples had formed untidily in the street outside the dance hall. The most famous and the best in Liverpool, so Sam was informed by Lynsey, who, as Hazel remarked drily, was something of an expert on such matters.

'Well, and why not? That's what I say,' Lynsey replied unabashed. 'Work hard and play hard, that's my motto. And thanks to the blinking ATS we certainly have to do plenty of hard work.'

'Oh, yes? Then how come I saw you painting your nails this afternoon when you were supposed to be typing all them memos for the War Office?' May asked her.

'What memos? I never saw no memos,' Lynsey gave the others a wink.

The ATS had been formed to train young women to take over the more mundane military support 'chores', such as cooking and general kitchen and domestic duties, typing, general paperwork, and sometimes driving military personnel or acting as messengers, in order to free up enlisted men for active duty.

'Lynsey, you really are the limit,' Hazel protested. 'There *is* a war on, you know.'

'Of course I know it!' Lynsey replied, digging her elbow into May's ribs. 'Get a look of them lads over there, May. Canadian fly boys, they are, all on their own, a long way from home. Need a bit of female company to cheer them up, they will, what with there being a war on and all.'

'Lynsey, really, you can do what you like but the rest of us don't want tarring with the same brush,' Hazel warned her, ignoring May's giggles.

'Oh, come on, Corp, we aren't in uniform now,' Lynsey grinned. 'Where's the harm in relaxing a bit and letting our hair down? I reckon that chap of yours won't be staying in, crying into his cocoa down in Dartmouth because you aren't around. What the eye doesn't see, remember, and if I was you—'

'Well, you aren't me, are you?' Hazel rounded on her.

'Oh, touched a sore spot, have I?' Lynsey asked. 'If I have you want to ask yourself why it is sore. If I were in your shoes—'

'But you aren't. Besides, he's only there on a course, and I'll be going down to see him soon.'

'Queue's moving – the doors must have opened at last,' May announced, determinedly moving forward.

'Lynsey really is the limit at times,' Hazel told Sam, falling into step alongside her and Mouse.

'She's fun, though, isn't she?' Mouse said unexpectedly, sighing as she added, 'I'd love to be fun, wouldn't you, Sam?'

Would she? It depended on what your idea of fun was, Sam decided. Certainly she liked a good lark and some jolly laughter, but fun for her did not include getting fresh with young men. The very thought made her shrink a little and withdraw into herself. But there was no denying that Lynsey's comments had brought Mouse out of herself and cheered her up a bit.

The interior of the Grafton wasn't at all what Sam had been expecting. For some reason she had thought it would look a bit like a church hall but it was unexpectedly elegant, even if a bit war shabby, with red walls and dim lighting.

'A proper dance hall, this is, with a really good sprung floor,' Lynsey informed her, seeing her amazement. 'Copied it from some Russian ballet theatre, the owner did, so I've bin told.'

'They get some really good bands playing here as well. The lot that are playing tonight have these girl singers. Ever so good, they are; good enough to be on the wireless,' May chipped in.

'Huh, I dare say I could sound just as good if

I were dressed up in one of them frocks they wear,' Lynsey informed them sharply.

'You? Don't forget I've heard you singing in the shower,' May laughed.

They had reached the top of the stairs, and were having to raise their voices above the noise generated by the people filling the dance hall.

Somehow they managed to find a vacant table not too far from the band or the dance floor.

'Right, what's everyone having to drink?' May demanded as soon as they were seated.

'Mine's a port and lemon, May,' Lynsey answered. 'What are you going to have?' she asked Sam and Mouse.

'Oh, I . . . just lemonade for me,' Mouse told her timidly.

'Have a port and lemon, Sam. I'm going to, and if we all have the same it will make it easier to share the bill,' Hazel suggested sensibly.

Sam agreed.

'I'll go to the bar to give May a hand with the drinks,' Lynsey offered, standing up.

'Give May a hand – that's rich. The only reason she's going to the bar is so that she can eye up the men,' Hazel told Sam wryly, waving to a group of girls from one of the other dormitories, who had just come in.

'Heavens, virtually the whole of the billet must be here,' Sam commented in the general chaos and bustle of exchanging names, and the newcomers getting seats and then drinks,

'Almost,' a lively-looking brunette agreed as she

sat down. 'Apart from Toadie and her favourites.'

Sam saw the way Mouse shivered and wished the other girl hadn't mentioned the warrant officer. 'Don't worry about her, Mouse,' Sam whispered.

'I can't help it,' Mouse responded. 'I know it must be hard for someone like you to understand, Sam, but she scares me so much, she and Captain Elland.' She gave a small shiver. 'They're just like my aunt, both of them. I thought it was going to be different in the ATS, that things would be better for me once I'd got away from her, but instead . . .' Her eyes filled with tears. 'I feel so afraid sometimes, Sam, that I'll never be able to escape from her; no matter what I do and that wherever I go, she'll make sure that there's someone there just like her to—'

'What tommyrot,' Sam stopped her firmly, sensing that she was on the point of hysteria. 'Toadie's a bully, I know, but if you ignore her she'll soon start leaving you alone, don't you worry.'

She could see that Mouse wasn't convinced, but before she could say any more, May leaned over and said, 'Put a sock in it, you two. They've just announced that the singers are coming on and I want to listen to them.'

It was always like this for her in those last few minutes before they went on to sing, Sally acknowledged as she felt the familiar mixture of exhilaration and apprehension gripping her insides, and yet she knew that once she was out there and actually singing the singing itself would be all that would matter. Even as a little girl she had loved to sing. When she felt unhappy all she had to do to make herself feel better was to sing. Somehow when she was singing there was no room in her heart for misery or worry, or at least there hadn't been. When she sang she could become another person, a person who had the confidence that her normal self did not. But tonight she was finding it hard to think about anything other than her anxiety over the debt collector's visit and the message he had given her.

She knew her neighbours on Chestnut Close, even those as kind as Molly and her mother-in-law, would be horrified at the thought of being in debt. She was afraid that they might be so horrified that they wouldn't want anything more to do with her. Being in debt was so very shameful, not the kind of thing that happened to decent respectable people. Her neighbours would, she knew, feel she was bringing disgrace on the Close and lowering its tone, and the inhabitants of Chestnut Close were very proud of their status, situated as they were right at the top end of Edge Hill, and so close to Wavertree that they could almost claim to be living there. She couldn't bear the thought of anyone accusing her of lowering the tone of the neighbourhood.

A sharp dig in her ribs from Shirley brought her back to her surroundings, as she hissed, 'Come on . . . we're on!'

An enthusiastic burst of clapping welcomed

them as the band leader introduced them. 'And here they are, ladies and gentlemen, the Waltonettes, Liverpool's own trilling larks.' One by one he introduced the girls by name and they each gave their audience a small teasing curtsy. Although in her normal life this kind of behaviour was something Sally would have shunned, here on the stage it was different. She was one of the Waltonettes, and it was all part of what the audience expected. The men wanted to feel that the girls were singing especially for them and the girls wanted to imagine themselves up on the stage, sparkling with confidence and singing that special song for their special man.

Sporting wide professional smiles, the girls clustered round the microphone ready for their first number, a slightly provocative breathy version of 'My Heart Belongs to Daddy', which always went down well with the audience, especially the men. Later on in the evening they would sing some lively upbeat numbers and then later still, everyone's favourite sentimental songs.

'See, I told you they were good, didn't I?' May demanded triumphantly, above the enthusiastic clapping of the audience at the end of the singers' first number.

Sam could only agree. How wonderful it must be to have such a beautiful voice, and to be so pretty as well, she thought as she watched the slender brunette singer the band leader had introduced as Sally. As she looked across at her, the brunette singer turned her head and smiled. What a nice genuine person she seemed, Sam decided, returning her smile.

'Huh, just look at them Canadian lads,' Lynsey hissed in a cross whisper. 'Can't take their eyes off the singers, they can't.'

'No wonder, the saucy way they were singing,' another girl sighed. 'My chap wouldn't half give me what for if he caught *me* carrying on like that.'

'They've got every chap in the place making sheep's eyes at them.' Lynsey was obviously aggrieved.

'I'm sure it isn't meant to be taken seriously and that it's just part of their job.' Sam surprised herself by sticking up for the singers.

Lynsey gave her an irritated look but before she could say anything Hazel pointed out, 'There's a chap over there who doesn't look like he's very impressed by them.'

'Where?' Lynsey demanded.

'On that table in front of the stage. The good-looking dark-haired chap,' Hazel answered. 'He's been watching that pretty brunette singer like he doesn't approve of what she's doing one little bit. Don't go staring at him, he'll see you,' Hazel warned her, but it was too late.

Lynsey was craning her neck and half getting up out of her chair to look across at the table Hazel had mentioned. Sam could see the man Hazel was referring to quite easily, and realised what Hazel meant. He was handsome but he was also looking at the singer with a very grim expression indeed. Was he the brunette singer's husband, perhaps, Sam wondered, angry about the fact that other men were admiring his wife? If so, Sam felt very sorry for her.

Normally once she had started to sing Sally was oblivious to everything but the music, including the audience, but tonight the music wasn't having its normal magical effect on her. She could see a girl on one of the tables, where the tall blonde girl who had given her such a nice smile earlier was seated, half stand up and look at another table and automatically her own gaze focused on that table as well. The people seated at it were smartly dressed, the women in silk frocks and those men who weren't in uniform wearing well-cut suits. One of the men was staring at her very grimly. Suddenly Sally stiffened in shock and almost missed a note, as she realised it was the new doctor.

It was no use asking herself what he was doing here. Sooner or later everyone who came to Liverpool visited the Grafton. It was famous as the city's best dance hall. Somehow, though, she hadn't had the doctor down as a dancing man. He had struck her as far too grim and cold. She was obviously wrong, though, because the woman seated next to him was placing her hand on his arm, obviously suggesting that they should get up and dance.

'What's wrong with you?' Patti hissed in Sally's ear, as the audience clapped their song. 'You missed your cue twice.'

'I . . . I'm sorry,' was all Sally could mouth back, as the band leader turned to announce their second song.

'You bloody well will be if it happens again,' Patti warned her sourly.

'I'm beginning to wonder if this was such a good idea after all,' Hazel said to Sam ruefully. 'I thought coming here would help take my mind off my chap, but all it's done is make me wonder what he's getting up to down in Dartmouth.'

'He's probably missing you as much as you're missing him,' Sam tried to comfort her, as she watched Lynsey jitterbugging energetically and expertly with her partner, envying her both her skill and her self-confidence. She could still remember the excruciating misery she had experienced as a little girl, attending the dance classes her mother had sent her to. She had always seemed to be out of step, much to the teacher's despair, and had never mastered the routines. Since then she had avoided dancing as much as she could. It didn't help that every time there was a family event of any kind with dancing, Russell would always make jokes about her two left feet and tease her that he had to bribe his friends to dance with her. Sam knew that he didn't mean to be unkind – after all it was the truth: she couldn't dance. She was relieved that Mouse's refusal to dance, on the grounds that her aunt would not approve, had given her a good excuse to stay where she was.

'You're a good kid, Sam,' Hazel told her, 'but

something tells me that you don't know very much about men. Being in the ATS will change all that. It's been a real eye-opener for me, I can tell you. I've lost count of the number of men I've heard of who have sworn undying love to a girl one night and then been seen flirting with someone else the next. If you ask me, it's out of sight out of mind with most of them, especially the navy lot.'

'What you want to do is give him a taste of his own medicine,' Lynsey advised her, coming back to the table just in time to catch the tail end of their conversation. She sank into her chair and fanned herself, exclaiming that she was 'puffed', before continuing, 'You know what I mean, Hazel; what you want to do is make up to some other chap and flirt with him a bit. Do you no end of good, it would, and you never know, you might find out that your sailor isn't the bee's knees you think he is. You'll never know what else is on offer unless you try a few out. Take that table over there, for instance—' She suddenly stopping talking and sat bolt upright, her eyes narrowing 'like a dog seeing a rabbit,' as May said later. 'Oh boy, just take a look at *him*,' she breathed.

'Who exactly are we supposed to be looking at?' May demanded. 'There's hundreds of men here.'

'Maybe, but this is one of a kind. Over there . . . that chap with the dark hair, all six foot of him, and will you take a look at those shoulders. Now there's a man who's got the goods and knows exactly how to use them, or my name's not Lynsey Wilkins.'

All the girls turned to look at the man she was pointing out, including Sam, who nearly betrayed herself by protesting out loud when she recognised that the man Lynsey was drooling over was none other that her own *bête noire*, Sergeant Johnny Everton. And what was more, he had seen her too, Sam realised as she tried to flatten herself into her chair.

'Gawd, Lynsey, stop showing us all up, will you? Any chap seeing you look at him like that is more likely to make a run for it than make a grab for you,' Hazel warned irritably, as Lynsey continued to look pointedly and invitingly in the direction of the uniformed Bomb Disposal sergeant.

'That's all you know. Look, he's coming over,' Lynsey crowed triumphantly.

If her chair hadn't been hemmed in so tightly between those on either side of her she would have been on her feet and bolting for the sanctuary of the powder room, Sam admitted, and yet there was no reason for her to feel like that. She wasn't on duty and answerable to him, and he certainly wasn't coming over here because he wanted to socialise with her, so why was she in such a silly panic?

'Oh boy . . .' Lynsey murmured ecstatically. 'Now that is what I call a man. I bet he dances divinely. Hands off, the rest of you, he's mine.'

'As if any of us had a chance anyway, with you making big eyes at him the way you are doing, Lynsey,' May whispered.

'I'm not at all happy with this,' Hazel muttered to Sam. 'Lynsey thinks she can get away with anything, but it's the rest of us that will end up getting a bad name along with her, if we don't watch out.'

'Would you like to dance?'

Sam could see the shock on the girls' faces, especially Lynsey's, as the sergeant stood in front of her and asked her to dance. She could feel that same shock zigzagging through her body like a hail of tracer bullets, illuminating the sharp rawness of her most private feelings. What was he doing this for? Was he *deliberately* trying to make fun of her, to humiliate her? A mixture of anger and misery gripped her.

'No, I wouldn't,' she told him shortly.

She could see the way his chest compressed as he breathed in sharply.

'Why don't you ask me instead?' Lynsey offered flirtatiously. 'I'd love to dance with you . . .' She was already on her feet, and reaching out to put her hand on his arm whilst she looked up at him, batting her eyelashes.

As though his appearance had opened the floodgates, within seconds the other girls, apart from Sam, Hazel and Mouse, had taken to the floor, dancing with one another, laughing and giggling as they watched Lynsey act the vamp with her partner.

'You were fearfully rude, turning that sergeant down like that, you know,' Hazel told Sam quietly.

'He didn't really want to dance with me,' Sam answered her. 'I could tell that from the way he was looking at me. He's already told me—'

'You *know* him?' Hazel stopped her, if anything looking even more disapproving.

'Not really . . . that is, I have met him before . . . he was introduced to me . . . by . . . by someone . . .'

'Oh, Sam, that makes turning him down like that so much worse.'

Sam could feel her face starting to burn. 'I didn't want to leave Mouse on her own,' she tried to defend herself.

'Mouse isn't on her own; I'm here,' Hazel pointed out, adding sternly, 'I really think you owe him an apology, you know.'

'An apology!'

'Yes,' Hazel insisted. 'It's awfully bad form to turn down a chap in uniform when he asks you to dance, don't you know? Not the done thing at all. Not . . .'

'. . . when there's a war on,' Sam chanted, causing Hazel to give her another stern look.

Outwardly she might be stubbornly defending her actions but inwardly she felt horribly guilty. She knew that had she been asked to dance by anyone other than Johnny Everton she would have accepted, and somehow or other forced herself to overcome her own self-consciousness at her lack of dancing skill. If it had been Frank who had asked her, for instance . . . Don't think about that, she warned herself. Sergeant Frank Brookes was married, and besides, all he had ever shown her was just a bit of good-mannered kindness, nothing else, and even if he hadn't been married she would have been a fool to have gone making something out of that that just didn't exist.

Sally could feel her hands trembling slightly as she folded them together behind her back and joined the other girls in their set line-up for 'You Are my Sunshine', the number that was proving to be one of the year's most popular songs. She wasn't going to look over to the doctor's table and risk getting caught in the glower of disapproval he had given her during their earlier number. Patti had given her a real old telling-off backstage, justifiably perhaps, Sally admitted. She hated being anything less than professional but what she hated and feared even more was that for the first time ever, something and someone had broken through the protective screen that singing had always previously allowed her to hide behind, away from whatever was troubling her. It was true that the 'something' and the 'someone' weren't related. After all, the summons to appear at 'the Boss's' party had nothing whatsoever to do with Dr Alexander Ross. Heavens, Sally could just imagine how a man like him would react to someone being in debt! He would treat them like they were a bad smell under his nose, she decided. And yet despite the resentment she felt towards him for showing her his obvious contempt, underneath Sally acknowledged there was pain. She had longed so much for her and Ronnie and their children to be a family who could hold up their heads; a decent respectable well-thought-of family who kept themselves to themselves and whom others admired, not like the families she had grown up amongst in Manchester. Good-hearted people she knew, but living on the breadline, never knowing if they would have enough money to pay the rent and often seeming not to care, taking their best clothes down to the pawn shop when they were short of cash, and then having to borrow from whoever they could to get them back again when they needed to wear them. Sally had spent her childhood anxiously aware that the very fine line that divided her mother's smiles from her tears and anger was because of her struggle to manage the family budget. Her parents may not have got themselves into debt but the threat that they might be had hung over her childhood like a dark cloud. Now that fear was hers, and she could feel the shame of having succumbed burning deep into her soul. Somehow the doctor, with his smart clothes, his posh furniture, his well-dressed wife and children, underlined for her all that hurt the most in her own marriage and life.

No, she wouldn't look at him, she wouldn't look at anyone, she told herself firmly as the band struck up the first notes of 'You Are my Sunshine'.

'Oooh, I love this number,' May said enthusiastically as the ATS girls joined in the approving clapping that greeted the opening bars of the Waltonettes' song. 'Lovely voices, they have, and

I'm not the only one that thinks so.' May nudged Lynsey in the ribs as she pointed out, 'There's that sergeant you was fancying, Lynsey, clapping like mad. He can't take his eyes off them girls neither, especially that brunette.'

Sam could see Lynsey scowling in the direction of the singers. Sergeant Everton certainly was responding enthusiastically to them. As Sam watched, the pretty brunette singer looked towards him, her lips curving into an open smile whilst he in turn smiled back at her, giving her a cheeky wink.

'She can smile at him all she likes, but it will be me that has the last dance with him,' Lynsey told them all determinedly.

'The last dance, mebbe,' May agreed, 'but I wouldn't bet odds on you getting to be the one he walks home, Lynsey.'

Sally had seen Johnny Everton smiling at her several bars into 'You Are my Sunshine', and now, with their spot finished, she did something she would never normally have done. Instead of heading backstage she went towards Johnny, who immediately left the table where he had been sitting with a group of other men in uniform and hurried over to her, taking hold of her in an enthusiastic hug. Her decision to go over to Johnny certainly didn't have anything to do with the new doctor sitting there watching her like she was the lowest of the low, Sally reassured herself, as Johnny kissed her firmly on the cheek.

'I'd heard you were back,' she told him warmly.

'Yup, turning up like a bad penny, that's me.'

Sally laughed. 'Go on wi' you. I dare say there's girls queuing up to welcome you home!'

To her surprise Johnny's smile vanished, to be replaced by an unexpected bleakness that was out of character for the Johnny she remembered.

'I heard about your Ronnie being taken prisoner when Singapore fell,' he told her, changing the subject.

'Yes,' Sally acknowledged. 'That's what the War Office have said, only there haven't been any letters or anything from him yet.' She tried to keep her voice light but she knew she hadn't succeeded when Johnny gripped her hand comfortingly.

'It's early days yet. And like they say, no news is good news. Them two little nippers of yours must be growing.'

'They are that,' Sally agreed. 'A real handful, they are at times, and I don't know what I'd do without Molly and Doris lending a helping hand. Been a true friend to me, Molly has, even though it was me and her June that palled up first. Expecting a kiddie of their own now, she and Frank, as well as having June's little 'un.'

'Yes, I'd heard.'

'A natural mother, Molly is. Her and Frank are really happy.'

'Frank's a good chap. I saw him earlier today at the barracks.' His voice was suddenly terse.

Sally's smile faltered slightly as she wondered what she had said to cause him to withdraw into himself so determinedly. 'So you're with the bomb disposal lot then now?' she ploughed on.

''S right,' Johnny agreed.

'You're very brave, Johnny, to take on such dangerous work.'

He gave a dismissive shrug.

'Look, I've got to go now,' Sally told him. 'We'll be on again in a few minutes. I'm having a bit of a party for my two boys, next Saturday afternoon. Tommy was three at the beginning of the month and Harry will be two the week after next,' she told him impulsively. 'It'll only be a few sandwiches and a cup of tea, but there'll be a lot there that you know and you'd be welcome to come along and have a beer with the men, if you feel like it.' She couldn't stay to say any more; she was in enough trouble with Patti as it was without risking appearing unprofessional, fraternising with the paying public.

Johnny had changed, she thought as she hurried backstage. The cheeky, almost too self-confident boy she remembered had been replaced by a man who, like all of them, had experience of the reality of a war behind him. The Johnny she remembered would certainly never have wanted to risk his life working in bomb disposal.

'Well, I wouldn't get too hung up on him if I were you, Lynsey,' said Hazel. 'You can see from his uniform that he's with that UXB lot, and I've heard that they reckon their life expectancy can be measured in weeks and months, not years. There was that case in the paper only a little while back of

118

a whole crew being lost when the bomb they were working on went off.'

Sam got to her feet.

'Where are you going?' Lynsey asked her. 'It'll be the last dance in a minute.'

'Ladies' room,' Sam told her briefly. It must be that last port and lemon that was making her stomach cramp so uncomfortably. It certainly wasn't anything to do with Hazel's comments about the danger of unexploded bombs.

As she came out of the powder room Sam heard the band leader announcing the last dance. Lynsey no doubt would already have secured her chosen partner, and he, Sam expected, would be only too delighted to share with her the intimacy afforded by the now dimmed lights and the slow sensual beat of the music.

'Oh!' Engrossed in her thoughts, she gave a small gasp as she cannoned into someone in the dimness. Immediately strong male fingers curled round her wrist, and equally immediately her heart beat out its own Morse code message of recognition to her brain. 'You . . .' she stammered weakly as she found herself confronting the very man who had just been in her thoughts. 'I thought you'd be dancing with Lynsey.'

What a complete idiot she was making of herself, gabbling away in a breathless voice she hardly recognised as her own, whilst he just stood there in front of her saying nothing.

'Because you turned me down?' he demanded grimly.

His anger underlined what Hazel had already told her, adding to her guilt. She took a deep breath, feeling like she had done as a child, faced with a spoonful of cod liver oil. 'That was rude of me. I'm sorry.'

He was still holding on to her wrist and she could feel a sensation like a hot wire jerking down her arm as he shrugged his shoulders.

'Wanted to put me in my place, did you?' he challenged her.

'No!' 'No, I would never do anything like that.'

'But you turned me down.'

'I . . . there was a reason,' Sam defended herself with as much dignity as she could summon.

'I see.'

Why did he keep on looking at her like he was, making it impossible for her to look away?

'That reason wouldn't be a certain sergeant by the name of Frank Brookes, would it?'

'No!' Sam was too horrified for pretence.

'No? Then what was it?'

He didn't believe her, Sam could see that.

'If you must know, it was because . . . because I . . . I'm not a very good dancer.' It had been very hard for her to make such an admission to him and when he started to laugh she could feel her whole body burning with humiliation and anger.

'Come on. Don't give me that. I've seen those pins of yours, don't forget. With legs like those you couldn't possibly not dance.'

Sam was too stunned to conceal her feelings. He was *praising* her legs? Those same legs that

Russell had always teased her were so long and skinny they were like pieces of string with knots where her knees were.

'It's true. I mean, I can't,' she insisted. 'Russell says I must have been born with two left feet.'

'Russell?'

'My brother. He's in the RAF.'

He gave her a curt nod.

'I'd better get back to the others.' Sam made to pull her wrist free but he refused to let her go. 'Why . . . ? What . . . ?' she began, but he wasn't listening. Instead he had turned towards the dance floor.

'Come on, anyone can dance,' he told her. 'It's easy.'

And then before she could stop him he was striding onto the dance floor, virtually dragging her along in his wake.

With the lights dimmed and the floor so full of couples swaying together in time to the music there wasn't going to be any room for them and he would have to let her go, but somehow or other, as though by magic, a space appeared for them. At least with the lights dimmed no one else was going to witness her making a fool of herself, or at least no one other than her unwanted partner, Sam told herself, as he swung her round so that they were facing one another, and then took hold of her.

This was going to be a world away from dancing with her brother, Sam sensed, stiffening in open panic as he closed the distance between them. She could feel the warmth of his breath against her hair, and she could feel too the firmness of his hand spread against the small of her back.

'Relax, you're dancing, not facing a firing squad.'

How could the sensation of a man's warm breath against her ear have such an extraordinary effect on her? Blindly Sam tried to take a step forward as she struggled to deal with the unfamiliar sensation flooding through her body, and then froze in fresh shock as she felt the hardness of the male thigh not just keeping her where she was but pushing her own leg back.

'No, *I* lead, you follow.'

Her body had now become obediently fluid, moving in time to the music, the unfamiliarity of the sensation forcing her to cling dizzily to him as he moved them across the floor. Somehow he was making it all seem so easy. And so unnerving. It was the most extraordinary sensation, scary and yet exhilarating. There was one thing for sure, Sam admitted to herself, dancing with her brother had never felt like this. The last notes of the song finally died away and the lights came on. Couples moved reluctantly apart. Sam was acutely conscious of the fact that inwardly she was trembling from head to foot.

'I must get back to the others.' She couldn't bring herself to look at him properly. All she wanted to do was to get away from him and yet when he didn't offer to walk her back to the table she felt unwarrantedly bereft.

'Well, you're a sly one and no mistake,' Lynsey accused Sam huffily as soon as she got back to the table, 'dancing with that sergeant, and after I said that I'd got me eye on him, and the last dance as well! I thought you were a decent sort, not the kind wot goes round pinching other girls' chaps.'

'I'm not. I mean it wasn't like that. I didn't really want to dance with him, he—'

'Oh, no, of course you didn't. I could see that for meself from the way you was cuddled up to him and holding him tight,' Lynsey retaliated sarcastically.

'No, really, you don't understand.'

'No, it's you that doesn't understand,' Lynsey told her sharply, the original warmth with which she had welcomed Sam to the dormitory giving way to angry hostility. 'We have a rule amongst us girls that we don't go trying to pinch a chap another girl's got her eye on.'

'Lay off, Lynsey,' Hazel warned. 'It's not Sam's fault if he asked her to dance.'

'Well, if you ask me it's that brunette singer he's really interested in 'cos he was ever so cosy and friendly with her earlier on,' May intervened.

'For what it's worth,' Hazel informed them sturdily, 'I always think it's best to steer clear of that kind of chap.'

'And what's that supposed to mean?' Lynsey snapped.

'I've seen his type in action before, Lynsey. He's got that air of danger about him that some men have, and he's too good-looking for his own good.

Men like that have girls hanging round them in droves, and they're best avoided unless you want to be one of a string of girls he's seeing. You might think you can twist him round your little finger, like them other chaps you've had going mad for you, but you won't, you know.'

'That's all you know,' Lynsey retorted smartly. 'You wait – come Christmas I'll have him eating out of my hand, and giving me a diamond ring, you see if I don't. And as for you,' she rounded on Sam, 'don't think I'm going to forget what you've done because I'm not.'

EIGHT

'I hope you know what you're doing, inviting Johnny Everton here,' Pearl Lawson, Sally's neighbour from lower down Chestnut Close, announced, giving a meaningful nod in the direction of the living room where Johnny was standing talking with the other men.

Sally looked up distractedly from the spoonfuls of jelly she was carefully counting into dishes. Her stomach was already so tied in knots of worry and dread over what lay ahead of her this evening that she could barely think about anything else.

'In fact I'm surprised that you have, seeing as how you're so pally with the Brookeses.'

Sally suppressed a small sigh. There was no real harm in Pearl but she did have a habit of gossiping about people behind their backs. It was perhaps no wonder that one of her closest friends and sometimes one of the biggest critics in the Close was Daisy Cartwright, who was also very fond of a good gossip.

'What's that supposed to mean?' she asked tiredly.

Patti had made the most fearful fuss when she had told her that she couldn't sing tonight, and Sally knew it would be a long time – if ever – before she was forgiven. But Sally had stood her ground and reminded her that she was only a stand-in, even if she was now singing virtually every Saturday night. She had been working all night at the factory and had only managed a couple of hours' sleep whilst Doris had the boys for her before she had to start getting everything ready for the party. And then tonight she was going to have to go out and sing at this party being given by 'the Boss' . . .

'Oh, come on, Sally, you can't have forgotten that Johnny and Molly were engaged?' Pearl reminded her.

'That was before the war. They were just kids then,' Sally pointed out.

'Well, my hubby was saying that if he was Frank Brookes—'

Sally had had enough. 'Oh, don't talk so daft, Pearl. Frank and Johnny are old friends, and everyone knows how happy Frank and Molly are.'

To Sally's relief, before Pearl could say any more, one of the other women demanded loudly, 'Here, Daisy, what the 'ell have you put in these fish paste sandwiches you've brung, only they don't half stink?'

'It's a special fish paste wot everyone eats in America,' Daisy answered, bridling slightly. 'Cost my hubby a fortune, it did. He had to trade two tins of fruit salad for just one jar of it and there were twenty jars in this box he brought home.'

'Well, I can't say as I'd fancy eating it.'

'It ain't for you, is it? It's for the kiddies,' Daisy told her, taking the plate from her and marching into the other room to put the sandwiches down on the table.

Through the open door Sally could see Molly, her arm round her late sister's daughter, Lillibet, the two of them watching the other children. Tommy was doing his usual big brother thing, only this time he seemed to be protecting Harry or, perhaps more realistically, the toy train Harry was clutching, from one of the other children. What was it about boys, Sally wondered ruefully. Whilst the girls were all looking pretty, neat and clean, the boys all seemed to have one sock half falling down, grubby hands and knees, and shirt flaps sticking out of jumpers. But then that *was* boys for you. And if she was honest she wouldn't change a single thing about her two, especially not the loving sticky kisses they gave her. Tommy was a softie really, running back to give her an extra cuddle when he thought no one could see him. If only Ronnie could have been here to see his sons. Her two weren't the only children in the Close whose dads were posted away from home, but what with Frank at the barracks, and Daisy's husband working down at the docks, Sally did sometimes feel as though she and her sons were the odd ones out.

'That's our Harry's train.' Tommy was standing his ground against the other boy, a young nephew whom Daisy had brought with her, even though he was a good three inches taller and more heavily built.

'Well, I want to play with it so give it here.'

Harry might not be contributing to the conversation but his tight hold on the train made it plain to Sally that he knew perfectly well what was going on. The other boy made a lunge for the train, but Tommy stepped in front of his younger brother.

'You're best letting him keep it,' he told him in such an exact copy of her own words and tone that Sally had to cover her mouth so as not to laugh. ''Cos if you don't he'll only start yelling, and then our mam will come and give you what for.'

'And then he'll really know he's in trouble,' Johnny murmured appreciatively at Sally's side.

She hadn't seen him coming over to join her but she could tell from his expression that he was as amused as she was herself.

'He's a corker, Sal,' Johnny told her, 'and as bright as a button.'

'Too bright sometimes,' Sally answered, but her pride shone in her eyes along with her love. 'I'd better go and sort this out,' she added, putting the dish down and excusing herself when it became obvious that the older boy wasn't going to give way.

'Why don't you let George play with your train for a while, Harry?' Sally coaxed, gently prising her younger son's chubby baby fingers away from the train. 'You and Tommy and Lillibet can play "Ring a Ring o' Roses" instead.'

'Ring a Ring o' Roses' was currently Harry's favourite game, especially the 'all fall down' bit – something he excelled in since he was closer to the floor than the others.

Having reassured herself that the children were playing together happily, Sally went back for the sandwiches. The men, including Molly's Frank and Johnny Everton, were standing together, laughing at a joke Johnny had just finished telling. The war had changed him as it had done all of them, hammering out the man he now was from the boy he had been. Frank was a good kind man, but he didn't have Johnny's raw sexuality, nor his charm, Sally acknowledged, her attention distracted then as Harry let out an outraged roar as one of the other children made a grab for the train.

'Time for those sandwiches, I think,' Doris Brookes advised Sally.

'Pity you couldn't get any more of that Velveeta cream cheese, Sally. They all like that.'

'I was lucky to get what I did. Mind you, it doesn't help having to have this new national loaf. The kiddies don't like the fact that it isn't white, for starters.'

'Huh, I've heard as how they're putting sawdust in it to make it go further.'

'Go on wi' you. Lord Woolton would never do that.'

'Well, they're saying it's all going to be different after the war, wi' new houses being built for everyone, and all the men in work.'

'See, Daisy, I told you them fish paste sandwiches

smelled rotten,' Betty Ryder complained as her daughter made a face and refused to eat her sandwich.

'Give over, there's nothing wrong wi' 'em. Look at the way Sally's Tommy is tucking into them,' Daisy defended her fish paste.

'Well, he must have a cast-iron stomach, that's all I can say.'

'Come on, Sally, you haven't had anything to eat yourself yet,' Doris pointed out, tactfully bringing the fish paste conversation to a close before it became too heated.

'I had a few bits whilst I was in the kitchen earlier,' she fibbed. With what she had ahead of her this evening she felt so sick with a nervous stomach that she couldn't have eaten anything.

'Nice to see Johnny Everton here,' Doris added, nodding in the direction of the men. 'I remember when he and my Frank first joined up together. Of course, your Ronnie was already in the army then.'

'It's only three years since war broke out. We've had Dunkirk, the Battle of Britain, then Liverpool being bombed, and Singapore falling, and now it just feels like we've been at war for ever,' Sally told her grimly. 'These little 'uns have never known anything else – only going without and bombs and rationing. Tommy can't remember his dad and Harry's never even seen him and now, well, to be honest, Doris, I wonder sometimes if my Ronnie ever will come home to us.' Tears suddenly filled Sally's eyes.

'Oh, Sally love . . .' Doris tried to comfort her.

'It's all right.' Sally fished out her handkerchief from her pocket and blew her nose determinedly. 'I'm just having one of them days. I'd better go and take some of these sandwiches over to the men before they all go.'

'Well, there's plenty of Daisy's fish paste ones left,' Doris laughed.

'Give 'em here,' Sally told her. 'I'll go and see if the men will eat them.'

'No, ta, Sally love.' Albert Dearden, Molly's father, shook his head when Sally offered the sandwiches. 'You keep them for the kiddies.'

'The trouble is that the kiddies don't want them,' Sally told Johnny ruefully, 'and there's that many left that Daisy is going to take offence.'

'Go on then, I'll have one,' Johnny offered, giving her a wink as he added, 'You've got to be ready to take a risk, working with the lot I've landed with.'

'Aye, I heard that a couple of your lads went and got themselves blown to bits over on Peel Street the other week.'

Johnny nodded. 'Had a type seventeen fuse in it, that one did. That means that by rights the bomb should go off within seventy-two hours of being dropped. When they don't, well, that means that they can be set off by the slightest movement and they can go off any time they like. Some of them have this extra ante-handling fuse as well, but not the seventeen. That's what happened on Peel Street.'

Sally gave a small shudder. 'I think you're very brave to volunteer for Bomb Disposal, Johnny.'

'Who said anything about volunteering?' he joked. 'When they said put up your hands all those who want to be in a unit where the officers get killed first, no one said anything about it being for bomb disposal. Of course, when they found out I was single that was me finished. They had me badges on and me on a train to Liverpool before I knew what was happening to me.'

'There's certainly plenty of work for your lot in the city,' Frank said soberly. 'Hardly a week goes by without someone reporting finding a new unexploded bomb.'

'Aye, what they didn't drop on the city the Luftwaffe dropped on Cheshire on their way home. Mmm, I see what you mean about these sandwiches,' he told Sally, adding when he saw her expression, 'Here give me them, Sally. I'll get rid of them for you.' He gave her another wink.

'What are you going to do with them?' she asked him uneasily.

'Well, I reckon just one sniff of these will have them two-thousand-pound so-and-sos lifting off for Frankfurt as fast as they can.'

Sally shook her head in mock disapproval whilst Frank and the other men laughed.

'I'll say one thing for Johnny,' she told Molly later on when everyone had gone and they were washing up in the kitchen, 'he knows how to keep everyone's spirits up.'

The sound of raised voices from the children in the living room had them breaking off from their conversation to exchange wry looks.

'I'll go,' Molly offered. 'It's time I was on me way anyway. I don't envy you having to go out singing tonight. You'd have thought the Grafton would have let you have a night off for once.'

Sally ducked her head, as she felt the guilty tide of red creeping up under her skin. She hated having to be deceitful, especially with such good and close friend as the Brookeses, but what else could she do?

'Chin up, Mouse. We're off duty for the rest of the day now, or at least we will be in another five minutes,' Sam tried to comfort the other girl, as the bus bringing them back from their work at the barracks came to a halt outside the school.

It was still light enough for Sam to sneak a quick assessing look at Mouse as they got off the bus together. As she had guessed from her now-familiar tense silence, Mouse looked pale and anxious. She had developed a small tick that rather cruelly made her look as though she was trying to wink.

'It's because she keeps getting picked on,' Sam had tried to explain to Sergeant Brookes only that afternoon. 'If it isn't Captain Elland having a go at her, then it's our own warrant officer.'

'From what I've seen of her, the poor lass isn't really Forces material,' the sergeant had said.

'She didn't want to join up. She had this auntie

who threatened to throw her out of her own home if she didn't. She lost her parents in a bombing raid, you see, and this auntie was her mother's stepsister, and I reckon she was jealous of Mouse's mother. I feel so sorry for her.'

'You've got a kind heart,' Sergeant Brookes had told her with that slow warm smile of his that made her feel all squishy inside. Just thinking about that feeling now brought an unwanted mental image of Sergeant Everton. She knew all too well what he would think of that squishy feeling. Well, he didn't need to go warning her off. She knew now that Frank was married and of course that meant that he was out of bounds to her, even if he had been interested in her in that way – which he wasn't.

She had meant to march into their billet right behind Mouse, knowing how terrified she was that Toadie might be waiting in the hallway to pounce on them, but now, thanks to Johnny Everton, she was two girls behind Mouse.

The hallway smelled of vegetable soup and damp wool. Sam wrinkled her nose against it. She could see that Mouse was well past Toadie's lair and had almost reached the security of the stairs. Poor kid indeed. Maybe tonight she'd eat her supper instead of staring sickly at it. Sam had perfected the trick of swapping their plates, so that by the time Toadie's carrionlike gaze was searching Mouse's plate it was respectably clean, as though she had eaten her food. Toadie did not, of course, make any comment on the fact that Sam still had food on her plate, but then it was poor Mouse she enjoyed picking on. 'It's as though she can smell out Mouse's fear and knows exactly when to pounce,' Sam had told Hazel. 'Mouse is so scared she isn't sleeping or eating.'

'Halt!'

All the girls in the hallway stiffened to attention as the warrant officer marched into the hallway.

'You aren't off duty yet. Call yourselves ATS, shambling in as though you'd never been taught on a parade ground? Well, you'll be on one tomorrow morning. Six sharp.'

No one moved, every gaze fixed firmly on the distance. No one made a sound except for Mouse, who suddenly gave a semi-hysterical bubble of high-pitched laughter.

Sam groaned inwardly. That had done it now. Sure enough, the warrant officer was marching over to the stairs where Mouse was now trembling so much Sam could hear her teeth chattering.

'So you think I'm funny, do you? Right, well, let's see how funny you find this. All off-duty time absent from barracks is cancelled forthwith for the next five days.'

Sam could feel the wave of emotion that surged silently through the other girls. Since they weren't actually living in a large or formal barracks, the girls had got used to making the most of their off-duty hours by going into the unbombed part of the city for their entertainment, generally either dancing or going to the pictures, just as though they were still living a civvy life, and so far their captain had turned a blind eye to this. They were a jolly bunch who liked to have a good time, and Sam could now sense their angry resentment.

Mouse, though, was oblivious to their reaction. She was staring at the door as though about to make bolt for it, a wild, blind look in her eyes that worried Sam. Toadie was watching her almost gloatingly as though she wanted Mouse to take the one fatal step that would give her the opportunity really to throw the book at her.

She had to do something to get Toadie's attention away from Mouse, Sam decided, before Mouse really got herself into trouble, but what? She thought frantically and then relaxed as she started to wriggle her body frantically, scratching herself and tugging at her clothes, whilst the other girls tried not to break ranks and turn their heads to look at her. She let out a sharp 'ow' and then pulled off her cap and dropped it onto the floor before scratching her head.

Sam knew that Toadie couldn't continue to ignore her behaviour. The girls closest to her were edging away from her as she slapped her hand down firmly against her middle, exhaled in relief, and then started scratching even more furiously.

Sam could hear the warrant officer walking towards her, footsteps heavy and deliberate, but still she affected not to notice her, as though she was too engrossed in what she was doing.

'You!' The command was barked into her ear. 'Stand to attention.'

'Can't, ma'am,' Sam gasped. 'Biting me all over, they are. Gawd knows where I've had them from.' Sam aimed another slap at her body. 'There, got it . . . oooh, no I haven't . . . Oh, you. Oh, ouch. It's just bitten me real hard . . .'

Sam could hear the indrawn breath of the other girls as the warrant officer told her coldly, 'Unfasten your jacket.'

Obediently Sam did as she was told. As soon as her jacket was unfastened the warrant officer yanked up her shirt to reveal the flesh beneath. Just as well she had remembered that trick Russell had taught her when they were young, Sam thought triumphantly as the warrant officer glared at the raised scratches on her skin and the small pinpricks of blood. Lucky too that she had just happened to have a safety pin in her pocket, and had been able to inflict a couple of 'bites' on herself.

'You will go up to your dormitory immediately and remove all your clothes, and put them in a pillowcase to be fumigated. You will also strip your bed and remake it – after you have had a shower. I am putting you on a charge.'

'It wasn't my fault, ma'am,' Sam objected, all injured innocence. 'I reckon I must have got them from the barracks. Some of the men that come in there . . .'

Someone gave a small spurt of laughter.

'Silence. The punishment I have already given your whole dormitory is now doubled.'

A ripple of dismay ran round the hallway.

*

'I take it there weren't really any fleas?' Hazel murmured to her as they all climbed the stairs.

Sam shook her head.

'You do like living dangerously, don't you?'

'I had to do something. Mouse looked as though she was about to bolt for the door, and if she had done, Toadie would have had her down as going AWOL and then thrown the book at her.'

Hazel gave a small sigh. 'It's to your credit that you want to protect her, Sam, but you know that isn't really helping her. She needs to stiffen her spine and develop a bit more gumption. This is the ATS, remember.'

'I don't think she can. She's not eating and not sleeping, and some days she doesn't even talk. I've watched her when we're working together – it's like she just isn't really there. She wants her bear back desperately. It's all she's got left of her mother. I couldn't tell her what's happened to it.'

'No, you mustn't,' Hazel agreed, frowning slightly as she added, 'Look, I've got a few days' leave coming up – fortunately for me, and for you, my leave won't be affected by Toadie cancelling your off-duty leave of absence. I'm planning to go down to Dartmouth to see my chap, but when I get back, if the situation hasn't improved, then I'll try and have a word with the captain and the MO. It's strictly against the rules to go over Toadie's head, of course, but in this instance . . . However, I want your promise, Sam, that you'll stop getting yourself into trouble. You're both in my dormitory, remember, and what you do reflects on me.

So no more "fleas" or any other kind of schoolboy pranks used as diversionary tactics.'

Sam nodded her head.

It was almost worth being put on a charge to have saved poor Mouse and put one over on Toadie, Sam decided irrepressibly, half an hour later as she stood under the shower, grinning to herself, even if Hazel had made her promise not to do it again.

'Mummy . . . please don't go. I want you to stay here with me . . .'

Sally's heart sank, as she hugged Tommy tightly and wiped the tears from his face. Normally he was such a stout-hearted little chap, never complaining and always sunny-natured with that impish, cheeky smile of his. He had started complaining of a sore tummy when she had gone upstairs to kiss him good night, and then just after Doris had arrived he had been violently sick.

'It's a pity you have to work tonight,' Doris said as Sally explained what that happened whilst she nursed Tommy on her knee. 'It looks to me as though he's got a bit of a temperature.'

Sally felt as though her heart was being ripped in two. She desperately wanted to stay and comfort him, but the threats that been made against them were all too hideously real for her to ignore. 'I can't not go now. It's too late.' That much was true even if Doris would think she was talking about the Grafton and not the real reason she was going out and leaving her sick child. 'Oh, Doris . . .'

'There, don't you go upsetting yourself as well. He'll be fine. It's probably just too much excitement,' Doris reassured her firmly. 'Come on, sweetheart,' she smiled as she took Tommy from Sally.

His sobbed protest tore at Sally's heart. She'd have given anything to stay with him and comfort him but tonight of all nights she simply could not do so.

Her heart was thumping as she hurried down the Close. Normally she looked forward to singing, and especially when she was asked to sing at something special like a wedding or a party, but tonight for the first time in her life she was almost wishing her gift away. What would happen if the accompanist she had been promised wasn't any good, or if the Boss didn't like the way she sang 'Danny Boy'? She had reached the end of the Close and she gave a shocked protest as a man loomed out of the shadows in front of her, blocking her path.

'You're cutting it fine, aren't you?'

'You said I had to be there for seven. What are you doing here, anyway?' she demanded as she looked up into the unwelcome face of the debt collector. He wasn't the most prepossessing of men, with his watery too-pale blue eyes and his over-red face with its ex-boxer's misshapen nose.

'The Boss sent me to make sure you got to her party safe and sound.' He leered at her, revealing broken teeth. 'Come on, get in,' he demanded, urging her towards a car parked discreetly almost out of sight. Sally's eyes widened. Private car owners were not supposed to be driving because of the need to conserve what petrol there was for the war effort. Some people, though, obviously lived by their own rules. Sally couldn't stop herself giving a small shiver.

'I'll make my own way there. The number nineteen bus—'

'Get in the car.'

Was she imagining that menacing tone in his voice? She certainly knew she wasn't imagining the grip he had on her arm.

The public house where the party was being held was on a street off Scotland Road, in what was well known to be one of the most run-down and notorious parts of the city. It was certainly somewhere that Sally would never have dreamed of going on her own, especially before the war.

When the Luftwaffe had bombed the city nonstop for a full week at the beginning of May 1941, these streets had borne much of the brunt of the attack. There was no sign of any war damage, though, on the corner of the street where the pub stood, music and light spilling out from its open door, with the same careless disregard for the blackout laws as the driver of the car had for the petrol shortage.

The driver brought the car to a halt outside the open door.

A thickset man appeared out of nowhere to bar her way as Sally headed for the open door, whilst a few yards away a man was standing in the gutter urinating. Quickly Sally looked away. This was even worse than she had feared.

'It's all right, Jack, she's legit,' the debt collector told him. 'The Boss arrived yet, has she?'

'Five minutes ago. She's upstairs, Sid,' the bouncer replied. 'The Boss says you've to go over and collect her Pete and Ryan. And get 'em here in double-quick time or else. She's bin complaining for the last five minutes that you've teken too long to get here. You know what she's like when she's in one of her moods.'

'Come on,' said the man called Sid to Sally, 'and be warned, the Boss don't tek kindly to them as don't jump to it when she says to.'

Sally could tell that he was afraid of the woman he worked for, and her feelings of anxiety and unease increased.

'Rules us all with an iron rod, she does, them as works for her and her own sons as well.'

Sally suspected that he wasn't so much explaining things to her as excusing his own fear. 'And she don't have much time for other wimmin neither,' he added, 'least not from the way she has them daughters-in-law of hers feared to death of her.'

He had taken hold of her arm as though she were a prisoner and he her gaoler, Sally recognised, as he hurried her into the narrow passageway that opened on to the two rooms either side of the bar. Ignoring those, he urged her towards the stairs. The pub smelled of stale beer and cigarettes, mixed with the rank sour odour of unwashed flesh and urine. The stairs were steep and uncarpeted, giving on to a windowless landing. The debt collector knocked briskly on a closed door.

'It's me, Eric, and I've brought the singer for the Boss,' he called out.

Almost instantly the door opened to reveal another thickset man much like the one downstairs. As he stood back Sally could see a long trestle table piled high with food whilst a temporary bar had been set up on an opposite wall. In the middle of the wall opposite the door a small elderly woman was seated in a wooden chair, one clawlike hand resting on the top of a walking stick. Her white hair was drawn back off her face into a bun and her eyes were the sharpest and the coldest Sally had ever seen.

'Here's the singer, Boss,' Sid, the debt collector, announced.

'Where the hell have you bin? You should have had her 'ere before now. Get yourself off and get them two lads of mine back here, and think on that it's you that I'll be holding responsible if neither of them is fit to stand up.'

Sid had been backing towards the door all the time his employer had been speaking, but she had lost interest in him now and was focusing her attention on Sally instead.

'So . . . you reckon you can sing, do you?' she demanded. Her voice was as cold as her eyes, unwarmed by its faint Irish brogue.

'I don't know. I . . . I stand in sometimes for one of the Waltonettes.'

'So I hear.' Without taking her eyes off Sally, she said sharply, 'Taken a real fancy to you, my

Pete has, but don't go getting any ideas. I like to pick me own daughters-in-law and my lads, all but Kieron, are already wed.'

'I'm a married woman myself,' Sally told her stiffly. 'My husband—'

'Went off, leaving you with his debts and then got hisself caught by the Japs. Yes, I know. Know all about my customers, I do. 'Sides, the old man had a bit of a soft spot for you, I reckon. Give you a better rate than he should have done. You'll find that I do business differently.

'Come on then, let's see if you can sing. Aggie,' she instructed one of the women standing behind her, 'go and find that pianist and bring him over here. Then tell Joe and Michael to leave that beer they'll be drinking and come and sit with their ma whilst we listen to a bit of singing. At least I've got three sons that had the decency to get themselves here on time like they was told. The other two are going to have the sharp side of my tongue when Sid gets them here.'

The pianist was a thin nervous-looking man in his fifties with a large Adam's apple and a bald head, and the piano a battered upright, which had to be wheeled out of a corner of the room and looked as though it would be out of tune.

'Got the piano from a client who was overdue with his payments,' Bertha Harris informed Sally. 'Said it had belonged to his grandfather. From the fuss he made about it you'd have thought it was the crown jewels.' There was no sympathy in her voice for the owner of the piano.

Sally did not think she had ever seen two more unprepossessing men than the two now standing with their mother watching her. Squat, with broad shoulders and long arms, they were plainly cowed by their mother's presence.

She was like a small but deadly spider sitting in the middle of her web, waiting to catch her unwary prey, Sally decided. There was something not just chilling but somehow almost hypnotic about that gaze of hers, and Sally could well understand why everyone seemed so afraid of her.

Only one member of her family seemed unafraid of her, going to stand at her side instead of behind her.

'That's her eldest, Kieron,' the pianist muttered under his breath to Sally. 'Watch out for him. He's his ma all over again, whilst the other four are just dumb lumps of meat that do what she says.'

Physically Bertha Harris's eldest son was very different from the other two present, being tall and thin, with his mother's hard eyes.

To Sally's surprise, both the piano and the pianist proved to be good, and as she launched into the opening words of 'Danny Boy' the whole room went quiet.

Don't think about this place or these people, she urged herself. Just think of the song and the words. Even here in this dreadful place the magic still worked and she could feel herself being lifted by the music, escaping to lose herself in it . . .

She was trembling slightly when she had

finished, oblivious to her audience, and its reaction to her singing, her own emotions reflecting those of the song.

'I've heard it sung better, but I suppose it will have to do.'

The grudging words brought Sally back to reality. 'I'm not a trained singer,' she felt bound to say.

'I'm not a trained businesswoman, but that doesn't stop me being the best there is – better than any man, an' all. Too soft by half, most of them are. Show 'em a pretty face and they lose all sense of what's right. Sing it again. Let's see if you can do it better this time.'

Mouse was crying. Sam could hear her as she lay wide awake in the darkness, her own eyes grittily dry. She couldn't bear it, she really couldn't. Something about the smothered muffled sound of Mouse's distress tore at her heartstrings. She pushed back the bedclothes. The linoleum felt cold beneath her bare feet, the draught coming in under the ill-fitting door sending chilly little eddies of air up her pyjama legs.

'Mouse,' she whispered, crouching down beside her bed. 'You must try to stop crying.'

'I am trying, Sam, but I can't. I'm so afraid.'

'There's no need for you to be,' Sam tried to reassure her, but Mouse shuddered, shaking her head.

'It's all right for you, you don't understand . . . you don't know . . .'

She was making things worse, not better, Sam cursed herself.

'I miss my mother so much. She used to tell me that when she was a little girl, her stepsister, my aunt, used to lock her under the stairs and then pretend she didn't know she was there. Can you imagine that, Sam? Being left all alone in the dark. I can. I think about it a lot. I hate the dark. That's why my mother gave me Bear. I want him back so much. I hate being here, and if I was brave like you I'd run away, only I'm not brave enough and I know now that my aunt would find me and make me come back.'

She talked more like a child than an adult, Sam reflected, a child who was more afraid of her aunt than aware that 'running away', as she called it, was a serious military crime.

'I expect I'll feel like running away myself on that parade ground tomorrow morning, especially since I've got a full week of jankers to look forward to, but I can't say as I'd fancy being reported as absent without leave, and then tracked down by the Military Police and hauled back to face the music.' Sam tried to inject a light note into her voice whilst at the same time tactfully making sure that Mouse was aware of the consequences she would be facing if she did try to 'run away'.

But the other girl seemed to be oblivious to what she was trying to tell her, insisting emotionally, 'I want Bear back, Sam. I can't get off to sleep without him, and when I do I keep on dreaming about him and how upset my mother would be if she knew that I'd lost him.'

Sam couldn't imagine how Mouse would cope if

she knew what had happened to her bear. It would be far better for her if she stopped thinking about it and accepted that she must learn to live without it, without having to know the truth. The destruction of the bear had been such a cruel and unnecessary thing to do, those viciously slashed and ripped pieces of fur surely indicating that the warrant officer actually enjoyed hurting others. Some people should not be in uniform, Hazel had told Sam, and in their different ways both the warrant officer and Mouse were two such examples, albeit at opposite ends of the scale. It was a malicious stroke of fate that they had been brought together.

'I know I'd feel better if he were here with me,' Mouse whispered weepily.

'Well, that's not going to happen, is it?'

'No it ruddy well isn't, not unless she goes and asks Toadie to give it back to her, and we all know she's too scared of her to do that,' Lynsey snapped, obviously on her way back to bed from the bathroom. 'And I'll tell you what else isn't going to happen either unless the pair of you shut up,' she added, 'and that is the rest of us aren't going to get any sleep. It's thanks to you that we've all had our off-duty time stopped, remember. We was fine until you two got landed on us; caused us nothing but trouble, you have, wot with one of you trying to pinch another girl's chap and the other going on about a ruddy kiddie's toy all the time.'

Sally exhaled in a silent sigh of relief as she watched the Boss take her leave of everyone, her sons at her side and her daughters-in-law very much in the background as they trailed behind her.

It was gone midnight. Sally's throat ached from the combined effects of anxiety and cigarette smoke. She had hated everything about the evening, but most especially the woman in whose honour it had been organised. There was no denying the fierce maternal love Bertha Harris felt for her sons, and their children, but their wives might just as well not have existed, and Sally had heard enough during the evening about her cold-blooded treatment of those who crossed her to understand why those wives were so cowed and obedient. Her sons were loud-mouthed bullies, who liked throwing their weight around, the strong-arm men she used to make sure that no one by whom she was owed money ever made the mistake of thinking they could get away with not paying her back. Sally had become more fearful with everything she had learned.

And as if that wasn't enough she was also worrying herself sick about her son. She couldn't get out of her mind the memory of how he had clung to her, crying, begging her to stay. She hated herself for having had to leave him but how could she have done anything else?

The Boss and her family had gone. Sally looked around for the debt collector and was relieved when she couldn't see him, even though it meant she would have to make her own way home.

She was halfway down the narrow steps when one of the Boss's sons – Pete, the one the Boss had warned her to keep away from and who Sally vaguely recalled seeing at the Grafton – came back into the pub and saw her.

'Not thinking of leaving us, were you?' he demanded, giving her a drunken leer. 'Fun's only just about to start.'

He started up the stairs, so Sally had to turn back. There wasn't room for both of them and besides, she had no wish to provoke him. She had overheard how he reacted to someone's comment about his wife's black eye, replying grimly, 'Aye, and she'll get another one if she doesn't watch out. Miserable good-for-nothing. Don't know why I married her.'

When she regained the top of the stairs, Sally turned to let him go past her but instead he reached out and grabbed hold of her arm, pushing his face so close to hers that she could smell his stale beer breath.

'How about giving us a kiss?' he demanded.

'I'm a married woman,' Sally told him firmly, just as she had told his mother earlier. 'My husband's in the army.'

'I'm a married man and my wife should be in the army,' he retaliated, roaring with laughter at his own joke, as he wrapped one arm around her, then pinched her cheek painfully hard with his free hand. 'Come on then and sing summat for us.'

'I really have to go,' Sally protested. 'My little boy isn't very well . . .'

'Aw, shame . . .'

He had dropped his free hand to her waist and

she could feel its heat as he moved it upwards towards her breast.

Sally could hardly believe this was happening. Her throat tightened and locked with fear and revulsion when he pushed her back against the wall and tried to kiss her, whilst a couple of the other male guests watched, laughing and cheering him on.

Sally didn't know what would have happened if one of them hadn't suddenly called out warningly, 'Watch out, Pete. Your Kieron's on his way back up.'

Kieron, Sally remembered from the pianist, was the eldest of Bertha Harris's sons, tall and thin where the other four were squat and broad, sober apparently where they were drinkers, and as Sally had discovered earlier in the evening, disconcertingly given to reading out aloud passages from the Bible he carried with him. He was also unmarried, and Sally had been told by his doting mother that he should have been a priest. It was Kieron, Sally had learned, who was his mother's first lieutenant and who put into action those orders she gave for beatings and worse to be handed out to those she felt deserved them. If it had not been for the weight of her maternal guilt and anxiety about Tommy, Sally knew that she would have spent the evening feeling even more appalled and scared than she had. For a mother, though, when her child was ill, that anxiety came before anything else.

To her relief Pete was now releasing her but so roughly that she fell against the roughly plastered wall, hurting her arm. She didn't waste any time. As soon as Kieron was on the landing, she slipped away and hurried down the stairs.

It was nearly half-past twelve and it would take her a good half an hour to walk home. Her head was aching and her heart thumping. *Why* had this had to happen to her? Why couldn't Ronnie have seen sense and kept his promise to her not to gamble or borrow any more money? It was all right for him; he'd had his fun and now she was left to pay for it. He'd reckoned to love her and their sons so much but he'd got a funny way of showing it, leaving her with a load of debt. It had been bad enough before, but now . . . And where was he anyway, going and getting himself made a prisoner of war of the Japs, and then not even bothering to write to her and let her know that he was safe? And he could have done. That was what the Red Cross was there for, wasn't it, to see that captured soldiers wrote home to their families?

The misery and anxiety the evening had brought her was driving her thoughts. It was all very well Ronnie doing his bit for his country but what about her and the boys – who was going to watch out for them? Who was going to protect them? How was she supposed to cope with someone like the Boss all on her own? There was no one for her to turn to, no one to help her or care about her.

Tears of anger and self-pity burned her eyes and hastened her footsteps, until suddenly she came to an abrupt halt, filled with guilt and shame. How could she be so unloving and selfish? It wasn't Ronnie's fault that he wasn't here, or that he was a prisoner of war. Poor Ronnie. Sally looked up at the night sky. All she knew about Singapore was the fuss there had been in the paper when it had surrendered – not because of the men killed and taken prisoner, but because now Britain would not have access to those much-needed supplies that had come into the country via Singapore. But what did she care about supplies when what she needed was the strong supportive presence of her husband to confront the threat she was facing?

What was she going to do? What could she do? She felt so helpless, so vulnerable and so very much in the power of Bertha Harris and her sons.

Things had been bad enough when she had been paying off their debt to old Mr Wade, but now . . . Fresh tears filled Sally's eyes. It's no use you crying, she told herself, and let's have none of that you don't know how you're going to manage. You'll have to.

She had been walking so fast that she had to stop as she turned into Chestnut Close because of the stitch in her side. Perhaps she could ask around and see if any of the other dance bands wanted a singer. If she could get a solo spot then she'd be paid more and she might even end up singing on the wireless like Gracie Fields or Vera Lynn. The thought that she could come anywhere near rivalling the success of two of the country's best-loved singers was enough to have her laughing.

There was no point in her feeling sorry for herself; she'd just have to pull herself together and get on with things as best she could.

No light showed through the blackout curtains as she turned the key in the lock of her front door, but Doris was obviously awake and waiting for her, Sally realised guiltily as the door was opened from the inside before she could turn the handle.

Only it wasn't Doris standing there in her hallway, it was her son, Frank, his expression sombre.

'Frank!' Sally exclaimed. 'What is it? What are you doing here? Where's your mother? What—'

'There's bad news, Sally. Mam sent word, and me and Molly decided that it would be better if I waited here to tell you. I'm sorry, lass, but it's little Tommy.'

'Tommy? What do you mean? What's happened?' She looked frantically towards the stairs, but Frank shook his head.

'He's not here, Sally. He's up at Mill Road Hospital – doctor's orders.'

NINE

'In hospital?' Sally shook her head. 'No, no, he can't be. There was nothing wrong with him when I left, not really . . . just a bit of tummy ache, that was all. All kiddies get that.' Her voice broke and she looked pleadingly at Frank. 'Doris said it was nothing, just a bit too much excitement, that's all.'

She could see that Frank was looking at her with a mixture of discomfort and sadness in his eyes but somehow she still couldn't take in what he was saying.

'Mam went to the hospital with him, and she took Harry along with her as well. Seemingly the doctor wanted . . . that is, he thought it best . . .' Frank told her awkwardly. 'Mam asked me to wait for you and tell you what's happened.'

'*Both* of them! Both of them are at the hospital?' She started to shake with shock so violently that her teeth were clattering together.

'You'd better sit down for a minute,' Frank suggested tiredly.

'No . . . no! I've got to go to the hospital. My boys . . . What's happened, Frank, tell me?' How could she sit down when her sons, her babies, were so sick that they had had to be taken to hospital? No one took their children there unless they were desperately ill.

'Mam said that he took bad after you'd left, being sick and crying for you,' Frank was saying. 'In the end he was that bad that she decided to send for the doctor, that new one, you know, that's taken over from Dr Jennings, especially with it being in the papers about them kiddies in Glasgow having smallpox back in June.'

Smallpox! Doris was a trained nurse; if she had felt it necessary to send for a doctor then that meant . . . Sally was still shivering, yet at the same time she felt as though she was burning up, being consumed by the fires of hell for going out and leaving her sick child.

'Mam told Dr Ross that she reckoned it was that fish paste of Daisy's, but she just wanted to be sure. The doctor took one look at Tommy and said that he was too poorly to stay at home and that he wanted him in the hospital, so Mam got them both wrapped up and then the doctor took the three of them down to Mill Road in his car there and then. Before she left Mam asked Mrs Brent next door to slip down to us and tell us what was happening, so I came straight up here and said I'd wait for you to get back.'

'Did the doctor say anything else – about it being smallpox?'

'I don't know any more than what I've told you, Sally,' Frank replied. 'Try not to worry. Like as not it will be them sandwiches.'

'But if it *was* just a bit of fish paste that was making him sick, then why has he had to go to hospital?' Sally asked shakily, unable to take in what had happened and in too much of a shocked state to think straight.

'I don't know. That's something you'll have to ask the doctor.' Was that disapproval she could hear in Frank's voice? If so, it was nothing to the guilt she herself was feeling.

'I should never have gone out and left him,' she whispered, more to herself than to Frank. 'I didn't want to, I really didn't, but I had no choice.'

'Come on, don't go getting yourself even more upset,' Frank urged her gently.

'I'm going to the hospital, Frank. I've got to see him – both of them.'

'They won't let you on the ward. Not until visiting hours.'

'They're my kiddies and no one is going to stop me being with them,' Sally told him defiantly, already turning to leave.

'Molly said as how you'd say that,' Frank told her. 'Hold up a minute, I'll walk you there.'

Sally gratefully accepted his offer.

How lucky Molly was, having her husband on home duties, and how lucky she was too to have a good steady man like Frank. Frank would never gamble or borrow money; he just wasn't the sort. Molly would never need to take on all the work she could get to pay off his debts, nor would she have to endure what Sally had had to go through tonight. Why had the doctor taken Tommy *and* Harry to the hospital? A bit of sickness, that was all he'd had, but what if it wasn't just a bit of sickness? What if was smallpox? Kiddies had died in Glasgow ... Her thoughts were going round and round inside her head, whilst her heart thumped with frantic anxiety. She started to walk faster, until she was almost running, causing Frank to lengthen his stride to keep up with her, but Sally was oblivious. All she could think about was her precious sons and her fear. What had *they* ever done to deserve something like this?

They had almost reached the hospital when an ambulance raced past them in the darkness, its doors opening almost before it had stopped. Sally could hear the low tortured groans of the man being stretchered into the hospital.

'Hello there, Frank,' the driver called out.

'What's happened?' Frank asked him

'He's one of them bomb disposal lot,' the driver said, nodding in the direction of the disappearing stretcher. 'Working on a bomb, they was, when it went off. He was lucky. He's lost his legs, but the rest of them didn't have a chance. Blown to bits, they was. That's the second lot gone inside a month. Oh, begging your pardon, missus, didn't see you there.'

Sally shook her head.

'You wouldn't know who they were, them as

was killed, would you?' Frank asked the driver, in concern.

Despite her anxiety to get to her sons Sally could well understand why Frank was asking. The moment the driver had mentioned the bomb disposal men she had thought of Johnny.

'Sorry, mate, no.'

'Look, Frank, there's no need for you to come any further with me,' Sally told him quickly.

'If you're sure . . .'

She could see that he was torn between wanting to stay with her and wanting to find out more about the bomb blast so she gave him a small push and told him firmly, 'I'm sure.'

The entrance to the hospital was busy with nurses coming on and going off duty, and it took Sally several precious minutes to find out where her children were.

'He's Dr Ross's patient, you say?' the sister on duty asked her, pursing her lips.

'Yes. That's right. All my little lad had wrong with him was a bit of tummy ache. I'm sure there wasn't any need for Dr Ross to go bringing him in here.'

'That's for the doctor to say, and doctors don't go admitting patients unless they think there's a need. He'll be up on the children's ward, but since it's not visiting time until . . .'

Sally wasn't listening to her. The nurse's words were beating a slow terrifying tattoo into her head like the dark measured beat of a funeral march.

Until this war had brought them its injured

soldiers and bombed civilians, the only time people like her had gone into hospital had been to give birth or to die, and sometimes, in the case of a woman, both at the same time, and just the fact that he was in a hospital made Sally feel as though the hand of death had already touched her vulnerable little boy. Inside her head there were so many treasured pictures of him: the day she had given birth to him, earlier than she had expected, her birth pangs mingling with the shrill wail of the air-raid siren, whilst Doris and a scared-looking Molly had helped her upstairs to Frank Brookes's old bedroom. How fearful and resentful of the new life causing her so much pain she had been then, and how little she had known about the true nature of the pain a child could cause its mother. She would go through those birth pains again a hundred, no, a thousand, times over now if in return she could know that her son was safe and well.

After hurrying along what felt like miles of disinfectant-smelling corridors, she saw the doors to the ward up ahead. Almost running the last few yards, Sally pushed them open. The smell of disinfectant was even more overpowering inside the dimly lit ward with its rows of beds. A nurse, with an angry frown and a thin pinched mouth, came hurrying towards her.

'What are you doing?' she demanded. 'You can't come in here. It isn't allowed.'

'I want to see my little boy. He's been brought in this evening by Dr Ross.'

If anything, the nurse was now looking even more sour and critical.

'You'll have to come back during visiting hours.'

'I want to see him now.'

'That's not possible. It's against the rules.'

A second nurse appeared out of the gloom, demanding in a cold voice, 'What's going on here, Nurse?'

'I'm sorry, Sister, it's the mother of that little 'un we've got in the side ward, the one Dr Ross brought in. She wants to see 'im but I've told her she'll have to come back at visiting time.'

'Yes, that's right,' the sister confirmed, but Sally wasn't listening, pushing past them both in her desperation. The sister caught hold of her arm, already bruised from the rough handling she had received earlier, but somehow Sally managed to break free.

'Nurse, go and call for a porter to remove this woman immediately.'

'I want to see my sons, and I'm not leaving until I have seen them. They're my children . . .'

'Nurse, the patient in . . .' a new voice joined the conversation, and it was one that Sally would have recognised anywhere, thanks to that Scottish accent! Still trying to free herself from the sister's painful grip she insisted, 'I want to see my sons,' at the same time as the sister was complaining, 'I'm sorry, Dr Ross, but she just burst in here without a by-your-leave and now she's refusing to go.'

'Where are my boys? What have you done with

them?' Sally was trying to remain steadfast and determined but fear was weakening her, making her voice tremble along with her body, and taking her to the edge of hysteria.

Ignoring her, the doctor turned to the two nurses, telling them calmly, 'Thank you, Sister. I'll deal with this matter now, seeing as the boy is my patient. And thank you for finding him a bed.'

'You're welcome, Doctor. I wouldn't have wanted to turn him away, not seeing as how poorly he is, and his mother not being there to look after him, poor little mite,' the sister responded, giving Sally an acid look of contempt before nodding to her subordinate to return to her post.

The doctor waited until they were out of earshot before acknowledging that she had spoken, looking past her rather than at her as he said coldly, 'Will you please stop making so much noise? There are children on this ward, who, unlike your sons, are not fortunate enough to have strong recuperative powers, and who, being extremely poorly indeed, need their sleep.'

In any other circumstances those cutting words would have filled Sally with guilt, shame and concern for the poor children and their mothers, but right now she couldn't think or feel beyond the relief his words had brought her.

'My boys are all right?'

A small inclination of his head was all the response Dr Ross gave her, as though he begrudged her the comfort of actual words. What kind of man was he? He seemed not to have any normal human feelings at all, at least not that Sally understood. It was almost too much for her to take in: such intense fear, followed by an equally intense relief, and now anger surging through her so powerfully that she felt physically dizzy.

'They haven't got smallpox then?'

'Smallpox? You mean you went out and left them thinking . . . ? No, they haven't got smallpox.'

The relief tipped her over the edge of self-control.

'Well, if they're all right, why won't you let me see them?' she challenged him furiously. 'Why are they in here, and where's Doris?'

'If you mean Sister Brookes, I have sent her down to the nurses' sitting room so that she can have a rest. She isn't a young woman, and being left with the responsibility of a very sick child whilst his mother goes out enjoying herself—'

Sally recoiled as though she had been hit. 'I had to go. Doris knows that. I had no choice . . . I was working. I have to work.'

'Working? At a dance hall, the way you were the other night?'

The scorn in his voice made Sally's face burn. 'I have no choice,' she repeated fiercely. 'There's a war on, you know!'

'No choice other than to leave a sick child so that you could go out and sing? Somehow I don't think that's what the Government had in mind when they said that the country's women had to enrol for war work. The age of your younger child means—'

'I know how old my kiddies are, thank you very much, but what I don't know is who gave you the right to go bringing them in here, especially seeing as you're telling me now that there's nothing wrong.'

'What I said was that they were all right now. When Sister Brookes called me out to see your elder son, he was very poorly indeed, extremely poorly in fact,' Dr Ross stressed, 'and his condition made it imperative in my opinion that he be nursed under the care of a responsible person. Since it was obvious to me that his mother could not be relied on to be that person, I had no option other than to have him admitted here. As for your younger child . . .' he paused, and now he was looking at her Sally caught her breath as she saw the condemnation in his gaze, 'if you can't look after your children yourself then why haven't you taken advantage of the Government's evacuation scheme and sent them into the country where they can be cared for properly and safely?'

'My kiddies' place is with me. I'm their mother.' Like every other mother she knew, Sally dreaded the thought of being parted from her children.

'I notice that your younger child has several bad bruises.'

'Him and Tommy are always fighting.' She wanted to see her boys, not listen to this man, whom she knew disliked her every bit as much as she did him, going on about a few bruises.

'And I found that when touched he has a tendency to cry out in fear.'

Sally's mouth compressed with growing irritation. 'That's because you're a man. He isn't used to men, on account of his dad being in the army, just like a lot of other kiddies' dads.'

'If that's true then surely that's all the more reason why you, his mother, should be with your children just as much as you possibly can.'

'What's that supposed to mean?'

'I should have thought my meaning was self-evident, Mrs Walker. This evening, despite the fact that you knew your elder son was feeling poorly, you went out to a dance hall—'

'I was going there to work. I don't have any choice, I need the money.' Sally regretted her emotional admission the moment the words left her mouth but of course it was too late to recall them.

'You have a job doing war work in a factory, so Mrs Brookes tells me, and your husband is a serving soldier, thus you will be receiving wages from your own work and service pay on account of your husband. Most women would find that ample income on which to manage under present conditions.'

'My husband is a POW, not a serving soldier, and as for how much money I've got coming in and whether or not it's enough, that's my business and not yours. What do you know about the needs of people like us? You're a doctor, living in a big posh house and—'

'During my training I worked in the slums of Glasgow, and let me tell you that what I saw there of the struggles of the true poor is something I will never forget. You don't sing in a dance hall because you need the money, Mrs Walker, you do it because you enjoy it, because a woman like you – attractive and alone – feels she deserves to have male flattery and attention. *That's* why you went out tonight, despite the fact that your little boy begged you to stay with him.'

Sally opened her mouth to defend herself and then had to close it again as her throat locked on choking emotions. How dare he say those things about her? How dare he judge her when he knew nothing whatsoever about her? Her pride stung from the lash of his harsh words. She took a deep breath and launched into a passionate defence of her actions. 'My kiddies mean more to me than my own life. There's nothing I wouldn't do for them, and if I say I have to go out to work, then that's because it's the truth. Of course I'd rather be with them instead of having to go out singing, but I haven't got that choice. It's all right for you to stand there and look down your nose at me. I saw that photograph of your wife and kiddies, and I'll bet those pearls she had round her neck cost more than someone like my husband could earn in a whole lifetime. It's all right for men like you and women like her. She doesn't have to worry about her husband getting killed or being taken prisoner, and of course she won't be doing any proper war work, leastways not working in a factory, just a bit of collecting for the WVS, and a nice hot meal waiting on the table for you when you get home,' Sally told him scornfully. 'It's a different world for them like you—'

Abruptly and without saying a word, the doctor turned round and walked away from her, leaving Sally standing watching him in open-mouthed disbelief. Deep down inside she felt shocked by her own daring in speaking up like she had. She wasn't normally the sort to make a fuss, never mind argue, especially not with someone like a doctor, but when it came to her sons . . .

She heard the doors to the ward open and she stiffened, expecting to be told to leave, but when she turned round it was Doris who was coming towards her, her plump face heavy with tiredness and strain.

'Oh, Sally love . . .'

'I'm sorry, Doris, I really am.'

Emotionally the two women clung together.

'Sister Brookes, this really is most irregular. We don't allow mothers on the ward other than at visiting time, you know that.'

'It's all right, Sister, I told Dr Ross that Sally here would be coming in to see her little 'uns the moment she heard, and he said that she was to be allowed to have a few minutes with them, seeing as it wouldn't disturb anyone else with them being in a private room,' Doris spoke up firmly.

Sally's eyes rounded. This was news to her, and surely at odds with the doctor's attitude towards her.

'Come on, love,' Doris urged Sally gently, guiding her down the ward. 'They're down here in a room off the main ward. That was the only space they had for them; a private room, it is, an' all. I thought Sister was going to refuse to admit them at first, but Dr Ross was that insistent, even—' she broke off, looking self-conscious, and then said hurriedly, 'I never thought I'd be saying this because I never thought anyone would be good enough to step into old Dr Jennings's shoes, but Dr Ross has proved me wrong. One of the best, he is, and no mistake.' She paused and shook her head. 'I never thought, wi' me being a nurse for all them years, that I'd ever need to call a doctor out to a sick kiddie, but I'll be honest with you, Sally, when I saw how bad he was getting I was that scared. I've never seen a kiddie being that sick before. I don't mind telling you, it fair put the wind up me. Dr Ross said straight off as how I'd done the right thing sending for him, especially when I told him about them fish paste sandwiches. Wanted to know all about them, he did, and if anyone else had eaten them. I said as how they hadn't – just as well really, an' all. Mind you, I didn't feel as though I could say too much, what with Daisy's hubby having given her the fish paste in the first place. And we all know how he came by it. Not that I approve of black marketeering for one minute, I truly don't, but Daisy's a neighbour and I wouldn't want to see her husband lose his job and get into trouble, especially not now, when it's fourteen years in prison if you get caught. Dr Ross said as how he'd have a word with you about it. Yes, that's it, through them doors, Sally.'

In the dark area through the ward doors, Sally could just about make out a door. She reached for the handle and then hesitated.

'You open it, Doris,' she begged. 'I'm in that much of a state . . .'

The room beyond the door, like the ward itself, was lit dimly, to aid the nurses in their work, Sally guessed absently. It contained a small bed and a cot, and in them . . . Sally pressed her hand to her mouth to suppress the soft moan of love and relief at the sight of her two sleeping children. Dim the light might be but it was enough for her to see the familiar and much-loved faces of her sons, in separate beds but sleeping in identical positions. She went first to Tommy, aching to pick him up.

As though she guessed what she was thinking, Doris touched her on the arm and said softly, 'Best not to wake them, Sally. Poor little lad needs his rest. I've never seen a child so sick, not even those that had had appendicitis. The doctor said himself that he didn't know if he could pull through. Stayed with him every minute, he did, right until he knew he was over the worst.'

Tears filled Sally's eyes, blurring her vision. She did not want to hear about how wonderful the doctor had been, nor how Doris felt that he had saved Tommy's life. She should have been the one to be with her son, not some stranger, even if he was a doctor, and she would have been with him if it hadn't been for . . .

The tears welled up and spilled over to splash down on her sleeping son. He turned over in his sleep, his forehead furrowing as he murmured, 'Mum.'

'Mum's here, Tommy,' Sally told him chokily, placing her hand on his forehead and smoothing away his frown, her heart pierced by the sharply sweet pain of mother love as he relaxed beneath her familiar loving touch.

'They've offered me a bed here for the night, in the nurses' home, so if you want to go home . . . ?' Doris offered.

Immediately Sally shook her head. 'I'm not going anywhere without my boys.'

'Well, the doctor's said that he wants to keep him in until the morning, just to make sure that everything's all right.'

'Very well then, I'll stay with them.'

'Sally love—'

'I mean it, Doris. I'm not leaving this hospital without my boys. I can sleep here on the floor. Not that I'll be doing much sleeping, after what's happened. I'll never forgive myself for not being there.'

'You mustn't go blaming yourself, Sally lass.'

'Who else is there to blame? I'm their mother, after all.'

'It was Daisy who made them sandwiches.'

'Mebbe, but it was me that went out to work and left him, even though he'd told me he felt bad.'

'You weren't to know. I didn't think anything of it myself at first, and I've bin nursing for over forty years.'

Sally shook her head. 'It's all very well you saying that, Doris, but I should have known.'

And if she hadn't been so worked up about having to sing, then she *would* have known, Sally admitted, after Doris had gone, leaving her to curl up on the floor between the bed and the cot, in the blanket the ward sister had reluctantly and disapprovingly produced at Doris's insistence.

Sally was as deeply asleep as her two sons when, just before dawn, the doctor eased open the door, frowning when he saw the unexpected third presence on the floor before turning away from her to stand in the shadows, listening to the calm breathing of his patient.

A live, healthy child snatched back from the maw of death. He wiped his hand across his face. His eyes felt gritty from lack of sleep, his unshaven jaw rough and itchy.

What had he expected? That saving other children would wipe out the burden of guilt he carried over those he had not been able to save? When was he going to understand that for him there could never be an easing of that guilt? He must carry it for ever, without a loving wife who understood, without a wife who cared enough about him to want to understand. What a fool he was to ache so intensely for that shared closeness, that oneness and completeness. He looked down at Sally. No one seeing her singing at the Grafton, as he had done, could have imagined that she was a married woman with children. She had sung like a single girl, using her smiles to tempt any foolish male to believe they were meant for him. This war was bringing out the worst in women like her, selfish women who felt that life owed them "a good time", whatever that was, and who were prepared to let their children suffer so that they could have one. He had seen the results of that selfishness so many times: in war-weary, heart-broken men, returning to find their wives had found someone else; in blank-eyed, unloved children, unwanted because they had the wrong father or had been born inconveniently. And yet this woman, whom he had judged as a selfish uncaring mother, had turned into a tigress in defence of her cubs when she had confronted him earlier, refusing to leave them and exhibiting a fiercely protective maternal love completely at odds with his assessment of her feelings for them. She was a singer, he reminded himself; a woman used to projecting her charms to deceive and delude.

The dim light etched hollows beneath the sharp slant of his cheekbones, emphasising his weariness as he studied the two sleeping children, and it was them that Sally saw first as she woke up and opened her eyes, sensing someone's presence.

Without moving she watched as Dr Ross bent over Tommy, checking his pulse and then gently smoothing his hair back from his face. The dim light revealed an expression of exhausted anguish shadowing his face. A lump formed in her throat, her chest seizing up with inexplicable pain at the sight of this man who was a stranger to him touching her son as a father might do, with tenderness and love. But how could that be when she had seen for herself his cold sharpness with them in the street?

He had turned away from the bed now, his shoulders bowed as though he carried the sorrows of the world on them, giving both boys a final look before he left the small room.

TEN

'Lord, but I'm glad today's over and done with. Had me running about all over the place, they have today,' May complained, dropping down onto her bed. 'Lend us a cigarette until I can buy some tomorrow when we're at the barracks, will you, Alice?'

'You said that last week and you never gave me one back,' Sam heard the other girl complaining.

'Well, that's not my fault. I came looking for you, only you was out with some chap. Speaking of chaps, what about that sergeant you was fancying then, Lynsey? Proposed to you, has he, yet?' May teased.

'I was supposed to be seeing him tonight,' Lynsey responded, glowering at Sam. 'Only we're all confined to quarters, thanks to a certain someone.'

'Give it a rest, will you, Lynsey? You've done nothing but go on about it all the way back on the bus,' Hazel told her sharply.

'Well, you don't expect me to be pleased about it, do you?' Lynsey demanded bad-temperedly.

'At least we haven't been given jankers, like Sam, and made to skivvy all day in the kitchens.'

'It's her own fault she got put on a charge, and I don't see why the rest of us should end up getting punished as well, having to get up an hour earlier and march round that ruddy parade ground, with Toadie watching us just in case one of us should miss a step.'

Since the former school wasn't a proper military establishment, its tennis courts had been adapted to make a parade ground. All the girls billeted at the school had to turn out for parade every morning before breakfast as a matter of course, but Sam and the others were having to spend an extra hour 'square-bashing' every morning as part of their punishment. And, of course, the other girls blamed her and Mouse for this.

Sam looked down at her hands, red raw from hours of peeling potatoes over a bucket of cold water.

'That's the army for you,' Alice sighed, adding with a grin, 'I hope you haven't gone and left any eyes in them spuds you've bin peeling, Sam.'

'Huh, it wouldn't matter how many eyes she left in 'em, they taste that bad. I reckon that the Naafi lot that does the cooking here must think that mash has to have lumps in it,' May said.

'It's because there's no butter to mash them with. I remember how, before the war started, my mother used to put in a good dollop of butter and a bit of onion and then—'

'Don't,' May groaned. 'You're torturing me. How do you think I'm going to be able to eat me dinner after what you've just been saying?'

'Same way you always do, I reckon,' Alice responded cheerfully. 'Come on, everyone, get a move on otherwise we'll be late for supper and that will be another black mark against us.'

'Where's Mouse?' Sam asked.

'I dunno. She came back on the bus with us,' May answered. 'She was sitting with you, wasn't she, Lynsey?'

'Driving me mad. She was going on and on about that ruddy bear. I mean, there's me not being able to go out on a date and all she can go on about is a bear. As if it were real or something. Told her straight, I did, that she wanted to stop going on to us about it and go and tell Toadie she wanted it back. That way we'd all get a bit of peace.'

'What's up with you?' she demanded defensively when Sam looked at her in angry disbelief.

'Do you really need to ask? You know how afraid of Toadie Mouse is. You shouldn't have said anything to her.'

'Oh, shouldn't I? And since when have you had the right to tell me what to do, may I ask?'

'That's enough,' Hazel warned.

'Oh, I might know you'd take her side. She's been sucking up to you ever since she got here.'

'That's not true,' Sam defended herself indignantly.

'Give over, Lynsey. You're just in a foul mood because you can't see your sergeant,' May objected.

'And whose fault's that?'

'I'm going to look for Mouse,' Sam announced.

'You're on a charge, remember, Sam,' Hazel reminded her, 'and if you get yourself into any more trouble . . .'

'I've got to find her. She'll be upset.'

'Oh, for heaven's sake! I don't know what you're making such a fuss about. She's probably crying for her mummy in the lav.' Lynsey pulled an unkind face. 'She gets on my pip at times, she really does. I mean, all this fuss over a kid's toy.'

'That bear isn't a kid's toy to her. Her mother gave it to her and she feels it's all she's got left of her,' Sam pointed out angrily.

Lynsey tossed her head stubbornly.

'Look, Sam, it's almost suppertime – why don't you leave it until after supper and then I'll go and look for her?' Hazel offered. 'We all know that she doesn't like the food here and that she tries to avoid eating it if she can. She probably won't thank you if she's deliberately avoiding having to go in for supper.'

Sam hesitated, then shook her head. 'No . . . If she did try to see Toadie and ask for her bear back,' she paused meaningfully and looked at Hazel, relieved to see from the small nod she gave her that she hadn't forgotten what its fate had been, 'I can run down now and be back before we have to go in for supper.'

'Very well then,' Hazel agreed, adding, 'She'd have had to make a formal request to see the warrant officer, so it's bound to have been recorded.

You could ask whoever's on the desk to check for you, but remember – no getting into any more trouble. You go straight down there, you speak to whoever is on the desk and then you come back and tell me what they said.'

Sam nodded, already halfway out of the room.

The girl on the desk looked up at her and then back at what she was doing, announcing mechanically, 'If you've come down to ask for a weekend pass, you're wasting your time. If you want cigarettes, you are also wasting your time. If you want—'

'I wanted to know if there've been any requests from Private Hatton to see the warrant officer,' Sam stopped her.

'That's not the kind of information I can give you,' the girl answered immediately, but Sam could see that she was looking at the book in front of her and that she had moved her arm as though to conceal something.

'She said that she was going to ask to see her,' Sam persisted stubbornly, 'but that was when she came in off the bus, and no one's seen her since. If she did see T— Is the warrant officer in her office?' Sam looked over to the closed office door.

'I really can't say, I'm afraid. What do you think you're doing?' the other girl demanded sharply when Sam started to head for the closed door. 'You can't go in there . . .' She made to bar the door but she was too late, Sam had moved too quickly for her and was already turning the handle. Only the door wouldn't open properly, as though there was something wedged against it.

'You're wasting your time. The warrant officer is not in there.'

'But Mouse did ask to see her, didn't she?' Sam demanded, still pushing at the door.

'It'll be a court martial you'll be facing, not a charge, and no mistake if the warrant officer comes down here and finds you trying to break into her office.'

Sam gave another firm push and then exhaled in satisfaction as she finally managed to get the door open.

'You can't go in there . . .' the girl repeated.

Ignoring her, Sam stepped into the small room, and then realised what had been jamming it.

Somewhere in the distance she could hear the angry voice of someone saying something to her, but she didn't pay it any attention. She couldn't. All she could do was stand and stare in paralysed disbelief and horror at Mouse's body as it swung from the rope with which she had hanged herself. On the floor beneath her feet Sam could see some small pieces of gold fur. She kneeled down and picked one up. Mouse's bear. Toadie must have kept some of the pieces after she had destroyed it. Had she shown them to Mouse? Tormented her by telling her that she had done? Sam shuddered violently, knowing what that would have done to Mouse.

'Can't you hear me? I said come out of there, otherwise—' the voice was getting louder as the other girl came towards her, her angry objections followed by a small silence, and then the sound of her screams tearing into the musty air filling the hallway, bringing girls and officers running to see what was going on.

Sam was distantly aware of the commotion going on all around round her, but it couldn't touch her. Without knowing she had done so, she had reached for Mouse's hand, and was trying to chafe warmth into it with her own.

'Let go of her hand ... Yes, that's a good girl ...' The captain's voice was quiet and calm, the medical officer taking her place at Mouse's side. Their faces shimmered in front of her as though they were reflected in a puddle, and it took her some time to recognise that the puddle was her own tears.

'She couldn't live without her bear. It was all she had left of her mother, you see,' she told the captain dully.

ELEVEN

'Mum . . .'

Immediately Sally was at her elder son's bedside, reaching for his hand whilst she smoothed back his hair from his forehead.

'What is it, love? Are you feeling sick again?'

'No. I want to go home.'

He wasn't the only one, Sally acknowledged. They had been at the hospital all day, confined to this small room, but the ward sister, still tight-lipped with a disapproval that Sally suspected had now turned into outright dislike of her, had refused to hand over the boys' clothes, saying that they couldn't leave until Dr Ross had been in to see them. And the truth was that much as she wanted to take them home, and healthy though they both looked, Sally was too much of a protective mother to want to risk Tommy having a relapse because of her impatience.

Harry, too young to understand properly what was happening, was hungry and grizzling, whilst Tommy was bored with being in bed and playing

the games Sally had made up to keep him occupied.

'Mum, I'm hungry,' Tommy complained.

All Sally had to give them were the egg sandwiches Doris had brought her when she had come
to see how things were before returning home. Still
too upset to feel like eating herself, Sally had put
them in her bag.

Carefully dividing them into two, she gave
Tommy the large portion before breaking the other
one into small pieces to feed to Harry, who finished
his in double-quick time.

She was just wiping the egg from round Harry's
mouth when the sister came in, a look of horror
widening her eyes as she demanded, 'What do you
think you are doing?'

'What does it look like?' Sally retorted. 'I'm
feeding my kiddies. Starving, they were.'

'Well, of course they are. Them was Dr Ross's
orders. No food until after he'd seen them.' The
thin lips pursed. 'You do realise what this means,
don't you? Dr Ross will have to be told, of course,
and he won't be pleased!'

Unlike *her*! She certainly looked pleased to have
caught her out in a wrongdoing, Sally reflected.

'I hope you realise that if they take sick again
it will be your fault?'

Sally's anger turned to fear and guilt, which she
disguised by snapping, 'If I'd been told they weren't
to have anything to eat then I wouldn't have given
them anything.'

'After all the trouble Dr Ross has taken with

them as well, insisting on paying for a private room for them himself when I told him I had no room on my ward for them. He won't want to be having to pay for them for a second night.'

Sally had gone rigid with humiliation and shock. The doctor had paid for this room?

'I'm taking my kiddies home right now.'

'You can't do that. They can't leave here until Dr Ross has given his permission.'

'These are my sons and I don't need anyone's permission to take them home with me, and if you don't give me their clothes, then I'll take them in what they're wearing.'

'Those nightclothes are hospital property.'

How dare someone, anyone, but most of all this doctor, who was a stranger to them, humiliate her by forcing on her unwanted charity? The whole of Liverpool probably knew by now that Sally Walker couldn't afford proper medical care for her sons and had had to be treated like a charity case. It was all very well having all this talk about what was going to be done for folk after the war was over, with free medical care for them that needed it, but what about what was needed now? Sally's pride was in open revolt. She stormed over to the cot, and reached into it to lift out her younger son.

'Sister, Dr Ross is asking to see you.'

Sally's heart sank and she could see the triumphant gleam in the sister's eyes.

'Stay here with this mother, Nurse. She is not to leave this room until I have seen Dr Ross.'

This nurse was a different one from the one Sally had seen last night, a pretty pert-looking girl with a wide smile.

'You're one of them singers from the Waltonettes, aren't you?' she said. 'I recognised you straight off on account of my cousin Cedric being mad on you. Goes to the Grafton every week, he does, hoping you'll be singing. Says you could put Gracie Fields in the shade and no mistake. These your kiddies, are they?'

Sally nodded.

'That'll disappoint him. Hoping you was single, he was. Not that he'd ever pluck up the courage to ask you for a dance, never mind a date,' she laughed. 'A proper softie, he is.'

Sally felt the small eddy of cold air against her calves and knew even without turning round and before she heard him speak who had entered.

'Sister tells me you wish to take the boys home. I would prefer it if they stayed here for another night.'

'In a private ward that you're paying for?' Sally shook her head and then stopped as she saw the betraying tide of colour seeping up under his skin. So now *he* knew how it felt to be wrong-footed. Good.

'Sister also told me that you've given the boys food, although I specifically said they were to be put on a starving diet for twenty-four hours.'

'No one told me.'

Ignoring her, Dr Ross had gone across to Tommy, who, to Sally's surprise, seemed pleased

184

to see him, greeting the doctor with a wide smile as he placed his hands on his stomach and gently examined him.

'Does that hurt?'

'No. Tell me some more about your train set.'

'In a minute. I want you to tell me first if this hurts.'

It seemed an age to Sally, waiting and watching anxiously before he had finished.

'The reason I did not want them to eat was because I wanted to make sure your elder son's system was clear of whatever it was that poisoned it in the first place. The Government takes this kind of thing very seriously indeed, especially in children.'

'He ate something that disagreed with him. I've never heard of the Government worrying itself about a fish paste sandwich.'

'Then obviously you don't read the newspapers, Mrs Walker, because if you did you'd be aware that earlier this year there were reports all across the country of people suffering similar symptoms to your son's. Several people died as a result of that outbreak.'

Sally put her hand to her mouth to stem her frightened protest.

'However,' Dr Ross continued, 'fortunately Tommy seems to be fine.'

'Does that mean I can take them home?'

'Not yet. Before you leave I have some questions I want to ask you about the source of the possible contamination, but first I have another patient I need to see. So if you'd just wait here for a few minutes . . .'

'I'll be needing their clothes then, so that I can get them dressed ready to leave,' Sally told him, giving the sister a challenging look.

When in response he gave a brief nod in the direction of the nurse, Sally felt her tense stomach muscles start to relax.

'But I want to see my doctor,' Tommy wailed as Sally hurried him into his clothes, one eye on her younger son, ready dressed and waiting in the cot the other side of the door. Heaven alone knew how she was going to find the extra money to repay the doctor, but somehow she would find it, she assured herself grimly.

'Come on,' Sally instructed her elder son, picking up Harry. 'We're going home.'

They had taken less than half a dozen steps down the corridor when the doctor appeared at the other end of it. Sally exhaled grimly, tightening her hold of Tommy's hand when he tried to pull free.

'You can't force me to let them stay,' she announced fiercely.

'Actually I could and would if I thought that there was any danger of them contaminating others. As it is, it's essential that the source of the sickness is identified so that we can make sure that no one else is affected by it. Sister Brookes made mention of some fish paste sand-wiches which she believed were the cause of

Tommy's sickness. Where exactly did this fish paste come from?'

Sally gave a dismissive shrug, remembering what Doris had said about not implicating Daisy or her husband. 'I'm sure I really can't say.'

'But surely you must have some idea? In these times of rationing most housewives know what they have in their store cupboards. My concern is that this fish paste could be part of a much larger consignment, which could pose the same threat to the health of others that your son suffered. If you can remember when you bought it . . .'

'Well, I can't,' Sally told him, not without some qualms at the thought of others – especially children – suffering as her Tommy had, but she quietened her conscience by promising herself that the first thing she was going to do once she got home was go round to Daisy's and ask her to get her husband to make sure that those who had had the tins were warned not to use them.

'How are you planning to get home, only it's raining heavily?'

Sally stared at him, surprised by his sudden change of subject. 'We'll get the bus.'

'I've got a better idea. My car's right outside the hospital – I'll drive you back.'

'No . . . no, there's no need for you to do that.'

'Your son has been very poorly; I think there is every need.'

Tommy took advantage of her confusion to pull away from her and run over to the doctor, clinging to his leg as he reminded him, 'You said you'd tell me some more about your train set.'

Sally was astonished by the smile that warmed Dr Ross's face as he bent down to pick up her son. 'So I did,' he agreed, 'but first I'm going to drive you home.'

'In your car?' Tommy was beaming from ear to ear with excitement at the thought, and Sally knew that she had no chance now of refusing the doctor's offer.

She could almost feel the heat of the two holes Sister's concentrated stare of dislike was burning into her back, Sally acknowledged a few minutes later when they left the ward escorted by the doctor.

His car wasn't as shiny and posh as the one Bertha Harris had sent for her, but the apprehension she felt at climbing into it was equal. Predictably, of course, both her sons were round-eyed with delight and excitement, Tommy chattering away nonstop, firing questions at the doctor about the car whilst revealing a knowledge of its technical workings that astonished Sally.

'You've got a very bright little lad there,' the doctor informed her quietly under cover of Tommy earnestly explaining something about the car to his younger brother.

'He gets it from his dad, and from Doris's son, Frank. He's with the Royal Engineers and Tommy's always pestering him about engines.'

'This country's going to need young men like him when all this is over.'

Sally didn't say anything. They were turning into Chestnut Close and she could well imagine the interest her return home in the doctor's car would be causing those who witnessed it.

'If you'd put the cost of the hospital room on your bill then . . .' she began as soon as the car stopped outside her front gate.

'There's no charge for the room. Sister gave you the wrong information about that.'

'Come on, Tommy,' Sally instructed, wanting to get out of the car and inside her own front door as fast as she could.

'Dr Ross said he'd tell me about his train,' her son protested.

'The doctor's busy, and he has to go and look after other sick little boys.'

'I've got enough time to come in for a little while,' he contradicted her, much to her dismay. 'There are still some questions I want to ask you.'

'About the fish paste? I've already told you.'

'No, with regard to who takes care of your sons when you are at work.'

He was getting out of the car before she could object, coming round to the passenger door to open it for her, taking Harry from her and holding him securely in one arm as he placed his free hand beneath her elbow to help her out.

Sally's instinctive reaction was to pull away from him but she was too conscious of her neighbours' curiosity from behind their lace-curtained front windows to do so.

'Mum, I'm hungry,' Tommy complained.

'I'll heat you up a bowl of soup,' she told him, as she unlocked the front door.

Leaving the boys in the parlour, she hurried into the kitchen and lit the gas beneath the pan of soup, which she, like so many other housewives, had learned to keep going with stock and leftover vegetables.

When she went back into the parlour to check on the boys and put coal and a match to the ashes in the grate, she could see that the doctor was looking round the room – and no doubt finding it wanting compared to his own home, she decided. Immediately her pride fired up.

'I dare say this isn't what you're used to.'

'No,' he agreed, 'it isn't . . .'

Sally's breath hissed out of her lungs in outrage. A sudden yell from Harry focused her attention back on her sons, who were rolling around on the floor, squabbling over a toy. Quickly she went to separate them.

'*This* is how Harry gets his bruises,' she informed him. 'Always scrapping, these two are. Doris and I do our best, but with their dad not here . . .'

'All the more reason, I would have thought, to send them into the country as evacuees for the duration of the war. I realise that you'd miss them but at least you'd have the comfort of knowing they were safe and being properly looked after.'

'They're safe and being properly looked after now. No one could take care of them better than Doris.'

'Sister Brookes may provide them with exemplary care now but, as I understand it, her daughter-in-law is due to give birth shortly.'

'What's that got to do with anything?' Sally challenged him.

'I should have thought it was obvious. Blood is thicker than water, as they say, and I dare say that Sister Brookes will want to be on hand to help her daughter-in-law.'

'So why should that make any difference to me? Molly doesn't work.'

'Sister Brookes isn't a young woman. She confessed to me how desperately worried she was when Tommy fell ill. I should have thought you could see for yourself how selfish it is of you to oblige her to carry that kind of responsibility, never mind the risk you're taking with your sons' health. A city that has suffered the bomb damage Liverpool has is not an ideal place for young children to grow up in, especially when they could quite easily be living in safety in the countryside. Any good mother would see that for herself.'

'If you're saying that I'm not a fit mother . . .'

The silence that followed her challenge made Sally's face burn.

'By your own admission you work long factory shifts, in addition to which you go out at night. That hardly leaves you with much time to spend with your sons.'

'I'm not having them evacuated,' Sally told him fiercely. 'And no one is going to make me.' Her heart was thumping unsteadily, driven by a mixture of anger, fear and guilt.

'Then maybe you should consider altering your own life to make sure that your children are properly cared for.'

'They are properly cared for.'

'And that you, their mother, are there when they need her,' he continued, ignoring her. 'You work in a factory when you don't need to, and then—'

'Who are you to say what I do and don't need to do?' Sally was beside herself with emotion. 'Obviously you have a wonderful perfect wife, who doesn't need to work and who would never leave your sons to go out anywhere, especially not a dance hall, but I'm not her and my life isn't hers, so why don't you go home to her right now, and tell her what a dreadful mother I am, and leave me to bring up my sons as I think? What . . . let go of me.' Sally demanded furiously when he suddenly took hold of her, gripping her upper arms so tightly that it hurt as he shook her, and told her savagely, 'Can't you see how you are endangering them, you stupid woman?' He released her abruptly, turning his back on her.

'Women like you should not be allowed to have children,' he told her bitingly, heading for the door.

'Just because I'm not like your wife that doesn't mean that I'm not a good mother, and I'm not having you or anyone else saying any different. My boys are hungry, and I dare say your wife will have your own dinner waiting for you, unless of course you've gone and made her evacuate herself and your kiddies to the country . . .'

'My wife and my sons are dead.'

Sally stared at him. A heavy silence filled the room, broken only by the hiss of the rain coming down the chimney onto the burning coal.

'I must go,' Dr Ross told her. 'If you do remember the source of that fish paste, please let me know.'

'I asked you if you would tell us what you know now about Private Hatton and if she had communicated to you anything that denoted that she might not be of sound mind. I appreciate that naturally what has happened has been a shock for you, Private Grey, but I would – indeed, I must – ask you to consider very carefully how much loyalty to a friend has guided your words.'

The captain was speaking quietly and very sternly.

Sam had no idea how long ago it was now since she had finally managed to open the warrant officer's office door and had found Mouse. Half an hour . . . an hour . . . She had lost all sense of time, her thoughts weighed down by leaden misery.

'Everything I've said is the truth,' she answered the captain bleakly. 'The warrant officer picked on Mouse horribly. She made Mouse feel that she couldn't take it any more.'

'She told you that?'

'Not in so many words,' Sam had to admit, 'but we could all see the state she was in, and we all knew why.'

Sam knew that it was almost unheard of for a lowly private to speak out as she was doing, but she had to do so for Mouse's sake. Only she knew how much she blamed herself for not having guessed what Mouse was planning to do, and somehow been able to stop it. Had she been there when Lynsey had lost her temper with Mouse and told her to go and ask Toadie for her bear back, she knew she would have made sure that Mouse did no such thing, but Lynsey, of course, had no idea about the bear's fate.

'You are making what amounts to a very serious accusation against a senior officer, Private, and I would ask you again to look very carefully into your own heart – and memory. When our emotions are disturbed we can all make assumptions and judgements that are not as correct as we like to think. We understand that when young women first join up and wear a uniform it can take some time for them to adapt to Forces life and its rules and regulations. The attitude of those in charge can seem harsher than one is used to in civilian life, but it is there for a purpose and that purpose is to train you all into a cohesive unit fit to work for the defence of this country. Inexperienced privates such as yourself cannot know and see as others can the very sound reasoning behind certain methods of discipline. You have told us about Private Hatton's distress at the removal of a teddy bear she brought here with her. Maybe to you this seems an unnecessary and even a harsh act, but I would say to you that it is a vitally important part of what you all must learn, and that is immediate obedience to orders. I would suggest to you therefore that what you witnessed in the warrant officer was simply a normal part of that learning process.'

Sam could hear the censure in the captain's voice but she had to stand up for her friend and defend her. 'I understand what you are saying, ma'am—'

'Good, then we will consider the matter closed.'

'But I do know what I saw. And I did see what Warrant Officer Sands had done to Mouse's bear. We could *all* see that Mouse wasn't strong enough to cope,' Sam rushed on, trying not to feel cowed by the captain's obvious displeasure. If *she* didn't stick up for poor Mouse then who would? How could she square her conscience if she didn't at least try to defend her? 'Mouse never wanted to join the ATS, you see. She'd been forced into it by her aunt. She told me that her bear had been given to her by her mother and that she treasured it because of that. She was terrified of the warrant officer and yet she was so desperate to get the bear back that she went to her to ask for it.' Sam could feel the tears threatening to clog the back of her throat.

The captain was looking at her very grimly. 'I see. We'll start again, shall we? Now, Private Grey, knowing that Private Hatton was suffering from personal worries, you felt that it was your duty to seek out Warrant Officer Sands and alert her to Private Hatton's disturbed state of mind.'

Sam was too shocked to conceal her feelings. 'No! I would never have betrayed poor Mouse to—'

As though Sam hadn't spoken the captain continued, 'I seem to be having difficulty making myself clear to you, Private. Obviously there will have to be a full report on the whole matter, which will naturally include a statement from you. Once written and filed, such a statement can never be unwritten, Private Grey, and remains to dog us and sometimes to damn us for the rest of our lives. I should warn you that contained in the verbal and informal statement you have just given me there are accusations which, if formalised, will do a great deal of damage to yourself as well as to others. People who let the side down and tell tales on others are not well thought of in the Forces. Now, I fully accept that you have had a bad shock. Therefore I shall consider that this talk between us has not taken place, other than for the purpose of my informing you that I shall speak to you again tomorrow when you have had the chance to think clearly about where your loyalties should lie.'

The captain wanted her to change her story, Sam realised.

'Someone will escort you to the sickbay where you are to spend the night.'

'The sickbay? But—'

'Until this matter has been examined in more detail I would ask you not to discuss it with anyone else. Dismissed.'

Automatically Sam stood up and saluted her,

but she couldn't stop herself from asking one anguished question. 'What will happen . . . to . . . I mean . . . she doesn't have anyone of her own, and—'

'Thank you for your co-operation, Private. That is all.'

The captain plainly wasn't going to answer her.

No sooner was she outside the captain's office and in the corridor than the medical officer's corporal arrived to tell her that she was taking her straight to the small sickbay, where she would be spending the night.

'MO's orders,' she informed Sam.

'Here you are, take this.' The corporal handed Sam a cup of cocoa. 'We've sent down to your dormitory for your night things.'

'My friend Mouse, the girl—' Sam began, but the corporal shook her head.

'Sorry, but we're under strict orders not to discuss it. I'll leave you to drink your cocoa.'

The small sickbay felt lonely after the bustle of the dormitory, and tonight the last thing Sam felt like doing was sleeping here alone. Poor Mouse. Had she been planning to take her own life when she had gone to see Toadie, or had it been a sudden decision made in the darkness of her anguish about her bear? If only she, Sam, had been here to stop her from going to see the warrant officer. But she hadn't been, and because of that Mouse was dead. What would happen now? Suicide was against the law.

The door suddenly opened.

'Hazel!' Sam exclaimed in relief.

'I've brought you your things,' the corporal told her.

'I'm so glad to see you,' Sam said emotionally. 'I wanted to come back to the dorm, but they won't let me. And, Hazel, the captain asked me to tell her what I knew about Mouse but when I did . . . She hasn't said so in as many words but I know she doesn't want me to mention Toadie in the formal statement I've got to make, but it was because of Toadie . . .'

Hazel sat down on one of the spare beds next to her and said quietly, 'Look, Sam, I know how you must feel about Mouse and how fond of her you were but, in all honesty, if I were you I would think very seriously about what the captain has said.'

'You mean you agree with her? How can you when you know what poor Mouse went through?'

'Sam, I shouldn't really be telling you this, but every now and again a girl joins up who shouldn't have done and sometimes she's silly enough to talk about being so miserable that she can't bear things any more. Perhaps she's used to having a lot more attention paid to her at home than she will get in uniform. More often than not that kind of girl goes out and buys a large bottle of aspirin, which she makes sure the other girls see. Sometimes she takes enough aspirin from that bottle to make herself unwell; sometimes she just talks about "ending it all". For the rest of us, those of us who have joined up to do our duty and not to make a fuss about ourselves, the outcome is always the same: her silly behaviour has tarnished our reputation.'

Sam had never heard Hazel speak so critically or unsympathetically, and it shocked her. 'But Mouse wasn't like that – you know that, Hazel,' she protested.

Hazel shook her head. 'This is the ATS, Sam, not a nursery. It's up to all of us to find a way of fitting in here, and those who can't or don't cause a lot of problems for themselves and everyone else. You may not have realised it, but Mouse wasn't exactly popular with the other girls.'

'You mean she wasn't popular with Lynsey,' Sam burst out.

Ignoring her outburst Hazel continued coolly, 'Anyone who draws officer attention to herself the way that Mouse did is seen as a problem by the other members of her unit, because that attention is turned on them as well. Several of the girls have told me privately that they couldn't understand why she had brought a nursery toy into the ATS with her in the first place, and I'm afraid that whilst everyone is shocked by what's happened, the general feeling is that whilst Toadie may have picked on Mouse, she made things far worse for herself than they need have been. Now we're all in danger of being tainted by the shocking thing she's done, of being thought of as not up to the mark, and are a potential cause of damage to the service because of that. It will take a long time for our dorm to live this incident down, I can tell you.

'I'm going on leave tomorrow morning, but when I come back I intend to make sure that the rest of us put our backs into reversing the damage Mouse has done to us all. Not that there will be any public reference to it. The powers that be can't afford to have it get into the newspapers that a serving member of the ATS was so lacking in backbone that she took her own life. The people of this country need to believe in the strength of the Government and those who represent it, which in a small way we in the ATS do. We all have our loyalty to our friends, of course, but our first and greater loyalty is to the ATS and to this country, and any girl who forgets that fact is not fit to serve in uniform, in my opinion.'

Sam was still too much in shock to say anything.

'Personally,' Hazel continued, 'I think it's a great shame that the MO didn't dismiss her as unfit for service right from the start, but I've been given to understand that when the matter was raised with her she pleaded not to be sent home and to be given a second chance.'

Finally Sam managed to struggle through her shock to defend her friend. 'You know how Toadie bullied poor Mouse.'

'What I know is that a member of my dormitory has done something that is unforgivable, and I would suggest *you* now need to think a bit more about others and a lot less about one silly weak young woman,' Hazel told her. 'By taking her own life, Mouse could undermine the morale of other girls here. That can't be allowed to happen. The services aren't about individuals and their needs, Sam, they're about the whole service working together to save our country.'

Sam looked blindly at the wall. She had thought of Hazel as a chum, but the way she was talking made Sam feel like an outsider and very alone.

'I did try to warn you about not getting too involved with Mouse. Of course your loyalty to a friend is understandable but, like I've just said, that kind of loyalty must never come before your loyalty to the ATS and to our country,' Hazel warned her sternly. 'Surely you can see the harm it would do, not just to those of us billeted here, but to the whole of the ATS if one of its number were to start making accusations that the actions of an officer led to a girl taking her own life. I'm not just speaking to you as a corporal, Sam. I like you; you're made of the right stuff.'

'You want me to lie to protect Toadie.'

Hazel shook her head. 'Have you thought of what will happen to you if other statements are taken, which they will be, and they do not tally with your own? I've already heard girls saying that they suspected that Mouse was unbalanced and inclined to be hysterical. I've even heard talk of some girls having heard her say openly that she intended to take her own life. I heard her say myself that she no longer wanted to go on living.'

'She did say that, but that didn't mean . . . She

was just upset . . . I can't believe you're saying any of this.'

'It's for your own good. Like I said, I like you, Sam, and I'd hate to see you take a fall out of misplaced loyalty to a girl who we all know was not really mentally fit to be in uniform.'

Hazel got up from the bed. 'Sleep on what I've said, Sam, and I'm sure that in the morning you'll see the sense of taking the captain's advice.'

'I have to tell the truth.'

Hazel walked towards the door and then stopped and turned round. 'But are you really sure you know what the truth is? Have you really not understood what I'm trying to tell you? Sam, if you don't take the captain's advice, if you persist in sticking to your own story, do you really think it would get any further than the captain's desk? You can't buck the system, Sam. You'll be labelled a troublemaker, and your life will be made a misery, and for what? You can't bring Mouse back; no one can do that. Once you're in uniform you have to live by the rules of that uniform, harsh though that may sound. It's like being in a family, Sam; if one member of that family does something that will bring disgrace on the family, it's hushed up and kept quiet; it becomes a secret that everyone knows about but no one admits to or talks about – especially to those outside the family. That's the way it is in the Armed Forces. Sometimes one of the hardest lessons we have to learn is that the reality of life is very different from our ideals.'

She opened the door, and then added quietly,

'Oh, by the way, you may not have heard yet but the captain has authorised me to tell you that Warrant Officer Sands received an overseas posting yesterday, and will be leaving us at the end of the week.'

Alone in the darkened room Sam desperately wanted to cry but the tears wouldn't come.

TWELVE

'Saw the doctor bringing you back from the hospital the other day,' Ida Jessop, one of Sally's neighbours, stopped her in the street to comment with obvious relish.

'Yes,' Sally agreed. Not for the world was she going to start gossiping about that thunderbolt of a statement Dr Ross had made to her before he had left, and which was still so fresh in her memory even now, two days later. There had been a look in his eyes when he had said those words to her that had broken through her antagonism towards him and her awareness that they inhabited socially different worlds.

'Doris was saying that it was them sandwiches of Daisy's that caused your lad to be ill.'

'The doctor couldn't say what had caused it,' Sally answered her diplomatically.

'Hmm, well, as to that, none of us know the truth of half of what goes on, if you ask me. Look at all that talk there's bin about this national loaf. None of us know what's bin put in it.'

'No, I dare say not,' Sally agreed.

'Well, I'd best be on my way. I'd heard that they've got biscuits at the grocer's up in Wavertree. Not that I'm registered there, but seeing as how I've got service people billeted on me . . .'

Sally had gone only a few more yards when she was stopped again, this time by Daisy, who came out of her front gate and crossed the road to come and stand in front of her, crossing her arms as she did so.

'I want a word with you,' she told Sally sharply.

'I can't stop now, Daisy,' Sally began. 'I'm already late—'

'What's all this I've been hearing about you going round telling everyone that it was my sandwiches wot made that lad of yours sick?' Daisy demanded, ignoring her plea.

'Daisy, that isn't true,' Sally defended herself.

'Isn't it? So how come everyone keeps going on to me about it?' she asked bitterly. 'Get my hubby into a real load of trouble, it could, and all over a kiddie being a bit sick.'

'Tommy was more than just a bit sick, Daisy,' Sally felt bound to point out. 'As it happens, Dr Ross did go on at me to say where I had the fish paste from—'

'What's it got to do wi' him? It's all right for rich folk like him, but the rest of us have to make do and mend as best we can, and if my hubby can help folk out by letting 'em have a few extra tins of stuff now and again, then why shouldn't he? If you was to ask me I'd say that the only reason

205

them like ruddy Dr Ross want to know things like that is because they want to keep all the decent stuff for themselves. My hubby says you should see what he's heard comes through the docks that we never get to see in the shops. So what if some of the boxes fall off the pallets by accident on purpose so that the men can have 'em as spoiled? What harm's that doing anyone, may I ask?'

Sally could understand Daisy's feelings but she still felt bound to point out, 'Dr Ross was telling me that there'd been cases of people dying from eating bad food, and that's why he wanted to know where the fish paste had come from. I didn't want to get your hubby into any trouble so I didn't let on about him getting it.'

'Well, you may have told him that but you've certainly made sure everyone round here knows different. My hubby had a nice little business going selling off them tins that we didn't want and now he's got people wot were keen to buy from him turning up their noses and saying they don't want it in case it makes them bad.'

Sally was beginning to lose her patience. 'Well, that isn't my fault, is it?'

'It's *your* kiddie that got took bad,' Daisy pointed out illogically, adding angrily, 'That's what happens when you get strangers moving into a street. We was all good friends round here and understood what was what before this war broke out and you come here. My hubby was saying only last night to him what lives three doors down that he feels right sorry for your hubby, stuck in a prisoner of war camp, whilst his wife goes out of a Saturday night.'

'I go out to work,' Sally protested.

'Oh, aye, of course you do, and what about that chap that comes round here at night? Don't think that we haven't seen him. Regular as clockwork, he is. My George reckons you could set your watch by him. But we haven't gone running round telling everyone that'll listen all about it,' Daisy finished, giving an angry toss of her head.

'You don't understand,' Sally protested, white-faced with distress.

'Don't make me laugh. Of course we understand. Your husband's bin taken prisoner fighting for his country whilst you've bin messing around wi' another fella. It's as plain as the nose on my face. It wouldn't surprise me if *he* was the one that made your Tommy sick.' With this parting shot she turned on her heel and marched back to her own house, leaving Sally standing watching her in shocked dismay.

One of the things that had touched her most after she and Ronnie had got married was the warmth with which his friends had welcomed her into their lives. She had felt more at home here in Liverpool than she had ever felt in Manchester, and she had cherished the friendships she had made, and the place in the community that belonged to her and her family. But now, with a few angry words, Daisy had destroyed all of that, making her feel like an outcast.

*

'You OK?'

It was the first sympathetic voice Sam had heard since Mouse's death and that it should belong to Sergeant Brookes made Sam's eyes blur with tears as she nodded and pretended to be busy checking items on the list she was holding.

'I heard about your friend.'

Sam dropped the list.

'She was a decent kid,' the sergeant said as he bent down to pick it up for her.

'You'd better not let the ATS hear you saying that.' Sam gave a bitter laugh. 'They want everyone to say that she did it because she was unbalanced, but that's not the truth. She killed herself because of what was being done to her by someone else, making her life a misery, even if I have had to give a statement saying different. I can't stop thinking about her,' she admitted. 'I should have been there. If I had then I'd have been able to talk to her, make her see . . . and she'd be alive now.'

'You can't go thinking like that, or blaming yourself.'

'Why not?' The lessons she had learned since Mouse's death had stripped her of the soft naïvety of idealism and the ability to trust in the system, and it showed in her voice. She was still raw with bitterness and shock.

'You couldn't have stopped her. I've come across folk like her myself. You learn a lot in the army, meet all sorts you'd not normally meet, and every now and again there'll be one like her, in the wrong place at the wrong time, out of step and scared sick, and being turned on by them as should know better. It's a fact of human nature and you can't do nothing about it.'

Tears stung Sam's eyes. At last Mouse was getting the sympathy Sam had expected her to receive from the other girls. Now that she was with someone who wasn't being critical and who seemed to understand, the emotions Sam had been bottling up came pouring out in a torrent of anguish.

'I feel I'm being so disloyal to Mouse, but the other girls – I had no idea they felt the way they do. I thought they sympathised with her like I did. But now when I think about it, well, *some* of them were unkind about her. Not as unkind or cruel as . . . *someone* was to her.' Sam caught herself up, almost having said the warrant officer's name. That, she knew, would draw down on her own head the sergeant's disapproval. Not for nothing was there a military saying: 'no names, no pack drill,' which loosely translated that if one never gave one's own name nor mentioned another's, then no formal punishment could ever be given to you or to them. 'Pack drill' was army slang for a punishing cross-country run carrying one's full kit in a haversack or, even worse, bricks, if the 'crime' was thought to merit such a punishment.

'Taking it out on you now, are they? Your mates? Lasses can be like that sometimes.'

'A bit,' Sam answered cautiously. 'A couple of

the girls from another dormitory have already sent me to Coventry. Not that that bothers me,' she assured the sergeant spiritedly. 'They were *her* spies and hangers-on so they were bound to be on her side, but even the girls in my own dormitory aren't the same to me any more,' she admitted. 'Mouse didn't fit in and shouldn't have joined the ATS, and now I'm beginning to think that I don't fit in either. The other girls are angry with me and . . . I suppose I shall have to ask for a transfer, but who is going to want me with a black mark against my name?' She paused and shook her head. 'I'm sorry, I shouldn't be telling you any of this.'

'Why not? It will do you good to get it off your chest and I'm as good a listener as the next person.'

He was wrong about that, Sam decided. His kindness coming so unexpectedly after the lack of sympathy and even downright hostility towards Mouse and her own defence of her was almost too much for her, and she fought valiantly against a sudden prickle of tears.

'I'm sorry,' she apologised again, searching frantically in her pocket for her handkerchief, accidentally removing with it one of the small pieces of fur she had retrieved from the floor of the warrant officer's office. Automatically she bent down to retrieve it, but the sergeant got there first.

'It's from Mouse's bear,' she told him, her voice wavering, as her eyes filled with tears. And then somehow she was in his arms, being held tight and cradled comfortingly, in a manner that reminded her very much of the way her father had comforted her as a little girl. 'I'm sorry . . . I'm sorry . . .' was all she could say through her tears.

'Cried my own eyes out, I did, after Dunkirk,' he told her, 'and I wasn't the only one, I can tell you. Look, what you need, I reckon, is to be working somewhere where you haven't got time to go dwelling on what's happened. Somewhere where there's a bit more happening.'

'Sorry to interrupt, Frank, but we've got a bomb to dig out before it goes off and blows out half a street with it. How's Molly, by the way? The baby's due any day, isn't it?'

The cold, curt and somehow accusatory words fell on Sam's ears like physical blows, and she was sure she could hear discomfort as well as surprise in the sergeant's voice as he exclaimed, 'Johnny!' immediately stepping back from her.

Released from the sergeant's arms, her face on fire with discomfort, and those telling words about the sergeant's responsibilities ringing in her ears, Sam took to her heels, disappearing as far into the murky depths of the store as she could. Not that she had been doing anything wrong, nor had wanted to do anything wrong. That female admiration she had been beginning to feel for Sergeant Brookes had been nipped in the bud the moment she had learned that he was married. He was a decent man, who she knew instinctively would never look at anyone other than his wife, and she simply would not have

211

wanted him to look in her direction, knowing that he was married. She just wasn't that sort.

It was Sergeant Everton's *attitude* that had made her feel so uncomfortable, not anything she had been doing.

THIRTEEN

'Charlie wants a word with you. He's in the office.'

There was no reason for her to have that uncomfortable feeling of anxiety, Sally reassured herself. That smug triumph she had heard in Patti's voice was just Patti being Patti.

She found the band leader in the small cluttered room at the end of the backstage corridor that everyone knew as 'the office'. Short and balding, with his patent black hair, which the girls swore was dyed, smoothed flat to his scalp, he looked like the good-natured family man he was. But there was no sign of his normal smile when she walked into the room, Sally noticed uneasily.

'Patti said you wanted to see me.'

'Yes . . . that's right.' He couldn't look at her and instead was fidgeting with a piece of paper on the desk in front of him.

Sally's small flutters of anxiety became a fist that squeezed her insides painfully tight.

'Thing is, Sally, that . . . well, you're a nice little

singer, and I've been glad to have you doing a bit here and there and filling in for Eileen.'

'A bit here and there?' Sally protested. 'I've bin singing for you as regular as any of the other girls these last few weeks, even if you haven't bin paying me as though I was one of them.'

'Well, you've hit the nail on the head there, Sally. You aren't one of them, and the truth is that there've been complaints from the other girls about you taking advantage. I'll be sorry to lose you, of course.'

He'd be sorry to lose her! It took several seconds for the meaning of his words to sink in.

'You mean you don't want me standing in for Eileen any more? But I thought . . . only the other week you said how good I was.'

'Aye, well, things change, and to tell the truth I've bin thinking for a while that a trio would work better than a quartet. And with you having them kiddies and working at the factory—'

'If it's because I've been late a time or two, then I'll make sure it doesn't happen again,' Sally pleaded desperately. She couldn't lose this job; she couldn't. 'Please give me another chance.'

Charlie's face had gone red with discomfort.

'I'm sorry, lass, but I can't. You'll soon find another band to sing with, happen one that will take you on as solo singer. You've got the voice for it.'

Sally wasn't taken in for one minute. If he really thought that then why was he so keen to get rid of her? She remembered that there had been some gossip about the band leader and Patti being a bit closer than they ought to be with Charlie being a married man, but she had dismissed it as nothing more than gossip, but maybe she had been wrong. She knew that Patti didn't like her, and the other girls had warned her that she had it in for her. But she had not been expecting this!

'Here,' Charlie said awkwardly, reaching into his pocket and removing his wallet 'Take this.'

Sally's eyes widened as she saw the twenty pounds he was handing her. Her pride badly wanted her to refuse, but twenty pounds was a lot more than three Saturday nights' wages, and more than she could afford to turn down.

'You know what I'd do in your shoes?' He was smiling now, obviously relieved to have an uncomfortable interview over and done with. 'I'd ask around some of the other dance halls, and see if there's anyone looking for a singer. I'll even put in a good word for you with the manager here, if you want.'

He seemed oblivious to the woodenness of Sally's quiet, 'Thank you.'

It was true that there were other bands that played at the Grafton – several of them – but Sally hadn't heard of any of them wanting new singers. The fact was that every girl with a half-decent voice was looking for work in the hope that it might get her into the BBC or ENSA, the Forces' entertainment arm, and turn her in to another Vera Lynn or Gracie Fields.

'Not rehearsing then, Sally?' Patti called out

maliciously when Sally was forced to walk past the band on her way out.

'You're back earlier than I was expecting,' Doris greeted Sally on her return. 'Not that I'm not glad. Molly's dad's bin round to say that Molly's bin that restless she reckons the baby might be about to start.'

Sally managed to force a wan smile. Why hadn't she noticed before how tired Doris was looking? And any day now, by the sound of it, Molly was going to need her help with her new baby. Perhaps instead of looking for another singing job she should be thinking instead about asking the foreman what the best shift to work would be to enable her to get both her boys places at the nursery Littlewoods ran for its workers' children. The problem was that with so many women wanting places, there just weren't enough to go round, unless you agreed to work on an unpopular shift. Sally even knew of mothers who worked nights and left their children at home alone asleep in order to do so, and then worried themselves sick all through their shift in case anything happened to them. But her children were far too young for her to be able to do that, even if she had been able to bring herself to.

But after what the doctor had told her, Sally felt she couldn't go on expecting Doris to look after them. After all, she and her kiddies were nothing to Doris, not like Molly and hers.

'I'd better take these two home then,' Sally told her mechanically.

'Are you all right, Sally, only you don't sound like your normal self.'

The temptation to tell Doris what had happened was almost too much for her, but she made herself shake her head.

'Oh, I nearly forgot, did you hear the news on the wireless about them poor kiddies before you went out?' Doris asked.

'No. What's happened?'

'It was Albert Dearden who told me about it when he came round. Seemingly a Luftwaffe bomber has dropped its bombs on a school this morning, with the kiddies in it. Somewhere down south, Petworth, I think he said it was.'

Sally pressed her hand to her mouth to stifle her shock, whispering in disbelief, 'Oh, no!' and hugging her sons to her so tightly that Harry wriggled in protest.

'Eighty-five boys, there was in it, and they aren't holding out much hope of getting many of them out alive.'

Sally badly wanted to sit down. It didn't take very much imagination to realise how those poor mothers must be feeling.

'According to Molly's dad they was saying on the wireless that the pilot must have known it was a school, he was flying that low. There's nowhere that's safe for children these days unless you send them off into the country somewhere . . . That reminds me,' Doris continued, 'I heard from one of the nurses the other day that Dr Ross lost his wife and kiddies in a bombing raid. Seems that one of the kiddies was rescued but died later in hospital. Poor man. Seeing as you've come back early, I think I'll pop down and see how Molly is. I wouldn't want to miss out on delivering this one when I've delivered your two and our Lillibet.'

Sally forced another smile. Bad as the news she had received this morning had been, it was nowhere near as bad as what those poor parents in Petworth were having to face. Or what Dr Ross had had to endure. Sally tried to imagine suffering the loss of one of her precious sons and acknowledged that it was impossible to imagine the extent of such grief. Kiddies were so precious, and so vulnerable, especially in a city like Liverpool, with its docks. Who was to say that the Luftwaffe wouldn't come back and blitz Liverpool again? And German bombs weren't the only danger to her children. Without the money she earned from singing how would she manage to keep up the payments to Bertha Harris? She had believed that Liverpool and this street were her home; that she had a place here where she belonged and where she was a part of a close-knit and caring community, but she wasn't, was she? As Daisy had pointed out, she was in reality an outsider.

As soon as she got home she tuned in the wireless, waiting to hear if there was any news about the bombed school. The dreadful fate of the children, along with Doris's comments about Dr Ross's wife and children, were weighing even more heavily on her than the fact that she had lost her job. At least things couldn't get any worse, she told herself in an effort to pull herself round.

Sam was acutely aware of the silence from the other girls as she walked into the dormitory, though she pretended not to be.

Lynsey, who was busy painting her nails, had turned her back towards her and it was left to May to say overbrightly, 'We were just talking about going dancing this Saturday—'

'You mean you were,' Lynsey interrupted her. 'Like I just said, I've got a date with a certain sergeant.'

'I thought you said you hadn't heard from him.'

'That was yesterday. I found out where he was working and I just happened to be walking past, so naturally when he saw me he made a date.'

'Are you sure it was *him* that made the date?' May queried wryly, before turning back to Sam and continuing, 'Well, anyway, if you want to come with us . . .'

'I won't, if you don't mind,' Sam told her quietly. 'It doesn't seem right, not with Mouse . . .'

Out of the corner of her eye Sam could see the looks May and Lynsey were exchanging.

Lynsey told her sharply, 'Look, you can go round with a face like a wet weekend if you want to, but don't you go expecting the rest of us to do the same. If you want to know the truth, some of us think we're well rid of her, getting us into trouble all the time.'

Ignoring her, Sam asked, 'Does anyone know what's happened to ... to her or what arrangements ... ?'

Putting down her nail polish, Lynsey stood up and turned towards her. 'Didn't you hear what I just said?' she demanded acidly. 'We don't care about what's happened to her, all we want to do is forget about her and we're sick and fed up of you going round with a long face trying to make us feel guilty. There's some of us who feel a whole lot happier and more comfortable now that she's gone. Got right on my nerves, she did, and like I've bin saying, anyone with a halfpennyworth of sense could see that there was summat a bit wrong with her in the head, always going on about that bear.'

'There was nothing wrong in her head. She was lonely and frightened, that was all, and if people like you hadn't turned their backs on her and pretended not to notice what Toadie was doing to her, and been a bit more understanding, then she'd probably be alive today,' Sam defended her late friend passionately.

Lynsey's face went red and then white. 'I'll have you know that the captain herself told me she was pleased that some of us had had the good sense to see what was what. No wonder the two of you palled up. Neither of you fit in and if you was to ask me I'd say it was a pity we'd only got rid of half of what's bin causing trouble for us all.'

Sam recoiled as though she had been hit.

'What's going on in here?'

They all stared at the corporal.

No one had heard her coming in and Sam's face was as pale with strain as Lynsey's was red with temper as they both turned towards the door.

'Oh, you're back, are you? Thought you wasn't due back until tomorrow. Well, seein' as you are, you might have come and told us, instead of sneaking in like that,' Lynsey announced angrily. 'Still, now you are here, *you* can tell her what *we* all know.' Tossing her head in Sam's direction, Lynsey picked up her nail polish and marched out of the room, leaving a highly charged silence behind her.

'All right, what's all this about?' Hazel demanded. Despite her own distress Sam could see that the corporal looked tired and not very happy, and she wondered if perhaps things had not gone as well between her and her chap as she had hoped.

It was Alice who answered, Hazel grimacing faintly and looking uncomfortable as she explained, 'May was asking Sam if she wanted to come dancing with us this Saturday, and Lynsey took the huff a bit when Sam said that she didn't on account of . . . of what's happened.'

Hazel's face tightened. 'Before I left I told you all of the captain's instructions that that certain matter was not to be discussed – by anyone.'

Sam could feel the weight of the other girls' accusations in the silence that followed.

'I . . . it was my fault,' she admitted guiltily. 'I didn't realise. I hadn't been told . . .'

'Well, you have now,' Hazel told her shortly.

*

'I've never seen a nipper in that much of a hurry to be born. Took *me* by surprise, he did, never mind his mother,' Doris chuckled. 'A big 'un, he is, an' all. I weighed him meself on Molly's kitchen scales and he was nearly ten pounds.'

'Have they got a name for him yet?' Sally asked as she handed Doris the cup of tea she had just poured for her.

'Well, as to that, Frank was saying that him and Molly had talked it over and said beforehand that if it was a lad they'd call him Edward Francis – that's Francis for our Frank and Edward for young Eddie that Molly was engaged to and got killed. Teddy, they're going to call him. You should have seen our Frank's face when he came in for his tea. Couldn't believe his ears, he couldn't, when he heard the baby crying. He was up them stairs two at a time.'

Sally looked away. Ronnie had been granted leave after Tommy had been born, but he hadn't even seen Harry.

'At least Molly wasn't in labour for too long,' she told Doris.

'Maybe not, but little Teddy came a bit too fast for my liking,' Doris informed her, switching from adoring grandmother to trained and experienced nurse and midwife. 'Molly lost a fair bit of blood and I was getting to the point of thinking she'd have to go in to Mill Road before it stopped. She's going to be feeling weak for a while, though, and it isn't going to be easy for her, looking after a new baby and getting her strength back, what with rationing an' all, and then she's got Lillibet to look after as well.'

Sally could see that Doris was now looking a bit uncomfortable, and couldn't quite meet her eye, and she guessed what was on Doris's mind, so she took a deep breath and, trying to sound casual, announced, 'I've bin thinking for a while that Molly might need you to give her a hand once she'd had the baby. You've been good to me and my boys, Doris, treating them like they was your own, but fair dos, they aren't. Molly's two are your own blood and it's only right and natural that you should want to do everything you can to help, especially with it turning out that poor Molly's not too good. I'd feel the same meself if I were in your shoes. So what I've done is, I've decided to pack in me job at the Grafton.'

Resolutely Sally ignored Doris's exclamation.

'And I've had a word wi' the foreman on my shift and told him how I want to switch to a shift that's got spare places in Littlewoods' nursery for my boys. He reckons that I've just dropped lucky and he can get me in on a daytime shift that's short-handed because a couple of girls on it are in the family way.'

'Oh, Sally!' Doris looked relieved. 'I've bin worrying that much about not wanting to let you down when Molly had this new baby.'

'I should have said something earlier,' Sally told her, hoping that Doris couldn't hear the bleakness in her voice and guess how she was really feeling. Of course, Doris's own grandchildren came before her boys, just as Molly came before her, but she still couldn't help feeling a bit raw on her boys' behalf. They thought the world of Doris.

'You should see Lillibet with the baby, Sally. A proper family, my Frank's got now. And as for little Teddy, hardly dropped an ounce, he has, since he was born. Really bonny, he is, and strong. You should see him kicking away. And he's that good, Sally. Molly was saying how she has to wake him up for his feed at night he's sleeping that well.'

Sally smiled and nodded as she listened to Doris's proud grandmotherly praise of the new baby. She could understand Doris's feelings, but at the same time she couldn't help thinking how lucky Molly was to have a grandmother like Doris for her sons. Ronnie's parents had both died before they got married, and her own mother was not the doting grandmother kind.

'Have you heard the latest news about that school?' Sally interrupted her, wanting to change the subject. When Doris shook her head, Sally continued, 'There's thirty-one kiddies dead along with two of their teachers. They've got some of the others out alive but injured.' She gave a fierce shiver. 'It doesn't bear thinking about.'

'No it doesn't,' Doris agreed fervently, before continuing, 'Did I tell you that little Teddy is the spitting image of my Frank when he was born? Oh heavens, is that the time?' she exclaimed guiltily. 'I'd better get back. I promised Molly that I wouldn't be long. Did I tell you about our Frank, Sally? Like a dog with two tails, he is, and no wonder.'

Doris couldn't stop herself from talking about the new baby, and although she tried hard to look enthusiastic, Sally's heart was heavy with sadness and envy. Maybe if she'd gone back to Manchester after her two had been born *they* would have had a doting grandmother, not that she could really see her mother in that role, and besides, she had a houseful now with Sally's younger siblings living there with their own families.

She had been so happy here and had felt so safe. But those feelings had been stolen away by the war and by the problems it had brought her.

'Fancy a cup of Horlicks?'

Sam looked up as Hazel put her head round the sitting-room door, where Sally was on her own, reading.

Before she could accept or refuse Hazel came in and sat down beside her.

'Look, don't go taking what Lynsey said to heart. She doesn't mean any harm really. If you want the truth I reckon she's fallen hard for this sergeant, and since he isn't running around after her like men normally do it's making her crabby.'

'I'm sorry, I didn't realise we weren't to talk about Mouse,' Sam apologised woodenly.

'You weren't to know. I'm glad I've caught you on your own. I've been wanting to have a quiet word with you. You're the sort the ATS needs, Sam, but there are some things you have to understand. Sometimes it's in everyone's interests to have a fresh start. Like with you and Lynsey. Nothing's going to bring Mouse back. We're at war, Sam, and in wartime people do, say and think things they wouldn't do normally. Sometimes . . .' she stopped. 'Sometimes, Sam, we all have to make decisions that we may not really want to make. We have to cut away from situations that are hurting us and aren't good for us, and draw a line under them for our own sake and for the sake of those around us. Sometimes life is unfair and unkind. War teaches us that, Sam.'

Sam knew that there was a lot of good sense in what Hazel was saying. She had heard her own brother voice much the same sentiments.

'You and Lynsey were good pals when you were first posted here.' Hazel's voice was persuasive now.

'I thought we were,' Sam agreed.

'I reckon part of the trouble has been on account of you dancing with her sergeant,' Hazel said unexpectedly.

Sam was too astonished to conceal her disbelief. 'But I explained to her that he isn't interested in me, and I'm certainly not interested in him.'

'He danced with you when she'd been expecting him to dance with her, with it being the last dance of the night and everything. Lynsey isn't the kind who would take kindly to something like that. In her eyes, him dancing with you showed her up. She isn't used to coming second best; it's other girls who are jealous of her normally, not the other way round.'

'She doesn't have to be jealous of me. I—'

'You might know that but I reckon Lynsey isn't convinced. If you want my opinion, for all that she won't admit it I think she's finding it harder to get this sergeant to fall for her than she expected. For once she's the one doing the chasing. The other girls can see that and they're not slow to tell her so, especially May. It's bad for morale when girls fall out over a chap. Lynsey isn't as tough as she likes to make out and my guess is that she feels pretty badly about Mouse, even if she isn't saying so.'

'I'm beginning to think that it would be best for all of us if I put in for a transfer,' Sam told her in a low voice. 'I don't seem to fit in any more and since we're talking of fresh starts . . .'

'Give it time,' Hazel advised her.

It was all very well for Hazel to tell her to give things time, but how was she supposed to do that when Lynsey was making it clear how much she resented and disliked her? Working here on her own at the barracks, where she had worked with Mouse, half expecting to hear her voice every time she managed to forget what had happened for a few seconds wasn't helping either, she acknowledged miserably as she stared at what seemed like a never-ending stock list.

'Frank told you yet that Molly's had a little boy?'

Sam almost jumped out of her skin. Sergeant Everton!

'Anyone would think you'd been trained as a

spy the way you go creeping up on a person,' she complained.

'Over the moon, he is, from what I've heard.'

'I'm sure he is,' Sam agreed, refusing to look at him.

'About the other day . . .'

The gloves were off now and no mistake. She had been waiting for something like this, Sam admitted. She had known that he wouldn't let what he had seen go without saying something about it. Not that he had any business telling her what to do.

'I'm going for my break,' she told him, knowing that whatever it was he planned to say to her, she did not want to hear it. What gave him the right anyway to keep on at her the way he did? It wasn't even as though she had done anything wrong.

'Heard about what happened to your pal.'

Sam was too taken off guard to do anything other than stare up at him in pain. Lynsey must have told him, she guessed.

'Bad do,' he added, causing Sam's shock that he should mention Mouse to turn to anger. Did he really expect her to believe that he meant that? Of course he didn't. Not a man like him. And besides, he was bound to agree with Lynsey's opinion of Mouse, as they were seeing one another.

'*I* think so,' she told him pointedly. His words had grated on her still-raw emotions like someone touching an exposed nerve in a bad tooth. 'But you don't. Not really. I expect you think the ATS is better off without her, just like Lynsey does.'

'Now wait just a minute—'

'No! Why should I? And why should people like you still go on criticising poor Mouse? Haven't you all hurt her enough? She's dead now. Can't you leave her alone and let her rest in peace? You don't care about Mouse at all. No one here does except me. No one! I'm not even allowed to ask what's happened to . . . to her, or if she's going to be buried with her mother, like I know she would have wanted,' Sam burst out wretchedly, filled with the misery of the last few days and her pain at the lack of any proper respectful mourning for her friend, even though logically she knew why this was not possible. To her chagrin she realised that she was dangerously close to tears. She could feel them clogging her throat and burning the backs of her eyes. The last thing she wanted to do was to humiliate herself by crying in front of this man.

'I'll bet that you and Lynsey had a wonderful time pulling Mouse to pieces, just like Toadie did her bear,' Sam rushed on, swallowing back her threatening tears.

'Lynsey?'

'And I'm sure she'll have told you as well how relieved everyone is that poor Mouse isn't around any more. Everyone but me, that is.'

'Hang on a minute,' he tried to stop her, but Sam was too caught up in her own feelings and her determination to show him that she cared about Mouse and she didn't care how unpopular that made her.

'Well, you can tell her that she won't have to

put up with me for much longer because I'm going to put in for a transfer. That should please everyone. And this time I'm going to ask for a posting as a driver, seeing as that's what the ATS have me trained to do.'

'You've trained as a driver?' he queried sharply.

'Yes,' Sam confirmed.

'Then how come you're working as a clerk?'

'You wouldn't understand.'

'Larked about and got rumbled by the wrong person, did you?' he guessed.

Sam stared at him. He had no right to make such an astute guess and be right. How could he have judged her so accurately when he barely knew her? Suddenly she felt vulnerable in a way that was totally unfamiliar to her. How could this man, who did nothing but criticise her and who always seemed to be there when she most wanted him not to be there, be able to know something like that about her? Certainly not from Lynsey, because Sam hadn't told the other girls about that. She felt thoroughly unnerved, not just by his assessment but by her own emotions, which she could neither understand nor control.

'I don't want to talk about it,' she told him, refusing to acknowledge that he had guessed correctly.

'But you do want that transfer?'

Why was he asking her that? Because Lynsey had told him about their fall-out? Because he harboured suspicions that she was trying to chase after Sergeant Brookes?

'I said I did, didn't I?' she answered assertively. 'Do you really think I'd want to stay here after what's happened?' she demanded when he made no comment but instead simply looked at her, subjecting her to a silent scrutiny as though he was weighing her up – and finding her wanting. 'Well, I don't,' she told him forcefully. 'In fact . . .' Sam stopped, her voice cracking, unable to continue, hating herself for her vulnerability, and hating him for being there to witness it. What was *happening* to her?

She started to turn away, wanting to get away from him before she broke down completely and then stiffened, inhaling in shocked disbelief as he moved, blocking her exit and then closing the distance between them, to take hold of her in an imprisoning grip. She could feel the strength of his hands as he held her upper arms and she could feel their warmth too.

'Now listen to me for a moment.'

'Listen to *you*?' Her heart was jerking around inside her chest and her pulse was racing. Humiliatingly she could feel tears prickling the backs of her eyes. 'Why? So that you can start criticising me again? So that you can make more accusations about me that aren't true? No thank you.' She must not let him see the effect he was having on her or how emotionally vulnerable he made her feel. No man had reduced her to tears, not ever, and she had never imagined that they might. Tears in reaction to male criticism belonged to a very different type of woman from her, and it increased her hostility towards Johnny Everton that he should somehow have managed to provoke them.

Sam wasn't prepared to listen to him any more. Abandoning her list, she pushed past him, ignoring his curt demand that she stay and listen to what he had to say. She could imagine all too easily the cruel way he and Lynsey would have talked about poor Mouse.

She *was* going to ask for a transfer, Sam decided. A fresh start was definitely what she needed.

FOURTEEN

'You sang lovely in church this morning, Sally, didn't she, Vicar?'

'Indeed she did, Mrs Brookes,' the vicar agreed. 'In fact I was hoping to have a word with you to ask you if you'd be kind enough to help out with teaching the little ones ready for the Christmas carol service. I know we're only just going into October this week, but it takes time to get them to learn all the words properly. Brown Owl does her best, but she isn't very musical.'

'Well . . .' Sally began uncertainly.

'You don't have to give me an answer right now. Oh, excuse me whilst I go and have a word with Dr Ross and welcome him to our community.'

Dr Ross! Sally couldn't stop herself turning round to look over to where the doctor was standing with the vicar's wife. Was it because she now knew of his personal loss that she felt he looked very alone? *She* was feeling sorry for *him*? Sally frowned.

'Well, I'm not having mine joining in any carol

singing, not if she's going to be teaching them after what she's tried to do to me and mine.'

As the strident sound of Daisy's voice reached her, Sally was well aware that it had been deliberately pitched loud enough for her to hear, and not just her; she could feel the sidelong looks she was being given.

'That's daft talk, Daisy, and you know it,' Doris responded immediately, coming to Sally's rescue. 'In your shoes I'd be down on me knees thanking God that I hadn't got more sick kiddies on me conscience.'

'That's a lie that it were our fault.' Daisy's face was bright red with temper. 'And if she's been saying any different—'

'Sally's said nothing,' Doris defended her.

'Sez you. If that's true then how come he's here?' Daisy nodded in the direction of the doctor. 'Let him just start trying to put the blame on us and I'll have a thing or two to say to him about her. Some mother she is, leaving her kiddies with someone else and going off out at night. You'd never catch me doing owt like that . . .'

'Oh, there you are, Mam,' Frank announced, hurrying over. 'Molly's told me to have a word with the vicar about the christening. I've told her there's plenty of time but she wants Teddy christened well before Christmas. Can you keep an eye on Lillibet for a minute for me?'

'How is Molly now, Frank?' Daisy asked, immediately solicitous, turning her back on Sally as she did so.

'Picking up a bit – but don't go bringing her any of them sandwiches of yours, Daisy,' Frank grinned, winking at Sally.

'Take no notice of Daisy, Sally,' Doris counselled Sally when Daisy had subsided. 'Allus had a bit of a temper on her, she has. How've you gone on with changing your shift at the factory?'

'The foreman says that he's sorting it out as fast as he can.'

Sally knew from Doris's expression that her words had been sharper than they should have been, but it wasn't her fault, was it, that all of a sudden she and her sons were just a nuisance?

'Dr Ross is coming over,' Doris told her quietly.

'He's probably heard that Molly's had her baby and he wants to have another go at me to have my two evacuated,' Sally returned, refusing to let go of her hostility.

'Well, there's summat to be said for it,' Doris told her. 'I can't pretend that I haven't been thinking meself that it isn't safe for kiddies to be living in Liverpool since that school was bombed.'

Sally was too busy trying to call back Tommy, who had seen the doctor and was making for him, to answer her, but it was too late, and she had to stand by in chagrined embarrassment as her son flung himself at his hero, clasping him round the knees as he beamed up at him.

'Well, you can certainly see he's used to handling kiddies,' Doris remarked approvingly as she too watched the doctor bend down and pick Tommy up.

'Huh,' Sally heard Daisy exclaiming sourly. 'I'm sure I know what to think about the kind of woman who uses her kiddies to go sucking up to a man, especially when she's already got a husband. Downright shocking, I call it, but then you allus get them sort wot has that much brass face they don't care what anyone else thinks. I never thought as we'd have one living in a respectable neighbourhood like ours, though.'

Sally had had enough. Turning round, she said to Daisy fiercely, 'If you're talking about me—'

'Don't let her upset you, Sally,' Doris intervened quickly. 'The trouble with Daisy is that she doesn't allus know when she's gone too far. She doesn't mean any harm.'

Sally didn't believe that for one moment but Doris's intervention was enough to have Sally recoiling from the recognition of how ashamed of herself she would have felt if she had been provoked into an exchange of insults, not just in public, but also having just come out of church.

'The doctor looks lonely. If it wasn't for Molly just having had her baby I'd invite him back to have his Sunday dinner with us,' Doris commented. 'Mind you, I expect the vicar will have asked him to join them.'

'Would you do me a favour, Doris, and go over and tell Tommy that we're going home now?' Sally asked. 'I'd go myself only I don't want Daisy making any more accusations.'

'Oh, don't pay any attention to her. No one else will,' Doris told her forthrightly, but Sally stood her ground, refusing to look across at the doctor, and hurrying Tommy away as soon as he came back.

Normally Sam enjoyed Sundays. There was something that always lifted her spirits about the bracing parade-ground-style march down to the small local church, followed by their shared singing of the traditional hymns that every schoolchild knew off by heart. But it would take more than singing hymns to lift her spirits today, she admitted as she filed into a pew behind May and then kneeled to say a few words of silent prayer. She had come down here to the church several times since Mouse's death, torn between the comforting familiarity of kneeling to say her prayers for her friend, and her wretchedness and guilt because of the manner of that death.

Her personal prayers said, she stood up, pity clutching at her heart as she saw the little black-clad family several pews in front of her: three young children, a girl and two boys, clinging to their mother.

Not very far away from them stood a young couple who were exchanging tender looks, and Sam wasn't surprised to hear their wedding bans being read in the service, nor the announcement of the loss of another brave fighting man – husband and father to the family she had already noticed.

'Pity you didn't come with us last night,' May commented once they were outside. 'You should have seen the way Lynsey was carrying on over her sergeant. All over him like a rash, she was. She's really got it bad. She's nuts about him.' She started to yawn. 'Gawd knows how I managed to get up in time for parade this morning.' She smothered another yawn. 'This time next week we'll be into October; I hope I get Christmas leave this year. Normally the whole family get together. My mum's got two sisters and a brother, and they all come round to us; there's always a houseful. We had some smashing fun before the war. I missed it last year. Have you got any plans?'

'No, I haven't thought about it,' Sam told her truthfully.

'An only one, are you?' May looked sympathetic.

Sam shook her head. 'No, I've got a brother. He's in the RAF. I can't remember the last time we got leave together, though.'

'This will be the fourth Christmas we've been at war,' May pointed out unnecessarily.

They exchanged looks and then May shivered.

'My dad said it'd go on longer than everyone said. Watch out,' she warned Sam, putting out the cigarette she had been smoking. 'Here comes the captain.'

Both of them were standing smartly to attention, ready to salute, by the time the captain, deep in conversation with the vicar, drew level with them.

Sunday afternoon for those girls who didn't have a pass out were normally spent in the shared sitting room, writing letters or engaged in some activity such as reading, knitting or sewing, the captain apparently having 'strong views' about the morality of playing card games on a Sunday.

Sam had just finished writing her weekly letter to her parents when she heard her name being called.

'Captain wants to see you,' the young lieutenant informed her.

Sam tried not to look as anxious as she felt. The soles to her better pair of shoes had started to come away and so she had had to wear her other less well-polished pair this morning, and no doubt the captain had noticed that fact when she had walked past them. Had there been any other faults with the smartness of her uniform, Sam worried uneasily as she made her way to the captain's office. She may still feel unhappy about the statement she had been pressured into giving after Mouse's death, but she was too sensible not to know that if she went ahead and asked for a transfer, it would not help her cause if she were to get on the wrong side of the captain.

'Private Grey, ma'am,' the lieutenant announced as they both saluted.

'Ah, Private Grey. Good. Sit down.'

The captain was actually smiling approvingly at her!

'Naturally I expect the women under my command to remember that we are all judged by the behaviour of each of us and put up a good show. We all want the country to be proud of us.

However, I must say that one can't help but feel pleased when a senior army officer applauds the pluck of one of one's gals. Well done, Grey.'

Sam was baffled by the captain's praise and felt sure that she had been mistaken for someone else, but she knew enough of the system now not to say so.

'In fact Major Thomas is so impressed with you that he has requested your transfer to his unit, as his personal driver and stenographer. It seems his existing driver is getting married and has requested a transfer back to Aldershot.'

'Major Thomas?'

Sam tried not to look too blank. She had no idea who Major Thomas was. She really *must* have been confused with someone else. A someone else she was already envying. There was nothing she'd like more than to leave the storeroom, especially for a role that involved driving. However, honesty compelled her to ask uneasily, 'Permission to speak, ma'am?'

'Yes?'

'I haven't met Major Thomas, and I was wondering if there could have been a mistake and—'

'The British military does not make mistakes, Private,' the captain told her severely.

'No, ma'am,' Sam agreed woodenly.

'You will report to Major Thomas at oh nine hundred hours tomorrow morning at Deysbrook Barracks and he will brief you as to your new duties then. I do have to tell you that there will

240

be some degree of danger involved in those new duties, although Major Thomas tells me that you will not be required to accompany him when one of his men is actually defusing any bombs. You can, of course, refuse this transfer if you wish. However, as I have already told Major Thomas, my gals do not flinch in the face of danger.'

'No, ma'am,' Sam agreed, more readily this time. Disordered thoughts were whirling round inside her head. She had managed to work out from what the captain had said that Major Thomas must be with the 'Ifs and Buts', as the Inspectorate of Fortifications and Directorate of Bomb Disposal was unofficially known. Normally that would not have put her off working for him in the slightest – quite the opposite – but there was the small matter of Sergeant Johnny Everton, who was also with the Bomb Disposal squad, and their mutual dislike and hostility. She could well imagine how he was likely to feel about them being in one another's proximity. The thought of that certainly put her off.

But what a marvellous thing it would be to get away from the stores, with its memories of Mouse. And what a marvellous thing too to be working as a driver. It was a dream come true. She couldn't think of a role that better fulfilled her longing for more action and contributing something of real value to the war effort. If it weren't for Sergeant Everton she would have been ready to jump over the moon. But then why should she let the thought of him spoil things for her? She'd be an idiot to turn down such an opportunity. As the major's driver she was hardly likely to come into much contact with him, she assured herself. She had learned from Sergeant Brookes that the work of Bomb Disposal's noncommissioned ranks involved preparing the bombs for defusing, whilst the officers were responsible for carrying out that defusing.

'Good-oh, Grey,' the captain was saying. 'Jolly good show.'

It was too late for her to say anything now. The decision had been made for her. Automatically Sam saluted, sensing that she was about to be dismissed.

She was still sure there must have been a mistake, and that the major couldn't possibly have really meant her, but she knew there was no point in continuing to try to say so. Maybe once he saw her the major would announce that she *was* the wrong person. She knew already how disappointed she would feel if he did.

'You're looking a lot more cheerful. Had some good news?' Hazel asked half an hour later when Sam went back to the sitting room.

'Sort of. The captain just sent for me to tell me that from tomorrow I'm going to be driving a Major Thomas and working as his stenographer,' Sam told her, but not adding that supposedly the major had asked for her to be transferred to his staff. 'It seems the girl who was working for him is getting married and has asked for a transfer back to Aldershot.'

'Don't mention marriage to me,' Hazel replied grimly.

Sam frowned. Hazel had hardly mentioned her naval boyfriend following her visit to see him in Dartmouth.

'If your chap's still holding back, I expect it's because he's thinking of things from your point of view and how it would be if you were to get married and something should happen to him,' she offered tactfully.

'You're very kind, Sam, but actually he isn't 'my' chap any more. That was decided before I left Dartmouth.' She gave Sam a wry look. 'The only thing he's been holding back from has been doing anything that would stop him from playing the field, as I found out when I was down there. He certainly wasn't holding back from trying to persuade me to go the whole way with him when I first arrived, if you know what I mean,' Hazel continued forthrightly. 'That's all he could go on about, until I caught him in a corner of the services bar with a Wren. It's sweet of you to try to make me feel better, though, Sam. I've been a fool to myself and I know it. If he'd thought anything of me, the 'yes' he'd have wanted from me would have been in answer to his proposal of marriage, not his proposition to take me to bed. Three months ago I might have been tempted to say yes, but thank heavens I used my head, otherwise I'd have been in a real state when I caught him with that Wren. Of course, he blamed me and said it was because I'd turn him down for you-know-what, and then he kept going on about how other girls were more "understanding" and accommodating. Well, he's welcome to them, that's all I can say. That's why I cut my leave short. There was no point in my staying on after that. I told him it was over between us and that I didn't want to see him any more. To be honest, what hurts more than ending it with him is knowing that I've been such a fool.' She was smiling bravely but Sam could sense that she was upset.

'Look, it's my birthday soon,' Hazel continued briskly. 'I'd like us all to go out together and put this wretched business between you and Lynsey behind us.'

'It isn't me that's caused it,' Sam pointed out defensively.

'I know that. The thing is that Lynsey's made so much of a fool of herself that she can't really back down easily – you can see that, can't you?'

'Yes,' Sam admitted reluctantly.

'So you'll join in, then?'

'All right,' Sam agreed, knowing she couldn't really say anything else. Poor Hazel, she was having a pretty bad time of it and naturally Sam didn't want to make things worse.

Privately Sam thought that Hazel was better off without her naval chap, but she could understand that her decision to end things, having caught him with someone else, must have been upsetting.

FIFTEEN

'Private Grey reporting for duty, sir.'

For such a very short man, not even as tall as she was herself, Corporal Willett had an extremely loud voice, Sam decided, managing not to wince as he bellowed out the introduction and saluted the major.

The corporal had been waiting for her when she had got off the bus at the barracks, a small, swift-moving, agile man with a weather-beaten, wrinkled face and bright blue eyes.

'Major Thomas said to wait for you and escort you over to our base, on account of you probably missing it if you was to look for it yourself,' he had informed her, part of a nonstop stream of information he had given her as he took short cuts through the maze of barracks buildings at a speed that left Sam almost breathless. 'Done much of this kind of thing before, have you?' he had asked her, and when Sam had replied that she hadn't, he had told her cheerfully, 'Shouldn't worry, you'll soon get the hang of it, just so long as you don't mind hearing a few ripe words now and then. Calls them ruddy bombs all sorts, the major does. Not that you'll get to hear that. Sticks to the rules like glue, he does. That's how we've lost only two of our captains and a lieutenant in the last six months whilst the other sections have damn-near lost every officer they've had. Good driver, are you?'

'I hope so,' Sam had answered.

'Only the major don't like to hang around, and that car of his is more like a ruddy tank than a car.'

'I'm sure I'll manage,' Sam had smiled with more confidence than she was feeling.

'Brought plenty of notebooks and pencils along with you, I hope, only he does a lot of talking, does the major. Bit of a character, he is, and no mistake. Likes to do things his own way. A "Sir" he was before the war. Seven Company are based here at the barracks on account of West Derby House being the Western Approaches Command Headquarters, and the major's over both sections. Give us this, they have, for a base,' the corporal had announced, indicating the shabby-looking building they were now approaching, a heavy-duty transport lorry parked to one side of it, loaded with worryingly sinister-looking equipment.

'The lads are all billeted out of the barracks, though. Not that any of us are complaining, not with a fair few of us having families living locally.'

*

'What ho, you're a deuced pretty girl to be in uniform, Grey. I don't want my chaps being distracted. Know much about bomb disposal, do you?' Major Thomas was asking her now.

'Not really, sir, only that the Inspectorate of Fortifications and Directorate of Bomb Disposal is under the charge of General Taylor and that it has the responsibility of defusing those bombs that fall on land.'

'Hmm . . . well, you've come well recommended. Jolly bad show, Lewis leaving. Know much about mechanics, do you, only the old girl gets pretty temperamental at times and it's a damned poor show when she takes against my drivers.'

Quick-wittedly Sam deduced that 'the old girl' must be the major's car.

'I know how to change a wheel, sir,' she offered, remembering the cause of her original downfall.

'Well, better take you to meet Boadicea then. This way.'

Five minutes later Sam was standing staring in disbelief at the car. A Bentley, long and low, with cream coachwork and red leather seats, the car was the kind that Sam knew her brother would have drooled over enviously, the kind that was temperamental and demanding.

'Rallied her at Le Mans before the war,' the major told Sam proudly. 'She's a bit petulant on the gears, though.'

'I'll take care when I'm double-declutching,' Sam assured him.

'Doesn't like too much brake either . . . in fact

to tell the truth the old girl prefers a man's touch, but I can't drive her myself these days, not since I lost the old hand.'

Sam hadn't realised until he spoke the significance of his rigid leather-gloved left hand.

'Right then, let's make a start, and see how many reports we've got in of new UXBs. Then we'll have a run out and take a look at them.'

'Yes, sir.' Sam was not for one minute deceived. The major obviously wanted to test out her driving skills for himself. Was she up to driving 'the old girl'? She hoped so, although she wished she could have taken a trial drive by herself before having to drive the major.

'Any news yet from One Section, Corporal?'

They were back in the Bomb Disposal Unit's barracks command post, and Sam's stomach was churning with a mixture of apprehension and excitement as she considered the challenge that now lay ahead of her. It was true that she could drive, but whether or not her driving skills were up to the major's Bentley's idiosyncrasies she wasn't so sure. It wouldn't do, though, to show lack of confidence.

'They've managed to find the bomb, sir. Dug itself right down alongside the building, it has, and the sappers say that they'll have to shore up the wall before they try to move the device.'

'Hmm. Any idea what type of bomb we're looking at yet?'

'Captain Melville thinks it's a big 'un – two

thousand pounds. He's not sure about the fuses yet but thinks it could have a seventeen and a fifty, but the sappers are still digging round it so he can get a proper look.'

Sam, who had been writing all this down in her notebook, looked up to find both men watching her. The major gave her an approving nod, whilst the corporal winked at her when the major wasn't looking.

'Any water showing?' the major asked.

'Hole's filling up a bit, sir, but they're getting a pump going.'

'Come on, Grey, we'll go and take a look at what they're doing.'

'Watch out for third gear,' the corporal muttered to Sam as she made to follow the major. 'Keep the clutch biting otherwise she won't go into gear and she'll stall on you. Major has it rigged that way when he's trying out new drivers.'

'Hop in,' the major commanded, handing Sam the keys, having unlocked the car.

Warily Sam settled herself into the seat and started the engine. To her relief it fired immediately. Now for the gears. The clutch was heavy and so strong that she had to use considerable force to depress it. She listened carefully to the revving engine whilst she pressed down the accelerator and let out the clutch, hardly daring to breathe until she felt the clutch start to bite. Holding both pedals with her feet she put the car in first gear and let off the handbrake. To her relief the car moved forward smoothly. Growing more confident, she changed up to second gear and drove out of the barracks, taking care to avoid the heavy transport lorries turning in through the gates.

'Turn left,' the major directed her. Obediently Sam did so, changing up again into second gear, and then reaching for third once they were on the open road. The clutch should bite now, she decided. Her hand was already on the gear lever when abruptly and without warning the clutch pedal kicked back and the engine protested as she missed the gear. Just as she was about to panic and let the car stall, Sam remembered what the corporal had told her and double-declutched as firmly as though she knew the clutch would bite, refusing to be daunted as she pushed the gear lever up and over into third gear, ignoring its attempts to defeat her.

'The old girl gets a bit skittish over third gear sometimes,' the major told her. 'Like the way you handled her, though. Good show.'

Making a mental note to thank the corporal, Sam kept her eyes on the road and said nothing. She could almost feel the car's sulky scowl at being bettered, she decided, hiding a small private grin.

The bomb site wasn't very far away, but driving the long-nosed Bentley, designed for powerful runs along straight roads, round corners and obstacles called for every bit of her skill and tenacity, as the car balked several times, and threatened not to go into third gear.

When they reached their destination the major ordered her to pull over and stop.

Getting out of the car, Sam hurried round to the major's door, opening it for him and saluting as he got out, then locking the car and hurrying after him with her notebook.

A group of men, their clothes and faces splattered with mud, were standing beside a hole in the ground, the debris they had obviously dug out piled up to one side. One of their number was hunkered down, examining something. His companions straightened up to salute when they saw the major, and as he got to his feet to do the same, Sam's stomach did a slow somersault as she recognised him. Oh, no! Sergeant Everton! Just her luck that on her first day in her new job, and whilst she was desperately trying to prove herself, the first section the major should want to check up on was the one Sergeant Everton was in.

'How's it coming along, Captain?' the major asked.

'Tricky situation with the rising water level, sir, but we're getting another pump on it.'

Sam started to make notes. If nothing else it would help her to stop feeling so conscious of Sergeant Everton.

Several of the men were wearing uniforms that identified them as members of the Noncombatant Corps or, as they were more often known, 'conscientious objectors', and Sam was slightly taken aback to see these men involved in such dangerous work, and even more surprised to witness the easy way in which the Noncombatant

251

men and the Royal Engineers got on with one another.

'Drove the major here, did you?'

She had been so engrossed in studying what she was doing that she hadn't noticed the sergeant detach himself from his companions and walk up to her.

'Yes,' she confirmed.

'Corporal Willett warned you, did he, that the major keeps the gear box rigged so that the clutch has a kick like a mule in third?'

Sam was so surprised that she almost dropped her pencil. 'He did say something of the sort,' she agreed, unable to resist adding sharply, 'I expect you'd have preferred him not to, so that the major would have asked for me to be replaced.'

Before he could retaliate the major called over, 'Sergeant Everton, you're our longest-serving member, come and take a look at this and tell us what you think.'

Ten minutes later the major was getting back into the car.

'Down to the bottom of the road, Grey, and then turn right,' he told Sam. 'We'll go and see how Two Section is doing. Made a note, did you, that One Section have requested a new pump?'

'Yes, sir.'

It had been Sergeant Everton who had informed the major of the section's need for this new piece of equipment, calmly listing the faults with the existing pump and the risks the men would run if they continued to use it.

It was so late in the afternoon when they returned to the barracks that Sam thought she might miss the bus back to the billet.

'Car behave OK for you?' the corporal asked her when the major had disappeared inside the building.

'Just about – thanks to your warning,' Sam told him.

'Nothing to do with me. It's Sergeant Everton you want to thank. He was the one that told me to warn you.'

'Sergeant Everton?' Sam was unable to conceal her disbelief.

'Down here first thing, he was, when he should have been off duty, and he said as how you'd be starting today and to warn you about that clutch, and the major's little trick to test new drivers.'

There must be some mistake surely, Sam decided. And then she remembered the sergeant's comment to her about the car's third gear – and her own less than gracious response – and her face burned. She hated the thought of being put under an obligation to a man she disliked so much.

'You were cutting it fine,' May told Sam ten minutes later as she clambered onto the bus just as it was about to leave.

'Didn't get back to the barracks until a few minutes ago,' Sam told her as she dropped into the nearest empty seat, which just happened to be behind Lynsey, after what had been the busiest and most enjoyable day she had had since her arrival in Liverpool.

'Me and the others were just talking about where we're going to celebrate my birthday. I hope you're going to come along as well, Sam,' Hazel said.

'I'd love to,' Sam agreed, mindful of what Hazel had said to her previously.

'Well, I don't know if I'll be able to come,' Lynsey said immediately.

'Oh, come on, you can do without seeing your sergeant for one night, can't you, Lynsey? I thought you liked keeping your men guessing,' May laughed.

Lynsey looked sulky but didn't, to Sam's relief, insist that she wasn't going to join everyone. Sam had a good idea that Lynsey had been going to refuse not because of her romance, but because she wanted to underline her dislike of Sam herself but, either accidentally or deliberately, May's intervention had prevented her from doing so.

'So where do you fancy going then, Hazel?'

'I thought we might go to the Grafton.'

'You wouldn't catch me going out with a crowd of girls if it was my birthday. I'd be wanting to be taken out by my chap.'

Was Lynsey just tactless and oblivious to other people's feelings, or was she deliberately trying to upset Hazel, Sam wondered, feeling sorry for Hazel, who was trying not to look as though she knew what Lynsey was getting at.

'Oh, that's typical of you, Lynsey, and I dare say you'd have been dropping hints to him about giving you another of them engagement rings to add to your collection as well,' May joked, once again diffusing the tension.

Hazel didn't go up to the dormitory with them when they got back, and as soon as they were out of her hearing May turned on Lynsey and said sharply, 'That was a mean thing to say to Hazel about her birthday, Lynsey, when you know that it's over between her and her chap.'

'Well, it's not my fault that she caught him with someone else, is it? More fool her for not realising what kind he was in the first place is what I say! So what was you doing today then, Sam?' she demanded, changing the subject. 'Only I heard that you was going to be driving some major around.'

And Sam could guess that she had heard it from a certain Sergeant Johnny Everton, although she wasn't going to say so.

'That's right. I'm standing in for Major Thomas's driver and I had to take him to various unexploded bomb sites.'

'That sergeant of yours is with that bomb disposal lot, isn't he, Lynsey?' Alice asked.

'Yes,' Lynsey agreed tersely.

'Has anyone got any ideas about what we can get Hazel for her birthday?' May broke in.

'P'haps Lynsey could give her some lessons on how to get the right kind of chap, and how to get him so mad for her that he proposes,' one of the girls suggested, making the others laugh until May said forthrightly, 'Well, if you want my opinion I think Hazel's done the right thing in ditching him.

She deserves better. I'm not going getting myself stuck with anyone until they prove to me that they're worth it.'

'Huh, you've got a high opinion of yourself all of a sudden, haven't you?' Lynsey demanded.

'So what if I have?' May retorted, unabashed.

SIXTEEN

'Oh, Molly, he's absolutely beautiful,' Sally smiled as she leaned over the crib to admire little Teddy.

'Pass him to us, will you, Sally? It's time he had a feed. I don't know where this week's gone. It's Friday already and yet it doesn't seem a minute since he was born.'

Once she had got the baby settled Molly continued, 'Frank's mam was telling me about Daisy having a go at you after church last Sunday. Don't you go taking it to heart, Sally. You aren't on your own. I remember the way she was with me over Eddie when it first got out that I was seeing him whilst I was still engaged to Johnny. Really nasty with me, she was. I reckon it's got something to do with the fact that her hubby isn't doing his bit.'

'I thought he'd tried to join up and been turned down,' Sally protested.

Molly gave a small snort. 'Well, Daisy likes to tell everyone that. Flat feet, he's supposed to have had, but if you want my opinion I reckon he knew he was on to a good thing staying working on the docks. He and Daisy don't go without much. I've nothing against Daisy. She's a good neighbour in her way, but she's got a nasty tongue on her at times and she's got no right to go round saying half the things she does and stirring up upset for other folk.

'Doris says you're changing your shifts and putting the boys in the factory nursery,' Molly commented whilst Lillibet and Sally's two boys were playing out of earshot.

'I'm hoping to,' Sally agreed. 'Doris has been a rock, helping me out with them so much, but I was thinking the war would have been over long before now.'

'You and me and most of the rest of the country,' Molly agreed.

'Anyway, I had a word with the foreman and he told me when I went to work last night that I could change me shift from the end of this week.'

'But what about your singing?'

'I won't be doing that any more.' Sally was too proud to tell her the truth.

'Oh, Sally, you can't give that up, not with that lovely voice of yours.'

'I'd better go,' Sally said, not wanting to give Molly the opportunity to ask any more awkward questions. 'I only popped in to see how you were going on.'

She was halfway home, when Tommy called out, 'Look, Mum.'

Sally didn't need Tommy's warning to alert her

to the sight of the telegram boy. No one could see the slight figure in his uniform riding his bicycle purposefully down their own street without their stomach turning over and that cold hand clutching at their heart, Sally felt sure, even if Tommy was too young to know the true significance of his presence. A telegram brought urgent news – good and bad. This time, though, the news wouldn't be for her, even if the sight of him brought back everything she had felt when she had received the telegram telling her about Ronnie being made a POW. No, this time it would be someone else's turn to unfold that piece of paper whilst sick dread filled them.

There were any number of households in the Close with loved ones in the services, even if the telegram boy was slowing down as he approached their house . . .

Without being aware of it Sally had started to walk faster, almost dragging Tommy off his feet as he struggled to keep up with her. The telegram boy was dismounting . . . right outside the house, but that must be a mistake . . . he must be going next door surely . . . Sally broke into a run, stopping to scoop up Tommy, who protested, 'Mum!' clutching him with one arm whilst she pushed Harry's pushchair with the other.

The boy was knocking on the front door as she pushed open the gate. He turned to look at her.

'Telegram for Walker.'

Sally nodded. She could see the familiar War Office envelope he was holding out to her. Putting

Tommy down, she took it from him white-faced, her throat muscles locked. She could hear front doors opening, her neighbours alerted by the sight of the telegram boy. Her hand was shaking so much that she couldn't get the key into the lock. Her heart was pounding. It could not be anything to worry about, she reassured herself. She had already had the bad news . . . 'Daft, you are,' she to herself when she had finally managed to open the door and get the boys inside. 'Just because it's a telegram . . .'

She waited until she was in the back parlour, though, to open it. The words wouldn't keep still, and it took her several seconds to realise it was because her hand was trembling so much. She put the telegram down flat on the table, trying to ignore the thudding of her heartbeat, as she began to read it.

'We regret to inform you of the death of Corporal Ronald Walker.'

No! No! That could not be! She read the words again, and then again.

'Mum, Mum . . .' Tommy was tugging anxiously on her coat, Harry was crying and someone was knocking on the front door.

Sally sat down heavily, still holding the telegram. There must be some mistake. Ronnie was a Japanese POW – how could he be dead?

Someone was knocking on the back door now, then she heard a key turning in the lock, but she could not drag her gaze away from the telegram.

'It's Nana Doris,' Tommy announced.

'I saw the telegram boy, Sally love,' Doris said gently, 'so I thought I'd best call round. I did try the front door first before I used me key. I hope you don't mind.'

Sally stared at her as though she didn't know her, her hands flat on the telegram, concealing its news.

Doris had come to stand beside her. 'Let's have a look, love.'

'There's nothing to see,' Sally told her desperately as Doris gently moved her hands so that she could read the telegram. 'They've got it wrong, Doris, they must have. Ronnie won't be dead. How can he be? He's a POW. They must have confused him with someone else . . . I'll have to tell the War Office. Some poor woman's lost her husband and she won't know about it yet. My Ronnie's a POW and they don't get killed, do they?'

'I'll put the kettle on and we'll have a nice cup of tea, and then when our Frank comes home off duty we can let him sort it out,' Doris told her gently.

'There should be a law against giving folk a shock like this, telling them that their husband's been killed when he hasn't.' They both looked towards the hall as someone knocked on the front door.

'You stay here, I'll go and see who it is.'

Through the open doorway Sally could hear voices, Doris's low and determined, although she couldn't quite catch what she was saying, the other voice, Daisy's, sharp and clear as she insisted, 'I

261

just come over to say that I hoped it wasn't bad news she'd had, what with her Ronnie already being a POW. I know we had them words the other day, but it's only neighbourly to come across when you see a telegram being delivered, and her on her own without any family around her.'

Sally got up and walked unsteadily into the hallway.

'There's bin a mistake,' she told Daisy. 'The War Office have got my Ronnie confused with someone else.'

Daisy and Doris exchanged silent looks.

'Bad news, was it then? I thought as much. That's why I come across. A person needs good neighbours when they get bad news. If you was wanting me to sit with you for a while or owt, Sally . . .' she offered.

'Thanks for offering, Daisy,' Doris responded for her, 'but I'm going to be here.'

'What about your Molly? I'd heard that she isn't too well after the baby.'

'Molly's doing fine,' Doris told her firmly, determinedly closing the door.

'Come on, love,' she instructed Sally, taking hold of her arm and guiding her back to the kitchen. 'Let's go and have that cup of tea, shall we?'

'It can't be true, Doris, I know it can't. Not with Ronnie being a POW. I mean, it's not as though he'd have bin fighting or anything, is it?'

'Let's wait until Frank comes home, then he can sort it out, shall we?' Doris suggested again.

*

'Frank, my Ronnie can't possibly be dead. I mean, it stands to reason, doesn't it, like I've already said?'

They were all crammed into Sally's small back parlour: Sally herself, Frank, still in his uniform, Doris, Molly's dad, listening whilst Sally paced the floor, still wearing the coat she had arrived home in hours ago.

'I'll tell you what, Sally, why don't you and me go and get some tea ready for your Tommy and Harry and then get them off to bed?' Doris suggested.

'Frank, you will go down to the barracks and tell them to tell the War Office that they've got it wrong, won't you? And make sure that you tell them that they've got no right sending people telegrams saying their husband is dead when he isn't,' Sally demanded, ignoring her.

Sally didn't see the looks Frank exchanged with his mother and Molly's father.

'The thing is, Sally,' he began heavily, 'there's bin some news in the papers . . .'

'What kind of news?'

'Well, it seems there's bin a bit of an accident with an American sub sinking a ship carrying British and Canadian POWs from Hong Kong. This ship, the *Lisbon Maru*, was being escorted by Japanese warships and . . .'

Sally watched as Frank broke off to control his own emotions.

'When she got hit the Japs gave the order to batten down the hatches with the men still down below, and then they abandoned ship. Them men as managed to break them open and get out were machine-gunned by the Japanese warships. That's no way to fight a war, drowning defenceless men and then shooting them as manages to escape.'

Sally shivered as she tried not to let her imagination picture the scene Frank was describing.

'But what's that got to do with my Ronnie?' she asked him blankly.

'Well, the thing is . . .'

'What Frank's trying to say, lass,' Albert told her gruffly, 'is that mebbe summat of that sort might have happened to your Ronnie.'

Sally looked at him, and shook her head. 'No, how could it. My Ronnie's safe in a prisoner of war camp. How could he be on a ship?'

'Sally, what Albert's saying is that them Japs don't allus treat their prisoners like we do. They see things differently to us. None of them surrender, you see. They don't hold with it. They'd rather kill themselves, and so . . .' Frank shook his head, unable to go on.

'You mean they'd kill my Ronnie because he surrendered?' Sally asked. 'But they can't do that.' When no one spoke Sally repeated, 'They can't do it . . . can they, Frank? They can't.'

'Sally love . . .'

When Frank went to put his arm around her Sally pulled back bursting out fiercely, 'No, no, no . . .'

'Come on, Sally, none of that now. You've got to be strong and brave for your kiddies' sake,' Doris told her firmly, stepping in quickly and giving

Sally a small shake. 'My Frank will go down to the barracks and see what he can find out. I'll tell you what, I'll get that fire lit for you, shall I? It must have gone out. It's no wonder you've still got your coat on.'

Sally looked blankly at the dead fire and then at her coat. It seemed no time at all since she had taken the telegram from the boy but now here was Frank home from work and it was already going dark.

'It's got to be a mistake,' Sally was still insisting. 'My Ronnie can't be dead.'

Sam blinked, trying to remove the tired grittiness from her eyes. It was nearly seven o'clock and well past the time when she should have finished off for the day, but a report on evidence of a potential unexploded bomb close to the railway line running to one of the munitions factories had resulted in it being given an A1 priority listing, and the major announcing that he wanted her to drive him over to the site immediately. It was the first occasion on which she had had to drive in the blackout and she had been thankful for her decision earlier in the week to start studying and memorising a road map of Liverpool and its surroundings.

Now that they were here, the major was talking to the section headed by Sergeant Everton, who were about to dig down to the bomb.

As Sam had quickly discovered, Sergeant Everton was held in high esteem, both by those who worked with him and the major himself, for his cool head in an emergency and his skill in judging how best to deal with bombs in difficult sites.

'If we tunnel down and we find the bomb's taken a trajectory under the railway line then we won't be able to reach it without risking destabilising the railway line and that's going to do as much damage as defusing the bomb on site,' he was telling the major.

'So what do you suggest?'

'We need to find out what angle it's gone in at. If it's not gone under the line then there isn't a problem; if it has then we're going to need to tunnel down under it and shore everything up so that the captain can work on the fuse.'

'Good-oh. I'll go over and have a word with him now. Wait here, Grey.'

'Oi, you over there, put them ruddy lights out,' an angry voice suddenly bellowed, splintering the silence between Sam and the sergeant after the major had disappeared to talk with the captain. 'Don't you know there's a blackout on?'

Sam heard the sergeant exhale. 'ARP, that's all we need.'

As the warden got closer and saw the Noncombatant Corps men standing together, he swore and marched up to them, saying contemptuously, 'Well, that's typical, isn't it? I might have guessed it would be you cowardly lot. Afraid of the dark, are you, as well as afraid of doing your duty? Ruddy cowards—'

'That's enough of that kind of talk. These men have a sight more courage than many another I could name.'

The sergeant had moved with such speed it made Sam blink. One minute he was leaning against the truck a few feet away from her, the next he was standing squarely in front of the ARP warden.

'Who the hell are you?' the warden challenged.

'Sergeant Everton, Royal Engineers, Bomb Disposal, and these men are part of my section.'

'Wot, ruddy connies, working on UXBs? Don't make me laugh. That lot'd run a mile if they heard a firework going off,' the warden jeered.

'You reckon? That shows how much you know, chum. Being in the Noncombatant Corps has nothing to do with any lack of courage. These men aren't conscripted, they've volunteered. It's *taking* human life they object to, that's all, not doing their bit to *save* lives.'

'Aw, you're making my heart bleed, you are, and no mistake, mate.'

'Keep on insulting my lads and it won't just be your heart that's bleeding,' the sergeant warned him grimly. 'And you can take that as a promise. Worth ten of the likes of you, they are, every one of them. There's no one I'd sooner have in a tight spot with me.'

'All right, keep yer hair on.' The ARP man backed off.

'Tell you what,' the sergeant said softly, stubbing out the cigarette he had just lit. 'How about you change places with them and let them do your job for a week whilst you do theirs? We've only had three Noncombatant lads blown to bits so far this month, oh, and a couple who've lost a leg apiece. Had to work on round the lad who lost his leg the other day.'

The major was coming back. Worried that the sergeant might get into trouble, Sam stepped up to the major, saluting smartly as she did so.

'Permission to speak, sir?'

'Yes, what is it, Grey?'

'Permission to ask Corporal Willett to check the oil tomorrow, sir?'

'What? Oh yes, of course . . .'

The car's oil didn't really need changing but it was all Sam could think of on the spur of the moment to enable her to stand in between the major and the sergeant and thus give the latter a chance to send the ARP man on his way before he tried to complain to the major.

She had driven halfway back to the barracks before it occurred to her to ask herself just why she had felt it necessary to protect someone whom she disliked so heartily.

She might not care for the sergeant but there was no denying how much his men thought of him. And now she could see why. It shocked her to discover her own reluctant admiration for the stance he had taken over the ARP man's comments. But that didn't mean that she had changed her mind over anything else about him!

SEVENTEEN

The room set aside as a sitting room for the girls had probably been both comfortable and warm when the house had been used as a home, but having been stripped of its furnishings once to become a schoolroom and then a second time when it was requisitioned, its shabby motley collection of second-hand chairs, none of which seemed to have been designed for comfort, and its thin threadbare rugs now gave it the air of an institution. Whatever colour its walls had once been, someone's unskilled attempts to distemper them had turned them a streaky green that clashed horridly with the puce velvet armchairs either side of the fireplace. Their springs were damaged and one had to know how and where to sit on them if one didn't want to risk feeling very uncomfortable. Half a dozen straight-backed wooden chairs with leather seats were scattered round the rest of the room, most of them empty as the off-duty girls tended to choose to sit on cushions on the floor instead.

Some wag had found from somewhere a particularly bad painting of Highland cattle grazing on a wet-looking Scottish hillside, which was hung above the marble fireplace. A very large fireplace, which currently contained a very small fire. The beasts were curiously badly proportioned, causing the girls to speculate on whether it was the artist's sight that had been at fault or his skill.

Outside, the wind drove rain against the windows and rattled the wooden frames. The fire had a tendency to smoke when the wind was in the wrong direction, as it was today.

'Oh, no,' May wailed as someone opened the door from the passage, causing a sudden gust of smoke to billow from the fire just as she had carefully placed a piece of bread on a toasting fork over it. May was doing the toasting, then Hazel scraped margarine over the toasted bread.

'Told you it was going to smoke and to wait a minute,' Hazel laughed.

'That was the last piece of bread as well,' May mourned.

'Grey, you've got a visitor,' the uniformed girl standing in the doorway informed Sam briskly. 'He's at the front desk.'

'He?' May queried, looking questioningly at Sam, her toast forgotten. 'Well, you're a dark horse, aren't you? You've never let on that you had a chap.'

'I haven't,' Sam assured her, refusing to get up off the worn leather chair on which she had been sitting darning her stockings ready for the girls' visit to the Grafton later on. It had been such a

270

wet day that they had decided not to go out for a meal prior to going to the Grafton but to make do instead in their billet and celebrate Hazel's birthday with tea and toast.

The mention of a male visitor, even one not for her, had Lynsey, who had been plucking her eyebrows on the other side of the room, dropping her tweezers into her bag, and reaching for her lipstick instead. After applying fresh colour to her mouth, she retracted the lipstick and put the top back on before returning it to her bag along with her compact.

'It's Sam who's got a visitor, Lynsey,' May pointed out, but Lynsey was oblivious to the warning in her voice, because she put her bag down to smooth her hands through her hair, before getting up to check her skirt. Whilst Lynsey was getting ready to make an impression, Sam continued to darn her stockings, convinced that Elsie must have made a mistake, since she could not think of any male who was likely to come looking for her here.

'What's he look like then, Elsie?' May demanded. ''Cos if he's good-looking . . .'

'Oh, he's that all right,' the girl who had made the announcement grinned, filching the last piece of toast. 'Says he's your brother, and that his name's Russell. He's wearing a fly boy uniform,' she informed Sam with another grin.

'Russ!' Sam was up on her feet, her darning forgotten as she headed for the door.

But when she tried to close it behind her, May

hung on to it, demanding, 'Bring him down here, Sam. We could do with a handsome chap to cheer us all up a bit.'

Sam could hear her brother's laughter even before she reached the entrance hall and she wasn't totally surprised to find him bantering teasingly with the girl on duty, her laughter and flushed cheeks showing how much she was enjoying it.

'Russ, what on earth are you doing here?' Sam demanded after they had exchanged hugs.

'Unexpected leave, and since one of the chaps was driving up this way to see his family I thought I'd hitch a lift with him and see how you are going on.'

He was speaking lightly enough, but Sam guessed the truth from the way he was scrutinising her.

Moving out of earshot of the girl on duty she protested, 'Mum wrote to you and told you about Mouse, didn't she?' She *knew* she shouldn't have given in to her emotions and written to her mother, pouring her heart out about her sadness over Mouse's death, Sally admitted. Of course she hadn't told her mother everything – how could she after the statement she had given, especially knowing that it wasn't always only overseas mail that was censored to make sure there wasn't any material in it that could affect the security of the country. 'I suppose she asked you to come and see me as well,' she continued accusingly, without giving him any chance to say anything.

'That's right,' Russell agreed. 'And I told my CO that I had to have leave so that I could come up here and comfort my kid sister. Come on, Sammy, yes, Ma did write and tell me about your friend – poor kid – but you don't really think I'd come rushing up here to hold your hand, do you? You're a big girl now, this war is tough on all of us, and as a matter of fact if anyone needs their hand holding it's me, not you. Lost three of our chaps and their planes on a night mission the other week. Pretty bloody show all round and those of us who got back only did so by the skins of our teeth. Had our own undercarriage shot half away.'

He was speaking lightly and self-mockingly, but Sam could see the pain behind his smile now.

'Oh, Russ.'

'Hey, Grey, I hope you aren't keeping that good-looking fly boy all to yourself,' a girl from one of the other dormitories joked as she walked past.

'Come on,' Sam urged her brother, 'we're celebrating our corporal's birthday with tea and toast, and the girls will never forgive me if I don't take you down and introduce you to them.'

Tucking her arm through his, Sam led the way to the sitting room. Her brother was a handsome young man with a twinkle in his eyes and a personable, easy-going nature, and so she wasn't surprised when the other girls clustered round him, wanting to be introduced, but what did surprise her was to see him half an hour later deep in conversation with Hazel, the two of them so engrossed in their shared conversation that they seemed to have forgotten about the rest of them.

'Well, Hazel's certainly taken to your brother,' May commented. 'Has he got a steady girl?'

'Not so far as I know,' Sam answered.

'Might be a good idea then to ask him to come along with us this evening. He's certainly cheered Hazel up.'

May was right, Sam acknowledged, but before she could say anything Hazel beckoned her over and told her slightly pink-cheeked, 'Russell was saying that he's going to be at a bit of a loose end this evening, so I've invited him to join us at the Grafton.'

'Great minds think alike,' Sam quipped. 'I was just about to ask you if you minded if he came along.'

'Have you warned him that he'll be expected to ask us all for a dance?' May asked, coming over to join them just in time to catch the end of their conversation.

'Why do you think I urged Sam to join the ATS, if it wasn't so that I could have the prettiest dance partners?' Russell joked back.

'So you're enjoying driving for this major then, I take it?' Russell asked Sam as she walked down to the bus stop with him a couple of hours later so that he could go back to his billet to get changed for the evening. 'Ma will be pleased to hear that.'

They exchanged understanding looks. As children they had had a pact about not telling their parents about the things they got up to that might worry them and that pact still existed even if neither of them referred to it any more.

'I am enjoying it,' Sam confirmed. There was no need to tell her brother about Sergeant Everton and the volatile atmosphere they seemed to create whenever they were together.

Head down against the rain, Sam tucked her arm through her brother's as he held the umbrella May had loaned them. The wind and rain weren't conducive to either a leisurely walk or a great deal of conversation.

'The other girls seem good sorts,' Russell commented as they neared the bus stop.

'They are, especially Hazel,' Sam agreed. There was no need to say anything about Lynsey. Sam had been surprised and then relieved when her brother hadn't paid any attention to Lynsey, despite her attempts to engage him in conversation. Once Russell had been talking with Hazel, Lynsey had flounced out of the room, announcing that she was going out.

'She's been a brick, especially considering she's had her own problems to cope with.'

'Oh? What kind of problems?'

So she hadn't been mistaken in thinking that her brother had been rather taken with Hazel, Sam reflected as she saw how keen he was to know more about her.

'A chap who treated her badly and who wasn't good enough for her,' she answered as they reached the bus stop and stood there together under the umbrella. 'We were all glad when she decided to end it with him, but it's left her feeling a bit blue.'

Luckily they were the only ones at the bus stop so they were able to talk openly, without being overheard.

'So there's no one at the moment then?' Russell pressed her.

His attempt to sound casual was nowhere near good enough to deceive a sister.

'That's right,' Sam agreed, taking pity on him as she added, 'I think it would cheer her up no end if you were to ask her to dance with you tonight, Russ.'

'If I can get a look in. A dashed pretty girl like her is bound to have chaps queuing up to dance with her once it gets round that she's not attached.'

Sam had never heard her brother sound or look so enthusiastic about any girl, and there had been plenty of pretty girls chasing him even before he had joined the RAF, so she found herself doing the kind of thing she had always laughed at her mother for doing, and getting involved in the kind of female mental arithmetic that involved adding two and two together to get five, adding a good pinch of sisterly intuition and then wondering if there might be a possibility that Hazel and Russ could really take to one another and become 'an item'. If so, she certainly wouldn't be complaining.

'Come on, Lynsey, the rest of us are ready, and if we don't get this next bus we're going to end up not even getting into the Grafton, never mind getting good seats.'

'Well, it's not my fault that it came on to rain so heavily it soaked right through my coat and shoes, is it?'

'You should have known it was daft going out in those flimsy things,' May retorted. 'Especially when we could all see how hard it was raining. You'd have done better staying in with us instead of going chasing after that sergeant, just 'cos you'd heard he sometimes goes in that Joe Lyons near Lime Street Station. Even if he had been there, there'd have been that many of them nippy waitresses wanting to serve him you wouldn't have got a look in anyway.'

'That wasn't why I went out, and don't you go saying it was. I'm getting sick of you keeping on saying I'm chasing after Johnny when it's not true. Huh, if anyone's doing any chasing it's you lot, making all that song and dance like you'd never seen a man before when Sam's brother was here earlier. I dunno why everyone makes such a fuss about the RAF.'

'So you saw your sergeant then, did you?'

'No I didn't! Aren't you listening to me? I just told you that wasn't why I went out. I'd heard they'd got face powder on sale in one of the shops, and I thought I'd try and get some.'

'Did you?'

'No, they'd sold out by the time I got there.'

'Aren't you ready yet, Lynsey?' Hazel demanded. 'I've just told her that she's going to make us late. Well, don't you look a treat Hazel?' May said admiringly, causing everyone else in the dormitory to look at their corporal. 'You'll put the rest of us to shame.'

Hazel did look lovely, Sam agreed. She was wearing a taffeta frock in a rich emerald-green that complemented her colouring, its boned, strapless bodice showing off Hazel's pretty shoulders and *décolletage*. She had styled her hair to curl softly onto her shoulders and darkened her eyelashes to show off their length, and she was wearing the pretty flower-shaped costume jewellery brooch the girls had clubbed together to buy her for her birthday.

'You don't think I've overdone it, do you?' she asked anxiously.

Immediately the girls gave a chorus of reassuring denials, Sam adding, 'It is your birthday, after all.'

Sam was wearing the dress she had borrowed from Hazel the last time they had gone to the Grafton. She was also wearing Mouse's belt, Mouse having insisted that she keep it. She had almost not done so, but then she had reasoned that Mouse would have wanted her to wear it and that by doing so she was in one way keeping Mouse with them, and fresh in her own memory. And that surely was the very best way of honouring her friend.

'You know, I reckon that Lynsey is going to come a cropper with that sergeant. I've never seen her like this before. Mind you, it will do her good, I reckon,' May told Sam half an hour later when they all finally got off the bus to queue up outside the Grafton, wrapped in their heavy ATS coats and clustering together under umbrellas. 'Here's your brother,' she added, giving Sam a nudge. 'Bet you sixpence he stops to have a word with Hazel.'

Sam laughed and shook her head, and sure enough the moment Russell saw Hazel he went over to her.

'I hope you've warned him that she's bin through a bad time and that the last thing she wants is another chap who's going to mess her around,' May told Sam sternly.

'Yes, I have.'

'Not that he looks that sort.'

'He isn't,' Sam confirmed.

'Come on then, girls, what can I get you all to drink?'

'You're buying drinks for all of us?'

Sam looked at her brother with sisterly concern. She could understand Russell wanting to treat Hazel and create a good impression, but she didn't want to see his generosity abused.

'Ah well, no, not really.'

Not really? What did he mean by that? Sam waited warily.

'You see when I went back to my billet and told the other chaps there what I was doing tonight, they said it wasn't fair that one chap should get to escort so many girls, and they insisted on coming along too. Don't worry, I had a word with Hazel outside and asked her if she minded.'

When Sam looked round she saw a group of beaming young airmen heading for their table, as Russell gave them a thumbs-up.

'Well, this is what I call a birthday celebration,' May smiled enthusiastically as a chubby-faced airman gave her a small bow and handed her a brimming glass of port and lemon.

The band playing tonight wasn't the one Sam had heard before but they were still very good. The Grafton itself was packed, with young women, all dressed up in their best frocks, their eyes shining with the excitement at the thought of a good night out, and young men, most of whom were in uniform although some were in civvies – those who were on leave perhaps, and those who were in one of the reserved occupations. But no matter how handsome they were, they could not match the good looks of the group of young men surrounding their table, Sam decided loyally as she studied her brother and his friends in their RAF uniforms.

From the glances they were attracting, other young women shared her opinion, Sam decided, when she saw how many members of her own sex were looking through the haze of cigarette smoke in their direction.

The American GIs, with their 'pinks and greens', as their uniforms were referred to, did stand out, she had to admit that – as much for their height as anything else, being in the main taller than the British service personnel, but she'd rather dance with one of their own brave boys any day. Even if that 'brave boy' happened to be Sergeant Everton? Now what had put that thought in her head, Sam wondered crossly. She certainly didn't want it there, or to be reminded of Sergeant Everton when she was out enjoying herself.

The dance floor was really crowded tonight. Sam heard someone say that Liverpool was full of men waiting to embark on overseas postings, and naturally they wanted to have a good time before they left. After all, some of them might not be coming back. Such sobering thoughts had Sam looking towards her brother. Russell had positioned himself very determinedly and indeed almost possessively right next to Hazel, angling their chairs so that they were facing one another. Whatever they were saying was causing them to lean very close together. As Sam watched she saw Russell lift his hand and place it on Hazel's arm, and then bend closer to her as he said something to her. Sam could see her shaking her head and she couldn't be sure but she thought she saw her brother discreetly pushing a white handkerchief into Hazel's hand. A small lump formed in Sam's throat as she remembered being comforted herself by a man in uniform. Only that, of course, had been very different because Sergeant Brookes was a married man. She *had* been held tight in another man's arms, though. Now the lump had become a tight ball of confusing emotions she didn't want to think about.

Turning to May she said, 'I'm going up to the powder room – coming?'

*

281

'Looks like Hazel is enjoying herself,' May remarked to Sam approvingly as they reapplied their lipstick together, leaning over the basins to look into the mirror whilst striving not to be accidentally jostled by the good-natured crowd of girls all trying to do the same thing. 'You couldn't say the same for Lynsey, though,' she added in an undertone as they turned to leave. 'I wouldn't want to be in the shoes of that sergeant of hers when he turns up – if he turns up, and she's not just making it up about them being an item.'

'He could have been called out on a UXB call, and that's why he isn't here,' Sam felt bound to point out.

May gave her a surprised look. 'I wasn't expecting to hear you defending him, not after the way you were with him the last time we were here.'

'I'm not, I'm just saying that he could have been called out.'

'Mmm, well, Lynsey won't take too kindly to coming second place to some bomb, and she won't take too kindly either to you perhaps knowing more about what he's doing than she does, so if you want my advice you'll keep mum about him and his bombs.'

Sam opened her mouth to tell May that she didn't need her warning and then closed it again as she saw her brother leading Hazel onto the dance floor, and not for an energetic dance either but for a romantic slow number. May had obviously seen it too because she gave Sam a meaningful nudge in the ribs.

'Well, it certainly looked like you enjoyed your birthday, Hazel,' Alice teased their corporal later than evening when they were all in the dormitory getting ready for bed. 'Only I hope that if you and Sam's brother become an item you don't start showing her favours,' she added with a grin.

Sam didn't know which of them looked more embarrassed, herself or Hazel, but Alice refused to take pity on them continuing chirpily, 'Going to write to you, is he?'

'Alice . . .' May objected

'I was only asking. No harm in that, is there?'

'Russell did ask me if he could keep in touch,' Hazel confided to Sam a bit later in a quiet whisper. 'I told him all about my navy chap and we agreed that we'd both enjoyed each other's company, so I said there was no harm in us being chums.'

'I can't wait to write and tell Mum.'

'No. Promise me you won't do that,' Hazel begged her, looking alarmed. 'At least not yet. It's too soon . . . I mean, we've both agreed that we're just going to be friends.' She was almost falling over herself in her desperation to prove there was nothing between them but Sam wasn't in the least bit deceived.

'It looked like Russell had more than friendship in mind when I saw him kissing you good night,' Sam told her mischievously.

'You saw that? Don't you dare go telling the others. I really liked him, Sam,' she added huskily, 'but it *is* too soon . . .'

'He's a fly boy,' Sam reminded her, 'and they don't like wasting time.' Her expression clouded as she remembered what Russell had told her about the deaths of his friends.

As though she guessed what was going through her mind, Hazel squeezed her hand comfortingly.

'He's going to write and let me know when he's next got leave and we're going to try to meet up somewhere – away from Liverpool.'

'I hope it does work out,' Sam told her, and meant it.

EIGHTEEN

'So you're not coming to church this morning then, Sally?'

Sally shook her head.

'It would do you and the kiddies good,' Doris tried to persuade her.

Still Sally said nothing. She hadn't spoken in anything other than monosyllables since Frank had come back on Friday evening to tell them that it was true and that Ronnie was dead.

Doris had wanted to stay with her that night but Sally had refused.

'Sally, I know how much the news has upset you, but sitting here isn't going to help. When did you last have something to eat?'

Sally didn't want to eat or sleep or talk to anyone; if she didn't then maybe she wouldn't have to accept the news in the telegram. And maybe just so long as she refused to accept it then somehow Ronnie could be alive.

'Come on, you know how you love to sing. It will do you good.'

Sally's mouth twisted with pain. Ronnie had loved to hear her sing, he had often said so. How could she ever sing again now?

Doris was saying something but Sally had stopped listening, and it was a relief when her neighbour finally left.

The fire was almost out but stoking it up wouldn't warm the icy cold out of her body and her heart. She looked over to where her sons were playing together: Tommy, who didn't understand yet that he would never see his father again; Harry, the son Ronnie had never seen. Poor little Harry, who didn't properly know what a father was, and never would know now.

She had no idea how long she had been sitting here in the kitchen, or how long it had been since Doris had come and then gone away again. She hadn't gone to bed last night, nor the night before either, knowing she wouldn't be able to sleep and unable to face the room and the bed she and Ronnie had shared. Had he known he was going to die? How had it happened? Had he been drowned like those men in the ship, or had he been hacked to pieces like she had heard other men had been?

When Ronnie had first been taken POW she had tried not to read the papers with their awful stories about the fall of Hong Kong and Singapore from those wretchedly few people who had somehow miraculously escaped, but somehow she had been driven by a compulsion to do so. Until now she had blotted out the horror of what she had read, burying it deep inside herself, but now it was as though a locked door had burst open, spilling out all the fears and horror she had tried to push away. All she could hear inside her head was the screams of dying men; all she could see when she closed her eyes was the torture of human flesh. A sound – something between a groan and a sob – bubbled up inside her throat, but she swallowed it back. The boys mustn't see her fear, they must never, ever see or hear inside *their* heads what she could see and hear inside hers. She must keep them safe from those horrors.

Doris had picked up some letters from the hallway and put them on the table. The top envelope just had her name scrawled across it. She knew what it was, and shivered. There would be no sympathy for her from the debt collector or the woman who employed him, just a demand for the money she still owed them. Money Ronnie had borrowed and would never now be able to give back. He had at least escaped from that worry and fear, which was more than she could ever do.

She could hear someone now, knocking on the back door, and was surprised to see that it was almost dinnertime. It felt like only a few minutes since Doris had left. How had so much time slipped by without her noticing? She wasn't going to answer the door, though. If she stayed here, small and quiet with her sons, and didn't let anyone in, then she could keep out all those things she didn't want to know, just as if she didn't go to bed and sleep she wouldn't be tormented by those night-mare visions of Ronnie that kept on trying to creep into her mind.

The key turned in the lock, and the back door opened.

'Dr Ross.'

He was holding her door key in his hand.

'Mrs Brookes has told me about your husband. I'm very sorry.'

'Doris told you about Ronnie?' She must have given him her key as well.

'It's my doctor.' Excitedly Tommy raced towards the visitor, whilst Sally looked past him and then said stiffly, 'It's a mistake. Ronnie won't be dead. I know he won't be.'

'Mrs Walker . . .'

'He can't be dead,' she protested as the doctor came towards her. 'The War Office have got it wrong. I know what the Japs do to them – they kill – but that can't have happened to my Ronnie . . .'

Tears had started to flood her eyes and pour down her face. Harry, sensing her grief, starting crying loudly whilst Tommy clung to the doctor's leg, trying to be grown up and brave.

'You've had a nasty shock.' The doctor's voice was calm and matter of fact. 'But life has to go on, and your late husband would be the first to tell you that, I'm sure. You have two children to look after. When did you last have something to eat?'

Sally looked at him blankly. 'I'm not hungry.'

'Have the boys eaten?'

Now his words penetrated the wall she had tried to build round herself to numb the pain, immediately arousing her maternal instincts. Was he trying to accuse her of neglecting her boys?

'Of course they have.'

'What did you have for breakfast, Tommy?' he asked, ignoring her.

'Porridge,' Tommy told him.

Sally had stood up when he had started to question Tommy and now she was shaking with fury and bitterness.

'You'd love to prove that I'm neglecting them, wouldn't you? Well, I'm not.' She bent down and picked up Harry, soothing him and kissing his forehead. 'That's why you've come here, isn't it? Because you won't rest until you've taken them away from me.'

'I came round because Mrs Brookes told me about your husband and said that she was worried about you. She said you'd refused to go to church.'

'Go to church? I should think I have refused to go, and have all them like Daisy asking me questions about my Ronnie, whilst her husband's safe and sound. They'd all be talking about me behind my back. Besides, what have I got to give thanks for? It doesn't bear thinking about what might have happened to my Ronnie . . . what he might have had to go through . . . and all for what? So that someone like you can take his sons away from their mother. And what does she mean by giving you my door key? She had no right.'

'Your husband was a professional soldier, a

brave man, loyal to his country and his friends, a man who chose to serve his country . . . a man his sons can be proud of. Do you think he would want to see you like this, or to hear such words? Isn't it the truth that it would hurt and upset him? Wouldn't he be relying on you to carry on as though he were still here, for the sake of his sons? They need you more than ever now. They need you to care for them and love them, and they need you to keep the memory of their father alive for them so that they can grow up knowing and loving him through you. You owe him that much surely, a man who has laid down his life for his country – you owe it to him and to his sons. You, his wife, the mother of his children – don't you think he would expect—'

'You can't tell me what my Ronnie would think or want. You didn't even know him.'

'I know that he was a brave and a good man. I know that he went to war because he believed in certain things, in certain freedoms, and that he laid down his life for those things. I know too that all of us, every single one of us, owe it to him and to all those others like him, who have paid the ultimate price for those beliefs, to be as brave in spirit and deed as he was.' The quiet voice rang with authority and conviction.

Sally looked at him, her eyes brimming with tears. 'Why does he have to be dead?' she wept. 'Why? I can't bear it . . .'

'Yes you can, and you must for your boys' sake. The human spirit has an infinite capacity to endure, no matter how much we may be called upon to suffer.'

Something in his voice broke through Sally's grief, reminding her that he had lost not just his wife but his sons as well.

'I couldn't bear that,' she told him as though she'd already spoken her thoughts to him. 'I couldn't bear to lose my sons as well.'

'Why don't I put the kettle on and make us both a cup of tea?'

Sally's eyed widened at the thought of the doctor performing such a humble task, and in her kitchen when he must be used to so much better.

'You'll do no such thing,' she told him roundly. 'I'll do it.'

She was filling the kettle when she heard him saying quietly, 'My boys would have been five and three now. Your Tommy reminds me a bit of Euan.'

'I heard that it was a bomb,' Sally said uncertainly, not sure whether she should make any response.

'Yes. A direct hit on the house in London where my wife and children were living.'

'London? But . . . ?'

'My wife was from London. I met her when I was working in a hospital down there. I'd made arrangements for her and the children to be evacuated to the country, but she hated living there. Without telling me beforehand she went to live in London with her cousin. They'd always been close, and she said that he needed someone to run the house for him – he was an artist. It took a direct

hit two weeks after she'd moved in. They . . .
Andrea and her cousin were killed outright, and
Euan too. Niall . . .' His voice caught betrayingly.
'It was for the best that he was taken too. His
injuries . . . Sometimes life seems very cruel in the
way that she doesn't spare us the pain of knowing
what our loved ones have suffered, and I know
that that is how you are feeling now, but believe
me, it won't always be like that. I was on my way
to see Fleur when the bomb hit, so I was able to
see Niall in the hospital. The poor little chap was
so badly injured but he still recognised me. I felt
he'd been waiting for me to get there before he
could go. He died in my arms.'

Sally gave a small sob, unable to endure hearing
any more. And if she couldn't bear to hear it, then
how must this man who had been that child's father
feel?

'How do you bear it?' she whispered.

'I don't . . . I can't . . . Sometimes my work
allows me to escape from it.' He took a deep breath.
'You're asking me questions that no one else has
asked, and compelling me to answer them with
the kind of honesty I find it hard to face. The truth
is that . . . The truth is that I don't think I shall
ever be able to bear the pain and the guilt of not
being able to protect my children. All I can do is
hope to be able to live with it.'

'Why must such dreadful things happen?' Sally
asked him emotionally.

'I wish I knew. I wish too that I knew how to
stop them from happening, but what I do not wish

292

is that I knew how to stop us from hurting when they do happen, because that is how we know we are human and that we care.'

Sally digested what he had said. 'It's not just that Ronnie's dead. It's thinking about what they might have done to him,' she explained.

'I know.'

'I can't bear to think of him . . . suffering . . . after all that he'd already been through. And I keep on thinking about those poor men in that ship, knowing they was going to drown and then them that escaped being shot in cold blood.'

'War is a cruel and bloody business.'

They looked at one another in mutual silence, and Sally felt as though something tight and hard and icy cold inside her was somehow relaxing its numbing grip on her, allowing life to seep back into her, slowly, painfully, but at the same time bringing with it a tentative recognition of a fellow sufferer and the realisation that she was not after all alone.

'Sally, it's only me, Doris . . .'

Sally's head snapped round as both of them turned towards the door. 'Oh, you're still here, Dr Ross. I didn't expect . . .'

Why, when it was Doris who was responsible for him being here, did she feel so guilty, as though somehow she was involved in something wrong and illicit, Sally wondered.

'I was just about to leave, Mrs Brookes.'

'Yes . . . thank you for taking the trouble to come round, Dr Ross.'

Sally couldn't look at him, the feeling that they were co-conspirators, in something secret that they needed to protect, refusing to go away.

She could hear Doris talking to him as she escorted him to the front door, the boys were playing together once again, the fire burning, everything on the surface just as it had been before he had arrived, and yet Sally knew that the reality was that deep down within herself something vitally important had changed irreversibly and for ever.

'Feeling a bit better now, are you, love?' Doris asked solicitously when she came back into the room. 'That's the spirit. Why don't you and the boys come up and have a bit of dinner with us? I've got Molly and Frank, and her dad and the kiddies coming round, and I've got a good-sized chicken cooking. Molly's auntie sent it up from the farm at Nantwich, so there'll be plenty to go round.'

Sally nodded. She wasn't hungry; the very thought of food blocked her throat and made her feel sick, but the boys needed to eat, and something told her that it would be safer for her to be with others instead of alone with her own thoughts.

NINETEEN

It was funny how it took only one thing to change, for others not really related to it to change as well, Sam reflected tiredly but happily as she made her way past the stores – until recently the cause and the scene of so much anger for her, and so much misery for poor Mouse. It seemed almost impossible to imagine now that such a very short time ago she had been on the point of requesting a transfer, so convinced had she been that she did not fit in and that she could not make a decent contribution to the war here in this posting. It was true that she would never be able to forget – or to forgive – the cruelty that had led to Mouse taking her own life, nor to regret that she had not been able to do something to prevent that tragedy and waste, but her alienation from the other girls, and the bleakness and despair she had felt had all miraculously been dissolved by her involvement in her new duties. Whoever it was who had put her forward for those duties – and she had a pretty shrewd idea she knew who that was now, the corporal having semi let the cat out of the bag by telling her that he had heard that 'someone' who had seen her at work and had felt she would be perfect for the job, had urged the major to give her a chance – had done her the best kind of favour.

There wasn't a morning now when she didn't wake up looking forward to the day ahead, and the challenges she knew it would bring. She and the Bentley had acknowledged a grudging respect for one another, and she was beginning to be able to interpret the meaning of at least some of the major's absorbed silences as he studied various bomb sites, and to understand how proud he was of the men under his command for their record not just of bomb disposal but also for their calmness and discipline under pressure.

She had just drawn level with the entrance to the stores when she saw a familiar figure emerging from them. Sergeant Brookes. Her heart leaped with gratitude. Here surely was the ideal opportunity to thank him for recommending her for her new duties.

Hurrying across to him, she called out, 'Sergeant Brookes.'

'Sam,' he responded warmly. 'How are you doing? How's it working out driving for the major?'

'I love it,' Sam assured him. 'I can't think of anything I'd want to do more. Oh, I'm so glad I've seen you. I can't thank you enough for what you've done, recommending me when the position became vacant, and everything.'

'Me recommend you?' He shook his head, and

gave her a rueful look. 'I'm not the one you should be thanking. It was Johnny's idea. All I did was agree with him that I thought the work involved would appeal to you.'

A handful of seconds ticked by and then a few more whilst Sam grappled with her shock.

'You mean it wasn't you who recommended me, it was Sergeant Everton?'

'Yes, that's right,' the sergeant confirmed cheerfully.

'Sergeant Everton?' Sam repeated unsteadily. 'But . . .' But that's not possible, she had been about to say, but of course she couldn't. 'But why would he do that?' she asked instead.

'Why don't you ask him?' Sergeant Brookes suggested. 'Here he is now.'

Sam turned round, dismayed to see the sergeant making his way towards them. Before she could do or say anything to stop him, Sergeant Brookes was hailing him.

'I was saying to Sam here, Johnny, that you're the one she needs to thank for recommending her for her new posting, not me.'

Despite the dour look the sergeant was giving her, Sam knew that it must be true. Sergeant Brookes was hardly likely to lie, which meant . . . which meant that she owed Sergeant Everton a huge debt of gratitude. Sergeant Everton, who always seemed to manage to be there when she was saying or doing the wrong thing, and who always managed to let her know it with that look that he gave her. He must really be enjoying this.

How it made her pride sting even to think of being in any kind of debt to him. She would have to grit her teeth and thank him, of course – it was unthinkable that she didn't – but she felt the same revulsion at the thought of having to do so that children felt towards the daily spoonful of cod liver oil the Government was so insistent they should have. Oh, why, why had this had to happen to her? She wanted to crawl away somewhere and stay there until the war was over.

'I was hoping I'd see you,' Sergeant Brookes was telling her *bête noire*. 'You probably won't have heard the news yet, but Sally Walker had a telegram on Friday. From the War Office. It's her Ronnie – he's dead.'

'Ronnie Walker's dead?'

Sam could tell from both men's expressions that the man they were discussing must have been a good friend.

'I knew the Japs had got him, of course – poor sod. What happened, Frank, does Sally know?'

'No, she doesn't. And it would be a good thing in my opinion if she never learns. She's in a bad enough way as it is, Johnny. She couldn't take it in at first, not even with the telegram there in front of her. She kept on saying that the War Office must have made a mistake. Told us over and over again, she did, how he shouldn't be dead because he was a POW. I tried to tell her that being a POW couldn't guarantee Ronnie's safety – not when it was the Japs that had got him, but without actually telling her too much, if you know what

I mean. No sense in making it even worse for her than it already is. She was in that much of a state that Ma promised her that I'd see what I could find out so I came back down to the barracks on Friday night and managed to have a few words with the CO. He made a few enquiries and it seems that Ronnie was took sick. The Japs' commanding officers don't keep sick prisoners, according what the Red Cross have managed to find out. If the men can't go on parade for work in the morning then their officers order them to go round the beds and . . . slice them straight down from the breast bone, apparently, and leave them with their guts hanging out. I haven't told Sally any of that, mind; she's got more than enough to bear. Just told her that it was true that he was dead.'

Sam's stomach heaved, but she didn't make a sound. She suspected that both the men had virtually forgotten that she was there and she didn't want to intrude on their private and very intimate anguish for a close friend by reminding them of her presence.

'I'd heard summat of the sort,' Sergeant Everton agreed curtly, 'but never thought. Ronnie . . .' He shook his head. 'I can see him now, that Sunday when you and me were first called up. Came to church, he did, with Sally; he was in his uniform. Put us wise to a few things and gave us the nod and a wink about how to go on . . . Sally's taken it bad, you said?'

'Yes, like I said, she wasn't for having it at first, Ma was worried sick about her. She even got the new doctor to go round and take a look at her. She's a good 'un, though, is Sally. Got a lot of pluck and she's got those lads of hers to keep her going. I wanted to have a word with you, though, and let you know.'

'Yes. Thanks for that, Frank.'

Sergeant Brookes nodded his head and then suddenly seemed to realise that Sam was still there. Forcing himself to inject a more hearty note into his voice, he told the other man, 'Like I was just saying, Sam here was just trying to thank me for getting her transferred, but I told her that she'd got the wrong man and that it was you she should be thanking.'

'Yes . . . yes. Thanks very much,' Sam agreed overbrightly, looking at a point well past Sergeant Everton's khaki-clad and extremely broad shoulders.

'I'd better go, otherwise I'm going to be late for me tea,' Sergeant Brookes told them both.

He was walking away before Sam could say or do anything, leaving her standing there feeling chagrined and angrily embarrassed, resentfully aware of what she owed to the man standing watching her and how much she wished she did not. But those were the wrong emotions for a young woman in uniform serving her country, and so she forced herself to put them aside and to say quietly, 'I'm sorry . . . about . . . about your friend.'

How stilted and awkward the words sounded but she still felt honour-bound to offer them. Who could not feel for those who lost loved ones and friends in such appalling circumstances? Who couldn't help but think that at any time they themselves could be the ones mourning a much-loved and lost life. The offering of sympathy, and the acknowledgement of a loss was a duty that now fell on them all, and it was one that everyone who had anything about them automatically respected. The fact that she and the sergeant didn't get on certainly did not in any way excuse her from doing so.

'He was a good soldier,' he told her bleakly. 'A professional soldier. He'd enlisted before any of the rest of us,' he added tersely by way of explanation. 'If he had to die then it should have been in the heat of battle, and not . . .' He cursed under his breath, and Sam could see the effort it cost him to drag air into his lungs as his chest rose and fell under the pressure. 'Ruddy war. Where's the sense in any of it, when a good man like Ronnie gets bayoneted like a piece of meat . . . ?'

He turned round, striding off into the gathering dusk, leaving Sam to do what she could to calm her heaving stomach before she went to join the other girls waiting for their transport back to their billet.

'What's up wi' you, Sally? When we was on the night shift together last year you was always singing like a lark. Fair cheered us all up, it did. Better than anything on the wireless and that's a fact.'

Sally couldn't answer Peg, even though she knew it must seem odd that she wasn't happier. After all, she had just been given a job that paid her more, and allowed her to work a day shift and have the boys in Littlewoods' nursery.

It had only been yesterday that she had been told out of the blue almost that she could start work on a new production line, working a day shift, if she wished, and that Littlewoods was providing extra nursery places for those women who agreed to be trained up for the new work, which was, so Sally had been told, making life jackets. Of course, she'd have been a fool to turn the offer down, so she had accepted it.

When she had arrived at work this morning she and the others had all had to stand and watch whilst they were given a demonstration of the full process and then they had been divided into three groups. The first group had the job of stencilling out the pattern of the jackets on the fabric. The second group had to cut out the jackets, whilst the third group had the responsibility of stuffing the jackets with kapok, which first had to be weighed accurately to ensure that exactly the right amount, no more and no less, went into each jacket before they were finished off. This work was paid on a piece rate, which meant that the faster a girl worked the more she got paid, although money would be deducted from her earnings for post-war credits, to be reimbursed after the war ended. Sally had congratulated herself at first when she had been picked for this final team, even though she had been warned that the Board of Trade would be sending an inspector to the factory to check every jacket.

Now, as she bent her head over her work, Sally saw the woman working next to the girl who had spoken to her give her a fierce nudge and mutter, 'Stow it, Peg, she's just lost her hubby. Haven't you heard?'

Sally could see how shocked Peg was and felt sorry for her. She was still sleeping downstairs at home, still unable to face the room and the bed that belonged to her role as a wife now that she was a widow.

'Eeh, Sally, I'm sorry . . . I hadn't heard,' Peg began, but Sally shook her head. She didn't want to talk about it. Not to anyone.

After several minutes of struggling with weighing her kapok, Peg sighed and grimaced and then announced, 'Bloody hell, I'm never going to earn owt doing this. I'd be better off seeing if I can get teken on in munitions.'

'What would you want to do that for?' Irene, the girl next to her and opposite Sally across the bench on which they were all working, demanded. 'Ruddy dangerous, munitions is, and no mistake. I've heard tales about what's happened to some of the girls wot work there that'd make your hair curl.'

'They pay a sight better than they do here, piece work or no piece work.'

'Aye, danger money, it's called, and with good reason. Anyway, what do you want getting more money for?' Irene continued. 'You've got your hubby on ARP duties and working down the docks, and that lass of yours is working now as well, isn't she? You must have more money coming in that they've got at Buckingham Palace.'

'Give over.'

'Come off it, Peg, I know what them men down the docks get paid. Aye, and how much they make on the side from what they get to sell off,' Irene said, refusing to be put off.

'Aye, well, if you must know, that's the trouble,' Peg replied miserably. 'Never had a bone of good sense in his body, my Barry hasn't, and the daft fool has gone and got hisself involved with a real bad lot. Only told me about it this last weekend. Well, he had to really, on account of him coming home with a cracked head and a couple of black eyes. Told me he'd walked into a lamppost in the blackout after coming out of the pub. As if I'd believe that. Knows its way home in a peasouper, that whippet of his does, and it has never once let him walk into a lamppost. So I told him straight that I wanted the truth out of him and no messing. Thought at first he'd bin up to his old tricks; allus had an eye for the wrong kind of woman, my hubby has. Sniffs 'em out like that dog of his does a rabbit, but no, he swore blind that it wasn't some tart's husband who'd given him what for, for mekin' up to his wife.'

'So what was it then?' Irene asked.

Peg shook her head glumly. 'Gone and got hisself into real trouble, he has this time. Shaking, he was, like a kiddie when he told me, and him weighing over sixteen stone. Mind you, he's more worried about his ruddy dog than he is about himself.

Seems that him and some of the others have had this bit o' business going supplying a bit of stuff as and when. Like he said, you 'ave to be careful. The bosses turn a blind eye to a few cans but there'd be hell to pay if there was a lot being taken. Anyway, like I was saying, they'd got this bit of a business going, and then this lot they were handing the stuff over to started acting all high and mighty, if you please, saying what they wanted and what they don't. My Barry told them straight that he wasn't being told what to do and for what they were paying him he might as well give the stuff away. Told them he didn't want no more to do with it and thought that was the end to it. Only now they've come at him and told him that unless he gets them what they want, he can expect more of what they sent him home with the other night, and he can forget having the dog to bring him home, 'cos he won't be seeing it no more.' Peg was in tears by the time she had reached the end of her sorry story.

'Your Barry wants to go and tell the police,' Irene stated roundly.

'How can he do that?' Peg demanded. 'Haven't you heard what I was saying? He'd be in trouble hisself if he did that. He said everything was all right before this woman and her sons started poking their noses in and taking over. Got their fingers into all sorts, they have, and none of it honest. She's got her lads sending their heavies round and threatening my Barry wi' all sorts if he don't do what they say. Even told him they'll get him sacked from his job if he doesn't go along with what they want . . .'

Sally, who hadn't been paying too much attention to what Peg had been saying, went still when she had heard the other woman mention the 'woman and her sons'. It had to be the Boss and 'her boys' who she was talking about. Everything Peg had had to say about the situation her husband was in confirmed Sally's own fears.

'Got no right threatening my Barry, they haven't. Heartbroken, he'd be if anything happened to that dog of his. Blubbing like a kid, he was, last night.' Peg's own face crumpled. 'Never seen him like that before . . .'

'Here, Peg.' Irene offered her a handkerchief. 'I can't see how you working in munitions is going to help, mind.'

'Well, I've told Barry that he might as well hand in his cards as be forced out, and I'm thinking that if I'm earning a bit more we can manage until he finds summat else. I've told Barry that we should perhaps think about moving away, some other part of the country, and having a bit of a fresh start.'

Sally's heart gave a fierce thud. Of course! Why hadn't she thought of that for herself? She'd even got the perfect legitimate excuse for wanting to move away. Hadn't the doctor said that she should evacuate the boys to a safer part of the country? Well, what was to stop her from going with them? Especially now. There was plenty of work to be had these days, even in the country. Sally's hands shook slightly as she bent over her work. It would be very wrong, of course, for her to disappear, leaving money owing to others, very wrong, and if it had still been the old man she was owing money to then she would never have thought of it, but she had to put her boys and their safety first, and after what Peg had said about her husband and his dog she was even more afraid for them than she had been before. The plain truth was that without the money she earned from singing she would not be able to find enough to pay the debt collector, and now with Ronnie dead things were going to be even worse. A widow's pension wasn't anything like the same as a serving soldier's wage.

The debt collector had called round again last night and this time he had gone on knocking for so long that she had had to let him in.

'Heard about your old man,' he had told her dismissively, 'but that don't alter anything, so don't you go thinking it does. Business is still business and you owe the Boss a tidy sum. Not that she would want anyone thinking she wasn't showing no charity. She says you can have a month off making any payments and that she'll add on a bit of extra interest to compensate her for what she's going to lose. Oh, and by the way, she said to warn you that it'll be the worse for you if you go sniffing around her Pete. She said to remind you that she don't hold wi' women tempting married men, so just because you haven't got no husband any more, think on that you don't go alley-catting after someone else's,' he had leered.

Sally shuddered now, reliving the outrage and horror she had felt, listening to him. His comments had sickened and disgusted her. The very thought of having Pete anywhere near her nauseated her. But she hadn't dared to say as much. Something about the Boss and her sons chilled her through and through, and her fear of them had been intensified with every word that Peg had spoken.

She had to get away. What, after all, was there to keep her here now anyway, without Ronnie? Doris had her new grandson; Molly and Frank had each other and their children. Thanks to Daisy, the rest of her neighbours had turned their backs on her. She had lost the singing job she had loved so much. What was there to keep her here in Liverpool? Tommy, of course, would miss 'his doctor', as he insisted on calling Dr Ross. Sally went still. She had no business thinking any kind of thoughts about Dr Ross, no business at all.

TWENTY

Sam's eyes widened at her recognition of the handwriting on the letter Hazel was pushing quickly into her pocket, as they all hurried out to get on the bus that would take them to the barracks. She'd have known it anywhere; it was her brother's writing. Russell certainly hadn't wasted any time in getting in touch with Hazel then.

'Do you mind if I sit next to you?'

Sam shook her head and moved further along the seat, making room for the corporal.

'Russell's written to me,' Hazel told her.

'I'm glad.' Sam meant it.

Hazel gave her a brief smile. 'I'm glad too,' she admitted, adding determinedly, 'Not that I want to rush into anything, and I've told Russell as much.'

'I'm sure he'll understand that, Hazel.'

'Well, I thought he did, but he says in his letter that he's got leave over Christmas and he wants us to get together.'

'He won't expect you to agree if it isn't what you want to do yourself.'

'Well, that's the problem,' Hazel said ruefully. 'It is what I want, but . . . well, the truth is that I'm scared, Sam.'

'Of Russell?' Sam felt slightly put out and rather protective of her brother. 'Hazel, that's the last thing Russ would want.'

'It isn't Russell who scares me, Sam, it's way he makes me feel.' Hazel dipped her head and said in a low voice, 'I think I'm falling for him, Sam.'

Sam swallowed uncomfortably. She felt scared sometimes too by the way Sergeant Everton made her feel, but *she* wasn't falling for *him*!

Determinedly Sam wrenched her thoughts away from the sergeant and told Hazel, 'You'll have to remind Russ that you want to take things slowly.'

'Yes,' Hazel agreed. 'The thing is, though, that there is a part of me that doesn't want to take things slowly at all, or be sensible one little bit, and I know that I've got to refuse to give in to it. For Russell's sake as much as my own.'

'Have you got that pump fixed yet?'

'No, Sarge.'

Sam listened idly to the conversation between the men who were standing beside the shored-up shaft several yards away from her, enviously admiring the motorcycle belonging to one of the team. She was keeping away from the shaft deliberately, knowing the effect standing too close to it was likely to have on her. Her fear of being trapped

310

underground was one she doubted she would ever be able to overcome.

She and the major had arrived at the bomb site over half an hour ago, and the major hadn't been too pleased to learn that far from having excavated around the bomb enough for the captain to defuse it, the shaft was now flooded, and the pump that should have been emptying it wasn't working.

'Why the devil haven't you got another pump working on this, Sergeant Everton?' The major's voice was sharp with irritation and impatience.

Sam knew perfectly well why the major was in such a vile mood. The news had been on his desk this morning of a defusing operation that had gone fatally wrong, killing not just the officer in charge but seven of that section's men as well.

The officer had been twenty-two and newly attached to the section. Sam had met him, a good-looking young man with a cheery insouciance.

As she had driven the major out of the barracks one of their trucks was being driven in, the wooden coffins clearly visible in the back of it. Sam had been working for the major long enough now to have heard the word-of-mouth stories about six-foot broad-shouldered men ending up in coffins so light a child could have carried them, whilst shorter thinner men were in coffins that took four men to lift.

'Fill 'em with sand, you see, when they can't find all the body parts,' the corporal had told her matter-of-factly. 'Nail 'em down as well so that the families don't get to see what's inside . . .'

'That's dreadful!' Sam had exclaimed.

The corporal had shrugged. 'What else can they do? There ain't much left of a person when they get it wrong when they're standing right next to a thousand pounds of German bomb. Working here in Liverpool, I was, during the May blitz, along with the sarge. Things we saw then. There was this one house, a woman and two kiddies in it – leastways that's what the neighbours told us. Couldn't find nothing, we couldn't, excepting one of the kiddies' feet . . . Only time I've ever seen anything get to the sergeant.'

'Three Section had an A1 to deal with last night, sir, and they were a pump short,' Sam could hear the sergeant answering the major now in an expressionless voice that Sam decoded as meaning that the pump had been blown up along with the men.

When the major didn't say anything, the sergeant turned his attention back to the excavation calling down, 'Come up then, Tweedey, and I'll go down and have a look at it.'

Under different circumstances she would have been itching for a go on the motorcycle, Sam admitted. Funny how much her priorities had changed just lately, especially since she had been driving the major. That change, she knew, had its roots in the hostility that existed between her and Sergeant Everton. No one had ever made her feel like this before, and when she was around him she felt on edge and wary, and yet at the same time something about his presence made everything seem sharper and more intense, more challenging and yes, more exciting. So much so that she knew that whilst a part of her hoped she wouldn't see him, another part of her hoped that she would.

Sam had no idea what to make of these extraordinary and contradictory feelings, and they weren't something she felt she could discuss with anyone else, especially in view of the proprietary stance Lynsey had taken about him. She didn't even want to have to think about her feelings, never mind acknowledge them or talk about them, she admitted. There were, though, times like right now when she had no choice, when her heart thudded and ached, and the woman she was now, emerging from the chrysalis of the girl she had been, grew impatient with that girl.

Stuart Tweedey, his face streaked with mud, had hauled himself out of the shaft, allowing the sergeant to take his place. Sam couldn't help giving a small shudder as she watched him lower himself into its depths. The major was signalling that he was ready to leave but Sam didn't really want to go – not yet; not until she had seen the sergeant's seal-black head as he pulled himself out of the diggings.

What kind of silliness was this? She started to walk towards the Bentley, refusing to admit how relieved she felt when she heard the now familiar sound of the pump starting up, telling her that the sergeant had succeeded in his task.

She opened the door of the car for the major, who was just on the point of getting in when Stuart

Tweedey called out anxiously, 'It's the sergeant. He's bin hurt and he's bleeding real bad.'

Immediately the major turned back, striding over to the diggings, calling back over his shoulder, 'Grey, bring that first-aid pack out of the car boot, will you, as fast as you like.'

When Sam reached the huddle of men, the sergeant was slumped against a barrel, his face paper white, whilst blood soaked through the sleeve of his shirt.

Her heart was pounding as heavily and unsteadily as though his injury somehow affected her personally.

'It's nothing much, just a bit of a scratch,' he was saying irritably, 'not a ruddy artery.'

Maybe not, but he was in evident pain. Sam realised that the waiting men were expecting her to deal with the injury. She had had first-aid training and normally would almost have enjoyed a chance to show off her prowess, but on this occasion she couldn't help wishing that there was someone else who could attend to the injury.

But there wasn't and the major was looking at her as though he wondered what was holding her back.

She took a deep breath and stepped up to the sergeant, and then stopped. She was too close to him. She could smell the scent of his skin and his hair, see the faint sheen of pain-driven perspiration above his upper lip, see the dark shadowing along his jaw where he shaved.

What was this? She didn't know, but she did

know that it was dangerous. Stop it . . . stop it, she warned herself.

Bending down, she opened the first-aid pack and removed a pair of scissors.

'You'll have to hold out your arm,' she told the sergeant without looking at him. 'I'll need to cut open the sleeve of your shirt.'

He'd made his arm rigid as he extended it, but Sam knew from her training that that wasn't enough and that she had to support the limb whilst she cut the fabric.

Reluctantly she moved closer to him, sliding her hand beneath his wrist. Her pulse rate was all over the place, skipping beats and then suddenly thudding. She started to cut open his shirt sleeve, laying bare the flesh beneath. His flesh had a slightly olive tone to it and still carried the fading warmth of a summer suntan. She could see beneath his skin the outline of the muscles he had made rigid, corded and strong. Something alien was happening inside her own body, some kind of weakening softness that made her tremble so much that the scissors slipped against his arm, raising a tiny pinpoint of blood. Automatically Sam looked up at him, her breath locking in her throat when she saw that he was looking back at her, trapping her in the web of his concentrated metallic gaze. She felt magnetised by it, unable to drag herself free, unable to calm that thudding race of her heartbeat and almost unable to breathe. And then thankfully he turned his head towards the other men, demanding tersely, 'Anyone got a cigarette?'

Sam waited until he had the lit Woodbine in his hand and she had seen the rise and fall of his chest as he took a deep drag from it before continuing.

She had almost reached the site of the injury when he threw the cigarette down unfinished, grinding it out beneath his heel as told her so quietly that no one else could hear, 'Disappointed that you didn't get the chance to spear them scissors through my heart, are you?'

'No.' Her denial was immediate and vehement, her hand jerking against his flesh as she pulled back the sleeve of his shirt to reveal a deep gash. Just looking at it made her feel slightly sick and dizzy. She was aware that his heartbeat too had picked up and that he was forcing his own breathing to appear even and unchanged.

The ragged edges of the wound gaped, the blood flow slower now, and Sam's heart thudded with a new anxiety.

'It's quite a deep cut, sir,' she told the major, 'and I'd rather not bandage it until it's been properly cleaned.'

The major frowned as he took a close look at the sergeant's arm. 'You're right. Get in the car, sergeant,' he instructed. 'We'll take you back to the barracks so that a medic can take a look at you.'

Sam was appalled. The last thing she'd expected when she had told the major that the sergeant needed to have the wound cleaned was that she would end up driving him back to the barracks. The last thing she wanted was the intimacy of

316

having him in the car. She gave a small shiver. She felt as though her nerve endings had had their protective covering ripped off, leaving her raw and far too vulnerable.

'Look, sir . . .' she could hear the sergeant beginning and she knew that he was going to refuse to go with them, but the major wouldn't let him finish.

'That's an order sergeant,' he told him firmly.

Five minutes later, with the sergeant sitting in the front of the Bentley next to her, Sam was driving away from the bomb site.

The major always sat in the back, using the car as an extension to his office. It was his habit to read his reports there, punctuating this with occasional grunts denoting either approval or disgust, and this was what he was doing now, his head bent over the papers he was holding, so that Sam felt almost as though she was alone in the car with the sergeant. She could feel the silence stretching between them as though it was a piece of rope slowly being tightened, and it was with great relief that she turned into Deysbrook Road and could see the entrance to the barracks ahead of her.

She had just slowed down to turn in when the major looked up from the papers he had been studying and announced, 'I've got a meeting at West Derby House at thirteen hundred hours, Grey. Going there with Lieutenant-Colonel Hartley in his staff car, so you may as well take your break now.' He paused and then added, 'In fact, you can escort the sergeant here to the first-aid station, to

317

make sure he gets there. And that's another order, Sergeant.'

'Thanks a bunch.'

They were on their own, sitting in the Bentley that Sam had just brought to a halt, having dropped the major off outside the officers' mess, and now the sergeant's angry words confirmed what Sam had already guessed.

For the first time in her life she adopted the nonconfrontational tactics she had seen her mother use to good effect during moment of domestic tension, and responded calmly, 'You're welcome. I owed you a favour for recommending me to the major.'

The sergeant, it seemed, was not as easily appeased as her father and her brother.

'This is a *favour*?' he demanded angrily. 'I've left ten men back there, with a thousand-pound bomb, a dodgy pump, and a captain who's still wet behind the ears.'

'I can see that you take your responsibilities to others very seriously,' Sam allowed, her normal outspokenness reviving as she added trenchantly, 'Shame that you don't take your responsibilities to yourself just as seriously. Do you want to walk over to the first-aid post, or . . . ?'

'Or what? You'll carry me?'

What on earth was her face burning for? And why for that split second had she had a mental image of his bare arm and her own awareness of the maleness of it and of him?

318

'You've lost a fair amount of blood,' she reminded him, pushing the image away, 'even if you are trying to pretend that you haven't. I could drive you there.'

'No, thanks, and what do you mean, my responsibilities to myself? Trust a woman to make a fuss over nothing. It's not as though I've cut an artery, after all.'

'No,' Sam agreed, 'if you'd done that you'd be dead by now. Still, at least that would have been a quick death, unlike the one you'll have if that cut gets infected and turns gangrenous.' Her stomach heaved and then clenched with horror whilst she fought not to let her voice wobble.

'And you'd know a lot about that, would you?'

'As a matter of fact, I would,' she told him truthfully. 'A friend of my brother's died from septicaemia. He cut his leg on a rusty scythe in his grandfather's garden. It was only a small cut, nothing much at all, but then his leg started to swell up. They tried to save him. They amputated his leg but it was too late and he died.' Sam spoke as briskly as she could, not wanting to remember the horror she had felt when the boys had talked about how Terry had died.

'I'll drive you over,' she told him.

He turned his head and looked at her, turned a smoky dark grey-eyed gaze on her that for some reason cause her heart to flip over. She half expected him to refuse to let her, and held her breath in anticipation of an argument.

'If you must,' he told her, giving in with a small shrug.

The medical unit was on the far side of the barracks, set apart from the other buildings. Sam parked the Bentley outside it and switched off the engine.

'Not coming in with me?' The laconic question caught Sam off guard.

'Well . . .'

'I'd have thought you'd want to make sure I see the doc, seeing as you seem to be taking personal responsibility for me avoiding death by gangrene,' he told her.

'It isn't something to joke about,' Sam insisted. Perhaps she should go with him just in case the major asked her to report back to him on the sergeant's condition.

'You looked as sick as a cat earlier at the site. What was up?'

'Nothing,' she denied.

'Liar. I've bin watching you: you don't like getting too close to the diggings. Why?'

'It isn't any of your business.'

'Everything that goes on around those bombs is my business, and if you were to go and do summat daft, like falling into one of them—'

'No!' Her sharp cry of panic had betrayed her, tipping her into the trap he had set for her, Sam realised as she saw the look in his eyes. 'Yes, all right,' she admitted angrily. 'I am scared silly that I might fall in. Go on, laugh if you want to.'

'I'm not laughing. What happened? And don't tell me nothing. Something must have done.'

He was using his free hand to remove his cigarettes from his pocket. He took two and lit them both, passing one over to her. Sam was too astonished to refuse it. She inhaled and then blew out the smoke, feeling it calm her nerves. He wasn't going to let the matter drop until he had got the truth out of her, so she might as well tell him, she acknowledged.

'I got trapped in a tunnel my brother and his pals had dug when I was a kid. It's stupid of me, I know, but now I can't . . .' Her voice was shaking again. She took another deep drag on the cigarette. 'I still have nightmares about it.'

'We all have those.'

Sam looked at him uncertainly. She couldn't imagine him being vulnerable in any way, never mind admitting it.

'Dunkirk,' he told her as though he had read her mind. 'The first boat I was in got hit and turned turtle. I thought I was going to drown.'

They looked at one another, and it was Sam who had to look away first. She opened the driver's door and got out of the car, leaving the sergeant to do the same, then she locked it. Sam was determined not to look at him again, but somehow or other she found that she was.

He threw down his cigarette and crushed it out with his foot, straightening up to lounge against the side of the car.

Putting out her own cigarette Sam went towards

321

him. As she reached him, to her shock he swayed and lurched forward. Immediately she went to support him.

He must have lost more blood than he'd admitted to, Sam decided worriedly when he sagged against her as they walked the short distance from the car to the Medical Unit.

'Here, let me help you.' She put her hand under his elbow on his uninjured arm. 'Mind the step.'

'What's all this then?' the nurse of duty asked briskly.

'Major Thomas asked me to bring Sergeant Everton over. He cut his arm whilst he was working on a pump,' Sam explained.

'Hmm, let's have a look.'

Sam saw the sergeant's mouth tighten slightly as the nurse briskly removed the bandage from his arm.

'Not very pretty, is it, but you'll live. I'll clean it up for you so that the doctor can get a proper look at it. This way.'

There was no real reason for her to stay and wait for him, but nevertheless Sam felt honour-bound to do so. It had shocked her when he had leaned on her. Somehow he just wasn't the sort of man she had expected to see give in to any kind of weakness, especially not in front of her.

He wasn't gone very long, returning in about ten minutes, a clean bandage on his arm.

'Now remember what the doctor said – no getting that wound wet or dirty until it's healed.'

'Cat got your tongue then, or are you just disappointed that they didn't keep me in to cut my arm off?' Sergeant Everton taunted Sam as they walked back to the car.

For some silly female, womanly reason, the thought of him without his arm made Sam's eyes sting sharply with threatening tears. Tears for him? This man who made her feel . . . but no, better by far that she didn't think of that. Just like she hadn't been thinking of it all week, pushing it out of sight because she was afraid? Quickly she blinked her tears away, not trusting her voice not to betray her as he opened the car door for her.

'The Bentley needs petrol,' she told him without looking at him.

'Fine,' he answered. 'I don't mind the ride.'

Sam said nothing. She had been going to suggest that she dropped him off first and then drove to the fuel store.

'You handle the car well.'

'For a woman?' Sam suggested through gritted teeth.

'I didn't say that. Turn left here,' he told her

Thinking he knew a short cut to the petrol store, Sam automatically did as he had instructed, only to find she had driven into a narrow cul-de-sac surrounded by windowless stores.

'What . . . ?' she began, but the sergeant shook his head.

'Switch off the engine for a minute.'

'What for?'

'There's something I want to talk to you about.'

Something . . . didn't he really mean someone,

that someone being Frank Brookes? He didn't know just how very badly he was getting things wrong, and she intended to make sure that he never knew, even if that meant letting him continue to think badly of her. If she had been in danger of having some kind of silly crush on the other sergeant, she definitely didn't have one now, and the reason she was so clearly aware of what her true feelings were was sitting right here next to her, and those feelings were becoming clearer – and stronger – with every hour, never mind every day, she spent in his company. Not, of course, that she could ever or would ever tell Sergeant Johnny Everton that she had done the most stupid thing she could and that she suspected she had fallen in love with him.

'What kind of something?' she asked him warily.

'This kind of something.'

For a man whose arm was heavily bandaged he was able to put it round her very quickly and easily, but Sam wasn't able to say so for the very good reason that with him kissing her the way he was doing she wasn't capable of thinking or saying anything.

So this was kissing . . . proper kissing . . . the kind that made a 'good', 'nice' girl forget that she was any such thing and ache very much to be something else. Her heart was beating so heavily and loudly it was drowning out any inner warning voice that might have been trying to make itself heard.

When Johnny lifted his mouth from hers she

made a small soft sound and declared in a wobbly voice, 'You kissed me!'

He still had his arm around her, and she could see his mouth curving into a smile.

'Yes,' he agreed, 'and I'm going to kiss you again.'

This time the pleasure was deeper and sweeter, running through her body like liquid heat, making her physically aware of herself as a woman; making her wrap her own arms around his neck and hold on to him whilst she closed her eyes and trembled under the shocking intensity of their intimacy.

She was still trembling slightly when the kiss ended, and so, she saw with swift hot pleasure, was Johnny.

'Why?' she asked him dizzily, both of them knowing that she wasn't asking him why he had kissed her so much as why this had happened to them; why they had both been caught up in this intense desire for one another, which neither of them had encouraged or wanted. 'We don't like each other.'

'You're not exactly my type,' he agreed.

Jealousy, sharp-clawed and sabre-toothed, savaged her, making her catch her breath. 'And you aren't mine.'

'Maybe not, but you haven't had time to experience what your type is. I have.'

'Meaning what?'

'Meaning that I should know better. Less than a month ago you were mooning around all big-eyed over Frank, looking at him like a kid with her nose pressed up against the window of a sweet shop, and with about as much understanding of men-and-women stuff as that kid. You're a baby still, a tomboy who hasn't learned yet to be a woman.'

'I'm twenty-one,' Sam defended herself.

'What I'm talking about doesn't have anything to do with age. Some girls are born as old and knowing as Eve, but not you. This is crazy. If I had any sense I'd walk away from it and from you right now, for your sake as well as mine.'

'I don't understand.'

She didn't. She felt as though her heart was being wrenched in two. How could he have kissed her in the way that he had and now be saying what he was?

'No, of course you don't. How can you? There's too much of a gulf between us for you and me to be right together. You're still learning things I learned long ago. By rights I ought to leave you to do your growing up with boys who are doing some growing up of their own, boys who you can flirt with and then walk away from. I've already done all of that. And more,' he told her meaningfully.

Sam's heart gave a funny little painful thud. 'I could do those things with you,' she forced herself to say.

He was looking away from her now, but she could see the way his mouth hardened.

'Yeah? The fact that you think so is just one of the reasons why you're too young for me. You haven't been to those places yet, and I need a woman who has. A woman, Sam, not a naïve girl. And even if I could find her I'd have no right to ask her to share my life, and even less right to ask you.'

Sam gave a small whimper of anguish. 'You can't say that.'

'Yes I can.' He swore savagely beneath his breath. 'Have you any idea what the average life expectancy is for someone working on UXBs?' he demanded.

Now it was her turn to look away from him. She knew perfectly well how dangerous what he was doing was and that on average the lives of men working on the ground in bomb disposal were measured in months and not years, and that that was why most of the men were unattached.

She heard him exhale, then saw his chest expand as he refilled his lungs with air. Out of nowhere she was filled with a longing to touch him, to press her hand against his flesh and to feel the beat of his heart beneath it. She knew that for as long as the war continued she would never be free of her fears for his safety, and that her love for him was what chained her to that fear.

'I should never have started any of this.'

'Yes, you should,' Sam told him.

'I should have left you to do your growing up with someone else. You're such a kid still.'

'No. I'm not.'

He looked at her in derision. 'You didn't even know that I wanted you until I kissed you, did you?'

'No . . . but . . .'

'But what?'

'I knew when you did kiss me how good it felt and how much I wanted you.'

It was the wrong thing to have said – if she had still been that girl he was deriding. But she wasn't, and it certainly wasn't wrong for the woman she now was. For her, that woman, it was entirely right, and she could feel that in the grip of his fingers on her arms, see it in the glitter of his eyes, hear it in the rapid way he was breathing.

'Don't,' he groaned. 'That's one hell of a dangerous thing to say to a man, especially when he's been thinking the thoughts about you that I've been thinking these last few weeks.'

He was weakening, Sam could sense it.

'We're living in dangerous times,' she reminded him. 'Life is dangerous and precious, too precious to be wasted, so why shouldn't love be the same?'

There, she'd said it, that one small word that changed everything between them beyond any going back.

'Love!' He breathed the word as though it was torturing him, sliding one hand into her hair, his fingers splayed against the back of her head as he twisted her round so that she was half lying against him; half lying *beneath* him, the weight of his torso pressing her into the leather seat whilst he kissed her fiercely and possessively, teaching her the potent intimacies of kissing as easily as he had shown her the sensuality of dancing. But even more extraordinary to her than how he felt about her was her own uninhibited and eager response to him, her complete willingness to be swept up and possessed by the feelings he had aroused within her. It was like flying, Sam decided helplessly, dizzy with joy and excitement, a kind of freedom and delight that took her soaring to heights that giddied her, into an atmosphere where what she breathed released bubbles of intoxication into her veins.

'You haven't the first idea of what love is, or what it does to a man.'

Her heart was thudding so heavily she felt sure he must be able to feel it. 'Then show me,' she urged him softly.

She could see shock, followed by excitement, darkening his eyes. He exhaled again as though in defeat.

'You're playing with fire now,' he warned her. 'Do you know that?'

Mutely Sam shook her head, although she knew perfectly well what he meant. He might call her naïve, but she wasn't that naïve.

'I've been wanting you like this ever since that first night,' Johnny was telling her, softly rubbing the pad of his thumb over the swollen contours of her mouth and then smiling when he saw her response to his touch. 'Even though I've fought like hell not to. All that blood I've lost must have weakened me, and now look what's happened.'

'What has happened?' Sam whispered.

'What has happened is that you've made me break my own rules and go crazy for the kind of girl who doesn't have the first idea of what she's doing to me. The kind of girl that a chap doesn't play around with. A wedding vows and for ever kind of girl. Because that's what you are, isn't it, Sam?'

'Yes,' she admitted.

'So there it is,' he told her lightly. 'You and me.'

His words brought Sam back to reality with a sharp jolt, guilt flooding her as she remembered what she ought to have been thinking about all along.

'But what about Lynsey?'

'Lynsey?'

'Yes. You've been seeing her, after all, and she thinks that you and she . . .' She could feel herself floundering.

'Seeing her? I haven't been seeing anyone,' Johnny denied.

'Lynsey's told everyone that you and she are an item.'

'Well, she's lying because we aren't.'

Sam looked up into his eyes and knew that no matter what Lynsey had said, Johnny was telling her the truth.

'The thing is, Sam, you've got a lot of growing up to do before you catch up with me, and I don't rightly know if it's fair to you for me to want you to do that growing up exclusively with me, or if it's fair to meself to take the risk that you won't take off and want to do it with someone else.'

'I'd never do that,' Sam protested.

'You can say that now but things change, people change.'

'I won't.'

'You shouldn't say that, Sam.'

'Why not, when it's the truth?' she demanded.

'Because like I said, a person can change. Any person.' He gave a small shrug.

The way he was talking was beginning to make her feel anxious and uncertain, plummeting her down into despair where only minutes ago he had taken her up to the heights of dizzy excitement and joy.

'I knew the moment I met you that you were trouble, the kind of girl a man could never relax around because he'd be forever wondering just what the hell kind of trouble she was going to get herself into next,' he was telling her. 'The kind of girl who a man needs to keep a constant watch out for in case she hurts herself. If you want the truth, when I saw the way you were going all big-eyed over Frank I was pleased, or at least I would have been if it hadn't been that I know he's married to Molly. You see, the way I looked at it, you wanting him should have made it easy for me to not want you myself.' He shook his head. 'You aren't my type.'

Sam tried hard not to let him see how much those last few words hurt her. 'So what is your type?' she asked him as brightly as she could.

'Quiet, gentle girls who don't keep a man awake at night.'

'I keep you awake then, do I?'

The look he gave her made her feel as though a jolt of electricity had struck right through her body.

'That's what I mean about you still having a lot to learn, Sam. If you had learned you wouldn't need to ask me that question; you'd know that I can't sleep at night for thinking of you and wanting you.'

She closed her eyes, excitement and joy sizzling through her.

Sally saw him whilst she was queuing up inside the butcher's. She was just looking through the window to check that Tommy was standing where she had left him with Harry in the pushchair, lined up between two large prams, when she saw him coming down the street.

It didn't matter she told herself, not even if he saw them. Why should it? He had told her himself that the Boss had said she would give her a bit more time – and charge a lot more interest. If she kept her back turned to the window then Sid the debt collector probably wouldn't even see her, but the problem was that she couldn't do that. Not with Tommy and Harry outside. Tommy was a good boy and she had told him to stay with Harry and the pushchair, but he was only three and easily distracted, and three-year-olds could wander off and get themselves into all sorts of danger and mischief.

Sid had drawn level with the shop now. Quickly Sally looked the other way but not quickly enough, and her heart sank when she realised that he had seen her. He was standing outside now and . . .

Sally's heart jerked on its maternal strings as

she saw him say something to Tommy, putting one hand on the pushchair handle as he did so.

'Excuse me . . .'

''Ere, wot's going on? There's a queue here, you know.'

'Hang on a minute, love, it's your turn next . . .'

'I'm sorry,' Sally apologised, ignoring the objections of the woman behind her in the queue packed into the narrow shop, as she caught her with her basket in her desperation to get to her sons.

'Watch what you're doing,' she complained, but Sally didn't have time to apologise or explain.

'Thought these must be your two,' the debt collector said to her. 'They've got a look of you.'

'Come on, Tommy,' Sally urged her son as she took hold of the pushchair, trying desperately to sidestep Sid.

'What's your rush?' He was standing in front of her now, blocking her exit, coming towards her so that she was forced to back away from him and into the shadows. 'I've bin thinking. Can't be easy for you with your hubby gone. I'll bet you're lonely too wi'out a man. Why don't I call round after I've finished me round on Friday and you and me could have a bit of a chat?'

The leer on his face told Sally everything she needed to know about his intentions. Her stomach curdled with loathing and disgust.

'I'll tell you what, why don't I walk back wi' you now? Come on, son, you hold my hand.'

'No!' Sally almost shouted her fear-filled denial but it was too late, he was already reaching out to take her son. Sally reacted with a strength and speed she hadn't known she possessed.

'Let go of him.' She pulled Tommy away from Sid, holding the little boy tightly to her side and slightly behind her in an attempt to protect him. In retaliation the debt collector stepped forward and put his hand on her shoulder, standing so close to her that she could smell the sour odour of his breath.

'I'm the one who gives the orders, not you, and don't you go forgetting it.' He squeezed her shoulder hard, making her flinch and cry out in pain.

Tommy's face had started to crumple.

'Leave us alone,' Sally snapped.

'Now that's not a nice way to talk to someone who wants to be friendly, is it? In fact if I was you I'd think about being a bit more careful, 'cos a person might just take offence, and we don't want that, do we?' His hand had moved from her shoulder to her throat, and as he finished speaking his fingers tightened, almost choking her. How far he would have gone if two women who Sally knew by sight and who lived a couple of streets away from Chestnut Close hadn't been coming towards them Sally didn't know.

As it was she made good use of the opportunity they had unknowingly given her to escape. Taking advantage of the debt collector releasing her, she pushed the pram towards them, saying with the kind of forwardness she would never normally have exhibited, 'You'll be walking back my way, I expect. I'll walk along with you, if you don't mind.'

She knew that Sid would not risk following her in broad daylight, but she also knew that the danger she was in now was far greater than it had been, and that the next time he came knocking on her door it would not just be money he would be expecting to collect from her.

There was only one thing she could do now, only one option left open to her.

TWENTY-ONE

The minute they were safely inside the house, Sally set to work. She had dragged a pair of heavy wooden step ladders in from the garden shed, locked both the back and front doors and then struggled to get the step ladders up the stairs so that she could drag down from the loft space the battered dust-covered suitcases that had lain there ever since her and Ronnie's honeymoon. She wouldn't be able to take anything she couldn't carry, so she would just have to take what was essential. The rest of their things she would have to ask Doris to store for them until such time as it was safe for her to come back and get them. Not that she intended to tell her neighbour what she was planning to do until the very last minute.

As she feverishly opened drawers and removed their contents, her mind raced ahead of her shaking hands, her body stiffening as she heard someone knocking on the front door. Before she could stop him Tommy got up from the floor where he had been playing and raced into the front room, pressing his face up against the window as he looked to see who it was.

'It's my doctor,' he told Sally excitedly. 'Mummy, let him in.'

'No, Tommy . . .' Sally began, but she knew that it was too late for her to pretend that they weren't in. The doctor had already seen Tommy at the window and if she refused to answer the door no doubt he would decide that she must be neglecting her sons and he'd keep on knocking on until she let him in.

Wherever they ended up going – and she had no idea yet just where that was going to be, except that it would be a long way from Liverpool and in the country – she intended to make sure that it was somewhere where they didn't have an nosy parker interfering doctor, who seemed to think that she wasn't capable of looking after her own sons just because he had seen her singing on stage in a dance hall, she decided angrily as she unlocked and opened the front door.

'I've been visiting a patient close by so I thought I'd call and see how—'

'Call and check up on me to make sure that I'm not being a bad mother, don't you mean?' Sally finished acidly as he stepped into the hall. Before she closed the door she looked outside quickly, fearing that the debt collector might be hanging around, but to her relief there was no sign of him, not yet. But it wasn't dark yet, and men like him preferred to slink out under the cover of darkness, using it to cloak what they were doing.

'I thought I'd call and see how both you and the boys are,' the doctor told her, ignoring her outburst.

'I suppose you'd better come through then,' Sally offered grudgingly. 'Only I'm a bit busy. I'm having a bit of a clear-out,' she added, acutely aware of the untidiness of the parlour with drawers and cupboards open, their contents spilling out. 'I'd offer you a cup of tea but, as you can see, I'm in a bit of a mess.'

'That's all right.' Ignoring her, Dr Ross crouched down so that he was on Tommy's level, a dimple creasing his chin as he smiled warmly at her son. Sally couldn't tear her gaze away from the picture the two of them made, their heads close together, Tommy leaning against the doctor, the doctor's arm around his shoulder, both of them engrossed in some kind of male communication that totally excluded her. A sharp pang of loss and pain struck at her heart. This was how Ronnie should have been with his sons, but they would never share a father and son relationship with him now; her boys would never know what it was to have a father's love, just as the doctor would never be able to see his own sons growing up. A man who had lost his children and two children who had lost their father – they were in a way united by those losses, her sons and the doctor.

Looking at them, Sally suddenly felt excluded, and even jealous that Tommy should make it so obvious how much he liked the doctor, running to him instead of clinging to her.

338

'I can see that both the boys are looking well and have some good healthy colour in their cheeks,' Dr Ross told her as he stood up.

'We've just come back from the shops,' Sally told him shortly.

Tommy moved closer to the doctor and told him, 'There was a nasty man at the shops. I didn't like him.'

'Tommy,' Sally tried to stop him, but it was too late.

'Didn't you, old son?' the doctor answered, ruffling Tommy's hair.

'No. He hurt my mummy and made her cry.'

How could something as simple as silence make her stomach churn as though she was about to be sick, Sally wondered as she struggled for something to say.

The doctor had moved closer to her son, and Tommy was leaning against him now, within the protection of his arm, both male gazes fixed on her but with very different expressions in them.

'How did he do that then, Tommy?' the doctor was asking him, bending to his level but without removing his gaze from Sally's guilt-ridden face.

'He did this to her,' Tommy told him, demonstrating the debt collector's grip of her throat with the small span of his own hand against the doctor's throat.

Another silence. Sally swallowed uncomfortably.

'Why don't you go and play with Harry for a minute, Tommy, whilst I have a word with your mummy?'

'No!' Sally protested, but it was too late, Tommy was already going over to the playpen she had put Harry in whilst she started to sort through their things.

'I'd better take a look at your neck. Come over here into the light.'

'No . . . no . . . it was nothing. I'm fine. Tommy got it wrong. It was just a bit of fooling around . . .'

The long cool fingers touched her skin with clinical detachment, whilst the sick anxiety in the pit of her stomach doubled and then trebled.

'A bit of love play from an overardent admirer, you mean?'

'No!' She jerked back from him, her eyes blazing with anger. 'Nothing like that! I've only just lost my husband and that sort of thing is the last thought on my mind. I've got my boys to consider.'

'So he attacked you then?'

'No! That is . . .'

'Well, he's certainly left his mark on you. You've got a bruise coming up already.'

A key rattled in the back door, causing Sally to jump nervously but it was only Doris, beaming at them both as she let herself in.

'I saw the doctor's car outside on my way back from Molly and Frank's so I thought I'd better call and see if everything is all right.'

'Everything's fine.'

'Tommy has just been telling me that his mother was attacked in the street.'

'What?' Doris sat down heavily, looking

340

shocked. 'After your purse, I expect. You'll have to tell the police.'

'Although Mrs Walker claims the man in question was merely being—'

'He was just someone who used to hang around the singers at the Grafton. You always get them – men who can't take a hint that you aren't interested in them,' Sally rushed in to stop him from saying any more. 'He'd heard about Ronnie and . . .' she gave a small shrug, 'it was nothing really.'

'It was enough to worry and upset Tommy,' the doctor pointed out.

Doris shook her head. 'Well, it's typical of you not wanting to cause a fuss, Sally love, but you'll have to watch out, you know. Sally, that sort don't know how to take no for an answer. What you need is a chap around the place to send him about his business. I don't like to think what could happen if he takes it into his head to come round here pestering you.'

'He won't, and even if he does . . .' she took a deep breath. This wasn't how she'd planned to break her news to Doris but now she felt she didn't have any choice. 'It won't matter. I've made up me mind. We're leaving here. I'm taking the boys away . . . to the country.'

Now Doris looked even more shocked, but it was Dr Ross who looked at her sharply and demanded coolly, 'Are you sure that's a good idea?'

'You were the one as said the boys would be safer evacuated,' she reminded him. 'Now that my Ronnie's gone, me and them may as well have a fresh start. The country's safer than living here.'

'I can understand that you might feel vulnerable living here on your own, but have you thought
this through properly? Have you got a job to go
to, for instance, and somewhere to live?'

Sally knew that her expression was giving her
away. 'Jobs are easy to find now there's a war on,
and I reckon I'll easily get a billet.'

'*You* might, but I doubt you'd find anyone
willing to take on a family. I've got a better idea.
It just so happens that I've been looking for a live-
in housekeeper to . . . to take charge of the house
and act as my receptionist. You'd have your own
rooms on the top floor of the house and there's a
fair-sized garden at the back for the boys to play
in.'

'*Me*, come and work for *you*?'

Sally shook her head in vehement denial, but
before she could refuse him properly, Doris stepped
in, insisting firmly, 'Don't be daft, Sally love. Dr
Ross is right; you'd be much better going working
for him than taking yourself off to the country,
and if this man does come looking for you then
the doctor will be able to tell him where to go.
She'll do it, Dr Ross, and a very good job she'll
do for you as well, even though I say it meself,'
Doris accepted, before Sally could stop her. 'A
good housewife, is Sally, and a good mother as
well.'

Sally still tried to protest, though, shaking her
head again and saying, 'No,' but she knew she
was wasting her breath. The doctor and Doris had

both made up their minds and Sally could see that they weren't going to change them.

'Right, now that's decided,' the doctor told her firmly. 'If you want to pack what you and the boys will need for tonight, I'll drive you home with me and then we can sort everything else out in the morning. I dare say Mrs Brookes won't mind asking her son to keep an eye on the house for you until you've had time to speak to your land-lord.'

Things were moving far too fast and in a direc-tion Sally would never have chosen but at the same time she was forced to admit that living under the doctor's roof would certainly protect her from Sid's unwanted sexual attentions. He would never dare to try to force himself on her there in the way that he would have done if she had been an unpro-tected widow living on her own with two small children.

She would still have her debt to repay, though, she reminded herself tiredly. It seemed that fate wasn't going to allow her to walk away from it in the way she had heard Peg describing, and deep down she knew it would be wrong for her to do so. Her stubborn pride wanted her to be able to repay the money and hold her head up high.

'Sam, are you listening to me?'

Guiltily Sam tried to drag her thoughts away from the pleasure of thinking about Johnny to focus on what Hazel was saying to her.

'You've been lost in such a daydream these last

few days that anyone would think you'd fallen in love,' Hazel joked, her expression changing when Sam went bright red and ducked her head, admitting, 'Well, they'd be right because I have.'

'What? Who with? Sam, what's going on? I don't want to throw cold water on anything but, well, Russell has asked me to watch out for you, and I do know that you haven't been seeing anyone.'

'I have, it's just that no one knew. Not even me. I've been seeing him nearly every day, but . . . well, not in the way that you mean. And he's only just said now that he . . .' Sam stopped and laughed self-consciously. 'The thing is, Hazel, he didn't want to fall for me and he's a bit worried that he's out of my league experiencewise. But that doesn't matter to me . . . well,' Sam's colour deepened. 'Personally I'd rather have a man who knows what's what, especially with me not knowing much at all.'

'Sam!' Hazel sounded faintly scandalised.

'It's the truth, that is how I feel.' Now Sam could see that Hazel was looking more concerned than convinced.

'It sounds to me very much as though he's giving you a bit of a line, Sam. My ex was pretty keen to let me know when we first met that he knew a thing or two he was more than willing to teach me. Men like that know how to turn a girl's head and how to steal her heart. Take it from me.'

'Johnny isn't like that,' Sam defended her new-found love indignantly.

Hazel shook her head. 'Sam, I do understand

how you feel, and I know too that war changes things, because none of us knows quite what tomorrow will bring or even if we'll have a tomorrow, but that doesn't mean that a girl should necessarily trust every young man she meets. Even pretty decent sorts can be tempted if they think they can sweet-talk a girl into doing something she shouldn't.'

Sam could understand that Hazel's own experience would make her cautious, and even a bit cynical, but she was determined to make sure that Hazel understood just how special and wonderful Johnny was.

'Johnny isn't trying to sweet-talk me into anything,' she assured her. 'In fact, he told me that he didn't want to fall for me and that he'd rather he hadn't done.'

Hazel was looking even more concerned. 'Oh, Sam, please do be careful,' she urged her. 'I'd hate to see you get hurt.'

'I'm not going to be hurt,' Sam insisted stoutly. 'Johnny would never hurt me.'

Hazel gave a small sigh. 'Why don't you tell me a bit more about him?'

Sam could tell that Hazel was not going to be put off.

'I wasn't going to say anything yet,' she answered her, 'but I can see that I'm going to have to come clean. When Johnny was just Sergeant Everton, I never imagined that he and I—'

'Sergeant *Everton*?' Hazel was looking at her as though she couldn't believe her own ears. 'You mean that good-looking bomb disposal chap that Lynsey's crazy about?'

'Yes,' Sam admitted. 'But it isn't like you think, Hazel. I'm not stealing him from her. Johnny says there's never been anything between them and that he isn't interested in her,' she insisted defensively.

'He might have told *you* that,' Hazel said doubtfully, 'but it certainly isn't what Lynsey thinks.'

'It's true,' Sam insisted fiercely. 'I know it is. He wouldn't lie to me. He isn't like that.'

'Well, I can see how you feel about him, and of course you're bound to want to believe him, but I can't help wishing that you'd fallen in love with someone else. He's obviously convinced you that there was nothing going on between him and Lynsey, and maybe there wasn't, but Lynsey's made it plain enough to all of us that she's got her eye on him and she won't take kindly to this.'

'Johnny didn't even recognise her name when I mentioned her to him, for all that she's been running after him and telling everyone that they're an item.'

'Oh, Sam,' Hazel repeated helplessly, 'do be careful, please. This sergeant of yours is a handsome chap. Don't let him sweet-talk you into doing something you might regret because he's telling you there's a war on.'

'I know what you're saying, and Johnny's behaving like a perfect gentleman,' Sam defended him.

'Mm, whilst kissing you breathless and making you wish that he wasn't quite so gentlemanly, I'll be bound,' Hazel guessed shrewdly. 'Don't go rushing into something you might regret, Sam.'

Sam couldn't help but feel a bit put out and hurt. 'I thought you'd understand. After all, you and Russell have only just met.'

'Russell isn't Sergeant Everton.'

'You're beginning to sound as though you're trying to say that you don't believe that Johnny could love me. I know that I'm not as pretty or curvy as Lynsey . . .'

Hazel looked horrified. 'Sam, no . . . I never meant to imply that you aren't every bit as lovable as Lynsey – of course you are. In fact you are a far nicer person than she is. It's just that men like him . . . well, I just don't want to see you get hurt, that's all. I'm sure he genuinely is attracted to you but men like him are very good at getting girls to fall in love with them. It's part of what they do best. Just . . . just don't . . .' Hazel shook her head. 'What am I saying? I can see that you're head over heels about him, and I'm sure he's everything I know you're burning to tell me that he is, but I still can't help worrying about you and feeling that you're going to end up being hurt.'

'Well, you needn't worry because I know I won't be hurt,' Sam told her lightly, not wanting Hazel to see how much her well-meant words had upset her, and how close she felt to tears. Hazel's comments had punctured the bright shiny bubble of joy in which she had been living since she and Johnny had declared their love for one another. Now she wished that she had kept her news to herself. She felt as though that she had been backed into a corner from which she had had to defend not only their love but Johnny himself as well.

First Johnny and now Hazel. Why couldn't they both see that she was perfectly capable of knowing her own mind and her own heart, even if what she was living through now was all new for her?

Her experience of men and falling in love, as both Johnny and Hazel had hinted, was less than that of other girls her age. But now that she knew he felt the same way about her, her whole world had become sky blue with golden sunshine.

Of course there would have been other girls; she was not so silly as to think any different. Johnny was well into his twenties and, as Hazel herself had already said, a very handsome and sexually attractive man.

A handsome and sexually attractive man who had once thought he loved someone else, she reminded herself. But that had been *then*, and it had been over and done with before he had met *her*, and anyway he would never have told her about it if she, whoever she was, had been really important to him, Sam reassured herself. Johnny was hers now.

Tiredly Sally sat back on her knees and surveyed the freshly scrubbed kitchen floor of what had become their new home.

She certainly had nothing to complain about in the spacious rooms on the third floor of the house, one for each of the boys, although she had kept them sharing a room as company for one another and because it was what they were used to, and a bedroom for her, their own bathroom and even a sitting room, although the doctor has insisted that they were to think of the kitchen and the morning room next to it, both with access to the large enclosed back garden, as theirs as well.

His surgery occupied one large bay-windowed room on either side of the front door on the ground floor of the large and elegant doubled-fronted house. As his receptionist and housekeeper Sally was to answer the door and the telephone for his patients, and to maintain a diary of their visits and appointments. Doris seemed to think she should feel overjoyed, but then of course Doris did not know the true situation.

But Sally realised that virtually everyone who knew her would share Doris's view, and consider her to be very fortunate indeed. She even had her own furniture in the top-floor rooms now, Doris having chivvied Frank and a couple of his friends to 'borrow' an army lorry and move it for her.

'But, Doris, the doctor might change his mind, and not want to keep me on,' she had protested, thinking that she would be looking for an excuse to leave just as soon as she could, and that leaving would be that much harder if she had her furniture to shift.

'Nonsense, of course he won't change his mind,' Doris had told her. 'In fact, the more I think about it, the more I reckon it's going to suit you both down to the ground. You'll have a steady job and be at home with your kiddies, and the doctor will have someone he can rely on to make sure he's properly looked after. A man needs that, especially a doctor.'

'Mrs Walker, I wonder if you could come into my office for a moment. I want to have a word with you . . . oh!'

The doctor might look disconcerted to find her on her knees scrubbing the floor but that was nothing to how she felt at having him stand there in his immaculate clothes looking down on her, her hair tired up in a turban and her face shiny with perspiration.

'I'll just go and get myself cleaned up first, if you don't mind, Dr Ross,' Sally answered.

'It wasn't my intention that you should scrub floors. I employ a daily to come in and do the rough work.'

Sally could hear the distaste in his voice. Did he think that having his housekeeper and receptionist do something as menial as scrubbing floors somehow belittled him, she thought angrily If so, she didn't share his views, not one little bit. She would be thoroughly ashamed of herself if the day ever came when she was too proud to scrub floors. Not that that was likely.

'Maybe you do,' she told him forthrightly, 'but whoever she is she doesn't do a very thorough job. There's no way I'd want me or my kiddies eating in a kitchen with a floor as filthy as this one was.'

It pleased her to see him looking taken aback. 'I see. I'm afraid I hadn't realised.'

'Well, there's no reason why you should, is there? That's my job, to notice things like that. Perhaps you'd like me to bring a tray of tea through for you when I'm cleaned up?'

'That's an excellent idea – make sure you put an extra cup on it for yourself, please.'

Didn't he understand that she didn't want him treating her nicely, Sally fumed as she stood in the cold bathroom to have a strip wash. It put her at a disadvantage and made her feel even more angrily resentful than she already was. She didn't want to have to feel grateful to him and to have to listen to everyone else telling her how lucky she was, and she most certainly didn't want those dangerous feelings that kept sneaking up on her and catching her off guard, like they had done this morning when she had thought how much better he looked now that he was getting some decent home cooking.

Washed and dressed in a clean blouse and skirt, she brushed her hair, tugging the brush through her soft brunette curls, before checking on the boys who were playing happily in their new surroundings, warmed by the good fire the doctor had insisted they were to have.

Ten minutes later she balanced the tea tray she was carrying carefully before knocking on the door to the doctor's office.

Instead of calling out to her to go in as she had expected, the doctor came and opened the door for her himself.

Startled by the unexpectedness of his action Sally looked up at him. He was looking straight back at her. Her heart started to beat far faster than she wanted. She could hear the china rattling slightly on the tray because her hands were trembling. She wanted desperately to look away from him, but somehow she couldn't. What was happening to her? This wasn't right. It wasn't right at all.

'Let me take that tray for you.'

Let him take the tray? How could she do that? He was her employer and yet here he was treating her as though they were equals. Sally shook her head.

'It's all right. I can manage.'

It was too late, though. He was already reaching for the tray. Their hands met, his covering hers, almost as though he were holding them.

Sally felt her heart jump. The only hands she held these days were those of her two sons. It was a long time since she had thought of the touch of another hand against her own as something that could make her heart beat faster and fill her with an awareness of a man's strength and tenderness.

It was a long time too since a man's hands had covered her own in this kind of simple domestic unintended intimacy. The kind of intimacy that might be shared between husband and wife.

A yearning she didn't want to feel ached through her. For *Ronnie*, and everything she had lost, she reassured herself. Not for anything else, or anyone else. But still she couldn't move.

A piece of coal hissed in the grate. The doctor released her and went over to the fire, freeing Sally to carry the tray to his desk, whilst he used the tongs to restore the lump of coal to the fire.

'I thought we'd be more comfortable having our tea here in front of the fire, Sally,' he said.

Sally stiffened before she picked up the tray and carried it over to the tea table close to the fire. He was treating her almost as his equal, which she was not, and she could only assume that it must stem from some peculiar Scottish practice. Certainly no one in Liverpool would behave like that to someone they were employing in their home. If he wasn't careful he could have her thinking all sorts of daft stuff, and that wouldn't do anyone any good, would it?

'Would you like me to pour for you, Doctor?' she asked him with extra formality, just to show him that whilst he may not know how to behave as an employer, she knew what her own role was. She could feel him looking at her but she refused to look back, determinedly focusing on pouring his tea, whilst equally determinedly not pouring a cup for herself.

She thought she heard him sigh faintly but he made no comment, saying only, 'We haven't talked yet about wages. That is my omission and one for which I apologise. I had thought that five guineas per week . . .'

Five guineas a week! That was a fortune. More

than she would have earned getting danger money working on munitions. It would mean, though, that living here in this house 'all found', so she wouldn't have to spend anything on food, rent or services, would allow her to save virtually all her earnings to pay off the outstanding debt on the money Ronnie had borrowed. Since, thanks to Doris making it impossible for her to refuse to take the job in the first place, and her own conscience, she couldn't run away from her debt, she could have been tempted to thank the doctor and take the money. But there was that 'conscience' and so instead she shook her head firmly, and told him, 'That's far too much. They'd be struggling to earn that much at the munitions factory, doing work that's dangerous.'

'You haven't met my patients yet,' he answered, so straight-faced that it took Sally several seconds to realise that he had made a joke.

'I think that five guineas is a very fair amount,' Dr Ross continued. 'After all, you are combining two roles, that of housekeeper and receptionist, and you will in effect have to act as my lieutenant, as it were, when I am away from my surgery at the hospital. I shall be relying on you to make a note for me of which patients I may need to see urgently.'

Sally gave a small gasp of protest. 'I don't know anything about people being sick.'

'Not in technical terms but you are an intelligent woman and a mother, and I am sure you have a very good instinct for what is genuine and what is not.'

Sally didn't know what to say. No one had ever told her before that she was intelligent.

Five guineas a week! With that amount of money coming in and no rent to pay she'd be able to save up enough to pay off her debt, provided the Boss didn't keep on increasing the interest. Perhaps as 'an intelligent woman' she ought to be firm and tell the Boss that the original debt was all she was getting!

'There is one thing that I must stress to you, though, and that is under no circumstances are either you or the boys to use the first-floor bathroom, which is set aside for the use of my patients, and which must be kept clean, and indeed should be cleaned after its use by a patient.'

Had she really thought he was treating her as an equal? Well, more fool her. He obviously thought that whilst she was good enough to get down on her hands and knees and scrub the bathroom upstairs, she was not good enough to use it.

'You needn't worry about that, Doctor,' Sally responded through gritted teeth. 'I shall make sure that we know our place.'

'I think you've misunderstood me. It isn't a matter of anyone knowing their place. I simply don't want you or your sons exposed to any kind of infection or disease my patients might bring in. That is why I insist on them having a separate bathroom and why I should like you to make sure that you keep separate cleaning things for it. Good hygiene is a very important tool in a doctor's armoury. I learned that very quickly in Glasgow's slums.'

Sally wasn't sure she liked the feeling that being wrong-footed by him gave her.

'Will you be wanting me to wear a uniform?' she asked.

'No,' he told her curtly, adding, 'You seem to think that your role here is to be one of subservience and servitude, whereas what I want is for us to work together as equals in a team.'

Sally couldn't believe her ears. Did he really think she was going to believe that? 'Equals!' she repeated scornfully, too infuriated to think about being careful. 'That's rich! You're a doctor, you live in a big posh house – how can you talk about someone like me being your equal?'

'You're right. The boy I was when I was growing up would be someone you would have looked down on with contempt. I can see from your expression that you don't believe me, but it's true. I grew up in a tenement block in one of Glasgow's slums. My father, a schoolteacher, died just before I was born, and my mother remarried. I didn't get on with my stepfather and I was always in trouble. I got more beatings that I got hot dinners. If it hadn't been for the kindness and generosity of our local vicar I'd still be living in that slum. He and his wife took me in; they fed my mind as well as my body. When they were moved to another parish they asked my mother if they could take me with them. She had other children by then with her new husband, and to tell the truth I think she was glad to see me go.'

Sally couldn't look at him. She didn't want him

to see the shocked pity in her eyes. 'I expect she wanted to do what she thought was best for you,' she told him quietly. 'It must have hurt her to let you go.'

'It's a kind thought, but I doubt that she did. She's dead now so I'll never actually know. My adoptive parents became close friends with the doctor in the small town we'd moved to. He was kind to me and encouraged my interest in medicine. I've been very lucky to have people in my life who've helped me to achieve my dream of becoming a doctor and in turn helping others, but make no mistake, nothing can change the beginnings I came from, or the way one is judged because of them, even if I was once foolish enough to think otherwise. Now, you will need some housekeeping money. How much do you think you will require each month for food and other necessities?'

Sally kept a close watch on what she spent and knew to the penny how much it cost to keep a roof over their heads and buy their food each week, but when she gave the doctor this sum he shook his head and told her, 'That won't be enough. I shall pay all the household bills, of course, but I don't want you to short-change the boys out of some foolish notion that you have to stick to a budget that isn't sufficient. No, I shall open accounts at any shops you wish to recommend and we will take things from there.'

'You're being very generous,' Sally felt obliged to say. 'Far too generous, in fact. It's no wonder the girl you've got coming in to do some cleaning doesn't do it properly. She'll have recognised that she can take advantage of you. She'll find that she's going to have to pull her socks up a bit.' There was a martial glint in Sally's eyes.

'Well, I've said my piece, so is there anything you want to ask me? Anything within the house you might want to see changed?'

Sally hesitated and then said quietly, 'Well, since you've asked, I'm a bit worried about the boys coming to live here, especially Tommy.'

'How so? They'll have more room and a bigger garden and—'

'It's nothing like that.'

'What is it then?'

She had known this wasn't going to be easy, but it had to be said, for Tommy's sake.

'It's the way Tommy is with you. He's only three and he doesn't understand things properly yet. He's . . . well, you don't need me to tell you that he's taken to you, what with him always calling you "his doctor", an' all. The thing is that now that we're living here I don't want him getting the wrong idea or making a nuisance of himself, and you having to put him straight.'

'What exactly are you trying to say?'

'Tommy can't remember his own dad. I don't want him . . . well, with you having lost your little 'uns . . . well, I know it can't be easy for you.' This was so difficult for her and she was beginning to wish she hadn't said anything but it was too late now. Her voice had become muffled because the truth was that she didn't think she could have borne to see too healthy little boys running around alive and well, and having to share a house with them, if her own had been in their graves.

'No,' Dr Ross agreed tersely, 'it isn't. But I wouldn't be much of a person if I blamed your boys for that, and besides, having you and them here can't possibly be compared with my life with my wife.'

Sally recoiled. Who'd said anything about wanting to be compared with his wife? Not her. All she'd tried to say was that she didn't want Tommy making a nuisance of himself, even if what she'd meant was that she didn't want the doctor upsetting her son by putting him in his place. There'd been no call for him to make that comment about his wife. There were some things that a person just didn't say.

'If that's everything you wanted to say to me, Doctor, then I'd better go and get on,' she told him, her pride smarting.

She was just about to pick up the tray when she suddenly remembered something she had needed to ask him. 'I was wondering what time you'd be wanting your tea. I was thinking maybe six o'clock or thereabouts.'

'My late wife always used to insist we had *dinner* at eight thirty,' he informed her.

Sally's face reddened with his stress on the word 'dinner'. Posh folk had dinner, not tea – she ought to have remembered that instead of having had him tell her.

'Then that's when I'll make sure your *dinner* is ready, sir,' she told him smartly, picking up the tray and making for the door before he could continue the conversation.

TWENTY-TWO

'Happy?'

The soft whisper caressed Sam's ear, causing the now familiar flutters of longing and excitement to race through her body. In breathless exaltation she daringly snuggled closer to Johnny in the darkness of the back row seats of the cinema, as he caressed the curve of her throat.

'Mm,' she answered him blissfully.

'Sure there's nothing else you'd like?'

He was teasing her, knowing how much she loved the intimacy of his touch, Sam knew, but there was something she would like very much indeed, so she took a deep breath and told him softly, 'Actually, there is. I'd love to meet your family, Johnny. I know you've told me that you mother is living in Wales now, but I heard Sergeant Brookes saying something to you the other day about your sisters.'

She wasn't going to say anything to him about how she'd felt a little bit hurt that he hadn't said so much as a word to her about his family, whilst asking her all sorts of questions about her own.

She felt the change in him immediately. His body tensed against hers and then he moved slightly away from her, no longer holding her quite so close.

'Well, you're not going to get to,' he told her so curtly that for a few seconds she was too shocked to speak.

When she did manage to speak she only got as far as protesting, 'But, Johnny—' before he interrupted her sharply.

'No. And that's an end to it. Apart from anything else, me sister Jennifer is the only family I've got living in Liverpool now, and her and me . . . well, she's got her life and I've got mine.'

'But she's your sister.' Sam was unable to take on board what he was saying. She and Russell might have quarrelled fiercely as children but there had always been a very strong bond between. All the more so now that they were grown up, in fact.

'Stow it, will you, Sam?' Johnny told her 'Let's watch the film.'

He obviously didn't want to talk about his sister, but why?

'Perhaps we could go and see her?' Sam suggested, unwilling to give up.

'No!'

His angry vehemence made Sam recoil, feeling confused and hurt. If her brother had been living close enough for them to visit him, she would have been both thrilled and proud to have had the opportunity to introduce Johnny to him.

'Well, if you'd rather not,' she told him valiantly, trying not to let him see how hurt she felt, 'then of course we won't.'

'There's no point.' His voice was still curt.

No point in her meeting his sister? Why not? The harshness in his voice suggested that his reasons were ones that caused him pain. Had there been a quarrel between them that they'd never made up – things like that did happen in families, she knew – or was it that they simply did not get on? Sam realised uncomfortably that she felt unable to ask him. Her closeness to her brother made her feel very sad for Johnny and for his sister.

She was so lucky with her own family, she acknowledged. Impulsively she reached for Johnny's hand and gave it a small loving squeeze. He was still sitting upright and slightly away from her, but she resolved not to allow herself to feel hurt.

'I wish your mum was still living in Liverpool,' she told him tenderly. 'I would have loved to have met her and heard all about when you were a little boy, and about all the little girls who wanted to marry you when they grew up,' she teased him, hoping to lighten the atmosphere between them, but instead, she could feel him tensing again.

He removed his hand from hers, withdrawing from her physically and emotionally, Sam recognised. Why?

'That's daft talk,' he told her. 'What's past is

past. It's us that matter now, Sam. Our future together, us.'

He obviously didn't want to talk about either his childhood or his family.

'And talking of us,' he added in a deeper and far more loving voice, 'how about I do what I thought we'd come here to the pictures to do in the first place?'

'Watch the film, you mean?' Sam enquired, mock innocently.

'You can watch the film if you want, but what I want to do is this,' was Johnny's response as he reached for her, drawing her back into his arms and bending his head to kiss her.

Sam still wasn't entirely used to the heavenly physical intimacy that being a girlfriend brought, not yet, but she was learning fast!

'Johnny, why don't we go back to your billet?' she whispered against his lips, surprising herself with her own daring. 'We could be alone there and—'

'Yes, and we both know what would happen if we were, and that's exactly why we can't,' he stopped her firmly.

Sam fiddled with the button on his coat. 'Why can't we? Other couples do.'

And it would mean that they were properly promised to one another, she told herself silently, and then surely those odd niggling little fears she had when he distanced himself from her wouldn't be there any more.

'There's a war on, after all,' she reminded him,

'and if anything should happen . . .' she gave a tense shiver at the reality of her own words. 'I don't want to lose you, Johnny, and I don't want to die without knowing what it's like to lie in your arms, knowing that I'm completely yours.'

She could feel his chest lift as he made a small choking sound and then she was being crushed in his arms as he kissed her very hard and for a very long time. Somehow or other his hand was cupping her breast and hers lay against his thigh where the evidence of his desire for her beneath her fingers made her heart thud with excited longing. When he finally released her she had lost all track of what was happening on the screen but she didn't care one bit.

'We could go back now,' she whispered eagerly.

'Don't tempt me,' he answered her thickly.

He was still touching her face, stroking her skin and then playing with the small feathery fronds of her hair where it had grown to curling round her ears, curling them instead around his finger.

'Why not, when I want to tempt you, Johnny, when I want you so very much?'

A sudden surge of music warned Sam that the film had finished. Soon the cinema lights would be going on, and the National Anthem would be playing and then there would be no privacy for them any more. She wanted desperately to understand why Johnny was blowing so hot and cold with her, but somehow she felt unable to ask him, and now with the film ending it was too late.

Sam's passionate nature meant that she had given herself over heart and mind to Johnny, and she wanted to give herself over to him with her body as well. Others might say that it was a sign of respect for her that he was holding back, but somehow all she could feel was rejected.

'You're quiet,' he commented later, when they had left the cinema and queued up to buy a bag of chips to share as Johnny walked her to her bus stop. 'What's up?'

Here was her chance to tell him how confused she had felt earlier in the evening – and hurt as well – but somehow instead she heard herself voicing another fear as she admitted, 'I hate it when I see you going down into a bomb shaft.'

'It's my job.'

'Yes, I know.' She gave a small shiver. 'You're so brave, Johnny. I couldn't do it. Just the thought of being underground scares me silly.'

He gave her a reassuring hug. 'I'd like to punch that brother of yours on the nose for what he did to you.'

Now thankfully he was her loving protective Johnny again.

A bus was coming down the road towards them, the blue glow of its blackout lights momentarily casting an eerie faint blue glow over their faces.

'He didn't mean any harm,' Sam assured him. 'We were always falling out as children, but he is my brother, after all, and I love him dearly.'

She bit her bottom lip anxiously as she realised

what she had said. She'd really gone and put her foot in it now. She hadn't deliberately mentioned how close she and Russ were as a way of encouraging Johnny to talk to her about his sister and why he didn't want them to meet, but she could tell from Johnny's silence that he was angry with her again.

She tried to snuggle up to him but instead he nodded in the direction of the bus stop several yards away, where half a dozen people were already queuing and told her briskly, 'Your bus is due any minute. We'd better go and get in the queue. You won't want to miss it.'

'Yes, Mrs Beddows, I'll tell the doctor that you've rung and that you want him to call round and see your husband,' Sally said firmly into the telephone receiver, before replacing it and then carefully checking the message she had written down in the notebook the doctor had given her, showing her how he wanted the caller's name, telephone number if they had a telephone, and their message recorded, along with the time of their call.

Although she wasn't fully prepared to admit it, Sally was rather enjoying her new role and the confidence it was giving her. Or at least she was when she managed to stop worrying about those elusive feelings and yearnings that sometimes managed to push through the barriers she had erected against them, reminding her of what it had felt like to play devil's footsteps, as a little girl, when no matter how quickly you turned you could never catch sight of the 'thing' you knew was stalking you. Most of the time it was easy to convince herself that those feelings and yearnings didn't exist, that she, newly widowed, had no right to have them for anyone, least of all someone like the doctor.

People treated you with proper respect when they realised you were a doctor's receptionist. Sally thought she might ask Doris if her Frank could come round and carry down a little table from upstairs so that she could put her notebook on it and a chair behind it for when she needed to record messages.

Christmas would be on them before they knew it. People were talking about it when they went shopping, worrying about what might be available and what would not. Sally, with her five guineas a week coming in, had put in an early order with Molly's aunt in Nantwich for a nice plump farm-reared goose for Christmas dinner, and the weight of the doctor's name on those accounts he had opened at the local shops in Wavertree had meant that she had been able to get in a few precious extras – all legal and proper, mind – none of that black market stuff, not after what had happened to Tommy.

She looked at her watch. Just gone midday. The doctor had said he would be coming home for his dinner today because he had patients to see in the afternoon. She had managed to get a nice bit of fish, which she had poached for him in some of the extra milk allowance she got for the boys. Her own mother may not have been much of a cook but Doris was, and Sally had not been too proud to learn from her.

She started to sing softly to herself as she ran up the stairs to check on the boys. Tommy was coming out with all sorts of big words now, and Harry had grown a full inch since she had last measured him not so long ago. She'd have to start letting down his little romper suits and knit them both some new pairs of mittens.

She'd have to get those old medicine bottles that patients had brought back washed out an' all, now that the doctor had checked through them.

She was still singing a few minutes later as she hurried back downstairs to check on the doctor's dinner, or 'lunch', as he called it, having reassured herself that the boys were all right, oblivious to the fact that the doctor had returned and was standing in the open doorway to his office until she was almost in the hall.

'Oh, I'm sorry, Doctor,' she began. 'I didn't know you'd come in.'

'There's no need to stop singing on my account, Sally. In fact I hope that you don't.'

He'd gone back into his office before Sally had time to react to what he had said and the fact that he had called her Sally and not Mrs Walker, and not for the first time!

She was acutely conscious of that, though, half an hour later when she knocked on the now closed door, waiting for him to call out 'Come in' before she opened it.

'I just came to tell you that your dinner . . . I mean your lunch is ready, Doctor.'

This was the first time he'd come back at dinnertime to eat and Sally had taken great care to polish the mahogany dining table before laying it.

'I'll be through in a minute,' he told her.

Sally hurried back to the kitchen, quickly serving the boys their own fish pie dinner, before carefully placing the doctor's lunch on the plates she had already warmed, ready to take through to the dining room.

When he opened the kitchen door, and commented cheerfully to the boys, 'Hello, you two. Started without me, have you?' Sally was so taken aback she could only stare at him before starting to stammer defensively, 'I've laid out the table in the dining room for you to have your lunch there.'

He was frowning now, the smile he had given the boys gone. 'I see,' he said curtly, making Sally feel that she had offended him.

'I thought that was what you would want,' she told him.

'What *I* would want? What would you know or care about what *I* wanted?'

Sally stared at him. 'I . . . it wouldn't be right, you having to eat here in the kitchen with us . . . People would think I was taking advantage, and getting above meself . . .'

'*People* would *think* . . . ?'

Was that anger or contempt she could hear in his voice, or was it a bit of both? Sally didn't know and she certainly couldn't ask him.

Without waiting for her to make any response he turned on his heel and strode out of the kitchen, leaving her on her own to answer Tommy's accusatory, 'Mummy make my doctor cross.'

'My, Sally, you must have worked like a regular Trojan to get this place looking so spick and span.'

Sally forced herself to smile back at Doris. The doctor's anger towards her at dinnertime still rankled and had destroyed her sunny mood.

'Well, it's thanks to you more than anyone else that I know how a house should be kept, Doris.' Sally told her truthfully. 'Been more like a mother to me than my own, you have, teaching me what's what after I had Tommy. Couldn't cook so much as a meat and tatty pie then, I couldn't.'

'Don't give me all the credit, Sally. You're a good hard worker and a willing learner, and me not having a daughter, and our Frank being married to June in them early days, and the two of us not getting on – not like me and Molly do – well, you gave me back as much as I gave you.'

'I'll put the kettle on and make us both a cup of tea,' Sally offered.

Doris had called round just after the doctor had gone out on some calls, and so Sally had offered to show her around her new quarters.

'Smells lovely of lavender polish. You were lucky to get your hands on some of that. I haven't seen any since they brought in rationing.'

'I found a load of stuff right at the back of one of the cupboards. I reckon someone must have put it there and then gone and moved and forgot about it. I'd give you a tin, Doris, only properly speaking it belongs to the doctor. I could ask him if he minds, perhaps,' she offered, seeing the look of longing on Doris's face. The smell of the polish had lifted her own spirits this morning when she had been polishing the heavily carved wooden banister rail. 'Funny how something as simple as a tin of polish can cheer you up, when you think we never used to give it a thought.'

'That's what war does for you,' Doris told her. 'Boys settled in all right, have they? What is it, Sally? What's wrong?' Doris pressed when Sally didn't reply.

Sally gave a small sigh, then told her grimly, 'They've settled in fine, especially Tommy, and that's what I'm worried about really. He's getting old enough now to recognise how much bigger this house is and all the things that go with that, and I don't want him getting too used to it, and having ideas above his station, Doris. His dad and me could never have afforded to be living somewhere like this. When I was at the grocer's yesterday I heard him telling another kiddie as bold as you please, "We live at my doctor's house now."'

Doris laughed. 'I shouldn't worry about it, Sally. You've got your feet on the ground firmly enough, and Tommy and Harry will look to you to tell them what's what.'

Sally tried to look convinced as she made the tea and poured her old neighbour a cup.

'China cups,' Doris sighed approvingly. 'My old matron when I was first training always used to say that you should drink tea out of a china cup and water out of a glass.'

'Doctor said to use them. Me own are still packed up, just in case we end up having to find somewhere else. I don't really like taking chances. You never know what might happen. It's all very well you and Molly saying that it's the best thing that could have happened to me, the doctor giving me this job, but if it doesn't work out and we have to leave then I'm going to be in a real old mess.'

'Give over, Sally, anyone can see what a difference you've made to this place. It will do the doctor no end of good having you and the boys around. I don't hold with a man like the doctor living on his own. It's not healthy for someone in his kind of work. He needs to come home to a decent meal and a properly aired bed. You're a good lass, Sally, and a strong one too, but don't you go being too hard on yourself. I'd better go, I promised Molly I'd call round. Oh, I almost forgot, Frank said to tell you that he'd seen a chap hanging round your old house the other night.'

Sally was glad she had her back to her so that Doris couldn't see her expression.

'It was too dark for him to get a proper look at him and he went off when he saw our Frank. If it's that chap that was making a nuisance of himself . . .'

'It won't be him. It was probably someone thinking of renting the house and having a look at

373

it,' Sally told her, but she knew that the man Frank had seen would have been the debt collector. She also knew why he had been looking for her, and it wasn't because of the money she owed to the Boss, after all, as he had told her himself that Sally could have a bit of a break from making any payments if she wanted to do so. No, what he had gone round to the house for had been to try to 'persuade' her to give in to him and let him into her bed. Sally gave a shudder of revulsion. Here under the doctor's roof, no matter what private doubts she might have about being here, she was safe from him in that respect. She knew Sid's type. They feared anything to do with 'authority' and kept away from it.

There was still the matter of the money she owed, though. Only last night she had been looking at the little book in which she had meticulously kept a record of the amount Ronnie had borrowed and what she had paid back. It seemed so unfair that the interest she was forced to pay meant that she had already repaid the full amount twice over but still owed more now than Ronnie had originally borrowed. At least now, with what the doctor was paying her, she could afford to pay back more. Not through Sid, though. No. She'd rather save up the whole lot and pay it back in one go, so that she could get the whole thing over and done with for ever. What a weight off her shoulders that would be.

'Is everything all right, Sam?' Hazel asked, falling into step beside Sam as they left the parade ground before breakfast. It still wasn't quite light, and whilst the nip in the wind blowing off the sea might have brought roses to Sam's cheeks, it had also left her fingers tingling with cold. 'Only you're very quiet,' Hazel continued. 'You haven't had words with that chap of yours or something, have you?'

Hazel's sympathy brought a quick surge of tears to Sam's eyes, which she hurriedly blinked away.

'Not words, no.'

'But something's been said that's upset you?' Hazel pressed her as they crossed the road to walk back to the house.

'Johnny didn't mean to upset me, I know that,' Sam defended him. 'It's just that we had a few words over his sister. She's living right here in Liverpool but when I said that I'd like to meet her . . .' she gave a small shake of her head, 'well, I could tell that he didn't want me to. I suppose I'm being silly.'

'You aren't being silly at all,' Hazel told her. 'And if you want my opinion, Sam, there's only one reason why a chap doesn't want to introduce a girl to his family and that's because they know things about him he doesn't want her to know.'

Sam was taken aback. 'Things? What kind of things?'

'Things like him having a different girl for every day of the week – or worse!'

'That's impossible,' Sam told her. 'I'd know if Johnny was seeing anyone else.'

'That's what I thought about my ex,' Hazel said

grimly. 'Look, Sam,' she added more gently, 'if he hasn't got something to hide then why doesn't he want you to meet his sister? It doesn't make sense. There's something fishy going on, and you must think so yourself, otherwise you wouldn't be feeling so glum.'

Did she? Surely not. She loved Johnny and she trusted him. But his way of blowing hot and then cold was confusing her and leaving her feeling unhappy.

'I thought they might just have fallen out,' she told Hazel.

'Then why didn't he say so?'

They had stopped walking as they talked, and now Sam realised that the other girls were well ahead of them.

'We're going to be late for breakfast,' she warned Hazel, glad of an excuse not to discuss Johnny any more. She felt disloyal doing so, and she felt unhappy as well, as though admitting her worries changed them from something vague to something far more important.

'Hang on a minute.' Hazel stopped her, putting her hand on Sam's arm. 'I know how much you love Johnny, Sam, but what do you know about him really? You're so young and . . . and inexperienced . . . and well . . .'

'I'm old enough to know how I feel.'

'Yes, but can you honestly say that you're experienced enough to know how *Johnny* feels Sam? He may tell you he loves you, but those are just words. Anyone can say them and sound as though they mean them. Remember what they say about actions speaking louder than words. Do Johnny's actions say that he loves you? And I don't mean the kind of actions that go with kissing you senseless either,' Hazel warned her, mock sternly. 'Not wanting you to meet his sister isn't the action of a man who loves you, Sam, and I think you know that yourself.'

Sam shivered but the icy cold feeling that was gripping her had nothing to do with the cold wind. Was Hazel right? Was there something that Johnny was keeping from her?

'The best thing you can do is talk to him, Sam. Ask him to tell you why he doesn't want you to meet his sister. There'll be an explanation if he hasn't got anything to hide, and I can't think of any reason why he shouldn't tell you what it is.'

'But you don't think there is an explanation, do you?' Sam challenged her miserably.

Hazel sighed, her exhaled breath making a white puff of vapour on the cold air. 'You know so little about him, Sam, and he seems very reluctant to tell you anything. That can't be a good thing, can it? When two people fall in love it's natural and normal for them to want to know everything about one another. He's old enough to know that.'

'He said when . . . well, he told me when he first said that he loved me that he wished he didn't and that he'd tried not to. Maybe he doesn't want to introduce me to his sister because he's not really sure whether he loves me or not,' Sam told Hazel miserably.

'You need to talk to him, Sam,' Hazel told her again adding gently, 'Come on. We'd better go and get our breakfast, before they send a search party to look for us.'

Normally Sam had a good appetite but this morning she just didn't want to eat anything. Her insides were churning with misery. She felt so confused. Being in love shouldn't be like this. She had been so happy at first, but now she was filled with doubt. Why didn't Johnny want her to meet his sister? Was Hazel right? Was he hiding something from her? She didn't expect him not to have had girlfriends – she wasn't silly. Perhaps she should tell him that. Maybe he was worrying that she might be upset to hear he had enjoyed the company of other girls before he had met her and that was why he was reluctant for her to meet his sister.

Her spirits started to lift. She dipped her spoon into her now congealing porridge. Yes, that was probably what it was. Poor Johnny.

Sally refused to look directly at the doctor as she took his breakfast into the dining room.

'Would you like me to pour your tea, Doctor?' she asked him woodenly as he sat down, holding the newspaper that had just been delivered.

'Yes, please.' His voice was as curt as her own as he opened the paper, but as Sally poured the tea, his expression changed, a broad smile talking the place of his frown.

'Sally . . . Mrs Walker . . . there's excellent news here from the Prime Minister, with a report of a speech he made at the Mansion House last night.'

Immediately Sally forgot her own hostility, sharing in his excitement as she leaned forward, trying to catch a glimpse of what it was he had been reading. Good news was something they all desperately needed and their shared eagerness for it transcended everything else.

'Well, things do seem to have been on the up,' she acknowledged, 'what with us having that victory at El Alamein, and then Malta being relieved.'

'Yes, and don't forget the success of the recent Allied landings in North Africa, and the fact that it looks as though the Russians shall win through. Here, let me read this to you. This is what Mr Churchill said at the Mansion House. "This is not the end. It is not even the beginning of the end. But it is, perhaps, the end of the beginning."'

Sally heard the emotion in the doctor's voice, and felt her own throat start to close up with the same feeling.

They looked at one another, separated by only a few inches as Sally had moved closer to the doctor to stand at his shoulder whilst he read the newspaper article to her, united in their shared pride in their fighting men, their country and their Prime Minister.

Neither of them moved. Sally could see the rise and fall of the doctor's chest as he breathed. Such a strong, dependable man. A man that any woman could easily be tempted to lean on. His sleeve brushed against her own and yet she could have sworn that neither of them had moved. Her heart had started to beat faster. She wanted to move away from him, indeed she knew she must, but somehow she felt too weak to do so.

'Oh.' Sally put her hand to her chest, suddenly feeling slightly breathless and dizzy. And not just because of the good news she had just heard, she admitted. The fact that she must have inadvertently moved so close to the doctor had at least something to do with her agitation and dizziness.

'Sit down, Sally,' the doctor told her gently, reaching past her to draw out a chair. 'Even good news can leave a person feeling shocked.'

Thankfully Sally seized on the excuse he had unwittingly given her. 'Yes, it did give me a bit of a shock. It's almost like a miracle, isn't it? Like it's too good to be true? We've been at war for such a long time that I can't believe, even though the Prime Minister's said . . . well, at least that's the way it seems,' she told him shakily. 'There've been so many terrible setbacks, especially with losing Hong Kong and Singapore.' She blinked back the tears that just saying the names of those places brought. 'So many good men lost and so much hardship for them and for everyone here at home. There's some I've heard saying that they don't know how they're going to get through another winter of rationing, they feel that worn down and worried, but now . . . I can hardly believe it . . .'

'The Prime Minister has a way of reaching our hearts and putting new strength into us,' the doctor agreed. 'This news can't bring back those who are gone, it won't bring an end to rationing or hardship, but it does give us something very precious indeed: it gives us hope, and that's something every human being needs. Without it . . .' he paused and shook his head, and in the sudden glint of emotion she could see in his eyes Sally's heart turned over and she wondered if perhaps he was thinking about his wife and his sons, just as she was thinking about Ronnie.

Instinctively she wanted to reach out to him, just as she would have done to Doris or Molly, or even Frank, a small touch that said she understood and felt the same way, but even as she began to do so a stronger need to protect herself stopped her, and made her step back from him, ignoring the sense she had that he was waiting for her to say something.

The silence between them now felt awkward and uncomfortable.

It was Dr Ross who broke it to say, 'You know there really isn't any need to go to all this trouble in the morning. I would be quite happy to have my breakfast with you and the boys. You've got more than enough to do as it is, without having to serve my breakfast in here.'

Eat with them, and have her on edge all the time because of what she was feeling? Sally certainly didn't want that.

'I should be doing twice what I am for what

you pay me,' she told him. She could feel him looking at her but she refused to meet that look.

Their brief shared moment of equality and intimacy was over, and so it should be, she told herself firmly.

TWENTY-THREE

'Huh, well, look who it isn't. We were just talking about you.'

Sam's heart sank as she and Hazel walked into the dormitory to find Lynsey sitting on her bed, along with a couple of the other girls. Lynsey had been on leave and Sam had known that she was due back today. Sam was not really surprised to be told that she had been the subject of Lynsey's conversation. She had known that sooner or later Lynsey was bound to tackle her about Johnny because Lynsey was that kind of girl.

At least now she was feeling a lot happier about her and Johnny than she had felt first thing this morning, Sam acknowledged, as she braced herself for the scene she suspected was to come. She and Johnny had managed to sneak a few precious minutes alone together at the barracks earlier in the day, whilst she had been waiting for the major, and Johnny had been so tender and loving towards her that she had wondered what on earth she had been worrying about. What did it matter if he didn't want her to meet his sister? He loved her. He had told her so when he held her in his arms and not just once either, but over and over again in between his kisses. Those kisses! A dreamy smile of blissful happiness curled her mouth.

'Still seeing Johnny Everton, are you?' Lynsey challenged her.

Sam had known that it wouldn't be long before Lynsey got to hear about her and Johnny. Personally she would far rather they had had this conversation in private, but it was Lynsey who had chosen to challenge her in public and she wasn't going to back down.

'Yes. Yes, I am,' Sam confirmed. 'Look, Lynsey—' Even though Lynsey had been running after Johnny without him giving her any encouragement, Sam didn't like to think of her being hurt, especially now that she knew what it was like to love someone, but before she could say so, Lynsey cut her off, turning to look knowingly at the two girls still sitting on her bed.

'Well, more fool you. Pity you didn't think to say anything before you went and got yourself involved with him, 'cos if you had I could have given you a few words to the wise about him. I just hope you haven't gone and done something you shouldn't have done, Sam – besides making a bit of a fool of yourself, I mean. It's like I was saying to Cal – that's my new chap, by the way, he's a GI – you learn to get to know the signs that tell you when a chap's trying to lead you up the garden path. Still I suppose it's too late to warn you now. It's like I was just saying to Babs and Lizzie here, I feel ever so sorry for you, Sam. I really do, 'cos it sounds like you've really been taken in. Of course *I'd* guessed that something wasn't right even before I'd been told all about him. That's why I dropped him.'

Sam was too taken aback to say anything. She'd been expecting Lynsey to be furiously angry and resentful, and yet here she was, all smiles and full of triumph, and talking as though she pitied Sam and knew something about Johnny that Sam did not.

Sam looked helplessly at Hazel, not knowing what to say. She could see from Hazel's expression that she had taken Lynsey's comments seriously because she was frowning.

'If you know something about Johnny that Sam ought to know, Lynsey, then you should tell her,' Hazel announced firmly.

'Well, since you put it that way, I suppose that I should,' Lynsey agreed, 'especially seeing as I heard it from his own sister.'

Sam's heart gave an unpleasant jump and thudded into her chest wall. The discovery that Lynsey knew Johnny's sister caused her stomach to churn and make her feel slightly sick with a mixture of shock and anxiety.

'You *know* his sister?' Hazel demanded, asking the question that Sam somehow could not.

'Yes,' Lynsey smirked. 'It just so happens that I do. Got introduced to her through a friend of a friend of her hubby's. Jennifer, her name is.'

Sam's heart was thudding even more painfully now.

'She filled me in about him. I don't know what he's told you, Sam, but if he's tried to fool you that he's fallen in love with you, he's lying. I know for a fact that he doesn't love you and he never will, and I'll tell you why he doesn't love you. It's because he's in love with someone else.'

'No, that's not true,' Sam protested, finding her voice.

'Yes it is,' Lynsey corrected her. 'His sister told me all about it. It seems that there was a girl he was crazy about. Engaged and everything, they were, him and this Molly, and then she goes and drops him for someone else. His sister told me that it broke his heart. Then when this chap she dropped him for got killed when his ship was torpedoed, and he thinks that the two of them can get back together, she tells him that she's going to marry her dead sister's husband so that she could look after her sister's kiddie. Johnny's sister reckons he'd be back with her like a shot if she gave him half a chance. Oh, and you'll never guess who this Molly's husband is,' Lynsey continued gleefully. 'It's only that Sergeant Brookes you were working with down at the barracks. Talk about it being a small world. Mad about this Molly, Johnny was, and still is, according to his sister. She reckons he always will be. Of course, him being a man he still has his needs, if you know what I mean, and if some girl is daft enough to let him have what she shouldn't off the back of him making out that he loves her when he doesn't, well then, of course he's not going to tell her the truth, is he? Stands to reason that he won't.'

Sam could feel a painful burning sensation in the region of her heart. Tears were threatening to blur her view of Lynsey. She tried hard to swallow against the lump of misery in her throat and found that she couldn't.

It was left to Hazel to ask Lynsey sternly, 'Are you sure about all of this, Lynsey, because if you aren't—'

'Of course I'm sure. After all, I heard it from his own sister. Not that she had any idea that he'd been trying it on with me before I got wise to him, and I certainly wasn't going to tell her after what I'd just learned. You look ever so pale and sickly, Sam,' she added with a too-sweet smile of concern. 'Still, it's best that you know the truth about him, isn't it? I'd never forgive myself if I didn't tell you and then you went and did something you shouldn't.

'Oh, is that the time?' Lynsey exclaimed, looking pointedly at her watch. 'My Cal will be round here thinking he's been stood up if I don't get a move on. He's taking me out to the pictures and then a bit of supper.'

'Come and sit down for a few minutes, Sam.'

Hazel's hand was on her arm, holding her gently as she guided her over to her bed. Sam was distantly aware that Lynsey had disappeared and the other girls were all tactfully pretending to be very busy.

'It can't be true,' she told Hazel shakily. She

could feel the hard frame of the side of the bed behind her knees as Hazel pushed her down to sit on it.

'I don't think that Lynsey could make up something like that, Sam, not when she's said she heard it all from Johnny's sister.'

'So you think it is true then?'

'You said yourself that he didn't want you to meet his sister.'

'Perhaps he just didn't want me to . . . to feel hurt because . . . because he'd been engaged to someone else before he met me.'

Sam knew that she was clutching at straws but she just couldn't bear to accept that Johnny did not love her.

'Oh, Sam.' Hazel sat down on the bed next to her and took hold of her hands in her own. 'I am so very sorry that you are being hurt like this, but you must be brave and strong. You must insist that he tells you the truth. Any decent man who genuinely loved a girl would want to be honest with her about his past. You do see, don't you?'

'Yes,' Sam admitted miserably.

Johnny, *her* Johnny, loved Sergeant Brookes's wife. Sam remembered how determined Johnny had been to make sure that she knew that Sergeant Brookes was married. To protect the woman he loved? For the second time that day Sam felt as though her heart was breaking.

Johnny. Why couldn't he have told her about being engaged to Molly Brookes? Why couldn't he have said that he had loved someone before her, but that she and that love were in the past now and she was the one who mattered; the one who had his love? If he had, then everything would have been all right. But he hadn't.

'I won't come down for supper tonight, Hazel. I've . . . I've got a bit of a headache.' She couldn't bring herself to look at Hazel, knowing that they both knew that she was fibbing, and to her relief Hazel didn't try to press her to change her mind, simply nodding and standing up.

Sam had to wait until all the other girls had gone down for supper and the dorm was empty before she could give in to her tears, crying until her pillow was wet with them and her throat raw from the effort of trying to suppress her broken-hearted sobs.

'Well, if it isn't the doctor's new receptionist.'

Sally could see the looks the other women in the queue outside the grocer's were giving her when they heard Daisy's sneering greeting and the way she had emphasised the word 'receptionist'.

'Got your feet well and truly under the table there, haven't you? But there's no point you thinking you can get away with giving yourself fancy airs and graces round here where there's folk wot knows you.'

'I was as surprised as anyone else when Dr Ross offered me the job as his housekeeper and said that he'd want me answering the door to folk as well,' Sally responded, deliberately playing down the 'receptionist' part of her duties. No matter how much Daisy's words annoyed her, there was no point lowering herself to Daisy's level by arguing with her or getting Daisy's back up even more than it already was. After all, she now had her position to think of.

'Oh, surprised, was you? Come off it, jobs like that don't grow on trees. I bet Doris Brookes had been angling for it for you for ages. Mind you, at least she's done the rest of us a bit of a favour as well. Wi' you gone from the Close we haven't got that chap who used to come knocking on your door of a dark night hanging around no more.'

Sally's face burned with angry pride. She could see a couple of women in the queue exchanging whispers, their hands close to their mouths. It infuriated her that she had to let Daisy get away with implying that she had been entertaining another man in her husband's absence, but there was no way she was going to betray Ronnie's indebtedness now that he was dead. It would be a rotten thing to do to him and to his memory, and he deserved better than that.

'Mind you, if I was you I'd not have bin so keen to move in there, not after what I've heard the doctor had to say about your kiddies. Had it from one of the nurses, I did, wot knows my cousin Ruby. According to her he was that worried about you going out the way you was and leaving them for others to mind for you that he thought they should be teken into care for their own good. Said it was no wonder they'd ended up in hospital, so I heard.'

'Well, you heard wrong,' Sally told her sharply, her good intentions overturned by her fury. 'The only reason they had to go into hospital was on account of the food poisoning they got from one of your sandwiches. Yes, and he wanted me to tell him where it had come from, an' all, but I didn't, having a bit more loyalty to others than some I could name.

'Wot the doctor said was that he thought that maybe I should have let them be evacuated, that was all, but then he could have said that to plenty of other mothers here as well, as I'm sure we all know.' *There*, that should put Daisy in her place, Sally decided angrily.

'I'm surprised you need to queue up to buy anything, Daisy, wot with your hubby being so good at finding them damaged tins. Mind you, I suppose you might as well use all them extra points you get for having him at home and not in uniform,' she added for good measure.

She might seem calm outwardly but her heart was hammering away as though she had run a mile. She wasn't going to let Daisy have everything her own way, not for one minute. That nurse had had no right to go saying anything about what the doctor had said to her about Tommy and Harry, and he had had no right to say that she wasn't looking after them properly. What did he or Daisy know about the worries she had to bear?

As Sally turned to leave, Daisy caught hold of her sleeve and hissed angrily to her, 'You want to keep an eye on that doctor, you do, 'cos what I reckon is that with him losing his own kiddies he's got it in his mind to take yours from you and adopt them. It was in the paper only the other week about someone doing that. Turned the poor mother's brain, it did, when the judge said that they was better off with someone else. If you want my opinion that's why he's given you that job. The next thing you know he'll be saying that you aren't a fit mother and he'll be keeping them two little lads.'

'Don't talk so daft,' Sally told her scornfully, turning her back on her and walking away.

'My, but you gave that Daisy Cartwright something to think about. That's the first time I've ever seen her lost for words.'

Sally tried to smile at the woman who had come up to her as she left the shop, but in reality now that she had calmed down she felt slightly sick and a bit ashamed of the way she had ripped up at Daisy.

'I perhaps said a bit more than I should.'

'No more than she deserved. It won't do her any harm. Was that right what she was saying about you working for the new doctor?' she asked.

'Yes, it is.'

'Thought I saw someone moving in the other week. Got two little kiddies, haven't you?'

'Yes, my sons.'

'Only I live opposite from the doctor and a few doors down. Not that our side of the street is anything like as smart as where you are. A lovely house, that one of the doctor's is. Your husband away fighting, is he?'

'He was,' Sally told her. 'Only he got made a prisoner of war by the Japs and now he's dead. I only heard a little while back.'

Immediately her companion's expression changed, her curiosity giving way to sympathy. 'Oh, love, I'm ever so sorry.'

'It's all right. You weren't to know and, besides, I'm not on me own. Sometimes I think there's more lost someone to this war than there are haven't.'

'Well, that's true enough. I've got two lads both in the navy and a daughter married into the Senior Service as well, and there's never a day when I don't wake up worrying about them. I'm Mrs Jessop, by the way.'

'Sally. Sally Walker.'

'Doctor not got a wife of his own then?'

'He's a widower,' Sally felt bound to tell her.

'Yes, I'd heard summat of the sort. House got bombed and killed her and their kiddies, so I'd heard.'

'I'd rather not discuss it, if you don't mind,' Sally told her politely. 'Not with me working for the doctor, you understand.'

To her relief Mrs Jessop gave her an approving smile. 'Quite right and proper. I shouldn't pay any mind to what Daisy Cartwright has to say, if I were you. Anyone can see how well looked after them little lads of yours are. I knew the minute I set eyes on them that they had a good mother. Never did have an ounce of sense in her head, Daisy didn't. If she had she'd have never married that lump of a husband of hers. She was at school

393

with my daughter, and she was allus causing a fuss about summat and nothing then. Tell you what, if you feel like you want a bit of company of an evening, feel free to come and give me a knock.'

'It's very kind of you,' Sally thanked her, 'but with the doctor having evening surgery some nights, and then the boys, I can't really go out in the evening. Maybe you could come to me? I'd have to ask the doctor first, though, if it's all right.'

She didn't really want to encourage a woman whom she suspected was probably only cultivating an acquaintanceship with her so that she could have a good gossip, but neither did Sally want to offend a new neighbour.

'Here's your wages for this week, Sally . . .'

'Thank you, Doctor.'

'Everything's all right, is it? You're happy with the arrangements we've made?'

'Yes, thank you, Doctor.' What else could she say? People would think she'd lost her wits if she complained about having a job they'd give their eyeteeth for. But it was thanks to the doctor that Daisy had been able to have a go at her this morning about Tommy and Harry. He'd had no right saying to her what he had at the hospital.

'Doctor! I hear that word so often I'm beginning to forget that I have a name. Doctor . . . even Tommy calls me "his doctor". I don't suppose I could persuade you to call me Alex occasionally, could I?'

Sally couldn't conceal her shock. 'I couldn't do that.'

'Why not?'

'It wouldn't be right, not with me working for you.'

Her heart was thumping all over the place and she could hardly breathe. What a thing to say to her – her calling him 'Alex', just like they were close. A funny little pain speared into her heart.

'So you could do it if you weren't working for me then?'

'No! No ... you're a doctor, and I'm ... it wouldn't be proper.' She felt angry now as well as in a panic, afraid somehow, although she couldn't explain to herself exactly what she was afraid of, only that it had something to do with the doctor and the way he made her feel.

She heard him give a small sigh. 'Very well, Mrs Walker and Doctor we shall have to continue to be. However, I hope you won't be too offended if I forget myself sometimes and call you Sally.'

Like he had done this morning, Sally wondered, remembering how he had called down the stairs to her, 'Sally, I can't find my collars and I'm due at the hospital in half an hour for a meeting.'

'They're in the tallboy, second drawer down,' she had called back, half irritably, for all the world as though he had been Ronnie. 'I put them there myself yesterday.' She'd had one foot on the bottom stair ready to go up and get the collar for him like any harassed wife, thinking it would be easier to get it herself rather than risk having her husband make a mess of her neat tidy drawers, before she had remembered what her position in the household really was.

She hadn't had time to question her reaction then, but later on it had made her feel really angry and uncomfortable with herself, just like she was now, to realise how easily she had slipped into a reaction that belonged to the intimacy of marriage and not the more formal behaviour expected between an employer and an employee. She'd told herself that she'd make sure she watched herself in future to see that it didn't happen again.

'It isn't for me to be offended, Doctor. Not with you paying me wages.'

'The fact that you work for me does not give me the right to abuse my position, nor would I want it to. However, I can't help wishing . . .' He stopped and looked out of the window. He looked tired, his shoulders slightly bowed.

Something she didn't want to admit she was feeling stirred in Sally's heart.

Still looking out of the window, he told her brusquely, 'I noticed that you gave me an egg for breakfast again this morning. That's the fourth this week, well over my ration.'

'I get extra on my ration because of the boys, but Harry won't always eat his so I thought you might as well have it.'

'I don't want you and the boys going without on my account. Children need their protein, that's why the Government gives them the extra egg allowance. If Harry won't eat his eggs as they are then we'll have to come up with some other way of getting them into him. Protein is important for growing boys.'

There was no reason for her to feel offended and that funny feeling inside her chest certainly didn't mean she was hurt because he was criticising her and rejecting her kindness in giving him the spare and precious egg, of course it wasn't.

'Yes, Doctor. Will that be all?'

'Yes, yes . . . You can go, thank you . . . Mrs Walker.'

'What's up? You look like you've lost ten bob and found a sixpence,' Johnny joked, as he joined Sam for a cup of tea in the Naafi.

Her heart lurched into her ribs. Her eyes still felt sore from all the tears she had cried last night and her head was aching. Johnny reached across the table to take hold of her hand. Immediately she tensed back from him so that he couldn't.

'Sam, what is it?' he demanded, his smile giving way to a small frown. 'What's wrong? And don't tell me "nothing" because I can see that there is.'

He was too quick for her, Sam acknowledged. She had planned to wait until they were alone before she talked to him about what Lynsey had said to her.

'There is . . . but well, I'd prefer to wait until we're on our own. It isn't something I really want to talk about here.'

'It sounds serious.'

'Yes.' Sam's voice was muffled as she bent her head to avoid having to look at him. 'It is.' If she'd known that loving him was going to hurt so much would she have been able to stop herself from falling for him? Sam wished desperately that her answer to that could be a firm 'yes'. She wanted to be brave and strong, but it wasn't easy. Not when more than anything else she wanted to be held tight in Johnny's arms and to stay there, knowing that she was loved.

'Serious, is it? Not changed your mind about loving me, have you?' he was asking her whimsically.

His words pierced her heart. How could he be like this with her if it was true that he loved someone else?

'No, I haven't changed my mind about that,' she told him, 'only . . .'

'Only what? Come on, Sam, out with it. I'm not getting up from this table until you tell me what's going on.'

Sam could feel herself starting to tremble. She would have to tell him now. She took a deep breath and then fixed her gaze on Johnny's as though it was her only lifeline to safety out of the darkness of some unimaginably frightening place.

'Why didn't you tell me that you were engaged to Molly Brookes before she married Frank?'

'Who told you about that?'

One look at his face told her that her lifeline had just been cut, plunging her into despair and misery. She could see his expression changing, the warmth leaving his eyes as though a shutter had come down between them.

'That's why you didn't want me to meet your sister, isn't it?' she plunged on doggedly. 'Because you knew she'd say something about Molly and how much you . . . about how you feel about her?'

Johnny looked at her in silence. His face had lost its colour, and his jaw was clenched. Because he was angry, or because he was shocked? Whatever he felt should not concern her now. It was Molly Brookes to whom he had given the keys to his heart and the right to care about what he felt, not her.

Sam pushed her chair back and got up, turning on her heel, almost running towards the door, half blinded by her own tears. She couldn't bear any more of this and she certainly couldn't bear to stay here and listen to Johnny telling her that he still loved Molly.

She could hear the sound of his boots on the concrete floor as Johnny came after her. He caught up with her just as she reached the door, leaning on it so that she couldn't open it and escape.

'All right, so I was engaged to Molly, but I don't see how that affects us.'

'How can you say that?' gasped Sam. 'Of course it affects us. You should have told me, and if you really loved me like you said you did then you *would* have told me. You'd have wanted to tell me because you'd have wanted to make sure that I heard it from you. You'd have wanted to protect me from being hurt by hearing it from someone else. But you don't care about me being hurt, because you don't love me. You still love her, Molly Brookes.'

This wasn't how she had meant to do this. She

had planned to be calm and dignified, not betraying with every word how much she loved him and how badly he had hurt her.

'Where the hell did you get hold of a crazy idea like that?'

'It isn't a crazy idea, it's the truth. Everything you've said to me about loving me was a lie.'

Someone was pushing on the door from the outside, wanting to get in. As Johnny stepped back from it Sam seized her chance and slipped through it ignoring his, 'Sam wait . . .' as she cravenly ran to take refuge in the one place where she knew he would not try to follow her – the ladies' lavatory.

Hazel was right to have warned her not to give her heart to Johnny, Sam could see that now. She had been such a fool. But she wasn't going to be a fool any more. She was going to be strong and she was going to show everyone, including Johnny, that broken heart or not she was still going to do her bit for the country and the war effort.

TWENTY-FOUR

'Will you just look at that,' Doris Brookes laughed, drawing Sally's attention to the game of football going on in the garden between the doctor and Tommy. 'The doctor's a good man, and him and your Tommy get on together like a house on fire. Stands to reason when you think about it, what with him having lost his own kiddies and Tommy having lost his dad.'

Doris swung round in surprise when Sally banged down the pan she had been scrubbing clean.

'What's that look for?' Doris asked.

'Me and the boys are only living here on account of me working for the doctor and I don't want anyone getting any other ideas. I've already had Daisy Cartwright saying that she reckons that the doctor wants me under his eye because he doesn't think I'm a fit mother.'

'Give over, Sally. That's nonsense and you know it,' Doris told her bracingly.

Sally's hands shook slightly as she scrubbed

even harder at the now clean pan. 'There's nothing more important to me than my two lads, Doris. I know I should have been there when Tommy took sick . . .' Her voice broke and she stopped scrubbing at the pan. 'I'll never forgive meself for not being there that night, Doris. Never.'

'Well, you should because it wouldn't have made a bit of difference if you had been there, and anyone who tries to say any different will have me to answer to, so don't you go getting yourself upset over Daisy's spite. And spite is just what it is. Everyone know what a good mother you are.'

Sally gave Doris a grateful look before determinedly changing the subject.

'How's Molly and the new baby?'

'Oh, he's coming on a treat, Sally. Ever such a good baby, he is,' Doris told her, more than happy to talk about her new grandson. 'Oh, and Molly said to tell you that she's having a few in on Boxing Day and that you and the boys are welcome to come along. She knows you'll be having your Christmas dinners here, of course, because you've got that goose ordered from her auntie at the farm.'

'The doctor asked me if I wouldn't mind working over Christmas, seeing as he's on duty with that emergency team up at the hospital he's joined up with as a volunteer. Seeing as it's voluntary work he's doing, I didn't feel I could say no.'

'He'll pay you a bit extra for working over, I expect,' Doris offered comfortably, 'and with

Tommy and Harry to bring up on your own you'll need it.'

'He did offer but I said no, he pays me enough as it is,' Sally told her. 'I'm not having anyone accusing me of taking advantage, especially when he's doing volunteering.'

'You're a good lass, Sally, I've always said so, but don't you go being so good that you lose out on summat that would bring you something good yourself,' Doris warned her cryptically.

'Hazel's been looking for you, Sam,' May called through the open sitting-room door. 'She said it was important.'

Sam nodded. She had thought she had already endured the worst day of her life with Mouse's suicide, but she had been wrong. Driving the major out to the bomb site where Johnny was working, knowing that it was over between them, had torn at her heart with all the devastating agony of a shrapnel blast tearing into vulnerable flesh to leave wounds that would never heal. Only her pride and her training had kept her from breaking down.

'Are you all right, Sam?'

'Yes, I'm just a bit tired, that's all,' she fibbed, miserably aware that May was bound to know the real reason she looked and felt so low. 'I'd better go and find Hazel.'

'She's with the captain at the moment.'

'I'll cut along to the hall and wait for her there then.'

Hazel probably wanted to see her to make sure that she was all right, Sam decided miserably as she made her way back down the corridor to the hallway.

The door to the captain's office was closed so she had no idea whether or not Hazel was still with the captain.

The girl on the reception desk was giving her a sympathetic look. 'Sorry to hear your bad news, Grey.'

Sam looked away. Did everyone know what a fool she had been over Johnny?

'The call came through whilst I was on duty. Corp's in with the captain now. She's putting a brave face on it but it's easy to see how she feels. Chin up, though, is what I say. Where there's life there's hope, and if your brother did manage to bale out . . .'

Her *brother*? The girl on the desk was offering her sympathy because something had happened to Russell, not because of Johnny?

Before she could ask her anything the door to the captain's office opened and Hazel came out. It was immediately obvious that she had been crying, and the moment she saw Sam her eyes filled with fresh tears.

'What is it? What's happened?' Sam asked her anxiously, pushing her misery over Johnny to one side.

'Your father telephoned. I'd just come back in – and so I was able to speak to him. Russell's squadron were sent on a mission to bomb Turin

– you know he's flying one of the Lancasters now and they've been using them for this mission. He was full of it in his last letter, boasting about how good the planes were.' Her voice shook, and she had to stop speaking for a few seconds to collect herself. 'Something went wrong, so it seems – they don't know what happened yet, only that Russell's plane is missing and there hasn't been any word. He didn't send out a Mayday or anything, but according to your dad they'd run into heavy fog coming back, and the last time anyone saw his plane was as they left Turin.'

'Oh, no.' Tears filled Sam's eyes as she and Hazel hugged one another tightly.

'We mustn't write him off yet,' Sam told Hazel chokily. 'It may not be as bad as it sounds. Russell isn't the sort to give up without a fight and, like they say, no news is good news. Chances are he's put the plane down somewhere . . .'

Hazel gave her a wan smile and Sam knew that neither of them believed there was really any hope of that happening. Hazel released her and stepped back from her. 'I spoke to your mum as well as your dad. I can't tell you how much it means to me that your parents were kind enough to let me know. I felt as though they already think of me as part of the family even though Russell and I aren't—' She had to break off as her emotions overwhelmed her but Sam knew exactly what she was trying to say.

Her own thoughts and emotions were in

complete turmoil. She had just discovered that the man she loved did not love her back as she had believed, and in the most misery-inducing and wretched of ways, and now she had to come to terms with not only that but the fact that her brother's plane was missing. All she could do now was pray that somehow, by some miracle, Russell might have survived, even if that meant that he had been captured by the enemy, but she knew how unlikely that was. And she knew that Hazel knew that too. How cruel life could be, letting you think you had found love and happiness, and then snatching it away, leaving you to live on with your broken dreams and might-have-beens.

'Your dad said he'd telephone just as soon as he got any news.'

Sam nodded, too miserable to trust herself to speak.

Sally wasn't sure just what had woken her. In the darkness of her bedroom some maternal sixth sense warned her that, despite the silence, something had disturbed her sleep. Harry still sometimes needed his nappy changing during the night, and as she pushed back the bedclothes she shivered, trying to make sure that she got her feet into her slippers, as she reached for her dressing gown. Even with her slippers on she could feel the cold coming off the linoleum floor as she picked up her torch and switched it on.

The first thing she saw when she opened her bedroom door was the light shining beneath the door to the boys' bedroom. Her heart thumped. Tommy couldn't reach any light switches yet, although she had caught him pushing a chair over the floor and then climbing up on it in an attempt to do so.

Quickly she opened the bedroom door, her eyes widening at what she saw. The doctor was seated in the too-small-for-him rocking chair from which she had nursed both her sons as babies, Tommy fast asleep on his knee. When he saw her the doctor raised his free arm, placing one warning finger against his lips to signify that Tommy was sleeping. Somewhere underneath the maternal anxiety rushing through her Sally was aware of another emotion, a mixture of anger, resentment and an aching sense of sadness and loss for both her own husband, who would never hold his sons like this, and the doctor himself for the pain his own loss must cause him.

'What's going on?' Sally whispered. Dr Ross shook his head again and stood up carefully, placing Tommy back in his own bed before coming to join her on the landing.

'Tommy came downstairs to tell me that he couldn't get to sleep because of a monster underneath his bed.'

'You should have woken me. I'm his mother.' What she really meant was, why had her son gone to him instead of coming to her? But she was too upset and angry to feel comfortable asking such a question.

'Tommy seemed to think that it was the kind of monster that would have frightened you as well and he didn't want that. He thinks that now his father's gone it's up to him to be the man of the family.'

'No,' Sally denied immediately, 'he can't think that. He's only three.'

'Children grow up fast in wartime, no matter how hard we try to protect them from its realities, and he's a very bright lad, very sharp and quick.'

'I'm sorry he disturbed you. I'll have a talk with him and make sure it doesn't happen again . . . He must have gone all the way down those stairs in the dark.' Her voice wobbled. 'He could have fallen.'

'He's got more sense than you give him credit for: he counted the stairs, so he told me.'

'He *counted* them? But I've only just started teaching him his numbers. He should have come in to me and he would have done if . . .'

'If what?'

'I know it must be hard to bear what . . . what you've lost, but *my* sons can't . . . I don't want you thinking that just because you've given me a job that means you can take over my boys . . . like . . . like they was a couple of stray mongrel pups. They aren't, and they aren't neglected either, no matter what you might be planning to try to prove. You might think you're doing them a favour, acting all charitable towards them like that vicar and his wife did with you, but you're not and I won't have it. They're my sons and that's the way they're going to stay. I'm really sorry about what happened to

408

your own boys. I can see that you must have been a good father to them. But my two have got a dad of their own, even if he is dead, and they don't need you or anyone else trying to take his place.'

There it was out! The fear that had been growing inside her ever since Daisy had had her say and destroyed her peace of mind with her hint that the doctor might be planning to take the boys from her.

'You can sack me if you want . . .'

'If I *want*? You don't know the first thing about what I *want*, Sally, because if you did . . .' He started to walk past her and then stopped and turned round. 'And for your information, no child, not even my own, if I should have any more, and certainly not yours, could ever take the place of the sons I've lost. And if you were the mother you keep on telling me you are, you'd know that for yourself. There isn't a day or a moment of a day when I don't mourn them and blame myself for what they and I have lost, but neither my guilt nor my grief can bring them back. All I can do is try to make sure that I do everything I can to protect those children who are alive, and whose lives for one reason or another are in my hands.'

He stepped through the door he had wrenched open whilst he was talking to her and closed it so firmly after him that Sally felt the draught blowing coldly against her skin, making her shiver.

His words had brought her up sharply, shocking her, and now that he had gone she was discovering that they were stuck into her conscience like so many painful little darts, to prick at her heart. Try as she might she couldn't dislodge them. She looked at the closed door. She had hurt him, she knew, but couldn't he see that she had to keep a safe distance between them and that it wouldn't be right if she did not?

Sally was still thinking about the doctor's outburst half an hour later, lying in her bed, unable to sleep.

He was wrong when he said she didn't have any idea of what he wanted. She had a very good idea indeed, because it was what she wanted as well. She closed her eyes and tried to steady her thudding heartbeat. However had it come to this, that she, a newly widowed woman, a mother, with more than enough problems in her life already, was lying awake at night sick with longing for a man she had no right to want? It made her go cold with dread to think of the scandal there would be if anyone ever got to know how she felt.

Even if she wasn't newly widowed, even if there were no other barriers between them, there was the gulf in their social stations in life. She had known it was the wrong thing to do when she had agreed to come and work for him, but foolishly she had not been able to help herself. What she was thinking . . . feeling . . . wanting was wrong – worse than wrong, it was a betrayal of Ronnie and their marriage. Poor Ronnie, who had had his life taken from him in the most cruel of ways through fighting for his country. How would he feel if he knew that she, his wife, the mother of his children, was lying awake in her bed at night longing to be in the arms of another man? She had tried so hard to fight it, and then, when that that failed, to deny what was happening to her. She had tried to turn her unwanted feelings from desire to angry resentment and dislike, and she had congratulated herself when she had thought she had succeeded. But then just when she had begun to think she was safe, something would happen, a look, a smile, her awareness of the scent of male skin, a dozen tiny different things, insignificant in themselves but with such an intense effect on her senses that they ripped through the foolish belief that she had conquered what she felt like tracer bullets tearing into a night sky. She should never have come here . . . never. If she had any sense . . . But she didn't, did she? And even if she did go, where would she go to now, so close to Christmas? What kind of mother would she be if she took the boys from the comfort of this house, just because she was afraid of her feelings?

'Bad show about your brother, Grey. Chin up, though. That's the spirit, eh?' the major told Sam as she held open the car door for him.

It had been raining all night and now this morning the ground around where Johnny's section were digging out a newly discovered unexploded bomb was filled with deep puddles and sticky with mud. A stiff wind was blowing the rain into her face like needles but it wasn't their cold sting that made Sam flinch so much as the tearing ache caused by the sound of Johnny's voice.

'Thank you, sir,' she answered the major, the etiquette of war taking priority over her personal feelings as she responded to his brusque words of intended comfort.

She didn't want to look at Johnny but she just couldn't help herself. She longed desperately for the comfort of his support and his closeness but he had his back to her. Deliberately, so she suspected. He was certainly making it clear that it was over between them. Perhaps he was even pleased. At least now he wouldn't have to pretend that he loved her when he didn't. And as for his reasons for taking up with her, so explicitly described by Lynsey, well, a good-looking man like Johnny wouldn't find it difficult to get himself a girl willing to share his bed.

It was just as well it was raining so hard, Sam decided. No one would notice that she was crying.

The telephone rang just as Sally was sitting down to eat her tea, but she got up automatically and hurried into the hallway to answer it.

'It's the hospital here, Mrs Walker,' she heard a crisp female voice telling her. 'The doctor has asked us to telephone you and let you know that he's been called out with the emergency team.'

'Oh, yes. Thank you for letting me know.'

'I can't tell you when he'll be back. Terrible accident, there's been,' the woman on the other end of the line told her. 'A double-decker bus coming from Lime Street full of passengers got hit by one of them American lorries and overturned.'

Sally sucked in a shocked breath.

'Bodies all over the place, so I've heard. Worse than if there'd bin a bomb gone off, so one of the ambulance drivers has said. Shouldn't wonder if the emergency team will be there all night.'

Sally shuddered as she replaced the receiver. Those poor people. What a dreadful thing to happen.

Her cup of tea had gone cold but she didn't feel in the mood to make herself another.

'Where's my doctor?' Tommy demanded crossly, playing with his food instead of eating it.

'He's gone to see someone who's very sick,' Sally told him. 'Hurry up and eat your tea and then I'll read you a story.'

'Don't want you to read it. Want my doctor.' Tommy banged his spoon down onto his plate, sending mashed potato flying onto the table, and the floor, which Sally had washed that afternoon.

'Tommy, that's very naughty, wasting good food like that,' Sally scolded him but her heart wasn't really in it. 'I know,' she told him. 'Why don't you finish your tea and then we'll sit down and write a letter to Father Christmas?'

He was too young yet to really understand about Christmas, which was just as well since the only toys to be had were second-hand and cost far more than she could afford, but his face had brightened up and he was giving her his normal sunny smile. *She* didn't feel like smiling, though, and not just because of the bad news about the bus. There was no point in her feeling sorry for herself because of her feelings for the doctor; she would just have to remember that saying of her mother's: 'What can't be cured must be endured.' After all, she wasn't some silly young girl who still thought that her life wouldn't be worth living if she couldn't have the boy she wanted, was she?

The sound of a key turning in the front door brought Sally out of the kitchen chair where she had been dozing in front of the fire.

It was gone midnight, and the last time she had opened the front door it had been raining cats and dogs, and a wind coming in off the sea that threatened to strip your skin from your bones.

She had switched off the light in the kitchen but the hall light was on, and that and the glow from the fire was enough to show her the weariness etched into the doctor's face.

He obviously hadn't seen her in the dimness of the kitchen and so she was at liberty to watch him, greedily absorbing every tiny detail to store away in her heart. He looked so tired and pulled down, his shoulders slumped, rainwater puddling from his coat onto the linoleum floor. She saw him turn towards the stairs, a look of such desolation on his face that her heart turned over with a mixture of pain for what she saw and guilt because she was seeing it without him knowing that she could.

Stepping back into the shadows, she scraped the

chair's feet noisily on the floor and then called out as though she had only just realised he was there, 'Is that you, Doctor?'

'Sally!'

The blaze of delight she could see in his eyes as she switched on the kitchen light tore at her heart but she affected not to notice it, busying herself by going into the hall and tutting over the mess on her clean lino.

'Yes, I'm sorry. I didn't realise . . .'

'It looks like you've brought half the Mersey in with you. You'd better give me that coat, and your shoes, although goodness knows how I'm going to get these shoes dry. I'll have to try to find some paper to stuff in them and then put them in front of the fire overnight.'

'You shouldn't have waited up for me.'

'I dare say I wouldn't have done if I'd known how late it would be but seeing as I'd made you a dinner anyway I thought I might as well keep it hot for you.'

'They telephoned you from the hospital, didn't they, to let you know? I would have telephoned you myself but there was such a rush.'

'Yes, they did.' She let the crossness drop from her voice as she said quietly, 'It sounded a really bad business, from what I was told.'

'Yes. Yes, it was. The bus was full . . . men coming home on leave, some of them with their wives and children who'd gone to the station to meet them and welcome them back.' He lifted his hand and rubbed it over his eyes. 'We did what

415

we could, but . . . the bus had slid along the road on its side, you see, from the impact of the crash.'

'It had been hit by an American Army lorry, so the hospital said,' Sally encouraged him, sensing that he needed to talk.

'Yes. Yes, that's right. The lorry was loaded with some heavy-duty equipment. No one knows yet just what happened. The driver, poor boy, was in a terrible state. He was only young – seventeen, he said, although he looked younger. Some of them lie about their age when they join us. His voice had barely broken. He'd gone through the windscreen.

'Still, at least the lorry driver is alive,' he continued, 'unlike some of the bus passengers. There was one family . . . the prettiest little girl. She looked just as though she'd gone to sleep. There wasn't a mark on her face, but her poor little body . . .'

His voice broke and automatically Sally went to him, only just managing to stop herself from doing what she had promised herself she would never do, and touching him. She was almost tempted to put her hands behind her back to make sure that she couldn't do so.

'I'll get your dinner out for you then, shall I, Doctor?' she asked, taking refuge in formality.

'Yes . . . thank you.'

He had turned to follow her towards the kitchen table so Sally stopped and turned round.

'I've laid the table for you in the dining room.'

She had lowered her gaze and was keeping it

fixed on the wall to one side of him but she knew anyway exactly the look that would be in his eyes, and how her sharpness would make them darken with anger.

'I'll eat in the kitchen, if you don't mind. It will be warmer than the dining room.'

This was the first time he had challenged her determination to keep him at a distance.

'Very well.'

He went to wash his hands in the downstairs cloakroom as she dished up the rabbit stew she had made earlier in the day. Molly's dad had brought the rabbit round, along with some veg from his allotment. As soon as she had put the plate in front of him Sally went to put the kettle on.

'I'll make you a cup of tea and then I'll be up off to bed. The washing-up can wait until morning.'

'Sally, don't go. Please stay and have a cup of tea with me. I'm not really in the mood for my own company tonight.'

She'd be a fool to stay, she knew that.

'Very well, Doctor.'

She could hear him exhale as though he had been holding his breath.

'You're always rushing around so much – come and sit down for a minute.'

'I've got the tea to make.'

'Then when you've made it. I feel so envious sometimes when I hear you and the boys laughing and talking over your meals, whilst I'm eating alone in the dining room.'

'Harry isn't exactly talking yet.'

'That's only because Tommy does his talking for him. Harry can understand what's being said well enough. They're two bright little chaps, Sally.'

It must be so hard for him always having to live with knowing that his own sons were gone. She knew she would not have wanted to be in his shoes. Losing a husband or a wife was one thing but to lose a young child, no more than a baby really . . .

She poured them each a cup of tea.

'Sit down, Sally, please,' Dr Ross repeated.

She shouldn't be doing this. It would lead to no good, she warned herself as she did as he had asked.

'I thought after losing my boys the sight of death could never touch me like that again, but tonight, seeing those children . . . as if they didn't have enough to bear with the war, without having their lives taken in a bus accident.' He put down his knife and fork. 'I'm sorry, Sally, but I'm just not hungry.'

The cuff of his shirt had turned bright red with blood. *His* blood, Sally realised.

'You're bleeding,' she told him.

'It's nothing.'

'Let me see.' She was up and out of her chair and at his side before she had time to think about what she was doing.

'I cut my arm on a piece of glass, that's all.'

Ignoring him, Sally unfastened his cuff and rolled back his sleeve, just as she might have done for

Tommy. Or Ronnie? She pushed that thought away. The cut was on the inside of his arm below his elbow, sharp and, she suspected, quite deep, the flesh gaping to ooze blood.

'It needs cleaning up and a bandage putting on it. Stay there. I'll go and get a bowl of water.'

She went over to the kettle, pouring what was left in it into a bowl and adding a bit of salt. Salt cleaned wounds; Doris had taught her that. And then she took a clean cloth from the cupboard and carried the bowl and the cloth over to the table, putting the bowl down and then dipping the cloth into it, working firmly and determinedly to clean the skin round the cut in exactly the same brisk fashion she would have done if he had been one of her sons. One of her sons – not her husband! A boy, not a man!

The only sound in the room was the occasional hiss of rain coming down the chimney onto the fire, and their own breathing, his slow and regular and her own equally steady. Each measured breath she took was an effort but if she gave in to what she was feeling her breathing would give her away.

'There,' she told him when she was satisfied that the cut was clean.

She was still holding the bowl and when he stood up and took it from her, she let him, not realising until it was too late what he intended to do.

'Thank you.' He bent his head and brushed his lips against hers.

'No!'

'Sally!'

She was in his arms and he was kissing her as she had dreamed and longed for him to do, a man's kiss filled with passion and need, his man's arms holding her tight, his man's body pressed hard against her own. It had been so long since she had known this, and that was why she wanted him so desperately – because he was a man and not because he was him – but even as she told herself her lies her heart refused to accept them, and tears spilled from her eyes because of her own guilt and despair.

'I'm sorry, I'm sorry, please don't cry. Sally, I'm sorry . . . I promised myself I wouldn't do that. I promised myself that I wouldn't do anything that would make you run away from me . . .'

It was wrong that she should allow him to bear all the guilt and blame. She pulled away from him but before she could speak he told her, 'Having you living here with me is part heaven and part hell. I feel like a man dying in the desert from the lack of water I can see but I can't touch or taste. Sometimes the torment of that . . . I love you, Sally. I've tried not to, God knows. Every morning I wake up telling myself that I mustn't love you, but then I see you and I know that I can't help myself. I think I fell in love with you the first time I saw you. You were walking past the house . . .'

'. . . and you were horrible to the boys.'

'Was I? I didn't mean to be. It was just that what you made me feel was such a shock. I swore after the way my wife lied to me and deceived me that I was better off being alone.'

His words jerked Sally out of her own pain and guilt. 'What do you mean, she lied to you and deceived you?' This wasn't how she had expected to hear him speak about the woman she had believed he considered so superior to herself, and had loved so very much.

He said quietly, 'I shouldn't have said that. We're always told that we shouldn't speak ill of the dead. And after all, she wasn't responsible for the fact that I was fool enough to believe her lies, or that I let my physical desire blind me to reality. But since I did say it, well, the truth about our marriage is an ugly one that does neither of us any favours. I rushed into it, driven by a mixture of lust and guilt because of that lust, and her fulfilment of it, never stopping to think or question why she might want to marry me. She never failed to let me know that in marrying me she had married beneath herself.'

'But your marriage brought you your sons,' Sally reminded him.

'My marriage brought me an expensive house that was too big for us, filled with a domestic staff that looked down on me almost as much as the wife who despised me. Like our marriage, the house was a barren cold place, controlled by my wife's never-ending reminders of how short I fell below her standards. I wanted a wife and a home that were warm and loving, the kind of home I had known with my adoptive parents. They were good friends to me, counselling me to think carefully about marrying her but, arrogant young fool that I was, I believed my wife when she told me she thought their concern sprang from a resentment that my marriage would take me away from them and into a new social strata. She was the daughter of an eminent titled physician, you see, a spoiled pampered adored daughter born after several sons. Sir Charles worshipped her and thought nothing too good for her. I own that I was surprised when she assured me that he would look favourably on me as a prospective son-in-law, but then of course I didn't know the truth.'

Sally waited, sensitive to his need to unburden himself.

'Fleur . . . what is it?' he asked when Sally made a small sound.

'Nothing really, just that it's such a pretty name, so delicate and elegant . . . not like Sally, that's so . . . so ordinary and dull.'

'No, it isn't. Sally is love and warmth and caring. Sally for me means home. As for Fleur being delicate, well, she liked to give that impression but in reality she was unyielding and selfish, determined to have her own way no matter what the cost to others. She told me shortly after she had discovered that she was pregnant that the only reason she'd married was because she couldn't marry her lover, because he was her cousin. She had tried everything she could to persuade her father to relent and sanction their marriage but he would not do so. It seemed there had been some intermarriage in the family in previous generations, which had resulted in the birth of a child with a number of physical problems. Her father, being a physician, was vehemently opposed to them marrying because of the risk of this happening again, as was his brother, who was her lover's father. They had both been told they would be disinherited if they didn't give one another up, and so Fleur had conceived this idea that she would find herself an amenable husband to marry so that they could continue with their affair in secret.'

'But she was your wife ... You had two sons ...'

His mouth twisted into a bleak tormented grimace. 'No, I did not have two sons. Those poor little souls had been fathered by her lover. That was why she had to tell me about him. You see, whilst our marriage had been consummated, we had ceased to share a bed within a few weeks of returning from our honeymoon. I could see no point in continuing with an act that brought me little pleasure and so much bitter self-disgust. She claimed that it was only the lower orders who expected to feel passion and delight in the physical side of their marriage, and that I should remember how much marriage to her had elevated me socially and professionally, and be satisfied with that. She pointed out the humiliation she suffered when her friends questioned her choice of husband and shuddered over my uncouth ways, and said that I should do more to show my gratitude.

'And then, of course, when she told me that

there was to be a child, she had to tell me the truth. I remember thinking then that perhaps her father had been right to forbid her marriage to her cousin because sometimes it crossed my mind that she herself was not quite . . . well, that her thinking was not quite as rational as it might have been. She was convinced that once her father had seen that the two of them had produced a normal healthy child he would relent and that with his blessing she could be allowed to divorce me on some trumped-up grounds so that she and her cousin could marry. Sadly within a year of his birth it was obvious that little Euan was not going to be the child she had hoped, but by then she already knew there was to be a second child, and I imagine she put her hopes on this coming baby . . . She took to referring to Euan, when addressing me, always as "your son". Poor little lost soul, I wish I might have been a better father to him, for God knows it is true he needed one.'

Sally was too appalled to speak. She remembered the photograph she had seen, and the two beautiful-looking children in it. Tears filled her eyes – for them and for their 'father'.

'Physically both children were perfect, good-looking replicas of their mother and their true father, but whilst they were gentle loving boys, they did not have that . . . that spark of intelligence that is so evidence in Tommy and Harry. I loved them, though – not perhaps as a father, but as their protector, for I could see that Fleur was bitterly resentful of what she could see they would become. I would often come home to find them locked in their nursery, unwashed and hungry, whilst Fleur had gone out with her lover.

'And then he was moved to London. His father obtained a post for him in one of the ministries to keep him out of uniform. Fleur wanted me to apply to a London hospital but I refused. There was the most terrible row. I told her that if she went to her lover then she would go alone, that the children must stay with me and that I would go to her father and put the whole sorry business in front of him preparatory to arranging a legal separation. If only I had known then that by delivering that threat I was sealing the boys' death warrant. She waited until I was out of the house and then she left for London, taking the boys with her. The rest you know. The house was bombed and she and her lover and their sons lost their lives.'

Now she could understand so much that she had not understood before, Sally's heart flooded with love and compassion.

'I never wanted to fall in love with you, Sally, but now that I have I can't bear the thought of living without you,' Alex told her. 'You and the boys have taken away the emptiness and loneliness inside me. You're everything I've ever wanted or ever could want in a wife. Just watching you whilst you've been here has shown me that over and over again. A doctor ought to be careful about choosing a wife, for her sake and for the sake of his patients.'

His wife! Sally's heart jerked against her ribs.

'So having me here as your housekeeper was just to test me out to see if I could measure up, was it?' she demanded in an attempt to cover up what she was feeling.

'No. Never! I am the one who needs to measure up to you, Sally, not the other way round.'

Somehow or other one of them had moved, or maybe even both of them, Sally admitted, because she was back in his arms, openly inviting him to kiss her for all that she knew she should be reminding him – and herself – that she was only newly widowed and had no right to be so much as talking with him like this, never mind anything more. But being here with him in the cosiness of the fire-lit room was so very, very sweet that she couldn't deny either him the comfort of her loving arms or herself the joy of their shared intimacy.

TWENTY-FIVE

It wasn't even six o'clock yet, but it had been pointless her lying in bed when she knew she wouldn't sleep. Far better to be down here in the kitchen, Sally told herself, busying her hands with tasks even if she couldn't busy her head with enough thoughts to distract her from what had happened last night.

She opened the back door. The sky had that depth of wintry darkness that warned that it would be a day when it couldn't lighten properly at all.

Like her heart?

She might have gone to bed as though dancing on clouds, warmed by love and deliriously happy, but it hadn't been very long before guilt had filled her, telling her how wrong it was for her to love Alex with poor Ronnie so recently dead. What kind of woman, what kind of wife was she? Ronnie deserved better from her than that. He certainly deserved that she mourn his memory properly and for a decent enough time instead of wantonly throwing herself into the arms of another man.

When she heard the hall door into the kitchen being opened she knew without turning round that it was Alex. Alex. How sweet and at the same time shocking it felt to be able to think his name inside her head, just as last night she had tasted it and him on her lips.

'My bed was very empty after you left it,' he told her softly.

Sally didn't speak or move, keeping her back to him. She had had to force herself to leave the warmth of his arms and his bed for the cold emptiness of her own but he knew as well as she did that they couldn't have Tommy waking up early and finding her missing from her bed. And they certainly couldn't have him taking it into his head, to go to 'his doctor's' room and find his mother there. Being the lad he was, ready to chat with anyone, he'd be telling everyone about it before she could stop him, too young and innocent to know what he was doing.

'I've been thinking . . .'

Sally stiffened as he came up behind her. 'So have I,' she said, evading him as he tried to wrap his arms around her. 'What happened last night wasn't right.'

'Of course it was. It was the most right thing that's ever happened to me in the whole of my life,' he stopped her tenderly.

'No!' Sally denied, panic sharpening her voice. If she could feel this weak and be filled with this much longing just because of the sound of his voice then how was she going to be able to do what was right if she had to look at him; if he touched her?

'You can't say that. You mustn't . . . I should never have let you . . .'

'My darling, wonderful, precious girl, what's wrong?' He was laughing tenderly, unaware yet of what had to come. Sally felt as though a knife was twisting in her own heart at the thought of how much she was going to hurt him.

'Everything's wrong. Me. You. Us. Can't you see that?'

'All I can see is the woman I love, the woman I want to spend the rest of my life with.'

'No! You mustn't say things like that to me.'

She turned round and then wished she hadn't because now she could see him her heart was telling her what she had already known and that was that she ached with love and longing for him. And that was wrong, so very, very wrong. Just as what she'd done last night – going to him, giving herself to him, loving him with a passion she had never ever experienced with Ronnie – had been very, very wrong, she told herself desperately, trying to whip herself up into the mood of self-disgust she needed to see things through.

'Why not? Last night—'

'Last night shouldn't ever have happened – it was wrong.'

'How could anything so beautiful be wrong? Last night when you gave me your sweet self, Sally, you gave me something I never imagined my life would have.' He reached and touched her face before she could stop him, causing her to make a small moan of protest and longing.

'I can't stay here now. Me and the boys will have to leave.'

'No! I won't let you go. You love me, Sally, you told me so last night, and I love you.'

'I can't love you. Not with me being newly widowed and you being the doctor. I can just imagine what folk like Daisy Cartwright would have to say about me getting ideas above me station.'

'Ideas above your station? What nonsense! You will make a perfect doctor's wife, Sally. Is that really all this is about? Some silly woman who doesn't know any better, gossiping about us?'

She could hear the relief and the love in his voice.

'Look, I'll tell you what we'll do. We'll have a fresh start, you, me and the boys. We could move away from here to somewhere where no one knows us. We could be married quickly and quietly first, and then we'd be Dr and Mrs Ross, and anyone who dares to think of upsetting my wife will have me to answer to.'

What he was saying was so tempting, and when he wrapped his arms around her she allowed herself to imagine that his suggestion was possible, but whilst he could protect her from Daisy's gossip, and they could run away from it, he couldn't protect her from her own conscience, and she certainly could not run away from that.

'It isn't just Daisy and what folk would say,' she admitted.

'What is it then?'

'It's Ronnie.' She felt his arms tighten round her. 'He's not even cold in his grave yet, and it would not be right me and you . . . I'd feel like I was behaving like one of them women what goes wi' other men behind their husband's backs.'

'You said you loved me.'

'I know . . . and . . . and I do . . . but that doesn't make it right. I may not be able to stop meself from loving you but I can stop meself from . . . from being with you and being disrespectful to Ronnie.'

'Sally . . .'

'I don't want to talk about it any more.'

But she knew that sooner rather than later they would have to talk about the future, Sally admitted later in the day when Alex had gone out to do his house calls.

She had just put both boys down for their afternoon nap when Doris arrived at the back door.

'You're looking a bit pale and peaky,' she announced as she sat down at the kitchen table and Sally poured her a cup of tea. 'What's to do?'

'Nothing.'

'From the look of you it seems to me like it's the kind of nothing that means an awful lot of "something". I'm not daft, Sally. Summat's bothering you. For all the attention you've bin paying to wot I've bin saying these last ten minutes I could have bin talking Chinese. It's you and the doctor, isn't it? Summat's happened.'

'No! Yes,' Sally admitted miserably, knowing that her red face was giving her away.

431

'Well, I can't say I'm surprised. I could see which way the wind was blowing with him, and that he was getting sweet on you. And summat tells me that you're every bit as struck on him.'

'Yes,' Sally admitted wretchedly. 'I should never have come here, putting temptation in front of both of us, but I didn't realise then ... I never meant anything to happen, Doris, I promise I didn't, no matter what anyone else might have to say. I didn't have a thought in me head of anything happening between me and Alex when I moved in here.'

'Of course you didn't, and neither did the doctor, I'll be bound, but things have a way of happening when there's strong feelings involved and there's a war on,' Doris assured her comfortingly.

Sally wasn't ready to be comforted, though. 'It's all very well for you to say that, Doris, but there's others that won't see it that way,' she retorted miserably.

'Come on, let's get that kettle on and have a fresh cup of tea, and then we'll have a talk about it,' Doris suggested.

Obediently Sally filled the kettle, and then burst out unhappily, 'I feel that ashamed, Doris. I've let my Ronnie down good and proper, and him dead no more than a few weeks.'

Instead of agreeing with her, Doris shook her head. 'Here, let me make that tea; you go and sit down,' she insisted.

'And it isn't any good me telling meself that I

didn't want it to happen or trying to lay the blame on Alex, 'cos I did, and it wasn't his fault,' Sally admitted.

'Well, you don't need to go telling me that anyone with any sense in them can see that you and the doctor aren't the sort to go getting involved in summat like this if you didn't have feelings for one another.'

'I don't have any right to have feelings for him, not with my Ronnie—'

'Sally, listen to me. There's no call for you to go making yourself miserable like this. I know it's only bin a few weeks since you heard about Ronnie, but it's bin over two years since he was last home.'

'That shouldn't make any difference. He was fighting for his country, and for me and our kiddies, and now he's dead, and I'm . . .'

'Things are different in wartime, Sally, and if you want my advice then I reckon you and the doctor ought to be able to have what happiness you can together. Anyone can see how much he thinks of you and them two lads. Boys need a father.'

'You brought your Frank up wi'out one, and that's what I'm going to do as well. I don't want my lads growing up hearing things said about their mother by other kiddies, like how she was off wi' someone else with their dad just dead. I couldn't live wi' meself if I did that to them, Doris. I've got me standards, you know. Me and Ronnie, we promised each other that we'd do the best we could for our kiddies, and I want Tommy and Harry to

433

grow up knowing what a good dad he would have bin to them.'

'Well, there's nowt to stop you telling them that, and giving them a good stepfather as well, is there? You'd be daft to turn your back on a good man like the doctor, Sally, especially wi' the way you feel about him.'

'I've got to think about what I owe my Ronnie.'

'What about what you owe yourself and the doctor? It's right that you should mourn Ronnie – I'm not saying it isn't – but you can't live wi' the dead, Sally, and your Ronnie would be the first to tell you that. If little Tommy hadn't taken to the doctor the way he has it might be different, but have you thought about what it's going to do to him if you was to tell him that he could have the doctor for his dad, but for you being daft? You're too young to spend the rest of your life mourning a dead man, lass.'

'It's all very well you saying that, Doris, but if you were in my shoes . . .'

'Well, as to that, I have bin, haven't I? Frank's dad was killed before Frank was even born.'

'That's as may be, but you've never remarried . . . or . . . owt . . . and Frank thinks the world of you, and no wonder.'

Doris looked at her and then said quietly, 'I'm going to tell you summat now, Sally, as I've never told anyone. Never thought I would do either, but seein' as you haven't got your own mother here to do a bit of straight talking to you then I reckon I'll have to do it meself. I can't let you go doing summat daft on account of worrying about what the likes of Daisy Cartwright might have to say.'

'What do you mean?'

'I mean that you aren't the first woman to find yourself in this kind of situation, not by a long chalk you aren't,' Doris told her meaningfully.

Sally stared at her. 'You're never trying to tell that you . . . that there . . . ?'

'Just listen to me, Sally, and don't say a word until I've finished. Me and Frank's dad grew up living on the next street to one another. Already walking out, we was, me and Frank's dad, Bert, when war was declared. I was doing me nurse's training and Bert had a good job, but of course what did he do but decide he had to join up? They was all doing it, of course, all the young lads, just like they have done this time. Well, of course, the first thing Bert said after he'd told me that he'd joined up was that he wanted us to get married, and I was just as daft, and said that I wasn't having him going off to fight without us getting wed – just in case. A proper fight we had on our hands wi' both his parents and mine telling us that we was too young. Bert was only twenty and me not even nineteen, but in the end they gave in and me and Bert got wed on his bit of leave after he'd done his training.

'There was plenty of lasses done the same, just like this time. I kept on with me nursing even though normally I'd have had to give it up on account of me being married, but Matron had an idea of what was to come and the Government had given orders that as many nurses as could be were to be trained up. I even lived at home with me mam and dad and me three brothers after I was married.

'Of course, we thought it'd all be over in a matter of weeks, and when it wasn't and the wounded started coming back from the Front, telling such tales . . .' Doris shook her head. 'Those were bad times, I can tell you. When my Bert walked in to me mam's kitchen late one night out of the blue, I thought for a minute he must have deserted, but it turned out he'd bin given home leave. We'd just had the bad news at home that our Fred, me eldest brother, had been killed, and Bert said he was going to rent a little house for us so that we could be on our own. That was how my Frank came about. Not that I knew until I was being sick half the day three weeks after Bert had gone back to the Front. That was in 1917. By the time Frank was born in 1918 both me other two brothers had been killed and then came the news that Bert wouldn't be coming back neither.

'A couple of weeks – that's all the time we'd spent together as a married couple.'

'Me and Ronnie didn't have much more than a few months, not with him being in the army even before the war,' Sally told her.

Doris gave her a sympathetic look before continuing, 'When the vicar asked if I'd take in this schoolteacher – Peter Marston, his name was – as a lodger, I thought nothing of it, only that it would be a bit more money coming in. The vicar told me about how he'd got this wound that still needed attention – dressing and the like – and that he thought I'd be able to do that for him, with me being a nurse. Quiet type, he was, not like my Bert, who'd been a bit of a one for a singsong and a drink, but I didn't mind him being quiet. It suited me, with Frank being only a few months old. Peter kept himself to himself at first, staying up in his bedroom and reading his books. They'd had to amputate the lower part of his left leg, and that was what had to be dressed clean every day. Never made a murmur, he didn't, even though I knew it must be hurting him when I had to take off the bandaging. Loved Frank, he did, and took to reading to him. He could get him off to sleep faster than I could.

'He'd been lodging with me for about three months when he said that he was going to leave. Wouldn't look at me at all, he wouldn't, when he told me. I can see him now . . . lovely hair he had, and the bluest eyes. Said as how he couldn't stay, not feeling how he did about me. Of course I felt the same about him. Three months we'd been living under the same roof. I knew him better than I'd ever known Bert, and I knew how I felt about him as well, but like you've just said now, Sally, him and me both thought that it wasn't right that we should feel the way we did, with Bert having been killed. There was a lot of chaps that came back from that war feeling bad about being alive on account of all them that didn't come back, and

Peter, well, he was the kind that thought a lot about things.

'He went and had a talk with the vicar. What he said to him I never knew, but the next thing was that the vicar had found him somewhere else to lodge.

'We'd agreed that he'd move himself out whilst I was working at the hospital, but then, well, there I was in the middle of having me dinner with the other nurses when suddenly I just stood up and said that I was going home.

'Ran all the way from Mill Road, I did – I was only a slim little thing in those days. When I got home I knew straight off that he'd gone. I could sense it even before I unlocked the back door. I sat down in me kitchen and cried me eyes out like me heart was broken, which of course it was. And then I heard this knock on the back door and when I went to open it, he was there. He'd got on the bus, he told me, but he'd only gone one stop, and had to get off and come back.

'Three weeks, we had together, and they were the most wonderful and precious weeks of my life, Sally. Of course the vicar came round and gave us both what for, but by then I'd got me courage up and I wasn't having it. Me and Peter had as much right to be happy as anyone else, I reckoned, and I didn't think my Bert would have begrudged me that happiness even if his mam had been telling everyone that I was no better than I should be for taking up with someone else.

'All sorts of plans, we made; he had such dreams.

He went over to Yorkshire for an interview with a school so that we could have a fresh start . . .' Doris shook her head, plainly battling with her emotions.

'I never saw him again. He came down with the Spanish flu, and what with him being weak from the amputation and everything . . . well, instead of coming back to me he let them send for a doctor over there, and he said he wasn't fit to travel, and then the next thing I knew the vicar was telling me that he'd died.'

'Oh, Doris . . .'

'Aye, it was a bad time for me . . . Without Frank to look after I don't think I could have gone on. I miss Peter still, Sally, I really do. But what I'm trying to say to you, lass, is that through all the years I've had without him, at least I've had the comfort of those weeks we had together in the way that nature intended a man and a woman to be together. I know there are those that would say what we did was wrong – we hadn't had any church vows, after all – but if you were to ask me I'd say it would have been more wrong not to do what we did.'

Sally couldn't find the words to express what she was feeling, and not just because of her astonishment that Doris, whom everyone thought of as so rigidly strait-laced, should have done such a thing.

'See, Sally, what I'm trying to tell you is that some things are more important than what the rest of the world thinks we should do. You say that you feel ashamed of yourself because you've fallen in love with the doctor when you've only just been widowed, but how would you feel if you were ever to be in my shoes? What I think is that at times like this, with a war on an' all, Sally, folk like you and the doctor what have a chance to be happy, should take that happiness, because you never know what's waiting round the corner. Sometimes there's precious little happiness to be had in life, and it seems to me that it's like being wasteful and throwing away something that shouldn't be wasted, when you don't take that happiness when it's offered to you. It's like God's giving you both the chance of a bit of happiness – yes, and your little lads as well, – and you're throwing it back in His face, and that's never right, is it? 'Cos what I reckon is that some things are meant to be, Sally, and that's that. Of course,' she added more briskly, 'if you don't love the doctor, then that's different . . . But if you do . . . well, you have a little think about what I've said.'

The room was silent now, the only sound that of their breathing and the quiet tick of the clock. Wordlessly they looked at one another, two women separated by a generation but reaching across that separation to share the same knowledge.

'I love him so much, Doris,' Sally said at last. 'It scares me half to death feeling like this.'

'I know, lass,' Doris told her gently.

'Oh, Doris.'

Tears welled up in Sally's eyes and the next

minute she was in Doris's arms, the older woman hugging her comfortingly.

Shaking her head, Sally released herself. 'I don't know what I'd have done wi'out you in me life, Doris, I really don't.'

They exchanged looks that were slightly embarrassed but wholly understanding, two strong women, who were both more used to keeping their own counsel than sharing their deepest feelings.

'I'd better be on me way now,' Doris announced determinedly, signalling both a return to their normal familiar relationship, and a sign that the time for confidences was over, 'otherwise Molly will be worrying.'

Taking her hint, Sally made no reference to what Doris had told her. She walked with her to the back door, and opened it for her.

But then, as Doris stepped through it, Sally reached out and touched her arm, telling her emotionally, 'I wish I could have met him – your Peter.'

'Aye, Sally, I wish that, an' all.' Sally could see the sadness in Doris's eyes. 'He was a lovely man.'

'Grey? You in there?'

'Yes,' Sam called back, shivering as the trickle of water from the shower suddenly turned icy.

'Well, get a move on. Captain wants to see you – pronto.'

Sally grimaced as she tried to rub some warmth into her cold flesh. Her towel was still damp from the morning, but she had got so muddy and wet driving the major from one bomb side to another that she had had no option but to have a shower. Her towel was beginning to smell slightly rank from overuse, but Sam knew there was no point in trying to get it laundered until the end of the week. Rules were rules, and one clean towel per week was all they were allowed.

Her clothes felt stiff with cold and slightly damp as she dressed as hurriedly as she could. Her shoes were wet inside – again – and she had no spare dry socks for the morning. But these small discomforts were nothing compared with the real reason for her current misery. How was it possible for a person to be so happy one minute and then to have that happiness torn from them the next? What did the captain want her for? If it was to tell her that she was being transferred somewhere else would she feel as glad as she ought to feel, or would she instead want to plead with her superior officer to be left where she was, in order to be close to Johnny?

'Private Grey reporting as requested,' Sam told the new warrant officer, as she saluted smartly outside the captain's office.

'Stand easy, Private,' the warrant officer instructed her, knocking on the captain's door to announce her.

'Good news, Private Grey,' the captain informed Sam without preamble when she had been shown into her office. 'Your father telephoned earlier to say that your brother is safe and well.'

'Russell is *safe*! I mean, yes, ma'am,' Sam managed to correct herself.

'Apparently your brother's Lancaster was damaged on the way back from a mission but he was able land it on a small airfield close to the coast, where he and the crew repaired the damage. They had to wait for the fog to clear before they could take off again, and of course they couldn't use radio communication in case they alerted the enemy to their presence.'

'He's always had the luck of the dev— I beg your pardon, ma'am.'

'That's all right, Grey. I too have an older brother who seems to have more than his fair share of our family good luck.' Was that really a twinkle she could see in the captain's eyes? 'Just as well really that they do, in these times. Dismissed.'

'Where's Hazel?' Sam demanded as she rushed into the dormitory several minutes later.

'She's gone for walk, she was feeling a bit low,' May answered. 'Try the chapel.'

The small chapel, which had been used by the school during its occupancy of the building, was tucked away down a long corridor on the ground floor. The house had apparently been built on the site of a much older dwelling, and since that dwelling had contained a private chapel, it had been decided to incorporate this within the new building, to be reached via a specially constructed windowless corridor, its walls half panelled and half covered in a sombre dark green wallpaper. Old-fashioned candle sconces still provided the only form of illumination for the corridor. Because of the war and the need to use candles sparingly, only every third sconce contained a candle and then only one where the sconce provided for two, so that long shadows haunted the passageway no matter what the time of day.

Sam wasn't overkeen on using the corridor with its darkness and silence, so she hurried down it as fast as she could, focusing on what her news was going to mean to Hazel, and what it would have meant to her had she been in the same position. Just as she reached the chapel she stopped abruptly. Life was so precious and so fragile, just like love. She put her hand up to her chest to ward off the spear of pain that had lanced through her.

If anything should happen to Johnny, she wouldn't even have the right to grieve. How could she live the rest of her life not knowing where he was or even *if* he still was? She loved him so much. But he did not love her, she reminded herself.

The door to the chapel was always left open, and although it was no longer used for any religious services there was still some sense of peace and prayer about the small panelled room, with its arched ceiling and simple altar.

Someone, no one knew who other than that it had been one of the first groups of ATS to be billeted here, had started what had become a tradition in placing in the chapel a lighted candle that was never allowed to go out, as a symbol of hope. Very often one would come here and discover that several candles were burning: silent witnesses to the hopes and prayers of some of their number for loved ones.

As she stood in the open doorway, Sam could see Hazel in one of the pews, her head bent in prayer, Russell's scarf, which he had given her the last time they had been together, clasped tightly in her hands.

What must it feel like to be praying for the life of the man one loved, not knowing what his fate might be, clinging to a hope so small and so frail that it was pitiful? Sam hoped she would never have to know.

Hazel was getting up. Although she was not particularly religious Sam waited in the doorway, feeling that to rush to Hazel with the good news would somehow not be right. So many people must have come here in hope and fear. You could feel it in the air and the silence. This was a place for humility in the face of terrible things, a place for acknowledging the heavy weight of human grief rather than celebrating human happiness. It commanded that there be silent respect for the fragility of those who came here to light a candle to ease the darkness of their despair. Gusting giddy careless laughter might blow out that light.

Sam waited until Hazel reached the doorway and then touched her arm gently.

'Dad telephoned,' she told her. 'It's good news. Russell is safe and well.'

'Oh, Sam!' Radiance illuminated Hazel's face. 'Oh, Sam!' she repeated emotionally, as they stepped into the corridor. 'I hardly let myself believe it. Tell me that I'm not dreaming.'

'You aren't dreaming,' Sam assured her, 'and it is true.'

'Oh, thank God . . . thank God.'

Tears were running down Hazel's face and Sam could feel her own eyes filling as well.

'Whilst I was praying for him I felt so close to him. Perhaps he was trying to tell me that he was all right. Love is such a precious thing, Sam, but it makes us so vulnerable. I don't know how I could have borne it if I had lost him. One must, of course, but to endure such a pain . . .'

Sam had to turn away from her so that Hazel couldn't see her own pain. It hurt so much, contrasting Hazel's joy and relief with her own despair. But then Russ loved Hazel, and Johnny did not love her.

She turned towards the corridor wall, and shaped her fingers to make shadows dance along the wall, making Hazel laugh.

'My father used to do that when I was a little girl. Do some more,' she encouraged her, laughing even more when Sam obliged.

At least she could make people laugh, even if she couldn't make Johnny love her, Sam told herself as she tried to force her unhappiness away.

Hazel was still laughing when they reached their sitting room, insisting that Sam showed the other girls what she had been showing her.

One thing led to an other and before too long Sam was larking about, persuading May to let her show her what a good gymnast she was by leapfrogging over her and then pretending that she'd got stuck.

'Oh, stop it, Sam, please,' Alice spluttered. 'I've

laughed that much my sides are aching. You're a real tonic, you are, and no mistake.'

A tonic for them, maybe, but whilst she was laughing on the outside and playing the clown, inside her heart was weeping tears of loneliness and loss as it grieved for Johnny.

It had grown so late whilst Sally waited for Alex to return that she had dropped off to sleep in her chair a couple of times, woken by the sound of the wind buffeting the house, and the ache in her limbs from the awkward angle of her sleep. Alex had been gone for so long that she was beginning to wonder if he was staying away deliberately. She knew what she had said to him had distressed him. She hadn't wanted to distress him but she hadn't been able to think past her own feelings of guilt until Doris had made her see that her duty now lay to the living and the future and that for their sakes she must put aside her guilt.

It was gone ten o'clock when she finally heard Alex's key in the door. She didn't wait for him to see her and come to her, choosing instead to go to him so that when he stepped into the hall she was waiting there for him.

Without a word she went to him and helped him off with his hat and coat and his muffler, all damp from the rain the wind was slanting against the windows.

'Sally . . .'

She could hear weary resignation and anguish in his voice, and she knew he was anticipating that she was about to resume their earlier painful discussion. They *would* have to talk, but for now something else was more important, and that something else was the gift that she had been waiting to give him; the gift of their future together.

She put her finger to her lips and shook her head, and then she went to him and stood up on her tiptoes to wrap her arms around him and tell him tenderly, 'I love you, and I want us to be together.' And then she kissed him.

She could feel the wild thrill of emotion grip him and run through him, his body shaking slightly as though he could hardly dare to believe what he had heard.

Tears filled his eyes and spilled down onto his cheeks. 'Oh, my love, my precious, precious love. You don't know . . .' He broke off and shook his head as though his emotions had taken him beyond mere words. 'When I left you earlier I was in such despair. I felt that all life could hold for me now was my duty to my patients, and that without that there would be no purpose in my going on. Not that that was a new feeling for me – it wasn't. After the death of the boys my guilt at not being there to save them filled me with such a loathing for myself that if it hadn't been for my doctor's oath only to preserve life I might have been tempted to take my own, although that of course would have been more of an escape than a punishment.

'And then there was you, with your loveliness and your spirit. If you hadn't stolen away my heart that day I saw you in the street, then you most certainly would have done when I heard you sing. You have a beautiful voice, I'm surprised that you don't sing in public more, although I admit I would be jealous in case I lost you to some handsome admirer.'

'That will never happen,' Sally assured him, sensing his vulnerability. 'I do love to sing, but I've never been that keen on being on the stage. I'm not ambitious enough, that's what I've bin told, and I reckon that it's true. I've certainly never wanted to be one of them singers wot travels round all over the place.' She shook her head. 'No, me kids and me home are what matter most to me.'

'And me – do I matter to you, Sally?'

'Yes,' she admitted huskily. 'You, me kids and us being together, that's all I really want, Alex. And p'haps singing in church now and again,' she allowed with a smile. 'Mind you,' she reminded him, 'you're saying now that I have a lovely voice, but you certainly didn't look like you was enjoying listening to it that night at the Grafton. Glared at me something fierce, you did.'

'That's because I was so jealous,' Alex repeated. 'There you were, looking and sounding so lovely, with every man in the place adoring you – what chance would I have, a dull doctor, when there were all those handsome men in uniform?'

'You are not to say you are dull, because it isn't true,' Sally chided him.

'I'm afraid it is.'

'Well, in that case we must just be dull together,' Sally told him lovingly.

'Oh, Sally.' Alex's voice was full of emotion. 'I feel like I've been granted a miracle – three miracles, in fact, with you and the boys.'

Sally laughed. 'I shall remind you of that the next time two of your miracles are making a nuisance of themselves disturbing your peace.'

'I shall love them as my own, Sally, and that is my solemn promise, not just to you and to them but to their father as well.'

Now it was Sally's turn to feel tears welling up in her eyes.

'I shall love them as my own,' he continued, 'but there must always be a place in their hearts where they can cherish Ronnie. It will be up to both of us to make sure that they grow up knowing about their father, and all that he was, all that men like him gave up for us and for this country. I take that as a sacred duty that I shall do my utmost to fulfil.'

How could she ever have thought of denying her sons the goodness of such a man in their lives? Doris had been so right to caution her to think beyond her own immediate guilt and fear of gossip. What did that matter when set against the loving kindness of a man like this? How fortunate she was, when she had done so little to deserve such good fortune.

'Promise me you mean what you've just said to me,' Alex insisted.

'I mean it,' Sally assured him.

He was bending his head to kiss her, but she stopped him, whispering, 'Not yet. There's something else I have to tell you . . .'

She could feel the anxiety he was fighting to conceal as he waited for her to continue and an even more intense surge of love welled up inside her.

'You've burned my dinner?' he guessed. He was making a brave attempt at seeming light-hearted but he was holding her hand so tightly that Sally knew how anxious he really was.

'No, but I have put *both* our hot bricks in your bed – instead of one in yours and one in my own, if that's all right with you?'

'Sally, *Sally* . . . oh, my love, you are my love now, and I will never, ever let you go.'

TWENTY-SIX

'Quick, Sam, catch.'

Automatically Sam made a dive to catch the deliberately low-flung rolled-up scarf that May had thrown her, as they climbed out of their transport at the barracks. The other girls laughed and applauded her skill, then laughed even more when Sam made a grab for May's gloves and started to juggle skilfully with the scarf and the gloves.

'Stow it, Sam,' Hazel warned her firmly. 'Top brass heading this way.'

With a swift flick of her wrist Sam sent the scarf and then the gloves flying in May's direction, and she struggled ineffectually to catch them.

'You're such fun, Sam,' May told her, still laughing as she came over to her. 'By the way, have you heard that Lynsey's asked for a transfer? Seems she's serious about that Yank she's going with, and since he's being posted down south she wants to move as near to him as she can.'

Sam nodded but didn't say anything.

Every day, or so it seemed to her, it got harder

for her to hide her unhappiness behind the mask of the joking tomboy she had always found it so easy to be. She was still that Sam, but now there was another Sam living inside her as well, and that Sam ached for her lost love.

She didn't know how on earth she was going to cope with seeing Johnny day in and day out, knowing that they were over, she really didn't. Just thinking about it blurred her vision with misery.

'Morning, Grey.'

'Morning, sir,' Sam returned the major's greeting along with a smart salute. No matter what her feelings might be it would never do to let the side down and show them.

His brisk, 'Got some meetings at Derby House today,' left her feeling slightly sick with relief at being spared the ordeal of having to see Johnny, if only for one day.

'And who did you see when we were out shopping, Tommy?' Sally asked as she picked him up and sat him on the kitchen drainer so that she could remove his Wellington boots.

'Favver Christmas,' Tommy told her triumphantly.

'Issmass,' Harry echoed with a beaming smile that made Sally laugh.

She had had ever such a nice time in town showing the children the decorations that the shops were putting up, after morning surgery had finished. Some of them were looking a bit war-worn now, but the kiddies didn't see that and the look on their little faces had been a treat to see. It had been a shame that Alex couldn't have been with them, but they had both decided that until they were ready to go public with their relationship it made sense not to go about together as though they were already a family.

As she had said to Alex, though, last night in bed, cuddled up to his warmth, what they did in private behind closed doors was no one's business but their own. Not that they wouldn't have to be a bit careful. Tommy was that age when he didn't miss a trick. Mind you, Sally admitted to herself, with her feeling that happy that she couldn't stop smiling there'd be others asking a few questions if she wasn't careful.

She put Tommy down on the floor to play with his brother. Alex was out doing his rounds, and with the rain lashing down like it had been he'd want something hot to warm him when he came in.

She was just turning the gas down under the vegetable soup she was making when she heard someone knocking on the front door.

'You stay here. It will be a patient wanting to see Dr Alex,' she instructed Tommy as she went to answer it, wiping her hands on her apron and then taking it off. She and Alex had decided that for now that's how the boys should refer to him.

'A sick person?' Tommy asked.

'Yes,' Sally agreed, opening the door into the hall and then closing it firmly behind her before going to open the front door.

It had been raining all day, a sharp wind icing the rain. A man was standing on the doorstep with his back to her when Sally opened the door, huddled into his raincoat, his hat pulled down and his coat collar turned up to protect him from the weather.

He swung round to face her, malicious pleasure in his small mean eyes as he said, triumphantly, 'Thought I wouldn't track you down here, did you?'

Sid! The Boss's debt collector!

Sally reacted instinctively, immediately backing into the hallway and trying to close the door, but he was too quick for her.

'A little birdie told me you were here. The Boss isn't very happy with you. It gets her goat when her customers try to cheat her.'

'I'm not trying to cheat her,' Sally denied. 'You told me yourself that she said I could have a bit of a holiday from paying her if I wanted to.'

'Bit of an *'oliday* mebbe, but you took off and disappeared wi'out giving us a forwarding address. Just as well I've got some good friends to give me a tip-off as to where you was.'

The confidence that came from having Alex's love gave Sally the courage to say determinedly, 'Well, you can tell her that by my reckoning I've paid her what I owe her three times over and more.'

She could see that her answer hadn't been what he was expecting and her hopes rose that he was going to leave, but instead he moved closer to her and snarled threateningly, 'Your reckoning won't hold water with the Boss, I can tell you that much. Does her own figuring, she does, and she reckons that you still owe her plenty. Mind you, she said to tell you that she's prepared to act generous towards you like on account of you losing your hubby.'

He was leering at her now, and remembering how he had behaved towards her before, Sally could feel horror and revulsion crawling through her stomach. She wasn't going to let him see how she felt, though, not for one minute.

'The doctor will have something to say if he comes back and finds you hanging around, you not being one of his patients.'

There, that should make him take himself off, Sally decided. But to her shock instead of reacting as she had expected the debt collector's leer deepened.

'Funny you should mention him.'

'Why should it be? This is his house, after all,' Sally reminded him sharply.

'And you're working for him as his housekeeper and that, so the Boss has heard.'

'Yes, that's right.' Sally's heart was thumping far too heavily for comfort now, as she sensed that somehow a trap had been sprung but not able to work out exactly what that trap was.

'That's why she's told me to come round and have a word wi' you, on account of you and her being able to do a bit of business together, wi' you working for the doctor.'

'A bit of business?'

'That's right. It's like this, see. Sometimes the Boss gets a bit of a business going wi' them she's teken a liking to. Helps them and her as well. There's allus a demand for things like bandages, and bits of medicine, towels, sheets, the kind of thing that doctors, and them wot works for them, can come by, wi' folk willing to pay good prices and not ask too many questions, if you know what I mean. Wot she said to tell you was that if you play ball with her then she'll forget about what's still owing. I'll come round with a list of the stuff she's wanting. A good-looking woman like you working for a single chap shouldn't have too much trouble getting him to sign his name to a few extra bits and pieces from the hospital and no one the wiser as to who's getting them. Then I'll come round and tek them off your hands and Bob's your uncle.'

He made it all sound so reasonable and above board, but of course it wasn't. Just the opposite, in fact.

'You want me to steal medical and hospital supplies from the doctor so that they can be sold on the black market?' Sally challenged him flatly.

His expression changed from leering satisfaction to irritation.

'If you want to put it like that, that's up to you,' he told her sharply. 'For meself I just say that it's a matter of you scratch the Boss's back and she'll scratch yours. There's no harm done, after all. You can't tell me that you haven't already helped yourself to a little bit of extra stuff here and there, and no one the wiser. I wouldn't blame you neither wi' them two little 'uns to feed and clothe.'

'No, I haven't. I wouldn't,' Sally denied. 'And as for me stealing hospital supplies for you,' she shook her head angrily, 'those things you're talking about are needed for . . . for sick people, and for all I know for our fighting men. So you can go back to *the Boss* and tell her that if it's a thief she's looking for then she's got the wrong person.'

'Oh, no, love,' the debt collector told her softly. 'The Boss don't make mistakes like that. She's got the right person all right, you just haven't realised that yet. You see, Sally – you don't mind if I call you that, I hope, only you and me are going to be a lot closer once we get this little bit of business up and running – well, like I was saying, Sally, the Boss don't make mistakes and when she offers a person a bit of business, then they'd better be ready to say yes, 'cos if they don't . . .'

'I'm not going to listen to any more of this.'

'That's a pity, 'cos I was going to warn you that if you don't act sensible and do as the Boss wants, then you're going to find yourself in a real nasty mess. You see, Sally, the thing is that the Boss has her little ways and she don't like being crossed. So if you was to think of going running to this doctor, for instance, or the police, then I ought ter warn you that you'd find yourself coming in to find a bit of a fire having bin started, by accident on purpose, like, whilst you was out ... or someone might take it into their heads to start writing letters to folk about you and the doctor, if you know what I mean, and then there's them two kiddies of yours ...'

He didn't need to say any more. Sally had already grasped the nature of the threats he was making. She clung to the door, her face robbed of its colour and her heart thudding heavily.

'Look, I'll tell you what I'll do,' the debt collector was telling her in a falsely kind voice. 'I'll give you a couple of days to think about it, and when I come back with the Boss's list of what she reckons she wants that you can get for her, I'm sure you'll realise what it is you have to do.'

With another leering smile he stepped back onto the steps and then turned to walk down them, along the path and out through the gate into the street, whilst all the time Sally stood clinging to the still-open door, unable to move.

He had gone. All that remained of his presence were the muddy shoe marks on the linoleum. Sick and shaking, Sally finally managed to close the front door. Why, *why*, had this had to happen, just when she had thought that she could allow herself to feel safe and happy?

What a fool she had been. That dreadful woman, the Boss, would never let her go; she would never be free of the hold she had on her. And it wasn't just her and the boys the black marketeer could hurt. There was Alex to think about now, a respectable, decent hard-working man, a doctor whose reputation could all too easily be ruined through his love for her.

Sally could just imagine how the old woman would gloat if she ever got to know about how she and Alex felt about one another and how she would try to use that to drag them both into the corrupt web she had spun around herself. How many other innocent people had she forced to steal to supply her with the black market goods she and her sons sold? Sally shuddered to think.

Well, she wasn't going to join their number, not for anything.

But if she didn't, the debt collector and those he worked for would make good those threats he had taunted her with, Sally knew. This was the underbelly of life for the poor. Sally had witnessed it growing up in Manchester as a child, although her family had never been involved with it, and now here it was again, threatening to reach out and drag her down into the dark underworld it thrived on.

Panic filled her as she realised how well they had got her trapped. She could not risk them making good their threats against her children, but she couldn't tell Alex either. She knew him so well now. His first action would be to protect her and the boys, and without thinking about himself.

The Boss was a slippery and evil person. Sally wouldn't put it past her to have plenty of strings to pull that could tighten on Alex and drag him down; whispered talk of things going missing from the hospital passed on along with Alex's name, even when no such thing had happened; other whispers about their relationship, false accusations and claims, things that meant nothing in a court of law but which in the court of human life, to which they were all subject, could mean a very great deal indeed. It wouldn't take long for a man's reputation to be left ruined once that kind of talk got going.

Sally walked blindly back through the hall, sick with fear for her sons, for the man she loved and for herself.

What on earth was she going to do?

TWENTY-SEVEN

It was a busy day. The major had had several meetings to attend, as a result of which Sam had arrived back at the barracks too late to catch the transport that would have taken her back to her billet. Now she had the option of hoping for a lift, getting a bus into the city and then another bus out again, or walking the three miles or so that separated the barracks on Deysbrook Lane from her billet up in Wavertree.

Sitting on her own in the Naafi cafeteria she pondered on what her best choice was whilst drinking her cup of tea.

It made sense to catch the bus, even though that meant going back into the city and out again. It had been raining virtually all day and now it was dark and the temperature had started to drop.

On the other hand, since she didn't feel like company or forcing herself to be pleasant and cheerful when she felt so unhappy perhaps she ought to walk. A brisk walk might even do her good. She could walk back via Tuebrook and the West Derby Road; that way, if she changed her mind, she could still catch a bus.

She finished her tea and stood up.

Outside the Naafi hut she could, if she had wished to do so, have looked across to where the Bomb Disposal Unit had their headquarters and parked their vehicles, but of course she did not want to do any such thing.

Keeping her face averted from them, she pulled up the collar of her greatcoat and walked briskly towards the sentry box, dutifully showing her pass as she left.

It took her a good fifteen minutes' brisk walking to reach Tuebrook, which, along with the railway sidings at Edge Hill, had been heavily targeted by German bombers, and the results of their attacks could still be seen in the damaged buildings.

Johnny's section of the Bomb Disposal Squad was monitoring several non-urgent bomb sites in the area.

Johnny! She came to an abrupt halt in the middle of the pavement, oblivious to both the darkness and the sleet. She hadn't known that it was possible for her heart to hurt so much.

She started walking again, her head down against the icy rain as she headed for Edge Hill.

She was close now to the bomb site that always filled her with secret dread because of the depth of the tunnelling. The Luftwaffe had bombed Edge Hill, hoping to damage the sidings. One of the bombs that had missed was now buried deep beneath the earth, with the site being monitored. The bomb had fallen into what had been a narrow street close to the railing cutting. The street and its houses had been demolished and the site was now an uninhabited wasteland with half-standing buildings, where no one except those with business there ever ventured.

As she drew level with the gap between the buildings that led to the site she glanced up it automatically and then stopped. An army lorry was parked close to the site, the number of Johnny's unit chalked on its side. What was it doing there, at this time of night? She would have known if there had been an emergency because the major would have had to have been informed. Without having had any intention of doing so, she discovered that she was walking towards the lorry, her heart beating far too fast.

Why? Because she thought Johnny might be here?

That was crazy. For one thing, just because she had seen a lorry from Johnny's unit that did not mean that he would be in it, and even if he was then surely he was the last person she wanted to see, wasn't he? He would certainly not want to see her! And for another, as she had been doing her utmost to avoid seeing him since they had broken up, walking down a potholed rubble-strewn road in the darkness, feeling sick with a mixture of misery and longing, hardly made any kind of sense, did it?

She gave a small gasp as she almost stumbled, grimacing as she stepped ankle-deep into a puddle.

What on earth was she doing?

She had reached the lorry now, which she could see was empty. Sometimes the men did leave a spare lorry at one of the sites, ready for use.

She switched on her torch, and swept the beam over the cordoned-off bomb site, registering its empty silence. The only sound was the noise of the wind-driven sleet hitting a piece of corrugated iron. Sam frowned. The opening to the tunnel was normally covered with corrugated iron held down by bricks. Could the wind have lifted them?

She stepped a little closer to the cordon and then stopped. She knew quite well that the real reason she was hesitating was because of her fear of this site.

The bomb had penetrated very deep into the ground. In order to get down to it the sappers had had to tunnel down a long way, shoring up the sides of the tunnel as they worked. The system with such a deeply buried bomb was that the sappers digging at the bottom of the tunnel, where there was barely room for more than a couple of men, had to spade what they dug up onto a shelf constructed above their head, which another sapper, working on that shelf, then removed.

She could see the bricks now. They were neatly piled up together. Neatly piled up? So it wasn't the wind that had blown that covering off, then.

Only human hands could have stacked them like that.

It was probably just some boys larking around who had removed the corrugated iron, not realising the danger they would be creating for the men who had to go into the tunnel. The most sensible thing she could do was put the covering back, put the bricks down over it, and then report what she had done to the barracks in the morning.

She went towards the corrugated iron and then stopped and looked back at the truck. A simple piece of mental arithmetic she didn't really want to add up was forcing itself on her.

Without the truck it might have been possible for her to convince herself that the removal of the covering over the tunnel shaft was the work of mischievous boys, but the truck was there and it must have had a driver.

Sam turned to look back the way she had come. There was no one in sight, no sounds of any human movement. Her lips had gone dry and her heart was pounding. She did not want to do this, she really didn't, but she knew that she had to.

Taking a deep breath she climbed over the cordon and walked towards the mouth of the tunnel.

A further hazard with this site was that water was gathering at the bottom of the tunnel, despite the men having installed a pump.

The pump! She couldn't hear the pump working. Maybe it had been turned off deliberately. She hesitated. There wouldn't be anyone down there – why should there be? She started to turn away, but her conscience was prodding her. If it had been any other bomb site but this one she wouldn't have hesitated to check it out, would she?

Taking another deep breath, she continued towards the tunnel mouth, gasping a little when she slipped on the sticky mud but not stopping until she was as close to the edge as she dared to get. She could feel her stomach churning sickly with her own fear as she shone her torch downwards, then forced her gaze to follow its beam.

Nothing! She exhaled in relief, started to turn away, then stopped, knowing that she should check again.

This time she shone the torch more slowly, panning its thin beam along the walls and then across the shelf platform, its boards sticky with mud. Down below it she could see the silent pump, and rising level of the water – nothing else.

Nothing else? Then what was that she could see shining in the beam of the torch through the boarding of the platform? She shone the torch yet more slowly, its beam picking out the badge that was the insignia of the Bomb Disposal Unit. She moved the torch beam upward from it over the uniformed chest, her heart leaping into her throat as finally it played over the face of the man trapped there.

Johnny!

Johnny. It couldn't be, but it was. Her hand was wet with sweat where she was holding the torch.

Her heart was drumming with fear and panic. She desperately wanted to believe that none of this was happening, but she knew perfectly well that it was.

Forcing herself to look down at him, she called Johnny's name, then when there was no response she called again more loudly.

Nothing. No movement. No sound, no awareness that she was there at all.

She could see that he was slumped over, his body almost submerged beneath the water, and she knew that if he was alive he must be unconscious. If he was alive? He must be. He *had* to be.

She had to get to him. Sam didn't hesitate. Driven by love and fear, not even the fact that she was shaking from head to foot, and half sobbing, could stop her from climbing down the rope ladder the men used to reach the platform.

It was like going down into hell itself, and several times she had to force herself not to panic and start clawing her way out again when her feet slipped on the wet, mud-coated rope, threatening to send her plummeting downward.

It seemed to take her a lifetime to reach the platform, and once she had she crouched there, feeling violently sick, unable to move, almost unable to breathe. What if the rain caused the mud she had left behind to start to slide into the hole trapping her, *burying* her . . . ? Don't think like that, she told herself. You mustn't.

She reached into her pocket for her torch, each movement an effort because of her fear and her icy cold hands. Switching it on, she peered down through the platform, her breath catching on a frantic sob as the first thing the light revealed was Johnny's face, closer now.

His eyes were closed, but to her relief she could see that he was breathing. Tears filled her eyes as she sobbed his name. He was lying on his back with rising water lapping all around him.

He was too far below her for her to be able to reach out and touch him from the platform. She would have to go down even further into the tunnel. She looked up the way she had just come. If she went for help would they get back in time? The water was rising fast.

If, instead of going for help, she could get to Johnny she might be able to lift his head clear of the water. They wouldn't have to wait long for someone to come looking for them. Someone at the barracks must know by now that he was missing, surely, and would send a search party out to find him? But what if they didn't . . . what if . . . ?

Don't think about it, Sam ordered herself as she started to make her way down to Johnny. Don't think about anything except being with Johnny. What if the worst *did* happen and the tunnel collapsed on top of them? At least they would be here together, and what was her life to her anyway without him?

But to die in such a way and such a place, slowly, gasping for air in the darkness . . .

She gasped, almost slipping into the pool, as she reached the bottom of the shaft, and managed to struggle through the muddy water to get to him.

Crouching down beside him she whispered his name in his ear and stroked the wet hair off his face, keeping her torch on and tucked into the breast pocket of her jacket so that she could at least see something of what she was doing as she struggled to lift his head up and support his upper body against her own to keep his head clear of the water.

It hurt so much to fear that holding him like this might be as close as she would ever get to holding him in a lover's embrace, and that this might be all she would know of him before death claimed them both.

But at least she was here with him. How many other women mourning the men they had lost would have been more than happy to change places with her, were this their man? She leaned forward and pressed her lips to his forehead, cold lips on cold flesh.

Suddenly his eyelids fluttered and then opened. For a minute Sam was too overwhelmed with relief to speak.

Johnny was looking at her, his gaze cloudy and confused. 'Sam . . .' he whispered weakly. 'Is it really you?'

'Yes, it's really me.'

'I've been dreaming about you. Perhaps I still am.'

'No, you're not dreaming. I am here.'

'The pump's packed up,' he told her.

'Yes, I know.'

'Part of the shoring fell in onto the pump. It's

on my leg and I can't get free. Hurts like hell, it does.'

Sam swallowed painfully. She'd realised that he was trapped, of course.

'Help will be here soon,' she told him. 'They're bound to send someone from the barracks.'

'I thought you said you're afraid of tunnels.'

'I am.'

'So why did you come down here?'

'You know me,' she answered as lightly as she could. 'Always ready to live dangerously.'

He didn't say anything for so long that she was afraid that he had lost consciousness again, but then abruptly he said, 'The water's rising.'

'Yes.' She managed to keep her voice calm but she knew that the way her arms tightened around him would have given her away.

'I want you to get yourself out of here, Sam.'

Now it was her turn not to say anything.

'Sam?'

'It's no use trying to boss me around. I'm staying here.'

'It's not going to be that long.'

'No, I'm sure the others will be here soon.'

'That wasn't what I meant. Is it still raining?'

Sam swallowed back her tears. 'No, it's stopped.'

'Liar. I reckon I've got an hour at the most. Water's rising fast.'

'No, you mustn't say that.'

'It's the truth, and you know it. I don't want you staying down here, risking your own life on account of me. I'm not worth it.'

'That's for me to say.'

'You're not crying, are you?' he demanded.

'No!'

'Must be raining then, seein' as me face is getting all wet.'

Sam gulped.

'I was thinking about you before . . .'

'Wishing you'd never met me?' Sam suggested, trying to sound light-hearted.

'No. Wishing I'd had a chance to tell you what a fool I've bin and how much I love you.'

'Oh, Johnny.'

She *was* crying now, but somehow it didn't matter and somehow too he had managed to put his arm around her and pull her down towards him until she was close enough for him to kiss her.

His lips tasted of cold and wet, and even a little mud, but Sam didn't care. Her heart swelled with love for him, and she kissed him back every bit as fiercely as he was kissing her.

'I've bin missing you,' he told her emotionally as he released her. 'Missing you and wishing I'd not acted like such a fool.'

'I've missed you too,' Sam told him.

'It isn't true that I still love Molly,' he said gruffly. 'There's only one girl I love, only one girl for me, and that's you, Sam. And that's the honest truth.'

'Why didn't you tell me about her? Why didn't you want me to meet your sister?'

She felt his chest lift as he breathed in and then exhaled on a deep sigh.

'It wasn't because I still love her. I don't. She's a nice girl and a good wife and a mother, but she's not my girl.' His hand tightened on Sam's. 'Yes, me and Molly were engaged, and I thought . . . but it was nothing more than a lad's calf love. The thing is, well, I've changed a lot from the lad I was then. I was a bit wild, a bit full of meself, and that. The army knocked that out of me and brought me to me senses. That, and this war. Me sisters, though, especially our Jennifer –' he paused again – 'they're good-hearted enough but they aren't your sort, Sam, and the truth is . . .' He swallowed. 'I'm ashamed of meself for saying this, but the truth is that I was worried that it would put you off me if you were to meet our Jennifer. She's married now but time was when she was off with a different lad ever week and our mam was at her wits' end with her.'

'You were ashamed of her?'

'Not so much of her, but of what I thought she might start telling you about me when we were kids, and that you'd not want me any more.'

'Oh, Johnny, how could you think that?'

'I could think it easily, Sam. When Molly turned me down it left me feeling that I wasn't good enough. Hurt me pride more than me heart, and that's the truth. But, well, a man's pride is important to him, Sam, and I swore then that I'd never set meself up to be brought down like that again. That's why I tried to put you off, saying that you was too young and that. I'd told meself that falling in love was for fools and that it wasn't going to happen to me a second time.'

Sam made a small sound of mingled pity and pain, and Johnny gave her arm a small gentle squeeze.

'I should have known better, but when you've grown up like I did, without a dad, looked down on by the neighbours, allus feeling that you wasn't quite good enough and having to put on a bit of a show about not caring what anyone thought, well, then there's allus a bit of that kid somewhere inside you, waiting for someone to give him a kick and tell him to take himself off. *That's* why I didn't tell you about me and Molly. I'm not saying that I didn't fancy meself in love with her, 'cos I'd be lying, but it wasn't anything like the way I feel about you. The truth is that I didn't want you knowing that she hadn't wanted me in case it set you off feeling the same.'

'Oh, Johnny,' Sam wept, 'I love you so much.'

'I know you do.' His voice wasn't as strong as it had been and Sam had to lean closer to him to catch what he was saying. 'You came down here, didn't you, and I know how hard that must have been for you.'

Sam gulped and then sniffed. 'I couldn't not do, once I knew you were here.'

'Don't you ever forget what I've just told you.' Johnny's voice was fading. 'I love you, Sam, and I allus will. Never think any different.'

'Johnny. *Johnny!*' Sam begged him frantically as she felt him slump against her. But it was no use, he had slipped back into unconsciousness.

*

Whilst they had been talking the water level had risen and now she tried to lift Johnny's head a bit higher. Why didn't someone come?

With Johnny unconscious she felt so alone and so afraid. Her kneeling position had made her legs go numb and now her eyelids felt so heavy.

What if help didn't come?

Maybe the best thing she could do for both of them was to let Johnny go into the water and then lie down beside him herself.

Johnny stirred in her arms, muttering something, and then said her name quite clearly and with such emotion, before losing consciousness again, that she wanted to weep.

Sam had no idea how long she had been down here in this icy tomb, her own senses slipping away from her as she kept being tempted into a dream state of warmth and safety.

'Next Christmas you and I will be taking the boys to see Father Christmas together, and when this war's over I'm going to buy Tommy the best train set I can find. Mm, this soup's good, Sally. Oh, no,' Alex groaned, putting down his spoon as they heard someone banging urgently on the front door.

'I'll go,' he told Sally, but she stood up, telling him, 'I'll do it. You finish your soup.'

She hardly dare look at Alex in case he guessed that something had happened and demanded to know what it was. She still had no idea what on earth she was going to do. She couldn't tell him.

She knew how he would react and how he would want to protect her. But he couldn't; not from someone like the Boss. Someone who didn't live by the rules.

Alex was such a decent upright man that he just wouldn't understand how easily the Boss could damage his reputation. Once rumour got its claws into a person it never let them go. It dragged them down and destroyed them. She couldn't let that happen to him because he loved her.

So what *could* she do?

There was only one answer, she knew that, but she could hardly bear to think of it, never mind act upon it. It ached through her like the slow painful spill of blood from a death blow. She could not, would not, allow Alex to be touched by this horror, or to be dragged down with her. There was no escape for *her*, she knew that; no law that could protect her from the kind of reprisals the Boss and her sort used to terrorise and control their victims.

No, this time she really did not have any choice than to take the boys and leave, to disappear. No choice at all. For Alex's dear sake she must do what she knew was the last thing she wanted to do.

She crossed the hall and opened the door to find Daisy Cartwright standing outside. She was in a pitiful state of despair, and had obviously been crying.

'We need the doctor,' she gasped. 'It's our Luke, teken real bad, he's bin . . .' She was shaking and shivering, her face the colour of old yellowing putty, and despite the way she had behaved towards her, and her own problems, Sally couldn't help but feel sorry for her.

'Wait here. I'll go and tell him.'

'Who is it?' Alex asked her when she went back into the kitchen.

'It's Daisy Cartwright. She's in a really bad way. It's her Luke. She says he's been taken bad.'

Alex was already standing up and wiping his mouth with his serviette, before pulling on his jacket.

As he opened the kitchen door to go into the hallway, Sally could hear Daisy telling him between sobs, 'Bin sick all day, he has, and the other as well, you know what I mean, that bad that I could have done wi' some nappies, and there's blood coming now, an' all.'

'All right, Mrs Cartwright. Let's go and have a look at him.'

'I don't know what time I'll be back,' Alex told Sally, putting his head round the door. 'If he's as bad as Mrs Cartwright says then it maybe that her son will need to go into hospital.'

Sally nodded, starting to turn away, and then unable to stop herself, she pulled him back into the kitchen, and kissed him fiercely on the mouth.

'You are the best thing that's ever happened to me and my kiddies,' she told him huskily.

'And you're the best thing that's ever happened to me.'

'No, I'm not . . .'

'Doctor . . . Doctor, are you there . . . ?' They

could hear Daisy calling anxiously from the hall.

He kissed her again, swiftly, before going back out into the hall. As soon as the door had closed behind him Sally sat down on a chair, put her head in her hands and began to weep.

TWENTY-EIGHT

The water was over her knees now. Sam knew that she needed to get Johnny sitting up, but she was afraid of trying to lift him in case he was too heavy for her and he slipped away from her and under the water. But if she didn't move him then he might drown anyway before help came.

Why didn't help come? Why?

She must get Johnny's torso upright, she had to. As she struggled to gently lift his unresponsive frame she could hear mud sliding from the sides of the tunnel and landing on the shelf above them. Her hands were so cold she could barely feel them any more, as she used her body as a prop to try to lever Johnny into a more upright position. But it was useless, she couldn't budge him, and the more she struggled the more she herself was getting sucked down into the mud. Her torch battery had run down what seemed like ages ago.

'Johnny, please wake. You've got to wake up . . . please,' she begged him, but he didn't answer her.

Wrapping her arms round him, she bent her head over his and let the tears come. She was so cold and so tired, too cold and tired even to be afraid any more, and certainly too cold and tired to hope.

She closed her eyes.

It was the beam of bright torches that woke her, and at first, confused by their brilliance, Sam wondered light-headedly if perhaps after all she was already dead and they were the lights of heavenly angels.

The voices that called down to her were anything but heavenly, though, in their rough anxiety, yelling her name along with Johnny's.

Collecting her bemused wits, she managed to call back, 'Yes, we're here!'

The torches went out and for a second she panicked, thinking that she hadn't been heard and that their rescuers were going to go away, not realising they were here.

'Please, please, don't go!' she cried out. 'Please . . .'

'It's all right, lass . . .' Corporal Willett's voice was warm and familiar, and much closer than she expected. 'We'll have the pair of you out in a couple of ticks. What happened? Fell in, did you, and Johnny had to rescue you?'

'Certainly not.' The accusation was enough to rally her to vocal indignation.

'So what happened then?'

She guessed that the corporal wanted to keep her talking and alert for her own benefit, so despite

480

her exhaustion she forced herself to answer him as lucidly as she could.

'I saw that the lorry was here and so I came to have a look, and then I saw that the corrugated iron had been removed and the bricks stacked up, so then . . . so then I came to have a proper look and I realised that Johnny was down here. So I came down, and then . . . then when I saw that he was unconscious and in the water, with it rising, I thought I'd better stay with him. I knew someone would come looking for us.'

'Unconscious, is he?'

'Yes. He is now,' Sam answered then gave a gasp as she heard a thud on the platform above her.

'Let's take a look-see then.'

Sam thought she had never known anything more welcoming than the warm touch of the corporal's hand as he leaned over the shelf and grasped her shoulder.

'Johnny's here,' she told him. 'I tried to sit him up but I couldn't so I thought if I could sit behind him I could at least lift his head. He told me that his leg is trapped.' Her voice shook with all that she feared and dared not say.

'Aye, it looks like some of the shoring's gone and collapsed,' the corporal said, adding, 'Let's have a butcher's at him, then.'

Sam winced in the bright glare of the torch he switched on. Its beam was much stronger than that of her own torch and in it she could see the way the side of the tunnel next to them was bowing in, pressing against the shoring with the weight of earth behind it, and then down into the water, where Sam could see now that the pump had somehow become wedged between two pieces of wood, trapping the lower half of Johnny's leg beneath them.

'Mm. Got himself in a real pickle, hasn't he? Looks like he must have slipped and knocked himself out. He was bloody lucky you found him. Right, let's get you out of here.'

'You'll have to get Johnny out first,' Sam told him.

'That's all right, lass, I'll take your place so as you can get out.'

'No! I'm afraid that if I move he'll slip into the water, you see. There isn't much room.'

'The thing is, Sam, because the pump hasn't been working some of the shoring's started to slip a bit.'

He was, Sam could tell, picking his words with care like a man with bare feet walking on glass, and she suspected she knew why.

'You're trying to tell me that the shaft might cave in, aren't you?'

'It's a possibility,' Corporal Willett agreed, 'so let's get you out first, shall we?'

'No . . . no, Johnny goes first . . . I mean it,' she stressed 'I'm not going anywhere until I know that Johnny's safe.'

For a moment she thought he was going to argue with her and then he gave a small grunt and called back up to the waiting men at the top of the shaft, 'We're going to need a sling to get Johnny up, lads. He's out for the count, and his leg's trapped. Should be able to get him free fairly easily, though, by the looks of it.'

'Hang on, there's a sling in the lorry,' someone shouted back.

'By heaven, if I had a daughter it would make me ruddy proud to have one like you,' the corporal praised Sam whilst they waited. 'Mind you, I'd probably feel like taking me belt to her for being so bloody stupid,' he added forthrightly.

'Go on with you,' Sam laughed. 'You're much too big a softie to do anything of the sort.'

Somehow it was easier than she had expected to keep up their shared banter and not to think about the warning he had given her, nor to hear the sound of the mud slithering down onto the platform above them, as the corporal worked quickly and competently.

'Keep a tight hold on him, lass,' he told Sam, as he started to remove the broken spars of wood.

Sam trembled, her stomach churning for him when Johnny cried out in pain, without opening his eyes, as the wood was removed from his legs.

'Just as well he's out for the count,' the corporal told her grimly as he put the broken spars in the sling, to be hauled up to the surface, and then started to remove the now submerged pump. 'Broken his leg, I reckon, from the angle of it,' he grunted, as he lifted the pump away.

'Shouldn't his leg be splinted before you move him?' Sam asked anxiously.

'Ideally, yes,' he agreed, 'but we ain't got ideal

conditions down there. He ain't bleeding, and that's a mercy and no mistake, so the best thing we can do is get him up to the surface, I reckon.'

All the men were trained in first aid, so Sam didn't argue.

As he had been doing intermittently throughout the time she had been in the tunnel shaft with him, Johnny moaned and muttered unintelligibly as though he was returning to consciousness, before going silent again.

It seemed to Sam that it took for ever before the corporal was satisfied that Johnny had been secured safely in the sling and he was finally being slowly lifted up out of their prison, the corporal following him to make sure that his inert body did not bang into the sides of the tunnel, pausing briefly as they reached the upper level of the platform, from which the men above had removed some planks to make the shaft wide enough for the sling and what it held to get through.

Now, as they rose slowly above it, their progress blotting out the reassuring brilliance of the torches being shone down by the men waiting above ground, Sam was once again trapped in darkness.

Then to her relief she could see a torch beam and a cheerful voice called down to her, 'On our way now, Sam.'

Shakily she exhaled her pent-up breath and then froze as there was a gathering sound of mud and debris trickling and then rushing towards her through the gap in the platform through which they had hauled Johnny to safety, in a roar of life-extinguishing darkness.

It had happened; just what she had always feared since that first time. She was trapped down here; buried alive. Panic clawed at her thoughts in much the same way that she wanted to claw her way upwards, but she forced herself to stay calm. The men up there above her knew she was there, and they knew far better than she how best to get to her. All she had to do was keep calm and wait . . .

But what if they couldn't reach her? What if the weight of the earth that that fallen on top of what was left of the platform forced it down on top of her? What if . . . ? She could taste mud mixed in with her fear; she could feel death hovering at her shoulder, waiting.

She thought of Mouse, and her parents. She thought too of Hazel and Russell, soon to be reunited and happy, but most of all, as the seconds and the minutes of her entombment crawled by, she thought of Johnny.

Sally tensed as she heard a car pulling up outside. Unable to settle after Alex had left, still filled with the shock and despair of the debt collector's visit and threats, as well as worrying about poor little Luke, she had started dusting the already dust-free furniture and then, when that was done, pacing up and down the kitchen, trying to work out how on earth she was going to find the strength to leave Alex, whilst knowing that for his sake she must.

'Alex!' She ran to open the door. 'How's Luke?' she asked.

'It's bad,' he told her grimly. 'I've had him admitted to Mill Road. The hospital didn't want to take him at first, but I managed to persuade them to find a bed for him.'

Because they thought so highly of him. Because he was a doctor, because he was a man who others admired and respected because of his decency and his devotion to his patients. But public opinion could be fickle. Gossip was easy to spread and could soon destroy even the best reputation.

Sally's thoughts ripped at her heart like so many knives. It was so unfair. If she left she would be depriving her sons of the best stepfather they could have, a man they already loved and trusted, and she would be depriving Alex of them, never mind her own feelings. But what else could she do?

'The ambulance has just collected him,' Alex was telling her. 'I'm on my way there myself now but I thought I'd just call here to tell you what's happening.'

'And Luke? I know you said it was bad, but he will get better, won't he?' she asked him.

To her shock Alex didn't reply straight away and then avoided looking at her. 'It's going to be touch and go.'

'What . . . what do you mean?' she asked him, but she already knew the answer from his bleak expression. 'No,' she protested, adding when he didn't respond. 'What is it? What's wrong with him?'

'Same as Tommy had, but much worse. His mother won't say what he's been eating, but my guess is that that husband of hers has been giving her tins of condemned food again. I just hope to God that this is an isolated case. He would have had a better chance if she'd got medical help earlier.'

'Oh, Alex. Why didn't she? It's not as though the Cartwrights are short of a bob or two.'

'She said something about her husband not wanting her to. Poor woman, she was in too much of a state for me to press her too hard for an explanation. I've got to go. They won't have any spare doctors down at the hospital to stay with him. The poor lad's very weak. If we can get him stabilised over the next twenty-four hours he might have a chance.' He rubbed his hand over his eyes. 'If only they'd called me out at the first. Don't wait up for me, Sally,' he told her. 'It's going to be morning before I get back.'

When he hugged her, Sally hugged him back fiercely, determined not to let him see her tears or guess what she was going through.

Maybe this was a 'sign' for her, she decided after he had gone. Maybe fate was telling her that she should leave, by providing her with the perfect opportunity to do so.

Alex had told her himself that he wouldn't be back until morning. All she had to do was go upstairs, pack their things, wake the boys and go.

No! No, she couldn't bear the thought of it, never mind actually doing it. It was so unfair. They had been so happy.

She had no idea where she could go or what she would do. All she did know was that she had to go to protect Alex.

She felt sick and somehow as though neither her head nor her body were working properly. It was a bit like having a bad head cold, a muzzy, vague, shaky sort of feeling that made her feel wretchedly miserable and weak.

It was dark and cold, and the mud was all around her, pressing in on her, filling her mouth and her eyes and her nose so that she couldn't see or breathe. It pressed down on her in a heavy crushing weight. Sam tried to cry out against it but it was too late, the darkness was invading her . . .

'There, it's all right, love, you're safe and sound now. You was just having a nasty dream, that's all.'

Sam forced open her eyes. They were sticky with something, and her chest hurt. A nurse was bending over her.

'Where am I?'

'Mill Road Hospital, love. Brought you in a couple of hours back, and a real state you was in, an' all, covered from head to foot in mud, looked like you'd been dug up out of a potato patch and according to them what brought you in you might just as well have been. Dug you out of some tunnel that had collapsed, they did.'

Sam could feel her chest starting to grow tight whilst her heart pounded.

'Johnny?' she managed to ask. 'My . . . is he . . . ?'

'Sister will have my hide if she comes in and finds you awake. You get back to sleep. Sister said to put you in a private room as a bit of a treat, seein' as what you've bit through.' The nurse started to move away.

'No, please wait,' Sam begged her. 'I've got to know. Was there . . . did they . . . Johnny . . . ?'

'You're asking me about that handsome chap with the broken leg and a bump the size of an egg on the back of his head?'

'He's all right?'

The nurse nodded.

Sam sank back against the hard mattress, weak tears of relief blurring her eyes.

'Unconscious, he was, when they brought him in but seemingly he's come round now and Dr Munroe says there's nothing wrong with him that won't heal, thanks to a certain someone not too far away from me,' the nurse told Sam meaningfully. 'Now, you'd better drink this medicine the doctor said you was to have. It will help you sleep. And no more nasty dreams this time.'

Reluctantly Sam took the glass she was holding out to her, grimacing as she drank its bitter contents.

Johnny was alive and safe. They were both safe . . . She closed her eyes and then opened them again, reluctant to go back to sleep in case she was dragged back into the nightmare from which she had just escaped. But the sleeping draught she had been given was too strong for her, and by the time the nurse came back down the ward Sam was fast asleep.

Weeping silently, Sally pressed the softness of Alex's shirt to her cheek. She had picked it up, meaning to wash it for him before she left, but she just hadn't been able to bring herself to part with it. It smelled of his skin and just holding it felt a little bit like holding him.

It was gone three o'clock in the morning and she still hadn't done what she had come upstairs to do. The suitcase she had dragged from under her bed was lying open on the floor, the boys' clothes folded neatly, ready to go into it, the drawers to her own cupboard open.

What was wrong with her? She should have had everything packed by now and be downstairs making up some sandwiches for their journey. She looked down at the case, her face contorting with grief. She just couldn't do this. She couldn't leave Alex.

But she must. She had to.

'Sally?'

She whirled round. Alex was standing at the door.

'What's this?' he demanded. 'What are you doing?'

Overwhelmed by her own despair she hadn't even heard her bedroom door opening, never mind his footsteps on the stairs or his key in the front door. And now all she seemed able to do was stand there clutching his shirt, caught between guilt and anguish, as he stood looking from her guilty face to the open suitcase.

'What's going on? What are you doing?' he repeated.

When she didn't answer, able only to shake her head in mute misery, he strode across to her, taking hold of her arm, tension darkening his eyes.

The smell of the hospital on his clothes jerked her out of her own despair, reminding her of where he had been and why.

'Luke, how is he?' she asked him urgently.

She saw his mouth compress as he looked away from her, drawing in a deep breath and then exhaling tiredly, and her heart went cold.

'He's gone.'

Sally could hear the heaviness of defeat in his voice. 'No,' she protested, her own position as a mother shrinking from the thought of any child losing its life. 'No, Alex. He can't be.' Inside her head she had an image of the vigorous, healthy child Luke had been. 'He can't be,' she repeated, but she knew from Alex's expression and his silence that he was.

Luke was *dead*. She started to shake, her fingers curling into the shirt she was still holding. She tried to put herself in Daisy's shoes, but it was too painful and she shrank back from the horror of such a reality.

'We tried our best, but it was no use.'

He looked down at the suitcase. 'You're leaving

me.' He said the words flatly, as though her going was something he had expected. Expected but not wanted – Sally could see that from the pain in his eyes. 'You were going to walk out on me without a word and leave me to come back and find you gone! Why, Sally, why? I thought you and I . . . You said you loved me.'

She could hear the torment in his voice. It tore at her heart and she knew she couldn't let him think she didn't care.

'I do love you. But I've got to go. I can't stay, Alex.'

'I'm not letting you go!'

'You must.'

He looked at her and shook his head. He looked so tired, so beaten down, that she ached to hold him and comfort him.

'I don't understand, Sally. You say you love me and yet at the same time you say you want to leave me . . . It doesn't make sense.'

Not to him, perhaps, but it made perfect sense to her.

Why had he had to come back like this, catching her when she was at her most vulnerable, making this so much harder for both of them? If she had just left without any explanation he could have hated her for going and that hatred would have set him free to find someone else.

'I want to know what's going on, Sally.'

'I can't tell you. Please don't try to make me. It wouldn't do any good, anyway. I have to go, Alex. I have to – for your sake.'

Sally felt as though she was being torn in two, her fear for him driving her in one direction whilst her longing for him was pulling her in another.

'You're not making sense,' Alex repeated. 'And I'm not letting you go, Sally, not until I have the truth.' His voice and his manner had changed now, becoming stronger and determined.

'You can't stop me.'

'No? You're still in my employ and if I were to report you to the authorities for leaving . . .'

Sally stared at him in disbelief. 'You'd do that?'

'Yes. Unless you tell me the truth.'

He meant it, Sally knew. She had no choice. She would have to tell him. Maybe only then would he understand that she had to leave and he had to let her go.

She looked up at him and took a deep unsteady breath. 'All right,' she told him, 'I will tell you.'

Slowly, haltingly, even stopping at times to shake her head when Alex, plainly moved by what she was saying, took a step towards her, she told him the full story.

'You planned to leave me because of that?' Alex burst out at one point when she had been describing how the debt collector had threatened her with blackmail.

'What else could I do? He said there'd be letters sent, and gossip spread, saying that you weren't a good doctor, and she, the Boss, she could do it . . . I know she could.' Sally gave a fierce shudder. 'You don't know her, Alex. She's wicked through and through. And if they found out about you and me

493

it would only make things worse. I couldn't let that happen, not even though I knew it would break my heart to leave you. I couldn't shame you and bring you down on account of you loving me, I just couldn't.'

'Oh, Sally, Sally! I can't bear to think of you suffering all of this . . . Listen to me. Nothing's going to happen to me.'

'You don't know what they're like and what they can do . . .'

'Oh, yes, I do. In fact, I know a very great deal now about this woman, her sons, their threats and their wickedness, and even if I didn't, do you really think for one minute I'd let anything or anyone part us?'

'What do you mean, you know a very great deal about them?'

Very gently Alex took hold of her and then drew her towards the side of the bed, where he sat down and pulled her down to sit beside him. Then turning so that they were facing one another he explained, 'Daisy Cartwright broke down at the hospital. She told us about this same woman, the Boss, and how she and her sons had been blackmailing some of the men working on the docks to force them to supply her with large amounts of tinned goods, pressuring them for more and more so that in desperation Daisy's husband has been giving them tins that are condemned. Daisy didn't realise this and opened one of them for Luke's tea. When he started to be sick her husband, guessing what had happened, panicked and told her that they'd have to keep quiet about it otherwise he'd lose his job. That's why she didn't come round straight away. Of course, once she saw how much worse Luke was getting she ignored her husband, but by then it was too late. I . . . I knew that as soon as I saw him, but one always hopes for a miracle, especially where a child is concerned.'

Sally could see how much the little boy's death had affected him. 'Oh Alex . . .' Instinctively she leaned towards him, wanting to give him comfort and receive it herself.

He moved towards her and then checked. 'What's this?' he demanded, looking at the shirt she was still clutching.

'Your shirt from yesterday,' Sally confessed. 'I was going to wash it for you before I left and then when I picked it up, well, it smelled of you and I . . . I knew I had to take it with me so that I'd have a bit of you with me.'

'Oh, my love, my love. How could you ever think that anything could matter more to me than you? Do you really think I'd ever let a bit of gossip, no matter how malicious or damaging, come between us?'

'Alex, you're a doctor – you've got your good reputation to think of, and your patients need you.'

'And I need you.' He removed the shirt from her grasp and wrapped her in his arms.

Sally didn't even try to resist, instead leaning her head on his shoulder and giving in to her own need to have this wonderful precious closeness to him. But her conscience still forced her to tell him,

'You know what the Boss can do to people, Alex. She'll try to blackmail me like she did poor Daisy's husband.'

'Shush,' Alex stopped her lovingly, as he held her close. 'She won't be doing anything to hurt anyone any more, Sally, I can promise you that.'

'What . . . what do you mean?' She moved slightly in Alex's arms and immediately they tightened lovingly around her.

'Daisy Cartwright and her husband agreed to tell the police what's been going on. In fact, the police were there at the hospital with them when they left, and I have it on good authority that the Boss and the rest of her gang will be behind bars in a very short space of time indeed.'

Silent tears of relief slid slowly down Sally's face whilst her body shook in Alex's hold with the force of her emotions.

'My dearest love, I can't bear to think of what you've suffered, but it's all over now.'

'Yes,' she began to say, but her assent was lost within the sweetness of Alex's kiss.

'I think I must have a very special guardian angel looking after me, Sally,' Alex whispered huskily against her lips. 'I nearly didn't come home tonight but after we'd lost little Luke all I could think of was how much I needed your tenderness.'

'Maybe it's not one guardian angle but a pair of them,' Sally suggested softly, knowing he knew what she meant when he looked at her and said huskily, 'My two lost boys? I'd certainly like to think they were looking down on me with love.

You mean so much to me, Sally. Everything, in fact. Promise me that from now on there won't be any more secrets between us?'

'I promise.'

The half-packed suitcase lay ignored on the bedroom floor as Alex lifted her onto the bed and then joined her there, the only sounds now breaking the night's silence not those of despair but the soft music of whispered words of love and shared kisses.

TWENTY-NINE

'Wake up, sleepy head.'

The soft words, whispered teasingly close to her ear in a familiar and beloved voice, had Sam opening her eyes and then turning her head on her hospital pillow in disbelief.

'Johnny!' she exclaimed with delight as she looked from his dear face to the wheelchair that he was sitting in, and in which he had, she was sure against hospital rules, managed to get himself into her small private room. 'Oh, Johnny!' she whispered, her eyes filling with tears.

'Well, that's a fine welcome for a chap who's managed to get himself a bit of transport out of a sister who's tighter that a duck's a—'

'Johnny!' Sam protested, giggling.

'That's more like my girl,' he told her approvingly. 'And you are my girl, Sam,' he added, his voice deepening with tenderness. 'Always and for ever. The only girl I could ever want, and just you make sure you understand that, and that you're mine. Savvy?' he told her, mock sternly.

'Savvy!' Sam agreed, giving a small blissful sigh of happiness when he reached out to put his arm around her so that he could kiss her.

It was a very thorough kiss and a very long one, and Sam, nestling against him, knew that she had never been happier nor more thankful to be alive.

'That was a bloody brave thing you did for me, Sam,' Johnny told her. 'And a bloody daft one, an' all, risking your own life like that.'

'Mine wouldn't have been worth anything to me without you in it,' Sam told him shakily.

'There you go, being daft again – how the devil is Mr Churchill going to win this ruddy war without you to help him?' Johnny teased her.

'He needs your help more than he needs mine,' Sam countered stoutly.

'Aye, well, as to that,' Johnny was holding her hand and now he held it tighter, 'I thought I was a goner down there, Sam, I can tell you. I knew that eventually the lads would find me, but I reckoned it wouldn't be before the morning, not with that bomb not being on the urgent list and me only having decided to take a look at it on me way home when I came off duty. And by that time I would have been drowned.'

Sam made a small sound of anguish and shook her head.

'It's the truth,' Johnny insisted.

'What about your leg? I know you've broken it.'

'Yes, but it's a clean break, luckily, and the doctor says that it should heal easily enough. Course, he's told me that seein' as they're short of beds here he's going to need to send me home, and that on account of me not being able to get around much under me own steam, I'm going to need someone around to look after me. Do you know anyone who'd be willing to take on that job, Sam?'

His words might be whimsical and light but Sam was only half listening to them. She was looking into his eyes, and what she could see there made her heart somersault as though it was in the hands of a juggler.

'I . . . I think I might do.'

'Mm.' Johnny was leaning closer to her. He was going to kiss her again. 'She wouldn't be a long-legged blonde with the most loving heart there ever was, and a smile that could soften iron, could she, this girl you know? 'Cos if she is . . .'

His free hand was cupping the back of her head now, his breath warm against her skin.

''Cos if she is?' Sam prompted him weakly.

''Cos if she is then I reckon that her and me are just about perfect for one another.'

'Oh, Johnny.'

'And what's going on in here, may I ask?'

They sprang apart at the wrathful sound of Sister's voice.

'When you told me that you wished to thank Private Grey for her part in your rescue, Sergeant Everton, this was not what I expected to find!'

To Sam's amusement, instead of looking chagrined, Johnny merely winked at the stern-looking woman standing in the doorway and said,

'Didn't want any other chap to beat me to it and propose to her before I could.'

'You've asked Private Grey to marry you?'

Johnny's smile broadened. 'Not yet, but if you give me another five minutes or so, I intend to.'

After Sister had gone with a disapproving rustle of her starched uniform and a firm, 'Five minutes and not a second more then,' Sam whispered lovingly to Johnny, 'It won't take me five seconds to say "yes", never mind five minutes.'

'No,' he agreed, 'but think of how much I'm going to enjoy kissing you, to celebrate, for the other four minutes and fifty-five seconds.'

'It's really kind of you and Russ to come and collect me and Johnny, Hazel,' Sam thanked her friend and her brother, as she checked that she had removed everything from her hospital bedside locker.

She and Johnny were both being discharged today and then the four of them were going to travel down south together to spend Christmas with Sam and Russell's parents.

'Johnny said he'd wait for us on his ward. He wanted to say goodbye to some of the other men.'

Sam's face clouded slightly. Although she and Johnny had been kept in hospital for only a few days, it had been long enough for Johnny to strike up friendships with some of the other soldiers on the ward, many of whom had very serious injuries indeed.

She and Johnny were so very lucky. Sam gave

a small shiver as the three of them left her small room and headed for Johnny's ward.

The first person Sam saw when Russell opened the ward doors for them was Johnny. The second was the pretty young woman who was standing talking to him, laughing up at him. There was something about her that was vaguely familiar but Sam couldn't put her finger on exactly what it was at first, and then she realised that she was the young woman she had seen singing at the Grafton the night Johnny had asked her to dance. A friend from his past, someone who knew all those things about him that she did not.

'What's up?' Russell demanded when he saw the way she was hanging back.

'Nothing,' she told him, but she knew that there was. Johnny hadn't seen her yet. It was obvious that he was relaxed and at ease with the woman, and that she was someone he knew well. She had even put her hand on his arm as she said something to him, as though to emphasise some point she had been making. Their intimacy underlined for Sam with painful sharpness the fact that a large part of his life – all of his past, in fact – was forbidden territory to her, and that hurt, even though he had explained his feelings to her.

Johnny looked up and saw her, a tender loving smile immediately curving his mouth. He was on crutches now and Sam saw him saying something to the woman, before starting to make his way towards her.

She felt Russell giving her a little push, and then

502

she was hurrying towards Johnny, meeting him before he had managed more than a few yards.

'Come and meet Sally,' Johnny told her. 'She was singing at the Grafton that night . . .'

'Yes. Yes. I recognised her,' Sam stopped him. 'You have a lovely voice,' she told Sally.

'Thank you.'

They exchanged slightly hesitant smiles.

'I must go,' Sally said. 'I've left the boys with my . . . with Alex, and since he really came in to see one of his patients, I'd better go and get them.'

'Sal just popped in to see how I was doing. I think she's been hanging on so that she can warn you about me.'

Johnny sounded as though he was joking but Sam could see the anxiety in his eyes and it brought her love for him surging through her, pushing aside her self-consciousness.

'No one could tell me anything about you that would change the way I feel about you,' she told him lovingly.

'See, Sal, I told you how it was.' Johnny was smiling happily now. 'Sam's the girl for me, and I'm damned lucky to have her. She's the best girl in the world.'

'Hey, wait a minute,' Russell joined in playfully. 'My Hazel's the best girl in the world.'

'I'm sorry, gentlemen, but I'm afraid I'm going to have to disagree with you there.'

Sally turned round to smile at Alex as he came into the ward with her sons, just in time to join in the conversation.

'Sally takes that title, in my opinion.'

Suddenly they were all laughing and joking together, the ice broken by each man's determination to speak up for 'his' girl, the girls themselves laughing and sharing that look that said how each of them felt about the man she loved and about being loved by him.

'No more going out playing in the mud for you,' Russell informed Sam in a lordly older brother way. 'You've still got some behind your ear.'

'What? No, I haven't. You beast, Russ,' Sam objected, joining in everyone's laughter when she realised he was teasing her.

'How long am I going to have to wait before I get you to myself?' Johnny managed to whisper in that same ear as they all left the ward. 'It's been for ever since you last kissed me.'

'Fibber. I kissed you at six o'clock this morning, when I brought you your breakfast and pretended to be a nurse,' Sam reminded him.

'Oh, that was you, was it?'

'Sam, Johnny, we're never going to get that train if you two stop walking to kiss each other every few yards,' Hazel scolded them as she turned round to see why they had fallen behind.